My Occasional Torment

To Tom—
Looking forward
to your novel!
Best,
Bruce

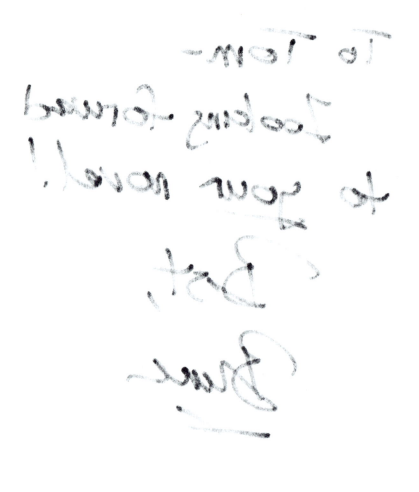

MY OCCASIONAL TORMENT

BEE ROBB

FIVE STAR
A part of Gale, Cengage Learning

GALE
CENGAGE Learning™

Detroit • New York • San Francisco • New Haven, Conn • Waterville, Maine • London

GALE
CENGAGE Learning™

LIBRARY OF CONGRESS CATALOGING-IN-PUBLICATION DATA

Robb, Bee, 1958–
    My occasional torment / Bee Robb.
      p. cm.
    ISBN-13: 978-1-59414-923-8 (hardcover)
    ISBN-10: 1-59414-923-2 (hardcover)
    1. Wives—Fiction. 2. Marital conflict—Fiction. 3. Domestic fiction. I. Title.
    PS3618.O29M9 2010
    813'.6—dc22   2010028397

First Edition. First Printing: November 2010.
Published in 2010 in conjunction with Tekno Books.

To April 25, 1987 and November 23, 2001
I thank God for you . . .

ACKNOWLEDGMENTS

I would like to thank the following wonderful and inspirational actresses because they are wonderful and have been inspirational to this process: Bonnie Hunt, Jamie Lee Curtis, Jane Kaczmarek, Geena Davis, Meryl Streep, Emma Thompson and Sela Ward. But unfortunately they have two traits in common with each other—(1) while they would each make a terrific Julia Connery in the movie version of *My Occasional Torment,* (2) as far as I can tell, not one of them knows this book exists.

Pity.

But there are other inspirational people who do know me or who have read the book, who don't stare blankly at the mention of my name. My mother, Joyce, who raised my brother, sister and me from young childhood after our father died, with a toughness that could take down any chauvinist pig at a hundred paces with one lightning-packed shout of "Let me speak to your supervisor!" And my sister, Lois, an advanced level certified Iyengar Yoga teacher to the common woman (and man) as well as to the stars; in our family photos, she's the one with the bulked-up triceps. To my brother, Larry, who is old enough to know what it was like to be an only child for a few blissful years, only to have his peace taken away by later arrivals.

My rough-draft readers—a fairly large and often naughty band of writers in the beautiful Fox River Valley town of St. Charles, Illinois, known as the St. Charles Writers Group, led by Rick Holinger, an exceptional teacher, writer, and happily married man. My precious librarians, Halle Cox, NancyLee Brown, and Mary Cella, each of whom has been waiting for this particular book to come out in print (it's their favorite, so they swear). Dee Solon who told me while holding my teeth hostage with her sharp dental hygienist utensils how hard she laughed reading the manuscript. To Judi and Steve Zeal, givers of superlatives along with their suggestions. And Kelly and Dave Stern, faithful readers.

New friends to this writing process include Tanya Meyers and her husband, Ted, (who can write me into riotous laughter 9 out of 10 tries). Keith Brown and Daniel Nigg, I wholeheartedly appreciate your confidence in me.

Lise Dominique—thank you for your kind words and your familiar voice over the radio for many years. I wish you good luck with the Harvey project.

To Cheryl Croasmun, who read the manuscript; to Cheryl's husband, Hal, who didn't read the manuscript but couldn't keep from telling me again and again that Cheryl and her mother, Joyce Ludwig, were constantly quoting this line and that scene, with laughter and tears in their eyes, from this thing called *My Occasional Torment*. These are comforting words for a nervous author to hear.

Thank you to extraordinary publishing point person, Tiffany Schofield, who manages issues with a deft, professional hand, as well as cover designer Deirdre Wait who has transformed a dream into a beautiful reality. Plus my appreciation of editor and novelist Gordon Aalborg who, I have found out, had put in a special request to edit any novel manuscript I ever submitted for publication regardless of genre. Also, a grateful smile of appreciation to Amanda Fowle Bindle, a talented editor who possesses not only the mechanics but also the music of writing. To Roz Greenberg, you are a sweetheart, and to her husband, Martin, who must be a fine man to have captured Roz's heart.

Acknowledgments

If I may, I acknowledge the inspiration provided by the married couples I've witnessed out there who adore their long-term love and commitment to each other; who still hold hands in their forties and will do so even when they make it to 100 years of age and beyond; who know that staying together for their children's sake is not necessarily a bad thing when it serves to remind each other why they fell in love in the first place; who know that the four walls of a house are not a prison, but rather a home holding all that matters in the world.

Last, and of course . . .

. . . to Scotland.

1

Sebastian Connery is my husband, my lover, my friend, my occasional torment.

This time the torment happens at the Gigaplex, our suburban twenty-three theater movie house. Sebastian and I sit together in theater number twenty-two, and I listen to him go on about the size of the screen.

"Like a television set," he says. "When we were kids, at least our movie screens were larger than our television sets." Then he complains about the size of his soft drink. "The small one costs two dollars. Two dollars for a thimble holding a couple of sips, for chrissake. And for a quarter more they give me a jug of it ten times larger than my bladder."

"You don't have to drink it all."

"Julia, of course I do," he says, sucking the last of it through the straw. "Now I've got to go to the bathroom, and the television set hasn't started yet."

So he leaves me for the bathroom, and I sit through three noisy commercials I don't understand and five movie previews that numb my ears. Sebastian still hasn't returned. I sink in my seat, waiting. I know it's coming. And it does. Just as the picture starts, the usher named Dillon comes up to me with his flashlight and shines it on my face for everyone in theater number twenty-two to see.

"Mrs. Connery," he says, leaning low to my ear.

I cough, stir in my seat, and ask him my pointless question. "What?"

"He's been kicked out again."

"Um hmm."

"The manager had him arrested."

"I see," I say, rising to leave. "Thank you for whispering this time."

With my hundred dollars in hand, plus a ten for jail processing, I ask the familiar desk sergeant what happened. He apologizes for laughing a bit. "Hello, Mrs. Connery," he says, and turns red with pity for me, and snorts through his nose when he tries to answer, so I ask Sebastian.

"Chrissake, I've been composting in the jail cell," Sebastian says, hefting his elbow-patched tweed coat over his shoulders. "What took so long?"

"Your suit's wrinkled," I say in the car. I'm driving for a change, and he hates it when I'm in the right lane, then hates it when I'm in the left lane, so I shoot him my disappointed-wife look which nails him and makes him shut up about it.

"Nobody wears suits to the cinema anymore," Sebastian whines.

I'm ready for his patter; his story of the days when citizens of America wore suits to ball games and picnics, and especially to the *cinema*, as he says, not *movie theater*.

"To hell in a hand basket!" Sebastian says it just like his father said it forty years ago, as his father still says it from his motorized wheelchair at the Saint Sister of Perpetual Care for the Inexplicably Alive Assisted Living Center.

Sebastian hisses my name as if I'm a co-conspirator in his plans to round everyone up and dress them in Sunday suits. "Julia, we shouldn't have to put up with it. You know I'm right. All those people in ripped jeans with their screaming tots, for chrissake, at a PG-13 cinema, throwing black Jujubes on my back and talking on cell phones and blaring about whose boss has the fattest ass at the office and thunder-chomping popcorn like a herd of starving Holsteins."

"Sebastian," I say, keeping my eyes fixed on the road. "Get on with it."

"Right," he says. "My arrest?"

"Go on."

"Cleanliness, Julia, is all I ask. A bit of clean in the bathroom. We do our worst in the public bath, and all you'd expect was a little organization, yet all I see are paper towels everywhere but in the trash and water spilt about everywhere but in the sink and nobody cleans up after themselves."

Even as I stare ahead I can see, and feel, Sebastian's caterpillar eyebrows squeeze together over his nose.

"So there I am, washing my hands, and in the mirror I see a man leave a stall, a stall still fresh with a flush, Julia. A man in a tweed coat just like mine, with the patches at the elbows, and wool slacks and oxford shoes. Almost civilized for an American at the cinema. He zips up over the waistband of his blue boxers. Surely you'd think he does the right thing, walking up to the sink beside me. But no, he doesn't do it, filthy bastard, not even glancing at the faucet, like it's as foreign a thing to him as a spoon is to a newborn. All he does is swipe his hands through his perfect gray hair, admires how it settles, and walk out unwashed. So I follow him to his cinema."

"You didn't!"

"Oh didn't I? I did. Television screen number eleven. And the cinema was nearly packed, but I found him and found a seat behind him. He's sitting next to a fine woman, a pretty woman as much as I could tell from behind and to the side. She wasn't yabbering or anything, just watching the cinema quiz questions on the screen, barely making a mouse's noise, eating her popcorn. And he does it. Without a thought he reaches for the popcorn bucket on her lap and plunges one of his filthy paws deep. Brings popcorn to his mouth, and palms it in as easy as if he had just bathed in the Garden of Eden. I leaned over between them."

"Sebastian, you didn't!"

"Didn't I? I did. 'Excuse me, madam,' I say before she eats another. 'Do you know where your man's hands have been, and unwashed afterwards, too?' To him I say, 'Don't you know where you just were? Don't you know what you just did? Don't you know where you put your paws? And there you go washing them in the lady's popcorn.' Then the lady says, 'What's he talking about?' 'He's a nut,' the man says. I say, 'Blue boxers. How come I know you're wearing blue boxers, just as sure as I know you brought your hands from your ass to her popcorn bucket with only a swipe of your hair in between?' "

In front of me is a car with a bumper sticker asking, *How Am I Driving?* How I wish I were in that car right now so I could have a chat about it with the driver. Sebastian squeezes my shoulder.

"So she says, 'How come he knows about your underwear, Howard?' She looks at her bucket of popcorn like it's full of viruses and worms, which it surely was. And she dumps it on his head and stomps out, and he gets up to stomp me, but I'm not letting either one of his dirty mitts touch me, not even for a friendly pat. So I jab my umbrella point quick into his chest, and he falls back over the next row, onto a lady, and his stinking hands touch everything about her trying to get up. I yell for her to run 'cause he's full of viruses and tiny worms. Pimply ushers start calling the cops on me even when it's the other guy violating everybody's sensibilities."

I say "Sebastian" like a falling bomb, but he's so used to it by now it hardly matters.

"They kept my umbrella for evidence. Evidence, they said, if you can believe it, and they left the polluted popcorn alone. There's the real evidence, any child's microscope would tell you. But I'll get my umbrella back. No way that man's coming to a courtroom to confess under oath about his dirty bathroom habits."

"I still don't understand why you insist on taking your umbrella into public bathrooms."

"Chrissake, I've told you before. Because you never know."

I can't help it. I can't. Sebastian makes me smile. After thirty-three years of marriage to this man, he makes me smile so hard I reach out to his arm, and I'm not usually one who drives with one hand.

In *Reader's Digest* I once read an article claiming eighty-five percent of all men don't wash their hands after one-ing it, and thirty-five percent don't after two-ing it. I'm not sure how anyone could run a survey like that, but how many of the unwashed percent share popcorn with their lovers at the cinema?

I tell Sebastian, "We're not going to the cinema anymore. Never."

"No, we're not." He nods and pats my shoulder and kisses at my ear. "Of course I always wash my hands."

"I love you too, Sebastian."

Like a cat after the dog leaves, Sebastian settles back in his usual way when he knows one of his torments of me won't lead to trouble. He pats me again with his clean hands.

2

Of course the assisted living center where Sebastian's ancient father lives isn't called Saint Sister of Perpetual Care for the Inexplicably Alive. That's only what I think it should be called.

In cheery yellow letters, with pastel flowers painted all about, the sign arching over the entry reads *Dignity Place.* Funny how the wrought iron gate and fence at the perimeter rise sixteen feet or more, with spikes atop, as if the Old Toots inside could ever hope to launch themselves over it.

Within the gate and fence, it's a forced beauty, a synchronous landscape carved into a chemical-smelling, weed-banished lawn. Square beds of tulips, triangles of irises, octagons of petunias, and sweeping ovals of rose bushes. I swear to my last dollar you could fold the place up on itself, like paper with wet paint on one half, and the resulting design would line up mirror-image perfect. Driving beyond the gated entrance is like mazing through a Rorschach test.

"They taught you well in high school," Sebastian says about our son's driving. Sitting in the back of our sedan, I watch Sebastian lean over from the front passenger seat and touch Roby on the shoulder. "Your history exam is another matter."

"What's so horrible about a B-plus?"

"So close to an A. It could have been an A-plus."

We didn't have Roby until Sebastian and I were in our late thirties, our only child. There's no second child to point out if the first one's a disappointment. We don't mean to feel this way, but it's probably why Roby's so thin.

"Don't they teach you anything Scottish in history class?" Sebastian says.

"No."

"Chrissake." Sebastian's voice goes from Chicago-nasal to bad Scottish lilt in one word.

"Dad, it's not as though Scotland has done anything important lately."

"Nothing important?"

"Tell me one thing Scotland's done lately that isn't a song or poem about misty skies or valleys of lush green."

"Scotland's learned to stay out of trouble. That alone is worthy of study."

Like a nail to Sebastian's heart, Roby says, "We studied Ireland for a whole month. Now *there's* some history."

"Don't go on about the Irish. They all wish to be Scottish anyway and have some peace and sobriety so they can sing about misty skies and valleys of lush green." Sebastian thumbs his tweed lapels. "A whole month's study wouldn't even touch Ireland's history of misery."

"Boys," I say. "Look at all the flowers."

"Same as always," Sebastian groans.

The groan of lawn mowers, lawn edgers, and weed-whackers fighting back nature's desire to grow as it pleases drowns out whatever else Sebastian says. Fresh cut grass, powered by chemicals, reminds me of a cemetery, and as we approach the whitewashed walls of Dignity Place, the Old Toots sit lined up in chairs on the veranda, looking inexplicably alive, eyeing the distant gate as though wishing they could find a way beyond it.

Roby parks our sedan. "I hate this place. Why can't Old Sebastian live with us again?"

"Because we have an honorarium paying half the costs," Sebastian says. "And because I've had to live with him half my life already. That's enough."

Roby grunts an ironic thought, and Sebastian, so oblivious, grunts back.

Three apartments down from the staircase and elevator, on the second floor, *The Godfather* blares through Old Sebastian's closed door.

We walk in just as James Caan's about to get whacked on Old Sebastian's television screen.

Although he's ancient and in a motorized wheelchair, fluffy blanket upon his lap, Old Sebastian raises his arms from his short-sleeve Chicago Bears T-shirt and shows off muscle by wiggling his hands to hush us.

"Think it's going to be different when you watch it this time, Grandpa?" Roby asks.

"Don't matter." With the rat-a-tat-tat of bullets into James Caan's car and body, Old Sebastian smiles perfect, bone-white teeth surrounded by his craggy face.

"We're here to visit you, Dad," Sebastian says.

Old Sebastian adores the gore on his television set. "I suppose you want me to put this on pause."

"Dad."

"All right, I'll pause. Don't shit your shorts."

"Please," I say, and nod toward Roby.

"Like the boy's never heard cussing before. Probably says a whole lot worse all the time himself. How old are you now, fifteen?"

"Seventeen, Grandpa."

Old Sebastian presses the remote's pause button and stares at me with his gray eyes sunrising over his nose-tip reading glasses. "Damn movie's a masterpiece, an opera."

"We brought you lunch," Sebastian says, raising a suitcase-sized paper bag with handles.

"Salisbury steak?" Old Sebastian sniffs the air. "Better not be. They served that crap here last week. Twice. A bunch of us chanted 'This meat is shit.' I used mine for a Frisbee."

"Beef ribs with spice sauce," Sebastian says. "Deboned."

While Sebastian sets up the eatery, including my fine china stuffed in the bag of deboned ribs, Roby runs his hands over a collection of gangster movie DVD cases lined up like the St Valentine's Day Massacre on a shelf beside the television set.

"There's an extra forty dollars on next month's tab," Old Sebastian says.

I say, "What now?"

"A hole in the wall behind my bed's headboard."

"Who made it?"

"I did. Me and my hammer."

"How'd you move the bed?"

"I had help, but I'm not naming names." With his mouth hitched over to one side, he says, "So there, yeah."

"Stop looking for gangster bones," Sebastian says.

"They're here, son. Al Capone lived here three years just to stash the bodies. You'll see one day."

"Where's the hammer?"

Old Sebastian raises his chin and narrows his eyes. "Someplace."

Robert DeNiro stares at Roby from a *Casino* poster, and beside DeNiro, James Cagney and Jean Harlow stare at each other on a *Public Enemy* poster. No plants. No books. Three look-alike pictures each supposedly of Scotland's shoreline hang on the walls, lakes with mist and green hills and rocks, although they could have been taken in Minnesota.

Marlon Brando is framed in silver, 8 × 10, on the bedside nightstand, wearing a tuxedo jacket, holding a drink, his jowls dragging like a basset hound's. Our family pictures gather in 3 × 5 cardboard frames behind Brando, and the tiny one I know holding Mrs. Old Sebastian, rest her soul, lies fallen on its face.

Thumbtacked to the wall hangs a gray photo of three men in stiff coats, each man older than the next. Old Sebastian's father, grandfather, and great-grandfather. Each one named Sebastian, all of them looking confused.

Sebastian sits on Old Sebastian's bed, admiring the clean way his father eats lunch at his wheelchair tray. The deboned saucy ribs he cuts with knife and fork, pinkies extended, a small towel tucked under his chin, and Moist Towelettes packages arranged like a hand of bridge cards.

"Where's *The Sound of Music?*" Roby asks, poking at the DVD cases.

Old Sebastian makes a noise, something like *Poohie!* and instantly dabs away a spot of sauce his gasp of disgust blew to his chin. "I won't watch a movie without tough guys in it."

"Austrian Nazis," Roby says.

Old Sebastian chews his last deboned rib. "Nazis? They're nothing but lipless lunatics dressed in matching outfits. Might as well be wearing tutus." His old fingers, cranky boned but still agile, tear open a Moist Towelettes package. To lips, to chin, to palms, to fingernails, he works the Moist Towelettes still folded in a neat square. Then another and another. He folds his chin towel bib into a Moist-Towelettes-shaped square, too.

Sebastian smiles misty-eyed at his father. "Was it good?"

"I ate it, didn't I? Didn't say it was shit, did I? Didn't toss it like a Frisbee, did I?"

Old Sebastian reaches to his nightstand drawer, takes a dental floss case, and pulls out a foot-long string. Sebastian looks like he's going to cry of happiness.

I say, "Dad, you can't floss dentures."

Old Sebastian flosses what he can anyway. Little glumps of stuff fly out with his spittle and he balls up the floss string before tossing it in the garbage can.

"Can I open the window curtains for you?" I ask.

"No."

"Why not?"

"The sun makes a glare on the television screen."

"But we're here to visit you."

"Fine. Close them when you leave."

It's a relief to open the curtains, heavy as chain mail, and the window for sunlight and air. On the grounds below me, like a ballet so orderly and choreographed, workers in white suits wheel Old Toots about the grounds. From the second floor, I see the paths they take, narrow tracks depressed into the lawn by the history of wheelchair walks from every day before. A breeze reaches me, sweet and clean, smelling like air from the Lake Michigan shore. Somehow it arrives untouched by the lawn chemicals below.

"You know I met Al Capone," Old Sebastian says. He twirls an index finger in the air toward Roby and Sebastian sitting on his bed. "On three occasions."

"Uh-huh," Sebastian says. "I thought it was twice."

"No. I'm pretty sure it was three times. The first time of course was, hmm . . ." Old Sebastian looks to the ceiling.

"1927," Roby says.

Old Sebastian gives his chin a scratch. "1927? No."

Roby opens a small, black book on the nightstand and grins at a list of names. His fingers are at the phone.

"Maybe it was 1926," Old Sebastian says. "Christmas Eve."

"Hello?" Roby whispers into the receiver, then twists his mouth up and starts in with gangster talk. "You dirty rat. You did my brother in. I'll get you for it, yeah. I'll get you for it, yeah yeah." He hangs up, shrugs and points to the black book. "It was Sam The Man Flounders. Local call."

"Shit, boy. Haven't you heard of caller ID? I'll be full of bullet holes by tomorrow."

"No way a man named Flounders could be a gangster,

nobody tough anyway." Roby reads from the little black book. "Three more Sam The Man's, three Del Greco's, two Little Nicky's, two Itchy Fingers, four Slicks, and a page full of Pretty Boy's."

"Code names." Old Sebastian smiles. "I'm dead by tomorrow."

"Put the gangster book down," Sebastian says.

I ask, "Would you like to watch the rest of your movie?"

"Might as well." How happy Old Sebastian's eyes glow at the thought of getting me out of his room and *The Godfather* back in. "Sure don't have much time left to live anyhow."

With his dentured mouth piped at me, Old Sebastian hisses, "Flounders will be coming."

We leave to the replayed track of bullets firing into James Caan's body. Sebastian wipes his eyes. "Dad seems happy," he says, then lets Roby get the car while we wait on the veranda. "Am I a bad son for putting him here?" Sebastian squeezes my hand. "The man knows his gangsters."

"The Old Toot is a nut," I think to say but know enough not to.

When Roby pulls up, Sebastian carries the bag to the car, dropping it with a sudden clank on the drive. Something expensive breaks in there. My fine china. But never mind, Sebastian has spotted a gum wrapper on the drive. He picks it up with a look of disdain for all the human race and stuffs it in his pocket.

As we drive away, I look for Old Sebastian's room. There it is, with the window and heavy curtains left open. Accidentally? Carelessly? Old Sebastian will think I want the wind to blow his old body out of his wheelchair to the floor. Funny how I don't think this way about the other Old Toots at Dignity Place. Those faces on the veranda stare their desperation at me, as if yearning to latch their wheelchairs to the back bumper and speed away for one more thrill.

There's a hum about Dignity Place, indistinct and distant. It's as though it sings to me: *Wait till it's your turn.*

I blame Frank McCourt, rest his lovely soul.

That's right, I do. Bad enough he was so adorable, but then he had to write *Angela's Ashes* and make the rest of the population want to squeeze the cheek of every Irishman in America. Although Sebastian hates the way Americans think Scotland is a suburb of Ireland, it doesn't keep him from falling into his pitiful Scottish lilt, nor from raising those bushy plaid eyebrows and balled-up cheeks and singing something Scottish that sounds Irish to people ignorant of the difference. He parades and croons his fake Scottish about to women ignorant of the difference even as he moans to me that Scotland is bigger and has more people than that miserable Ireland.

And I blame Mitch Albom. Maybe more than Frank McCourt.

This blame is for writing *Tuesdays With Morrie,* which may be somewhere on the best-sellers list till the earth explodes, and makes Sebastian's history students from the junior college swoon at our door weepy-eyed and wanting to hug him. Usually women. Anytime our doorbell rings there's a chance it's a woman enrolled in his classes this year, or last year, or the last decade, or from the first moon launch, wanting to get to know their old history teacher before he dies.

I say to this teary group, "He's only fifty-seven, and he has no sickness."

Between moistening sniffles they say, "But he will die one day. At least can we touch him?"

Sebastian calls out from somewhere in the house, "Who's there, Julia?" and the women lean through the doorway, hoping to catch glimpses of him before the Lord or Satan snatches my Sebastian away. Then Sebastian figures out what's going on and raises the Scot from his soul, his fake lilt and bushy plaid eyebrows and cheeks, and he no longer cares if Ireland rises into the sky and settles over all of Scotland.

"Hiya, Lassies," Sebastian begins.

I say, "These women want to touch you before you die so they can write books about the experience."

It's the compactness of Sebastian, his warmth contained in the size of a man I can wrap myself around twice in one embrace. When I look at him, it's not the hairy nostrils some wives look up to with their taller husbands, but his bright blue eyes flashing a bit below level with mine, telling me with their quick twitches how he cannot get enough of me. It's the smell and crunch of mousse I know he's been using to keep his thick, tussled hair brown. And it's the sight of his laugh wrinkles both time and our marriage have deepened at his eyes, mouth and brow.

This man has loved me long before best-selling books made him irresistible to strangers. With his torments of me and his old father wearing on me, I wonder what Sebastian sees in my face. But he soon enough closes the front door on his procession of worshipers, wraps me up with his clean hands, Scottish lilt, rising cheeks, and bushy plaid eyebrows, and says he hopes he dies a very old man before I die because he couldn't stand the thought of a day without me.

I remind him, though. My worst torment of all. "That particular woman."

"Chrissake, Lassie. Lola was long ago. Before we were married."

"We were engaged. There's no difference."

He scratches at his chin. "Will you ever let it go?"

"I have."

"Doesn't sound like you have."

"I've let it go. I haven't forgotten. There's a difference."

"I'm confused between your differences and no differences."

"On this there's a difference, and you shouldn't remember her name."

"All right," he says. "But try not to bring her up when I'm throwing myself at you."

Sebastian kisses me in his way, withers my seed of doubt until the seed is almost gone. The space this withering creates allows other torments to rush in. I remind myself these other torments are the surface kind. They shouldn't bother me, but they do. How our bedroom furniture is topped with endless Scottish trinkets and books, corn silk and thistle, and photos of rolling mist from the sea. There's a map of all of Scotland beside our closet where Sebastian has cut out most of Ireland and all of England, or buried them beneath the matte and wood frame. It's the last thing I see when we turn out the light at night.

In dreams I'm tormented by the map, in particular the circle of red Sebastian has drawn around the point of a peninsula in the lower left corner, the Mull of Kintyre. The map, trinkets and books come alive and start talking to each other in Sebastian's horribly fake Scottish lilt—*Hiya, Lassie! Hiya, Lassie! Hiya, Lassie!*—to all the pining women wanting to squeeze my Sebastian. The dream shows me our beautiful living room Berber carpeting, nightmared from neutral beige into Scottish plaid, and I scream because it looks like the fat ass side of a golfer's pants. Sebastian wears a pleated tartan kilt, and he ignores me as he answers the front door. *Hiya, Lassie!* he says to the gorgeous Julia Roberts standing on our front porch. And the actress gets all teary-eyed and begs to touch him before he dies and hugs him against her push-up bra and wants to know for the book she's been writing whether there's anything he's wearing under his wonderful tartan kilt.

Between my dream and waking, I find my pillow and use it to thump the lump beside me.

"For chrissake, Julia!" Sebastian says.

"Which Julia?" I scream. "Me or the movie queen asking about your kilt?"

"I don't own a kilt!"

"You do in my dream."

"Oh? And what was I doing?"

"You know," I say, huffing back under the covers. "Watch yourself, Sebastian Connery."

"In your dreams?"

I feel his eyes trying to burn a gaze into my brain for some reasoning and common sense. It's bad enough having the torment of hopelessly loving Sebastian when I'm awake, and the Frank McCourts and the Mitch Alboms making him irresistible to the rest of the world, and my seed of doubt that refuses to wither away completely. But the things he does to me in my dreams can only make me into a saint one day when the next century's priests consider it.

"You're Scottish, too," he says. "Three-quarters of you anyway."

"It's different for a woman."

Sebastian settles under the covers, and in a Scottish lilt sounding almost right, he says, "Wish I knew that last quarter of you. 'Tis right I find out for real rather than in a dream."

His arm and hand sliding over me, not understanding his torment of me, he makes me melt all over again.

3

When I turned fifty, it didn't seem like such a big deal at the time. After all, I wasn't far gone from my forties. Fifty-one, though. Fifty-one hit me hard.

Turning fifty-one told me I was marching toward sixty. *Sixty!* Sixty sounds a hundred years older than fifty-nine. Fifty-one told me there was no going back. My parents turned sixty and seventy and eighty, and then died two years ago. First her, then him. This aging thing was for them, not for me.

Then *she* came along.

Like a child's imaginary playmate, she popped out of my mind. I thought my brain had created her for my own comfort, to talk about things I found difficult to share with Sebastian.

She showed up for the first time after my father's funeral, watching me in the bathroom while I freshened my makeup. Back then, her voice was like a whisper. *They weren't happy together, you know.*

"Who?"

Mom and Dad.

"Of course they were happy."

She shook her head. Nameless and plain, a pleasant smile, thin like a waif, and so pale and ordinary up and down, as if she were a canvas waiting for a brush. *Tell me, could you ever imagine them doing it? You know what I mean, doing it?*

"I know *doing it,* and I don't think of such things about my parents."

Since I'm saying it, you must be thinking it.

"I suppose. Well, of course."

Because you know they stayed married for fifty-two years for the sake of you and your sister. More than half the time your father would rather get drunk in a fishing boat and your mother would rather walk barefoot through a landfill than look at the other one naked.

I dropped my lipstick in the sink and considered slapping this figment of my imagination. I insisted, "Well I'm not thinking it now!"

Of course you are. You have to be or else I wouldn't have mentioned it. She laughed and moved her hands to her hips. *Nobody makes it happily to fifty years of marriage. Nobody.*

"Sebastian can't keep his hands off me after thirty years!"

He's been disappearing every now and then, ever since Old Sebastian went off to Dignity Place.

"He always comes home. Always."

You know better, Julia honey. Those extra gaps of time between Sebastian leaving work and Sebastian coming home.

"Maybe once a month. Twice at most. He's my husband, not my property. Men have their friends and hobbies."

Name the friends. Tell me his innocent hobbies. What makes him disappear?

"It's not a disappearance. It's a few hours away after work once a month or so, maybe to clear his thoughts."

It took only a few hours for Sebastian to find his hobby, with the first Lola. Lola One. I noticed at that moment it was no longer a pleasant smile on her face. She gave me a nasty smirk and a devilish wink. She then offered, *Call me Lola Two.*

I moved to slap her, but my hand was like a hammer falling through a cloud.

Still with the smirk and wink, this Lola, Lola Two, said, *Did that hurt?* I squeezed the sides of the sink, focused on water droplets gathered around my lipstick in the basin.

I'll show you what men really want. All men. Including Sebastian.

At the time of my father's funeral, this is what my lovely brain brought to me. Lola Two. Not a comfort, but a new torment to remind me of my parents' miserable marriage. Something new to water and fertilize my seed of doubt.

The next time I saw Lola Two was a few months after her first appearance. She decided to show up, sit beside me on my front porch, and say nothing for a while. Together we sniffed at the summer breeze and watched the houses across the street tucked away in their solid splendor. In Highland Park, Illinois, my home is typical of the older neighborhoods; brick and stone, two stories, garage in back in a large yard, lots of trees and shrubs filling the lawns. The branches overhead hum with cicadas, and the streets echo with voices of children at play.

You could have been anything you wanted to be.

I looked at Lola Two and saw something different about her.

You made it through graduate school. You earned excellent grades and had your own opportunities. But you married Sebastian instead and have been nothing but a housewife ever since.

"What do you mean by nothing?"

She smiled at me, and I saw. Her teeth blindingly white, her nose thinned down so you could spike it through paper. *Don't get so defensive. There's nothing wrong with being a housewife. Nothing at all.*

"What did you do to your face?"

Her smile broadened, and she closed her eyes, and she looked as though I'd paid her a compliment.

I've been to Dr. Plastic. The type of doctor you've been wondering about since your early thirties. Let me tell you, the man's a genius. Teeth bleaching. Nose job. Don't they look wonderful on me?

"What was wrong with the way you looked?"

She tossed her head back and laughed. *Oh, Julia. I'm just*

showing you what you've always suspected. Dr. Plastic is making me into what men really want.

"Sebastian's happy with the way I am."

Where is Sebastian?

"At the college teaching summer classes."

Are you certain? Don't you want to check?

"There's no need to check."

Of course you have to check. We've read the same magazines. You stand a twenty-five percent greater chance of getting divorced because you're a housewife is all I'm saying. Some husbands insist they don't want their wives to work outside the home, but then they turn around and get bored with their housewives. But don't worry, working women stand a thirty-five percent increased chance of getting cheated on. I don't understand the numbers, but they must be true if they're printed in Cosmo. I'm certain Dr. Plastic would agree.

"There's no Dr. Plastic. Maybe I've thought such a person, but he doesn't exist."

Trust your thoughts, Julia honey. Just look at the house across the street. The Martins'. Beautiful home. Three kids. A dog, an apple tree in back, picket fence. About as Norman Rockwell as you'll find in Highland Park. But you don't talk to the Martins. Why? Because you know about them. He's cheating on her with Mrs. Marbry next door, but Mrs. Martin doesn't care 'cause she's got it going on with Mr. Havlicek in the house to the south of yours. And two houses to the north, Mrs. Winthrop told you something personal a few months ago, something you never wanted to hear. She told you her husband's so fat he hasn't seen his own pecker in ten years. You know what she's doing with Mr. Kramer in the house across the street and one over to the north. And even Mr. Winthrop found somebody's housekeeper on the block west of here who doesn't mind showing him exactly where his pecker is.

Lola Two yawned in her chair and touched at her new nose. *Then there are the three divorces, four separations, and the couple you know as the Screamers with their poor, eldest son and the twins who have to listen to it all, the Unkers, five houses to the north.*

Of course I was stunned by what she knew. What I knew. She raised her feet to rest them on the brick banister, breathed in sweet summer air, and slouched low in her chair.

What a neighborhood we've got here. After fifteen years on this block, no wonder you keep to yourself. You think you'll catch the infidelity germ and infect Sebastian. But it's airborne, honey. You can't avoid it forever. After all, Sebastian's proven he's susceptible.

I told her we're happy in our home, and she waved her hand at a fly. I told her my bed is busy enough, and she snatched the fly in her hand and crushed it, only to watch the fly reappear and flit away from her imaginary flesh.

You could've been anything you wanted to be. She pointed her Dr. Plastic pixie nose at me. *But you chose Sebastian and this neighborhood.* With a wink, she said, *No marriage makes it happily to fifty years. Passion always dies and marriage is the cause of death. Marriage turns romance into misery. Always.*

"What about the Newberrys?"

The Newberrys over there? Lola Two nodded at my neighbor's house next door, to the north. Brown brick, vines up and down the porch, heavy gray-purple curtains sealing the windows. *You've got to be kidding. He's dead and buried!* Her laughing fit hit my ears so hard the sound of it remained in my head long after she faded away. And I remember the last thing she had said that afternoon.

Don't kid yourself, Julia Connery. When it comes to Sebastian and all other married men in the world, Dr. Plastic is very, very real.

As soon as she vanished, I called the college, asked the front desk for Sebastian and waited. When he answered, he said, "What a pleasant surprise."

"I love you, Sebastian."

"Well. I love you too, Julia."

There was nothing more to say. I knew I had failed.

It wasn't until my fifty-third birthday last February when Lola Two came out again. *I've got something new to show ya,* she said, and she swung her chest around. Naked. They looked barely attached to the rest of her chest, as if they were planetary spheres stuck to Velcro, shining and upturned.

"They're unnatural."

I know—so fabulous! Dr. Plastic says I can get them made larger if I wish. What do you think Sebastian would say?

She tortured me on my fifty-third birthday with her Dr. Plastic breasts, and me standing before my bedroom mirror, half-dressed, getting ready to go out to dinner with Sebastian. "It's not fat; I'm just large. That's the way it is for me."

I think this is what Sebastian wants, she said, cupping her hands beneath them. *Maybe a bit more upturned.* Then she leaned toward me, her pointed nose, neon-white teeth and planetary breasts, and sneered at my bra and the largeness of all of me. *If I were to lay down with Sebastian,* she said with a hiss, *at least mine wouldn't flatten out.*

I cried at the mirror, before my reflection of moles, veins softly blue below my skin, and stray hair I have to pluck every other week. Lola Two went on even as I wept. *Men get fat, they turn gray, they go bald, they sag in the face and over their belts. And what do people call them? Distinguished-looking, that's what. But when these things happen to women, what do people call them? Old, Julia. Women get called old. Not fair, but it's a fact.*

"What part of me are you?"

For the first time with her about, Sebastian walked in. He floated through Lola Two and stepped quickly to me, wiped my tears away and kissed my lips.

"Why're you crying on your birthday, Lassie?"

I needed his touch, his unclasping of my bra and his hands light upon my breasts. He kissed me again and apologized. "It's difficult for me, Lassie. When I see you this way, you're a magnet."

"You're right; it's my birthday." I loosened his belt, clasped his pouting face in my hands and kissed him. I led him to our bed, saying, "This is what I want."

I'm the part of you who understands what Sebastian really desires. Lola Two vanished.

Sebastian turned out the light and sighed to the sound of his slacks and belt hitting the floor. "Ah, Lassie. Happy birthday to us both."

Now in late September, Roby's busy with his senior year at the high school and Sebastian as a professor and head of the history department at the junior college. Lola Two chooses to appear right as I step out of the shower. At least she's covered this time, even if the jeans and T-shirt are much too tight.

Look, she says. She pats her hips and her rump, and she's lost her waif appearance forever. *Butt pads sutured in by Dr. Plastic. If you weren't imagining me, something like this would hurt like hell.*

"You've ruined yourself."

To the contrary. God made woman. Dr. Plastic makes her hot.

"How do I get rid of you?"

Lola Two juts her hips to the left and her breasts to the right, smiles her snowy teeth and taps her elfin nose. *Find us a couple married at least fifty years who can't keep their hands off each other and I'll go.* She looks at herself in my bathroom mirror and wonders aloud whether Dr. Plastic could tack her ears back a bit. *Do we know such a couple, Julia Connery?*

I watch her watching herself in the mirror, and she's so smug smiling at my hesitation. *Honey,* she says, kissing at the air. *Looks like I'm here to stay.*

4

My kitchen was once photographed for *Highland Park Homes* magazine. The article praised the ceramic floor and the marble counter tops and the airy feel. It approved of my table, a square made of bleached oak, and bench seats the magazine had said, "Require parents and their children to sit close together, encouraging meaningful family conversations."

Monday morning, another start of a school week pulling him further away from summer freedom, Roby says, "Toast. For the third time, Mom. Just toast."

I've got oatmeal and scones and jelly pastries, a dozen different kinds of cereal, bacon and ham, potatoes, eggs, and copper bottom pots and pans hanging over our kitchen table island ready to serve it all. Slugged upon our wonderful bench seats at the kitchen table, Roby grunts for his toast.

"We've got raisin bread," I say.

"Plain, white bread toast. No jam, no butter. Plain. It's all I can stomach this morning."

Sebastian sits on the wonderful bench seat across the table from Roby and raises his eyes over his Monday morning Chicago Tribune. "Not feeling well?"

"I'm fine," Roby says.

Sebastian chews and reads his paper, and all the while his fingers sweep breakfast bits crumb by crumb into a neat little pile beside his plate. When the load reaches a certain size, he sweeps it into his palm and dumps the crumbs into a pail he keeps beside him for breakfast. He starts a new pile.

I sit beside Sebastian, my elbows leaning on top of the fabulous table suitable for magazine photos, and I'm bored waiting for white bread toast to pop up in our fancy kitchen. Sebastian reads the sports section, chews a strip of bacon, and finds errant crumbs for his pile.

Along with his jeans, his T-shirt beneath an untucked and unbuttoned shirt, and untied ratty gym shoes, Roby wears his back-to-school Monday morning teenage angst as solid around him as any steel shield. Where is the boy who drew cartoons at the table, who taped graded homework papers with yellow smile faces on our refrigerator door, and who asked to be quizzed on multiplication tables and spelling bee lists and capitals of the states of the union?

"You guys were noisy last night," Roby says. "Worse than before."

"Chrissake," I say.

His father flaps down the top half of his paper. "A loving son among loving parents becomes a loving husband and father himself one day." Up goes the paper, and from behind it, Sebastian finishes, "We were better than before."

The toaster pops before I do, and Roby chomps a bite out of his plain white toast. He settles back, chewing, his eyelids closed a sneaky bit the way teenagers do when they're showing their parents they're smarter than everyone else in the world. His eyes slither back and forth between Sebastian and me, and it's no wonder why he can only stomach plain white bread toast. The thought of Old Sebastian doing it with Mrs. Old Sebastian, may she rest in peace, would make me fast for all of Lent.

Roby eats half his toast and prepares to leave for the school bus. Sebastian raises his stare from his newspaper. "You painting a house today?" he asks, watching Roby move about in his layers of rags and wrinkles.

Our son slugs away from us, his book pack over his shoulders, a mass of untied straps, unzipped zippers, unbuttoned buttons and dangling shirttails and denim. He leaves us for the street curb to wait for the school bus.

From my front porch, I see Roby's best friend, Brian Unkers, the brother of younger twins, son of the Screamers. Brian is a handsome boy with dark, uncombed hair and a swirl of pimples around his mouth. Roby calls him Bean-Dip, a name Brian gave to himself. I suppose he's resigned to the way his pimples look around his lips, the same way he's accepted his parents' voices screeching through brick walls into the neighborhood.

Brian hands Roby a cupcake, and Roby shoves it all in his mouth. He chews it twice and it's gone.

When the bus arrives, Brian jumps on. Something slows Roby down, stops him like a scent he can't resist. For a moment, his eyes are wide and calm, and he's the boy I remember at our table drawing cartoons. With a grace so irresistible to watch, he bends over to pick some paper litter off the pavement and stuffs it into his pocket.

Sebastian gives me a kiss on the lips. A long one. He cups my breasts in his palms and says to them, "I'll be home at four."

Before he steps off our porch, I grab his arm. "Remember your first words to me?"

"A test?" His eyes widen. "You were holding your bra up with the other co-eds and their bras, and you couldn't get yours to ignite. I told you there was too much material even for a torch to light, let alone your puny match."

"My breasts aren't toys. They're not worms on a lure to catch fish."

"And what would you think if I swam by your lures so oblivious and ignorant?" Sebastian kisses me again. "By four," he says, this time watching my eyes, then leaves me on the porch.

It's not a story to tell Roby if he ever asks me how his mother and father met and married. To Roby, I'll say, "We protested the war together."

I stand on my porch, looking down the length of the street. The manicured brick homes with their chair-swing porches the size of living rooms and towering tree canopies connecting endlessly one to the other. Inside all this outward serenity I wonder how many former bra-burners on this street are lucky enough to have husbands who still get all chauvinistic over their breasts.

Nothing should ruin this moment for me. Certainly not a dusty memory of one infidelity that happened so long ago, technically before we were married, as Sebastian occasionally dares to say. I am grateful for this morning's absence of Lola Two.

When Sebastian's car leaves our garage and he drives for the junior college, with his history class lesson plans and homework assignments and his mind racing on about four o'clock this afternoon and my breasts, I lean against the porch banister in my gardening jeans and sweatshirt and feel naked.

The early fall breeze, like Sebastian's hands, caresses me head to toe.

5

John Newberry married Iris fifty years ago because he was too afraid of her not to.

In my unmanageable backyard garden, I remember John Newberry as I shake a hybrid tea rose bush and yellowed leaves shower off its stems. Each fallen leaf wears a fatal black spot in its center, discoloring green life into brown death. A hundred black spots, like evil eyes, stare up at me from my rose bush flower bed. Again, I think, poor John Newberry.

"Black spot," Iris Newberry says.

Her face shaded below a straw sombrero she never takes off, her button denim shirt with multiple pockets storing seeds in packets she never plants, and a pocket gardening book she never reads, Iris Newberry stands at our shared picket fence. With her arms folded, she holds a spray bottle of Armageddon-strength fungus killer, a finger on the trigger, like a Martha Stewart action figure.

How I wish Sebastian had ordered the six-foot fence instead of the neighborly three-footer. Each time Iris Newberry snoops her nose into my yard, I feel my home's property value plummet.

"Black spot kills rose bushes," Iris says. She tilts her head back and her pale, wrinkle-free face glows in the shade beneath her gardening sombrero. In the fifteen years I've lived as her next-door neighbor, I've never seen her let the sun touch her face. She keeps her curtains drawn, and I swear I've seen her slather on her bullet-proof sunblock just to dine with me in her living room near sunset. Why she keeps inviting me and my family to her Friday dinners, with her passionate hatred of my garden, I'll never understand.

Sebastian thinks she's seventy, maybe seventy-five. With her bullet-proof sunblock vampiring white on her cheeks, she makes me believe she's centuries old, living until a stake finds her heart. I search her face for a soul only to find her sunglasses, like the black spot on my rose bushes, have taken her eyes.

She hangs her hat brim and nose over the fence and sniffs at my garden. "Your strawberries are growing into the ajugas, and the ajugas are springing up everywhere, and your periwinkle is getting choked, and those daylilies are not much better than weeds. At least take care of the black spot, Julia."

I'm suddenly holding her bottle of fungus spray, and Iris lowers her sombrero and moves into the proof of her personal worth that she finds in her own garden. She's somewhere beneath the pile of clothes and pointy hat she wears. Her yard surrounds her, sprayed, powdered, fertilized, and aerated, and as impervious to black spot, crab grass and dandelions as it is to butterflies and finches.

I let nature fight it out in my backyard. Ever since her husband died, Iris hires out mercenaries. Even with her arty fish pond and winding cobblestone walk and rose bushes and miniature plum trees as perfect as wax imitations, she doesn't have a gardening stain on her, not a touch of dirt on her hands. Every Monday and Thursday, spring through autumn, she raises an index finger all day long at young men she cannot name and wags them around her yard with a promise of payment in cash.

Four years ago, the obituary said John Newberry died of natural causes at sixty-six. But I'm convinced he exploded from all the things building up inside him that he wanted to say to Iris but couldn't.

I remember John as a large man. Tall and broad-shouldered. His sixties touched him with white in his hair and brought handsome dignity to the lines on his face. A kind man, an accomplished musician and music teacher at the high school. But I could see it in his eyes, how they blinked less and less, how the whites grew large and the pupils shrunk to pinpoints, especially in the few years before his death. He lived his final days frightened of his own retirement—*More time with Iris!*—forced to wear a gardening sombrero, ordered to slather on bullet-proof sunblock cream, living not afraid of the sun but of her. I'd catch him ducking to a spot beside a perfectly coned bush, hiding from Iris, tipping his hat back to tilt his face toward the sun and smiling like a babe discovering his fingers and toes for the first time.

"Caught the black spot," Iris said at his funeral. "I warned John again and again." (And again and again and again and again, I'm certain, poor John Newberry!) "Skin cancer."

But there was no proof of skin cancer and no proof of natural causes, not that I saw. His death was as sudden as a door slam. He exploded to escape Iris; that's the way John Newberry died four years ago. The murderer reclines on a chaise lounge chair in her pile of clothes.

"Spray the black spot, Julia. I won't have it coming into my yard."

"And I won't have your poison coming into mine," I want to say, but I don't. Making war with the neighbor, especially one who can look at an apple and insist it's an orange, is not in my best interests. "Yes, Iris," I say. So I accommodate. I hiss, I hiss and I hiss again, and Iris' ears, tuned for the sound of her own voice, can't distinguish my onomatopoeia bullshit.

"Very good, Julia," Iris says beneath her umbrella, sombrero and sunglasses. "Spray from the bottom to the top."

From my dying rose bushes, Iris appears small between my

thumb and index finger, and I squish her and she reappears, and I squish her and she reappears, and she remains unchanged.

"Taking care of the dandelions today, Julia?"

"There are no dandelions in my yard, Mrs. Newberry."

"Of course there are. And the clover? What about the clover? Clover spreads like wildfire. I won't have any of it in my yard."

"There's no clover, Mrs. Newberry."

"Of course there is. By the side of your garage and the walk. And you'll have to pull the crabgrass this late in the season. Can't spray for it now. I had warned you."

"There's no crabgrass in my yard, Mrs. Newberry."

"Dear, you sound just like my husband."

For my own ears, I say, "Just before he exploded?"

"My poor Jonathon would go on about how dandelion flowers are a pretty yellow and clover is green just like Kentucky Blue Grass. He never understood."

"I suppose he didn't."

"Are you and your little family coming over for dinner tonight?"

"It's not Friday."

"I have a special dinner in the works. You'll love it."

"I'm afraid we may have other plans."

"Four-thirty, then."

"Mrs. Newberry," I say, and my temperature rises, blood pressure, too, and there's a vein throbbing in my neck just thinking of what Sebastian wants to do with me when he comes home at four, but instead we have to sit on Mrs. Newberry's Queen Victoria chairs to eat whatever goulash a seventy-five-year-old vampire makes for dinner. "All right, Iris."

She nods the rim of her sombrero hat. "Hand-pull the crabgrass. Fall fertilize."

Stepping over dandelions and crabgrass and clover to my door, I leave my yard before I explode like poor John Newberry, and I sit at my fabulous table in my kitchen where the clock tells me it's only ten-thirty. Tomorrow's the first day of October. I'll wait for winter to come and kill my weeds.

In my kitchen, *God Investment* plays on the AM radio station I found far to the right on the dial. Less about God, more about investment as the Bible sees it. I listen to two male voices tell me how the woman is subservient to the man in all things, and if the husband wants to speculate the college fund in technology upstarts, the wife is supposed to stand by in silence and obey and iron his shirts while their portfolio goes *blooie* and their children have to go to Internet correspondence college. *It's God's way, bless you. Thanks for the question, caller.*

Five hours to dinner with Iris Newberry, and I will the telephone to ring just to get my mind off of her. It's Sebastian.

"Julia, you won't believe it!"

"Why so angry?"

"I've been summoned to court. Hand-delivered at the college."

"Again with jury duty? You know they always kick you off."

"Not the jury. I'm the defendant. Chrissake! Battery, Julia. It's a final notice to appear, or else. The man didn't wash his hands. It was self-defense. It was defense of the poor woman beside him!" His breaths tremble at my ear. "My afternoon classes are covered. I'm coming home early."

With determination and anger in his voice, and his worst Scottish accent, I know I'm going to hear about it. His comparisons between his plight to William Wallace rising from the ranks of downtrodden Highlanders to lead a revolt against the oppressive England and how the Australian Mel Gibson never should have made his *Braveheart* movie, which he never saw but criticizes anyway. *Click*, goes the phone. No *I love you* first, and it's the sound of a starting gun announcing a new torment of me.

A woman caller on *God Investment* asks about speculating in a gold mine in New Jersey. Her husband's about to cash out their certificates of deposit too soon, take the penalty hit, and give it to a man in a pale blue suit passing out ownership deeds in the East Coast Prospecting Company.

The male voices let her know what's what. *Who are you to say there isn't undiscovered gold in the hills of New Jersey? Follow your husband. It's God's will.*

"Remember," I say to Sebastian after he bounds his sedan over our curb, clips a side mirror entering the garage and hurries into our living room. "William Wallace was hunted, captured and separated into parts for the downtrodden people to see."

"What a glorious six years he had," Sebastian says and begins his battle cry. "Nobody has dared before! Everyone before knew they were wrong and unwashed and too embarrassed to oppose me in court!" He rattles a paper proclaiming *The State of Illinois versus Sebastian Connery.* Poor State of Illinois, I know.

"I'll call our lawyer."

"None of that," Sebastian says. "I'm representing myself."

I want to say, "A man who represents himself has a fool . . ." but the army of right and might has already mounted up, its commander resolute and armed in his elbow-patched tweed coat. Sebastian takes me like his damsel, and I think to protest his chauvinism. Then his smell, his touch and his kiss make me think otherwise. Another day, maybe, I'll revolt and burn a bra. But I want him, along with his torments of me. It's my want of him that takes us to our bed at one in the afternoon.

The sound of *God Investment* carries from the kitchen radio into our bedroom. A woman's saying, *I know my position is to relinquish all financial control and leadership to my husband. I accept that.* And a husky-voiced man responds with words you just know come from a smiling mouth. *God bless you, caller. You are correct and righteous.* And the woman says, *But he's going to a tea leaf reader for stock advice.* Another man says, *Give him guidance, my pamphlet you can buy through my web site, and may God serve to show him the way. So who's our next caller?*

"Silly buggers," Sebastian says, and he flips on our bedroom radio to the FM, and the dial to 87.7, *WLFM*, which might as well advertise itself as the make-love music station. It drowns out *God Investment* below us.

I stand before him, my weapons exposed and armed. "We're invited to dinner with Iris Newberry at four-thirty," I say.

"But it's not Friday."

"I know. Iris insists it's a special dinner."

"I'm glad I came home early," Sebastian says, and I pounce on him.

6

Sebastian phones in our excuse to Iris Newberry. Whatever I hear half-asleep into my pillow doesn't work. We're going, the great Sebastian William Wallace Connery defeated by a wrinkle-free vampire. Roby bangs on the other side of our bedroom door, closed and locked.

The door speaks to us. "I see Dad's car is in the garage before I got home. Again." Roby's sneakers patter toward his own room.

"Does the boy think we're doing something illegal?" Sebastian asks. "Everybody else is divorcing or behaving like they should be divorcing. He should be happy with us."

Rising from our bed, Sebastian opens our closet door and reaches for an ancient box on the top shelf. There stand his chicken legs, nude, splayed, and completely hairless, and his fanny pale and small, capped by protruding love handles like muffin tops on his hips; his torso reaches straight and narrow to his thick, short neck and hairline. Not a terribly pretty sight, I suppose, but I recognize the parts and areas I remember by rote and by touch and how every time we embrace it's like the youthful magic of connecting puzzle pieces. Whenever I rise from our bed first, I sense Sebastian inspecting me, and the feeling swells the faults I know are there—my thighs like bowling pins overturned on their heads, puckered, and my fanny and breasts not standing like they once did, larger and in need of firmer undergarments.

It's the ancient box I despise Sebastian pulls down from the closet shelf, a handsome wood carving, ornate and pretty. It once served as someone's fine silverware case.

"Don't put that thing on our bed," I say, but he does. He opens it, standing naked over his dead relatives. Ashes of Mrs. Old Sebastian, and her father and mother, and Old Sebastian's father and mother, and great uncles and aunts and cousins stretching back to the day great-great Sebastian Connery first arrived in America with his bride, now also in the box. Not the entirety of them, but a pinch of them, each in their own miniature urn. The Urns of Connery, he calls them, as reverent as if they were the Lord's own tea cups.

I hide under the covers, thinking of all those old Victorian faces, so stern and disapproving of a woman who has a quarter of her not being Scottish, so naked before them.

"I promise you all," he says. "I swear I will win this battle in court. For the clean and the proper and the dignified." And he says like he always says before returning the Urns of Connery to the top shelf beside my dress shoes, "I'll be taking you back to Scotland one day soon. You shall see, to be released into Scotland's mists and the breezes of Kintyre."

He caresses our map of Scotland beside our closet door, rests his palms upon the Mull of Kintyre, the Mull stretching southwest like a tube into the ocean. Even in his pitiful past-middle-aged naked self, he appears like a humbled lamb receiving absolution from a priest.

When I think about the Urns of Connery, I, too, think of William Wallace. Like William Wallace, the Connery ancestors have been drawn and quartered. Rendered to ashes and separated. Parts of them rest in miniature in our urns and await their release in Scotland, the rest of them fly in the breezes of America. I'm a Connery by marriage and I wonder if part of my ashes will wind up in an urn alongside the pieces of the ancient Connerys. Roby will be in charge of my ashes one day. Chrissake.

The bedroom door speaks to us again. "When's dinner?"

"We're eating at Mrs. Newberry's," Sebastian says. "Four-thirty."

"But it's not Friday!"

"She's making a special dinner for us."

Our door says, "Blast!" and Roby's sneakers pound down the hall like he's carrying the weight of disaster on his shoulders.

With Sebastian's love and torment and his dead relatives powdery in my closet and Roby's teenage sullenness moping about and a vampire waiting for us to attend dinner in her lair, I cannot keep from laughing, and hard at that.

"I make you happy?" Sebastian asks.

I answer, "You're not boring."

He smiles. "Same thing."

Visualize the pall of a funeral parlor during a wake, or the dreariness of a museum for things nobody wanted to see when they were new, and the dreadful image could not outdo the suffocating atmosphere of Iris Newberry's dining room. Heavy, dark furniture tipped with gargoyle figurines at every chair and table foot, mottled curtains sealed tight absorbing sunset like black holes over the windows, wood floors stained turpentine brown, dotted by islands of regurgitated fur balls which may have been throw rugs two hundred years ago. The bulbs in the floor lamps and ceiling fixtures struggle as if light were not welcome.

"It smells like formaldehyde in there," Roby says not so secretly, perhaps hoping Iris might hear him and kick him out.

Sebastian says the same way as Roby, "It would put me to sleep if I weren't so concerned about the herd of gargoyles coming to life."

We leave the outside's sunlight and airy porch and enter

Bleak House. The space exhales doom and the sound of energy being sucked from my soul is almost audible outside my imagination. The home of a true vampire. The solid door slams shut behind us, and there's Iris Newberry. The sombrero is still on along with her baggy gardening clothes without a drop of sweat on them, and a slathering of bullet-proof sunblock is still white upon her cheeks. Sunglasses are off, her eyes blue and sharp, aiming like laser beams.

"The whole family, how nice," she says.

"Fifteen pints of A-positive plasma for her," Sebastian says in my ear.

Iris smiles. "What's that?"

I say, "He wants to see the surprise you've prepared for dinner."

"Don't be in such a hurry to find out or it won't be a surprise." She excuses herself for her kitchen, which we're never invited to see and we don't wish to go to anyway.

"Why do we do this?" Roby asks.

"Because she's alone," Sebastian says. "And quit slouching."

"That's how I stand."

"Chrissake almighty," Sebastian says. "The pictures on the walls are watching me again."

I want to scold my family, tell them to hush, but a stronger voice inside my head keeps me quiet in the hope Iris might overhear one day and stop inviting us for dinner. Who knew the explosion of John Newberry would mean our entombment for two hours every Friday, and now on a Tuesday for a special dinner?

"She's a lonely woman," I say. "We're being good neighbors."

"What's that?" Iris asks, returning with a dome-covered serving tray, far too large for an old woman to carry unless she's Iris Newberry. Her reflection (at least there is a reflection) stretches distorted over the top of the silver lid. In the image, her teeth move like a cave with teeth. "Sit. Let's eat."

In a whisper, Roby says, "Still smells like formaldehyde."

"What's that?"

"I said I became a vegetarian this morning."

"You can vegetate tomorrow," Iris says, setting the server down. She lifts the lid and we're greeted by four lobster tails, succulent and fresh, their smell inviting us to eat and savor them. They're surrounded by four different types of butter sauces in bowls for dipping, and fresh-steamed vegetables framing the whole delectable feast.

"There's more in the kitchen," Iris says.

Guilt. I feel it. And it's in the eyes of Roby and Sebastian while they sit at the gargoyle-infested dining room table and forget to put their napkins on their laps and rush for first crack at the best tail.

"Iris," I say. "You're full of surprises."

She sits and smiles at the men's hands cracking into the lobster tails. Beneath her hat brim, her smile is not like a vampire's, not even a vulture's, but that of a sad old woman. "I'm moving," she says. "Putting her up for sale tomorrow. So there's my surprise."

Sebastian and Roby freeze, mid bite, butter sauce dripping from their lips. How we complain about this place, our obligated entombment, yet we come here anyway, like going to church, hating it before arriving, abiding the service, then feeling invigorated for having gone. I expect Roby to jump out of his seat and fly around the room, but I see sadness in his eyes.

"But why, Mrs. Newberry?" Roby asks.

"Because I've heard my house smells like formaldehyde, young man." She taps her right ear.

"Oh."

"It's because the house is too much, the yard too much, and there's too much of my husband still here. And it's full of gargoyles." She turns her laser-stare to Sebastian and taps her right ear at him.

"Oh."

"I'm going to sell her. After forty years in this house, she'll probably make me a rich woman. I'll buy one of those condos in Florida or Arizona where old ladies are supposed to migrate to and die."

I say, "Don't go. We'll take care of you," even as I ask myself why I'm saying such strange things.

"Please, dear. You'll be glad. No more complaints about your yard from me. Maybe someone else will let the sun shine into this place. I can't."

Iris Newberry takes a lobster tail and mauls it with her bare hands. We eat without much conversation, listening to Iris preach about how good a man John was and how she misses him and wants to repent to him for all her unkind words and prays his soul in heaven will forgive her and want her in heaven beside him when it's her turn to go.

"I didn't deserve him," Iris moans. "He certainly didn't deserve me."

Thoughts of vampires and my garden of weeds and black spot and the dreariness of this house leave me instantly. I want to hug Iris Newberry, and I do hug her. Within our embrace, I feel frailty in her bones and the smell of men's cologne, the scent I remember on John Newberry whenever he stopped by for a visit.

"John died four years ago to the day," Iris says. "I have to sell her."

Through her mound of thick denim, I feel the vampire Iris Newberry tremble.

"I wonder," Sebastian says as we step away from her porch toward our house, "who in the world would buy her place the way it looks?" I want to answer, *Hopefully nobody,* and I think about and ponder the pros and cons of Iris Newberry.

A familiar voice behind me pulls at my ears. *She's the woman you offered as proof of a happy marriage?*

I stop to let the men go on home, and pivot back toward the Newberry house. Lola Two looks like a figure eight in a mini-skirt and halter top standing on the steps to Iris's porch. Her eyes now in the shape of a cat's, she says, *Eye job and brow lift. What do you think?*

Sebastian waits for me at our front door, and I turn from Lola Two. *Have you asked your loving husband yet where he goes off to now and then?* Her laughter scratches at my back. *God Investment is your present, and Iris Newberry is your future.*

7

Why is it that all these young people working at Dignity Place have such contentment on their faces? They wheel the Old Toots around the grounds in pre-set tracks no faster than a snail's crawl so the Old Toots don't get too worked up, and they deal with spit and drool and stories from times nobody cares about concerning people who are dead now or living at Dignity Place. Yet the young people smile. Real smiles—not like the fake smile I wear here—even as they wipe and clean and spray and mop and soak up all the horrible things the Old Toots trail behind themselves.

In the visitor's day room, I see a paper tacked to a notice board that reads, Help Wanted.

Perhaps it's an S-O-S from an Old Toot suffering misery while nubile workers show off their youth around her. So I read the smaller print:

Inspired person wanted to manage fitness program activities.
Must be energetic, tender with our Residents, and patient.
Aerobics Instructor certification preferred, but not required.

Someone had scrawled in red ink below it: Must look good in leotards.

★ ★ ★ ★ ★

I might consider myself good-looking in leotards—in the dark, without my reading glasses and if I lie to myself. But I'm not a waif. I'm covered in puckering skin. I don't have the aerobic instructor's face, the young actress's face, or the model's face. Those faces, gaunt and skeletoned about the eyes, with mouths cosmetically altered to look like one of those fish forever lip-stuck to the inside of aquarium glass.

"You're beautiful," Sebastian tells me every morning.

To Sebastian, I always answer, "That's because your standards are low."

I turn from the help wanted sign and see Old Sebastian in his wheelchair and Sebastian and Roby huddled with him. They're agape watching a young woman read a *Cosmopolitan* magazine as she sits so daintily on a fold-out chair beside an Old Toot. The Connery men seem preoccupied with her beauty, their jaws hanging stupidly at a short skirt made shorter by the crossing of her legs.

As I walk to them, Old Sebastian whispers to Sebastian, "That's Poof Butt, just wait and see."

Poof Butt?

So I flit my eyes as if to look at a picture on the wall, spying on the woman Old Sebastian calls Poof Butt. With her straight nose, high-arched brow, youthful skin and narrow waist and those fish-lips sucking air over her magazine, she'd be perfect to answer the help wanted sign. Beside her, the Old Toot has the same nose and brow, set deep in wrinkles, and her posture is the same, only shorter. The Old Toot glances at Poof Butt with a longing, a memory perhaps of her own features during their unwrinkled days. Poof Butt turns a Cosmo page and ignores the Old Toot.

"Bitch," Sebastian says.

"Just wait," Old Sebastian says.

Roby asks, "Wait for what?"

Then it happens. Poof Butt finishes her *Cosmo* and stands to get another on a rack across the day room. She passes me, gives a smirky smile, and bends low to inspect the rack of *Cosmopolitan*, *Good Housekeeping* and *People* magazines.

"Christ," she says in a snit. "Nothing from this year."

Old Sebastian squirms in his wheelchair, his body jumbling about even as his face fights back laughter. In their chairs, it's the same with Roby and Sebastian.

"Poof Butt," Old Sebastian says.

She walks by me toward her chair with the same awful smile, her hips overdoing the swaying, and the rolling mound of each fanny cheek pushes back against her skirt. Between each cheek, dead center, shines the bright red color of a flat-topped tack.

Old Sebastian says, "Bulls eye."

"Poof Butt," Roby says.

The Old Toot beside her raises her stare to me, then to Old Sebastian, and she smiles her perfect dentures at him and raises a conspiratorial thumbs up.

"Good shot, Marie," Old Sebastian says across the room, and the Old Toot blows him a kiss, all going on in the ignorance of Poof Butt as she flips a magazine page and sits as comfortably as can be.

"Serves her right," Sebastian says, "ignoring her mother the way she does."

Old Sebastian looks at me, just a glance, but enough to make me worry, enough to make me inspect my fanny for tacks. Finding none doesn't keep me from thinking Old Sebastian plots to put one there.

"I punched another hole in a wall in my room."

Roby laughs, "Find any gangster bones?"

Old Sebastian shakes his head. "They're here somewhere. I know it."

"I want to work," I say to Sebastian in bed. Seeing the glow in Sebastian's eyes, I add to stop his lust, "Outside the house I mean."

"Oh," Sebastian says, and he curls up beside me. "What would you like to do?"

"There's a help wanted sign at Dignity Place for an exercise instructor."

"I saw," Sebastian says. "Must look good in leotards."

"Don't you think I can do that?"

"Of course I do. But I worry you don't think so."

Sebastian draws near, his head upon my pillow. It takes a few minutes, but I ask him. My words come out after tripping through my throat. "Where do you go off to now and again?"

He's fallen asleep, so easy and content. He sounds as though he snores through a smile.

Why can't I dream about George Clooney? That's what I want to know. It's bad enough to go to Dignity Place and think about working there, but do I have to dream it, too? I see all the Old Toots lined up in their wheelchairs with their walkers and their canes, ready to do their exercises. The music plays, Tchaikovsky's *Swan Lake,* and with each twin beat of the waltz an Old Toot topples over and curses me for it.

"Play something slower!" Old Sebastian demands in my dream. "You're killing us!"

I say, "Slower than *Swan Lake?*" And I see myself in leotards, vainly trying to flatten my cellulite and tummy, and my fanny's covered in tacks, the Old Toots laughing and congratulating themselves.

I wake up screaming.

"What?" Sebastian says, jolting from his sleep.

"Nothing."

"Definitely was something."

"They covered me in tacks."

"Who?"

"You worry I think I don't look good in leotards? What did you mean by that?"

Sebastian presses against me and starts to speak then hesitates. "Can I answer without getting hit?"

"Depends on the answer."

"How about if I go back to sleep?"

"Answer me."

He sighs and holds me tighter. "We all get old. We all become Old Toots if we're lucky to live long enough. Things fall apart, but you'll still be my Julia."

"I'll get ugly and crumbly and my teeth will fall out and my breasts will take turns covering my navel."

"I promise not to put my glasses on," Sebastian says.

"You'll leave me."

"I can't live without you."

"Why do you say such things?"

"Because I mean it."

"I know someone who gets plastic surgery all the time. What do you think about that?"

"I think you wouldn't be my Julia."

"I'd be better."

"How?"

"My breasts wouldn't flatten out in bed."

"Lassie, let me enjoy you every way you are, everything you become, until the day I die. That's what I want."

"I may take that job at Dignity Place."

Eyes dilated, unbuttoning my nightgown, he says, "Looks damn good in leotards. Even better without leotards."

There's another question I'm supposed to ask him. Can't think of it, though. Not now.

8

There's a woman at the front door early this morning, probably forty, but dressed in a short skirt, tight blouse and far too many cosmetics to pretend she's thirty, or younger, and she's clutching her precious copies of *Angela's Ashes* and *Tuesdays With Morrie*, both. She's weepy and sighing up a storm on my porch, and says even as I hold my wedding band to my chin, "I'm writing a book about the best teacher I ever had. Is the dear Sebastian Connery at home?"

To her I want to say he died, but saying so might make her explode, leaving nothing but buckets of tears on my welcome mat. "It's Monday morning," I say. "He's teaching at the junior college."

"But it's seven-thirty."

"Teachers' meeting."

"The college office told me Friday he would be off today."

"They lied to you. They get so many book writers pestering the teachers."

She's sneak-peeking around me, checking for proof I've lied. Her perfume, Chanel No. 5, 6, *and* 7, it seems, blasts around my face and into the living room, like fingertip-searching pheromones in the high rutting season, hunting for my Sebastian.

"Gone," I say. "I'm his wife. I'm Julia," and I extend my hand to hers and squeeze to let her know I'm not someone to mess with. In my mind I'm flipping her about with the strength of ten Amazons, a judo throw to the ground, then one of Roby's Wrestle-Mania show's throat-stomping pile drivers into the mat, and I finish with a *Crouching Tiger, Hidden Dragon* rapid fire kick to her chin while she stays frozen in time.

Walking away, down the porch steps, she passes through Lola Two. *You see? There's plenty of opportunities for dear Sebastian, especially at a junior college.* Lola Two winks at me and fiddles with an earring flat against the side of her head. *Dr. Plastic finally tacked them back.* She looks at my ears as if they were built to catch radio waves, and I slam the door on her.

With another torment tearing at my heart, Sebastian appears from our hall, sniffing the scent the latest weeper left behind for him. "What's that awful smell?" he asks. And with proof of his good taste, he opens the living room windows to let the late summer air blow her odor away.

"A wrong address."

"Some people cover up their stink with more stink," he says, and another torment feels like it's about to pass. Then Sebastian, in his best blue suit, pressed and clean, adjusts his tie and tells me what I've worked so hard to block from my mind.

"Ready for court," he says.

"It's today?"

Sebastian shoves a CD into the living room stereo and a tartan bagpipe battle march loads up the troops in our home. He freezes there with a stare to faraway Scotland, his eyes dreaming to right the wrongs done to Scottish soil by the Romans and the Vikings and the French and the English, and the poor soul who doesn't wash his hands before eating his girlfriend's popcorn.

Roby appears. "Is it today, Dad?"

Sebastian doesn't answer. He can't. His spine hardens, his heart races, the plaid rises in his brain, the whole of him embraced by the song and soul of the tartan bagpipes.

"I'm going with you," Roby says, "school or not."

Breaking his trance, Sebastian says, "Roby can come with me." Then turns to me and orders like a warrior, "Call my father."

Throughout history, the Scottish were lucky to survive any battle, let alone win one. My whole family is off to the slaughter.

For six years, William Wallace rose from the ranks of the common Highlander and fought brilliantly against the English. He became a folk hero, a true hope of the people to rid Scotland of the pretenders to Scottish soil. William Wallace won an occasional battle he had no business winning. Yet he could not bring himself to win the big one. He could not reach the top despite the unwavering loyalty of the people even in the face of repeated defeat and the utter hopelessness of the truth.

"Like the Chicago Cubs of the thirteenth century," Roby once said about William Wallace. "So loved by the fans, always promising, blindly believing, and usually drunk." A twenty-first century analogy Sebastian agreed with but added that both the Cubs and the Scots were alive and kicking and still trying.

"Right, Dad," Roby said. To the agony of his father's heart, Roby cheers on Notre Dame and the Yankees.

As I drive my family to court this morning, my sedan holds all the torment I can stand. Old Sebastian talks legal strategy with Sebastian in the back seat, and Old Sebastian's dentures *click* and *squish* out a noise that reminds me of a butcher handling raw meat.

"Don't let them intimidate you, son." *Click click. Squish squish.* "Don't let them see one bit of fear in you."

"I have no fear," Sebastian says.

Click click. Squish squish. "That's my boy!"

Roby says beside me, "Are you all right, Mom?" I want to

hug him and squeeze all the wrinkled, baggy clothes he's wearing.

"Thank you. I'm fine."

"Liar."

"I know."

From the back seat: "Object to everything the prosecutor says, even if you're not supposed to."

"Thanks, Dad. I will."

I turn on the radio, tuned to *God Investment. We're heading for bankruptcy,* a desperate woman says in tears. *Can't I take charge of anything?* The male hosts answer together, *Take charge of your role as the woman and,* with gusto they say, *Stand by your man!* The woman nearly screams, *You guys quoting the Bible or Tammy Wynette?* And she hangs up.

"Why do you listen to this garbage?" Roby asks.

"Because it makes me remember your father isn't so bad and I'm not that stupid."

Click click. Squish squish. "Now don't let the judge push you around either, son."

"I won't, Dad. I won't."

"The Cubs are in last place again," Roby says.

I turn off *God Investment* and consider the history of the Chicago Cubs, Scotland and the generals in the back seat. "How far out of first?" I ask.

Roby says, "A whole lot."

Metal detectors, German Shepherds and guards with holstered weapons at the gates keep the endless line of zombie-faces in order, more like a march into prison than a courthouse of supposed fair play and justice.

"Where are the pillars?" Old Sebastian asks. "Isn't this a courthouse?"

"It's new," Sebastian says.

"Looks like a shopping mall." *Click. Squish.* "Where's the old-man-in-the-wheelchair line?"

"Only one line, Dad," I say.

Old Sebastian sneers at the gray-suited man in front of us and whispers to Roby, "This one looks like a lawyer." With a nudge of his wheelchair toggle, Old Sebastian bumps his wheelchair forward.

"Hey!"

"Are you a lawyer?" Old Sebastian asks.

The man shakes his head. "I'm a salesman with a speeding ticket."

"I'm truly sorry." To Roby, he says, "Wait till I find some lawyers," and wiggles his wheelchair like a car anxious to start a demolition derby. He stiffens his back and pushes at his dentures. "I think I see Sam The Man Flounders. Hope these metal detectors work."

"There're no gangsters here, Dad," Sebastian says.

"Right," Old Sebastian says, grousing. "Bet I don't leave this building alive."

After Roby, I go through the humming metal detectors. My purse appears on the x-ray screen showing my wadded up tissues, car keys, lipstick balm, nickels and pennies, checkbook and wallet, and my three rolls of Tums. Old Sebastian's wheelchair sounds the alarm like an air raid siren and three guards pounce with their metal detector wands.

"He's harmless," one guard says to the others.

"Mostly, but not completely," Old Sebastian says. "You fellahs know where I can find some lawyers?"

Sebastian shouts, "I'm not putting my satchel on the conveyer!"

The guard at the conveyer barks, "You have to or you can't enter the courthouse."

"Sebastian," I say, "let them do their jobs." The guard, with his security patches and emblems, gives me a smile.

Sebastian clutches his leather satchel, cracked and tied with leather strings, like a weaning baby to the breast. "I am not x-raying the satchel!"

"Buddy," the conveyer guard says. "Either you do it now or you'll have to leave, and if you don't do either of those, I'll arrest you."

Roby says something about how funny it would be to get arrested while on your way to prove to a jury why you shouldn't have been arrested.

"Please, Sebastian," I say.

"Urns of Connery," Sebastian says in a rush.

"What?"

"I brought the Urns of Connery."

"You didn't!"

He squeezes the satchel tighter. "I did."

No pads of paper in his satchel, no pens or pencils. Just particles of the dead side of his family to help in the battle, Sebastian would say if I were to ask him, so I don't ask him.

Guards surround Sebastian now and the line behind him grows and grumbles. With the tears of a hundred ancestral Connerys, Sebastian gives up the satchel holding the thimble-sized containers of dust, of Great Grandpa Sebastian and his wife and aunts and uncles and brothers and sisters and cousins and who-knows-who else as long as they're Scottish and Connery by blood or by marriage. Sebastian cringes at the satchel's pitiful clank into a vault, piled in with the common possessions of the dirty and the unwashed—the Urns of Connery!—and Sebastian sadly places a parcel identification tag into his suit pocket.

"Like a pauper's grave," he says.

"We'll get them back," I say. "Like a resurrection."

A shout across the atrium—*Hey!* Old Sebastian smiles at the shins of two lawyers he's nailed, apologizing, clicking, squishing, and faking senility. "Sorry. I thought one of you was Sam The Man Flounders."

Roby takes my hand. "Saint Julia Connery," he says. "Have a Tums."

We're packed and sweaty in the front row of courtroom 200, traffic and misdemeanor court, and whoever built these public pews has a passion for stiff right angles and a complete disregard for the human body. Old Sebastian parks in the aisle beside Sebastian. The bailiff calls case after case, first the traffic tickets, then the jailed misdemeanants, then the free misdemeanants.

Judge Marcus Eastman looks as bored as a math genius who's been explaining what one plus one equals for an eternity. His shock of white hair makes him look the judge, but his down-turned mouth appears ready to drool out of boredom. Jailbird after jailbird says the same thing: "Please, Judge. I want to get my life back together." "Please, Judge, I want to get my life back together." With each "Please, Judge," the Honorable Marcus Eastman further dulls his eyes, increases the jailbird's fine, adds another day in jail, until the last "Please, Judge" seems ready to earn life in prison for stealing a watch.

Old Sebastian eyes three young men and one young woman in gray suits sitting at attorney tables, right and left. Each snickers at the unrepresented fools making things worse for themselves. All have pads of paper and pens in front of them.

"Lawyers," Old Sebastian says beside Sebastian.

"Prosecutors," Sebastian says, pointing to the man and woman seated at the table to our right. "Public Defenders," he then says, pointing to the two seated at the table to our left.

Click click. Squish squish. "They're all lawyers to me."

"Why don't they do anything?" Roby asks.

The woman prosecutor stands. "We have one trial, Your

Honor. The People versus Sebastian Connery. Misdemeanor battery."

Judge Eastman calls out, "Sebastian Connery!"

There's just our little family left seated on the torture-pews. Sebastian raises his hand.

"Why don't you talk to the nice prosecutor and work things out?"

To the prosecutor, Sebastian negotiates, "I want the case dropped and an apology."

Back to Judge Eastman, she says, "Ready for trial."

"For crying out loud," Judge Eastman says.

"We must be ruining some important golfing plans," Old Sebastian whispers to the family with a *click* and a *squish* and a low snarl. "After all, judges are lawyers too, you know."

"Have you signed a jury waiver form, Mr. Connery?"

"Why would I do that, Your Honor, if a jury trial is what I want?"

"You want a jury trial, Mr. Connery?"

"Yes, Your Honor. If it's still a right in this country and not an imposition."

"Good one," Old Sebastian says.

"Suicide," Roby says.

Judge Eastman leans toward his bailiff, his mouth shaping into curse words so it seems, then straightens. "You sure you want a jury trial?"

"It's my right, and I want one."

"Where's your lawyer?"

"I'm doing this myself."

The public defenders and prosecutors turn to us and smile, and not the smile-with-us kind.

"You've got your jury instructions ready, Mr. Connery?"

Sebastian says, "What?"

Again Judge Eastman leans toward his bailiff, and there come the private curse words again, with exclamation points this time. "Is the prosecution ready?"

"Yes, Your Honor," she says. "The victim is in my office."

"The victim?" Sebastian nearly sings with his palms pressed over his heart. "I'm right here."

"See you at one," Judge Eastman says, "for the trial of the century, I presume," and leaves without an "all rise" or a bang of his gavel. The public defenders scamper away like they're excited tattletales, and the prosecutors, to each other, whisper, laugh, whisper, laugh, and look at us with their evil prosecutor smiles.

"How are you going to do this without any pens or pads of paper?" I ask Sebastian. "At least you need pens and paper, not the Urns of Connery."

"Did you ever see the winning lawyers on TV use pens and a pad of paper?" Sebastian says. "Perry Mason, Ben Matlock, Ally McBeal? None of those lawyers ever used a pad of paper or pencil in court."

"You watch Ally McBeal reruns?" Roby asks.

"That's TV!" I say.

Sebastian folds his arms and huffs. "I know what's right and I can do this myself without a pad of paper and without pens. I've got it all figured out in my head and the facts aren't about to change."

The prosecutors leave and Old Sebastian takes off after them. Why bother trying to stop him? How can I? He has the advantage of being an Old Toot on a speedy motorized wheelchair and the presumption of senility on his side. From the hall, we hear one of the prosecutors yelp and Old Sebastian apologize and ask about Sam The Man Flounders.

Sebastian begins to hum some battle hymn of William Wallace, the brave and ultimately defeated, and I swear there's a tartan bagpipe inside Sebastian's throat loading up for righteous battle, oblivious once again to the odds against him.

9

"I'll take all twelve," the prosecutor says of the first panel of potential jurors. She has asked not a single question of them, not a single one booted off, even though Judge Eastman said each side could boot off five during the selection without giving him a reason. Behind us sit over a dozen more potential jurors, and almost two dozen men and women in suits, holding pens, pads of paper, and smiling at each other and pointing at Sebastian.

"Who do you think they are?" Roby asks.

"Lawyers," Old Sebastian says. "With nothing better to do than watch the show."

"I recognize someone from Fox News."

"Better still."

We sit behind Sebastian who sits at the counsel table without a pen or pad of paper but with sixteen hundred years of righteousness on his side. The Honorable Marcus Eastman wants to know if Sebastian has any questions for the potential jurors.

"Can I kick any one of them off?"

"We say 'excuse,' Mr. Connery. As I said before, you may excuse up to five jurors."

Without asking a question of any juror, Sebastian says, "Then I excuse Mr. Davis, Mr. Jensen, Mr. Alberts, and Mr. Peterson," leaving eight women and four empty juror chairs.

The suits behind us go on again with their giggles and smiles and say things like Romeo and Don Juan and idiot and lamb to slaughter. I want to stand up and beg for mercy, plea insanity on Sebastian's behalf, but I can't do any of that. Sebastian's living William Wallace's last stand, and he keeps smiling at me and winking and nodding at Roby with his chest puffed out and returns Old Sebastian's thumbs up.

The clerk calls the next four jurors from the pews to replace the booted-off Mr., Mr., Mr., and Mr. They are *Mrs.* Carol Johnson, *Mrs.* Bettina Pattock, *Mrs.* Marybeth Friel. But then— *Mr.* Dave Jones.

Mr. Dave Jones is the last to sit in the jury box, and he's an older gentleman covered in a gray beard and long gray hair with only his forehead, eyes and nose showing through, and his baggy blue jean overall disguises whether he's heavy or thin. Sebastian has a reaction to this man, a double-take. We all do, it seems, because he's like Bigfoot showing up to court.

"I'll take all twelve," the lady prosecutor says, again without a single question, again with the assurance of a bazooka aimed point-blank at prey inside a tea cup.

Sebastian rises, buttons his coat, and says, "So do I, Your Honor," then sits.

"He let a man sit on the jury," Old Sebastian says, his loose dentures churning with their clicks and squishes.

Roby asks, "Is that a mistake?"

Maybe it's my imagination, my understanding of Sebastian's powers, or his torment of me, but all eleven women in the jury box seem to blink at my Sebastian, smile and appear ready to launch their panties at him. Mr. Dave Jones sits like a mushroom festering on a log, head down and hidden.

Click, squish. "I recognize that hairy man from Dignity Place. Didn't know he had a name. Just sits all day outside looking up at the sun, even in the winter."

Sebastian leans to me, far over the battlefield railing. "Julia," he says with the secretive talk of a spy. "That man, that man," he goes on. "He's none other than our dear departed friend. I could smell him, see it in his eyes. I swear it."

Roby bends close. "Who, Dad?"

"None other than Iris's very own John Newberry."

"No," I say.

"Yes," Sebastian says.

"Is that legal?" Roby stutters. "He's dead."

"The prosecutor didn't ask him a single question," Sebastian says. "Her smug face is not my fault."

"It can't be," I say. "We saw Iris bury him."

Sebastian reminds me. "Closed casket."

"What's with Iris Newberry?" Roby shifts uncomfortably on the pew. "What's in the coffin?"

"Dave Jones?" *Click, squish.* "What kind of fake name is that?"

"We have an ally behind enemy lines," Sebastian says, and he rolls his seat back to his lawyer table.

Mr. Dave Jones raises his stare for a second, and through all the hair, John Newberry nods the slightest hello to me, like an accident, then buries himself once again.

Sebastian Connery, like William Wallace in his final days of life, has been chased through the Lowlands and the Highlands, taking direct hits, looking for places to hide, discovered and routed again and again. We gather by the drinking fountain, huddled, Sebastian preparing final strategy while I consider how much bail money is left in our checking account.

"Why didn't you give an opening statement?" Roby asks.

Sebastian answers, "Why should I show my cards before the game begins?"

"How's it going, son?" Old Sebastian pushes at his dentures.

It's the one thing that keeps Sebastian smiling, his father blind to the truth of disaster. Sebastian strokes his father's face, cuddles wrinkles over old cheekbones. "We'll get those dentures fixed tomorrow, Dad."

It's lost now, and I know Sebastian understands. Even if all twelve jurors were Dave Jones or John Newberry or whoever the pitiful man wants to be, all is lost. When lost, Sebastian tightens his grip around his family because his family is his victory among all else.

"I'm getting tired," Sebastian moans. "I'm tired of hearing the prosecutor and the judge and their little conversations. 'Objection,' she says. 'Sustained,' he says. Over and over like gongs in my ears."

"Those were just the police witnesses and the theater usher," I say. And I know I shouldn't say such things. My talk only encourages him, but Sebastian, to me, is at his most powerful when he's the whimpering pup in a storm. I remind him, "You still have Howard Dirty-Hands to cross-examine. He's the prosecutor's entire case, so you haven't lost a thing."

In front of Roby groaning and complaining that we're on security video and Old Sebastian saying there's nothing wrong with his dentures, Sebastian holds me close, cups one hand on my bottom, the other behind my neck. He kisses me. "Howard Dirty-Hands," he says, tickling my ear. "Very clever of you."

There's a flush in the men's room beside the elevator, and a moment later Howard Dirty-Hands appears, running a hand through his perfect gray hair.

"No time for a wash," Sebastian whispers to me, turning toward him from our embrace.

I expect a war, a fight in the hall, another arrest, another trip to the desk sergeant at the police station. But no. Sebastian smiles at Howard Dirty-Hands, watches him ignore us and straighten his tweed sport coat with the patches at the elbow as he heads back to court.

"What?" I ask.

"Victory," Sebastian says.

I kiss Sebastian again because I fear it may be a few days, weeks or months before the next one.

10

Standing before witness Howard Dirty-Hands (smug and fresh from telling the prosecutor and the jury how my Sebastian attacked him like an animal, and for no good reason) Sebastian turns to Judge Eastman. "May I ask a question, Your Honor?"

"That's the whole idea of cross-examination, Mr. Connery."

"I mean of you."

Judge Eastman glances at the prosecutor. She smirks toward the lawyer-filled pews, her familiar men and women lawyer friends in suits with lunch stuck between their teeth, so excited to watch a defendant make a complete boob of himself. They wave and grin at her and wink their *Why nots? More fun for us!* She returns an I-don't-care shrug to the judge.

Judge Eastman says, "Ask me your question, Mr. Connery."

"What exactly is a battery?"

Leaning long over his raised bench to the giggles of the lawyers, Judge Eastman drones, "Don't you think you should've known the answer to that question before you started representing yourself at this trial?"

"But there are all kinds of batteries, right? I mean there's the sock-them-in-the jaw kind. There's the push-them-down-the-stairs kind."

"So?"

"Then there's the don't-touch-me-like-that kind, too, even if there're no bruises for that kind of battery."

"Correct, Mr. Connery." Judge Eastman, to the music of

lawyers giggling and snorting, eases back and asks, "Are you thinking you're ready to defend murder cases now?"

"No, sir. Just checking about battery. I don't want to ask anything likely to get you and the prosecutor going on that objection-sustained conversation again. It's very annoying."

This time Old Sebastian and Roby giggle and snort and the lawyers keep their yaps shut. Sebastian straightens his tie, tugs at his sleeves and takes a step closer to Howard Dirty-Hands. For Sebastian, it's hard standing so close to a pile of rubbish, and he asks his questions like he's trying to hold his breath.

"Just before, as you say, I struck you mercilessly, you were eating popcorn from a bucket you shared with your date, am I right?"

Howard Dirty-Hands tilts his head to look beyond Sebastian to the prosecutor. She's doodling with her pen on her pad of paper and doesn't object.

"That's correct."

"By the way, where is your nice woman friend? Why isn't she here to testify on your behalf or at least come for support like my family over there?" Sebastian points to us and waves. Old Sebastian waves back and the women jurors smile at him. Dave-Jones-John-Newberry stays hidden in his hair.

"She couldn't make it," Howard Dirty-Hands says.

"Couldn't make it? Why not?"

"What's she got to do with this?"

Judge Eastman interrupts. "That's a good question, Mr. Connery."

Sebastian scratches his chin and strikes a pose the way Perry Mason and Ben Matlock and Ally McBeal all do, and I just know he's recalling a television-lawyer answer. "I'll tie it all up before it's over, Your Honor."

"I'll give you one minute."

"Well, sir," to Howard Dirty-Hands, "seems I only have a

minute. So to the point and under oath. Is it true your lovely girlfriend broke up with you that night at the cinema?"

"For unrelated reasons."

"I see. You're at the cinema, the victim of a merciless battery, and the nice lady breaks up with you?"

Howard Dirty-Hands squirms and pulls at his coat's elbow patches. Old Sebastian growls, "Now hit him with an uppercut, boy."

"It's private," Howard Dirty-Hands answers.

Sebastian says, "My guess is you can't say that under oath."

Judge Eastman, for the first time looking at Sebastian without a scowl, says, "I've noted that the witness's answer to your question is evasive. Go ahead, Mr. Connery. I'm giving you another minute."

"Again to the point, sir. I suppose if I ask you about your bathroom habits, you'd say you were a clean man, a man who washes with soap and water after every flush."

There's urgent coughing behind us from the lawyers waving their pads at the prosecutor. She's doodling away on her pad a second longer before she finally looks up and says, "What?"

"Object!" a lawyer in back says.

"Zip your yapper," Old Sebastian says. A slam of the gavel shuts everyone up.

"For the first time in years," Judge Eastman says, "something new is happening in my courtroom, and I would appreciate it if the rest of you would give your mouths a rest." With a moment's threat of contempt of court, nobody breathes until Judge Eastman says in a kinder voice, "Go ahead, Mr. Connery."

"Sir. Do you wash after every bathroom flush, soap and water?"

"Of course I do."

"And you washed your hands at the cinema before dipping them in your lady friend's popcorn bucket?"

"Of course I did. I always do."

"Your Honor," the prosecutor says. "How is this relevant to the fact that Mr. Connery beat this man up with an umbrella?"

"Defense of the poor lady," Sebastian says.

"Ridiculous. Even if he didn't wash his hands, it's no defense to this case."

Sebastian steps toward the center of the courtroom and posits to the air around him, like Perry, Ben, and Ally. "We've established that a battery can be an unwanted touch, even the kind that doesn't leave a bruise." Sebastian waits the dramatic pause, and as if directed by Steven Spielberg himself, hits his next line. "So I give you this choice—would you rather get the unwanted push or eat popcorn intentionally infested by this witness's unwashed hands?"

Of course everyone would choose Howard Dirty-Hands' popcorn as the more vile battery, and the prosecutor looks down at her pad, littered in doodles, as if there were a different answer there for her to find.

"But Mr. Connery," Judge Eastman says. "Can you prove the state's witness used the toilet and didn't wash his hands before shoving them in his date's popcorn?"

"Myself, Your Honor," Sebastian says, "and these other honest witnesses." He points to the Connery family, all of us close and looking doe-eyed, and Old Sebastian pushing his dentures back into place. "Each would testify they saw Howard Dirty-Hands come out of the bathroom not a minute before recess was over and he took the stand."

"Objection," Howard Dirty-Hands says. "My name is Howard Carruthers, and he heard me say that!"

"We'll see what your name is," Judge Eastman says. "And stop objecting, you have a prosecutor." Judge Eastman stretches himself close to the witness box, and waves Sebastian to go on with his questions.

"Sir. Did you use the bathroom during the last recess?"

"Well. Yeah."

"And it was a stall you used, wasn't it?"

To the judge, Howard Dirty-Hands begs, "Do I have to answer? I mean, isn't that why they put doors on bathrooms?"

"Humor us," Judge Eastman says. "You're under oath."

"Fine then. Yes. A stall. Yes."

"And," Sebastian says, "you washed your hands right after, soap and water, just like your mother taught you?"

"Of course!"

"Just like you say you always do. Just like at the cinema before plunging your hands into the lady's popcorn?"

"Yes! Of course! Yes!"

To the Judge, Sebastian asks, "So I don't do this the wrong way, Your Honor, can I now have the witness approach the jury?"

Howard Dirty-Hands goes pale. "What?"

"Objection!" the prosecutor says.

"Whatever for?" Judge Eastman says.

Sebastian says, "I want the jurors to sniff his hands."

"Christ!" the prosecutor says.

The jurors, except Dave-Jones-John-Newberry, laugh nervously at this and lean far back in their seats. But the lawyers sitting behind us interest me most. With their glorious education and bravado and suits and pads of paper and pens, they are as quiet as babes asleep in their cribs.

"Objection," the prosecutor says again.

"But why object, Your Honor?" Sebastian points into the air. "This man testified under oath that he washes his hands all the time, washed them at the cinema, just like he says he washed them not ten minutes ago. If he's telling the truth, his hands ought to smell like the nice lemony-fresh soap you have in your bathroom dispensers. If not, well, Lord only knows."

Jurors gasp and shudder away, like it's a maggot instead of a man they're watching squirm in the witness chair.

"It's as certain as a blood test," Sebastian goes on. "Lawyers use that all the time, don't they? And if a man can't defend a woman against this gruesome sort of battery, then what kind of world do we live in?"

Judge Marcus Eastman, with his black robe and high-rise judicial bench and shock of white hair, sits and ponders the attack of Sebastian Connery and the proof not just of his innocence, but of his bravery. "How do you know what our bathroom soap smells like?"

Sebastian poses as if swooping Superman's cape over his shoulders. "I, Your Honor, always wash my hands."

"He does indeed," Old Sebastian calls out.

To the helpless Howard Dirty-Hands, Judge Eastman orders, "Step to the jury."

"Oh my God!" says a juror in the front row.

Howard Dirty-Hands yelps, "No!"

"No?" Judge Eastman barks. "You're telling me what I can and cannot order in my own courtroom?"

Howard Dirty-Hands shrivels in his seat.

"Objection," Sebastian says. "I think he's wiping his hands on his pants."

Judge Eastman pounds his fists. "Let me see those hands!"

"No." Howard Dirty-Hands says again. "Leave me alone."

From the jury box comes a voice, low and scratchy as if it belongs to a man who long ago decided to give up talking. "Not guilty," the lone man says, and I know for certain, from all my years hearing his voice speak volumes of Iris and her war against weeds and dirt and sunshine, that without any doubt I breathe in the living presence of the dead and buried John Newberry.

"Objection!" the prosecutor screams. "I get closing argument. I get jury instructions. I get the right of jury deliberation."

"Not guilty," Dave-Jones-John-Newberry says again, and he raises his sad face from all his hair. "Not guilty."

One by one the remaining jurors say "Not guilty" until the last, all nodding their heads along the way, more and more thanking God they don't have to sniff the evidence against Howard Dirty-Hands.

"What's the point of deliberation?" Judge Eastman says and bangs his gavel. "Not guilty!"

Sebastian falls to his knees, clutches his fingers tight, and calls for me; I run to him and go to my knees beside him.

"I've won, Julia! I've won!" The strength of William Wallace and all his brave and righteous men live in the blood flowing through the heart of my Sebastian. All around us hums the noise of mopping up; jurors sighing their continued relief, and the Honorable Judge Marcus Eastman ordering Howard Dirty-Hands out of his courtroom and to not touch anything on the way out, and to security to disinfect everything he may have touched. There sits the prosecutor with her pen and doodled pad of paper, looking ill, perhaps at the memory of a handshake with Howard Dirty-Hands and of all the things he touched while waiting in her office before the trial started. Roby stands by us saying, "Wow, Dad! Wow, Dad!" and Old Sebastian's wheelchair whirs away at the shins of lawyers, not one of them able to do what my Sebastian just did this afternoon.

The man Roby knows from Fox News runs out of the courtroom with a smile broad over his face.

I raise my stare to the jury box. They're all there applauding and smiling and wiping tears from their eyes, except for John Newberry. Like a sainted spirit, again the man has vanished.

"They can keep my infected umbrella," Sebastian says. "Let's get the Urns of Connery."

Together we rise, the Connerys, and we move down the courtroom aisle amid smiles and applause from jurors and lawyers alike. Glorious victory, for Sebastian, our family, the Urns of Connery and, of course, all of Scotland.

"I bet," Sebastian says, "everyone here today will wash after every flush for the rest of their lives."

11

Sebastian wants a victory dinner and Old Sebastian suggests someplace Italian.

"You always suggest someplace Italian," Sebastian says.

"He won't be looking for me in an Italian restaurant. He wouldn't think I'd dare."

"Nobody's looking for you."

"Sam The Man Flounders."

"Right."

With a "Hoo-hoo, fancy-fancy" from Old Sebastian, our victory dinner ends up at Andaggio's. Our waiter reviews our menu choices and specials with her lips patting together like sighing a lover's poem. Sebastian orders everything for us from the menu's Family Style Dinner selection. Appetizers—bruschetta and baked shrimp oreganata. Salads—low-fat creamy Italian over spinach and chopped salads. Pastas—fettuccini alfredo with broccoli and mostaccioli eggplant marinara. The main course—chicken saltimbocca and New York strip Contadina. Desserts—chocolate zuccotto cake and tiramisu. And drinks—champagne for all, even Roby.

After ordering, Sebastian and Roby leave me for the bathroom, and I'm abandoned with Old Sebastian. Such a thing rarely happens. When Old Sebastian's around, I'm seeking shelter in the company of others. The background music and the clanking of forks on plates and humming restaurant conversation do nothing to shelter me. He's on the other side of the table with the tossed-about hair he insists is his own natural brown color at ninety-one years of age and his mouth seemingly unable to close over his dentures, a smile distorted by frowning lips.

"I have to tell you, Julia. There's going to be an extra eighty dollars on next month's tab from Dignity Place."

"What now?"

"I made two more holes in the walls, one in my room, one in the day room."

"Why in the day room?"

"Thought I'd give it a try."

"Stop looking for gangster bones."

"Capone put some there." *Click, squish.* "I know it."

"Who's helping you with the hammer?"

"Ain't telling."

"Fine. Would you like a roll?"

He says among his clicks and his squishes, "I'm going to have to take them out."

"Out?"

"My teeth. They're loose. I'm going to have to take my teeth out."

"Oh."

"They've been making a lot of noise today."

"Hadn't noticed."

"I can see things, Julia."

"Things?"

"Grimaces and smirks and shudders. Your body language."

"You're imagining things."

"Why do you hate me?"

"Hate?"

"I'm an old man. I don't have time for sideways answers to my questions."

"I don't hate you." My discomfort grows as huge and as oafish as an ogre. My limbs puff up and feel as heavy as clay. Why does he do this to me? If he gets me going, I'll never stop with my complaints and ruin our victory dinner, yet he glares at me through eyes that still work without glasses. They're Sebastian's eyes, the shape and color and glow, but I don't feel their affection from Old Sebastian's face.

"Watch me take them out," he says, and I think, Take out your eyes? He reaches for his mouth, a cloth napkin covering the process, and covertly removes his dentures.

"You're grimacing, Julia. Smirking. Shuddering."

How his face has shrunk without his dentures, his chin too close to his nose, and I reach for a roll with my oafish, blobbing clay hand. I do grimace and I do feel the smirk on my face and the shudder in my shoulders. He says, "If you'd spend a little time looking at me, you'd get used to it."

"I've looked at you plenty," I say. "I watched you sleep in my bedroom for seven years while Sebastian and I had to sleep on a fold-out couch in the sun room."

"You never said anything the whole time."

"Because you always complained about the twenty pills you had to take for the fifty ailments you suffered over a hundred percent of your body. How could I ask you to sleep on the couch?"

"It's not my fault I have bad bones." Old Sebastian pushes at his water glass. "You should have named my only grandson Sebastian."

"What?"

"It's a tradition. You broke tradition."

"How long have you been waiting to tell me this?"

"Forever."

"Maybe if you didn't sleep in my bedroom for seven years, I would've had a second son to name."

"Well," he says, again fiddling with his water glass. "Guess

83

it's good we finally got all this out in the open."

My lips begin to quiver as I say, "Let me tell you exactly how I feel."

But I'm stopped.

Shouts of men barrel toward us. Waiters and waitresses and bus boys scamper to the side and patrons spin to view the commotion heading our way. First a large man in a dark suit, looking important and dangerous, halts and spins about to point a finger. At Sebastian! The large dark suit growls, "You don't know who you're messing with, man."

Roby tries to pull his father back even as men in matching dark suits sitting at a table in a shadowy corner begin to rise with scowls etched into their faces.

"Holy Hell's bells!" Old Sebastian says. He toggles his chair into reverse, turns to the aisle, and takes off.

It's all too much for me to stand, one torment to the next. I hear Sebastian's voice go on about unwashed bathroom hands—"Do you plan to eat with those filthy mitts?"—as if he has learned nothing once again. I bury my head in my arms, remembering a torment from a thousand torments before, and I play over and over in my head what I wish to say to Old Sebastian.

I'm afraid of you.

There's a bang and a yelp and I have to look. Old Sebastian's gone and run his wheelchair into Sebastian and Sebastian's hopping, limping in circles, saying, "Pop, why?" But Old Sebastian's too busy apologizing to the large dark suit, saying things about his son, how he's a bit insane and off his medication and growing nuttier by the day and for the man not to take it personally and he'll take care of his son and force medication down his throat.

The large dark suit considers this, the heavy face grinding its teeth as if anticipating the taste of Sebastian's bones. A wave of his hand sends the other dark suits retreating to their corner table in the shadows. He tugs at his lapels with a sniff of importance and says, "My nephew's got the same problem. But don't let it happen again."

Sebastian hobbles to our table and Roby slouches like he wants to slither under it. To his father, Sebastian says, "Why'd you stop me? Why, Dad? Look at that man. He's eating steak fries with those polluted hands!"

Roby says, "Must be Sam The Man Flounders."

"Little Nicky," Old Sebastian says.

Roby scoots up in his chair. "Really? Which one?"

"The second to the worst. If he had been Little Nicky Number One, your father would have been blown out of his shoes by now."

"Come off it with the gangsters, Dad."

"Makes Sam The Man Flounders look like a day camp counselor."

"Dad."

"Believe what you want. These things I know about."

Roby can't stop taking peeks at the man who may be the second worst Little Nicky in town or just a man with friends, and they all like to dress in dark suits and keep scowls on their faces.

"Old Sebastian," I say, and I stare at him, at his wrinkles and bones and his chin too close to his nose, and it's not so hard this time to behold his withering face. "Thank you."

Even with the distraction of the second worst Little Nicky, as Roby sees it, or, as Sebastian sees it, the man eating with polluted hands, Old Sebastian's mouth raises a toothless smile and his eyes show a bit of affection.

"I'm thinking of working at Dignity Place," I say.

Old Sebastian's smile vanishes and he stuffs a piece of a roll into his mouth, smooching at the bread with his gums. "Stop calling people Old Toots," he says. "Especially me."

"But it's a term of endearment."

"Not the way you say it. Sounds like spit in my ears."

The noise he makes, eating without his dentures, I cannot deny, bothers me more than the clicks and the squishes he makes with them in. "Still," he says while he chews. "I'm glad we finally had this talk."

Iris Newberry calls after the 9 o'clock news. "I heard Sebastian won his little trial," she says. "Fox News said so."

"Yes," I say.

"Dinner tomorrow at my house?"

"It's not Friday."

"Another surprise meal."

"I see."

"Julia, get those flower beds weeded. Put the fall fertilizer down. I'm trying to sell my house, you know. Things have to look good in the neighborhood."

"Yes, Mrs. Newberry." And I have to ask, perhaps out of curiosity, but more out of cruel fun. "How long has it been since John passed?"

"Oh, my precious," she says. "Four years, one week and one day."

"Yes, Mrs. Newberry. I remember now. A beautiful funeral. Seems to me the pallbearers weren't working so hard carrying the casket. Such thin and mealy-looking pallbearers, too."

"Of course. The black spot got John. Shrunk him down to a shell of a man."

"I don't recall seeing that before he died."

"So quick. It's the black spot, like your rose bushes have. Shrivels up the leaves."

"See you tomorrow for dinner. Four-thirty?"

"Right. Weed the flower beds, dear. Fall fertilize." The phone clicks off.

Sebastian places the Urns of Connery in our closet with promises of release of their ashes at the Mull of Kintyre. In bed, Sebastian pulls beside me. "Poor Iris," he says. "Poor John."

With a knock, our closed bedroom door speaks to us. "I've put my ear plugs in, stuffed tight, just so you know."

"Thank you, Roby," Sebastian says.

"What?" the door says. Roby's feet patter lightly to his room.

At my ear, nibbling, Sebastian says, "When you get that job at Dignity Place, you can investigate the history of Dave-Jones-John-Newberry."

"You think I'll get the job?"

Sebastian kisses me tenderly along my neck, and rather than saying yes or no, he says, "I caught you smiling rather nicely at my father."

12

I've never been to Dignity Place by myself before. Feels like guerilla warfare somehow, with the Old Toots—excuse me, Old Sebastian—the *Residents*. The Residents shoot dirty looks at me fired from eyes filled with ammunition. Parked in a visitor's spot near the front door, I sit gripping the steering wheel. It's like a life preserver in my hands.

Three Residents watch me from their wheelchairs on the veranda. Their gray heads, with pink ribbons tied in their wispy hair, barely rise above the backrests and appear lost beneath pink blankets draped over them. Pink ribbons, like tags, to remind the staff that these Residents are women. I wait for them to blink. They don't blink. They make fists and place them on their chairs' arm rests.

I wave. They squeeze their fists.

"May I help you?"

In a white shirt, white cap and black tie, looking like a milk-man from the 1950s, a young man offers to escort me from my car. "My name's Harry," and he is hairy with his black, steel wool hair poking from under his cap, eyebrows meeting over his nose, a mustache like a rectangle of Shredded Wheat, and arms I could set hair curlers in. I know, from Old Sebastian's few stories that aren't about gangsters, that this young man goes by the name Hairy Harry, and he's all right with it.

"Need help?" he asks.

I get out of the sedan with Hairy Harry inspecting me for

luggage, so it seems. And he floors me with his question. "Resident or visitor?"

"What?"

"Resident or visitor?"

One of the Residents in her wheelchair smiles and waves for me to come over. "Need a fourth for bridge," she says.

"What?"

"A fourth for bridge!"

Another Resident leans toward her, says something, and they share a joke of some kind, then both shoot a hard look at me.

Hairy Harry throws daggers at my soul when he asks more insistently, "Resident or visitor?"

"Certainly not a Resident," I say with a snap.

As I walk, Hairy Harry scampers about me, apologizing and explaining Dignity Place's minimum tenancy requirements. "You can be mobile," he says. "Independent. With a medical condition or not." Then he stops me with a tap on my shoulder. "And you only have to be fifty-five years old."

"I'm fifty-three," I say. "I'm here to see about a job."

"Oh," Hairy Harry says. He hangs there like he's nailed to a stake and waits for the blindfold, last cigarette, and bullets to the heart.

"Why don't you stay here and let me go in by myself."

"Don't tell them, Miss."

"Don't tell who?"

"Mr. Grissly and Mrs. Grissly. The managers. Your interviewers."

"Don't tell them what?"

"How I insulted you. I didn't mean to." He kicks one of his black polished shoes into the walk. "I'm kind of new here, so I make some mistakes. It's only been three years for me. I mean four. I've been here four years. Five years actually. So I'm pretty new and I make some mistakes. Not many but some. In a month it'll be six years. I'm the host. My title is the Greeter but nobody calls me that 'cause I do the laundry, the sweeping and everything needing taking care of in the basement." He smiles. "I make two dollars over minimum wage."

"Don't ask people if they're Residents or visitors. The visitors won't like it."

"The Residents like it."

"But if the Residents already live here, they don't need to be greeted."

Hairy Harry scratches at his neck. "I never said I was a *good* greeter."

"How old are you?"

"Twenty two."

"Why aren't you in college?"

He smiles and looks at his shoes. "C'mon. You can see for yourself, can't you? Some people say I'm an idiot."

"Who tells you such a thing?"

"Teachers. School counselors. Just about everybody. Not my dad, though. He's never said anything bad like that to me or nobody. And I'm not in school anymore, not for a long while, so I haven't been called an idiot in five years, maybe six." I swear the black stubble on his chin grows as he talks, and he scratches at it. "I remember them people calling me an idiot. Nobody at Dignity Place says bad things. Dad's seen to it."

"Do you know a Resident named Dave Jones?"

"I greet him every day, Miss."

I shake Hairy Harry's hand, expecting bristles on his palm, but I feel only his perspiration. "Mrs. Julia Connery," I say. "And I won't tell on you."

"You don't look any older than the last school counselor I saw, Mrs. Connery. Not when you're up this close."

Without telling me how old this counselor was the last time he saw her, a counselor who called him an idiot, Hairy Harry tips his hat and smiles beneath his mustache like he's paid me a compliment bigger than the earth. I haven't gone twenty feet from my sedan and already I've been turned into a Resident and I feel like running home to wait for Sebastian to make me feel young. There goes Hairy Harry, back to the veranda, getting goosed by a Resident in a wheelchair, with a pink bow in her hair. He smiles and waves at me, overdoes it a bit, as though I hold his career at Dignity Place and his two dollars over minimum wage in my hands.

Hairy Harry likes to talk and greets the Resident Dave Jones, so I pass through the doors of Dignity Place without Sebastian and without Roby for the first time in my life.

Mr. Grissly and Mrs. Grissly sit side by side in chairs behind a battleship-sized desk in their office, and if he were to hold a farmer's pitchfork in his hand, I would swear I am being interviewed by American Gothic. Their lips stay horizontal and hardly move while they talk, and I have to watch closely so I know for sure who is asking the question.

My resume sits alone on the deck of the desk, although the paper reads more like a history report on the 1970s.

"Why do you want to work at Dignity Place?" Mrs. Grissly asks.

"To help people."

Mrs. Grissly turns to Mr. Grissly, and it's a surprise not to hear creaks rise from her neck. Mr. Grissly, I think, nods.

Mrs. Grissly doesn't blink. "Why do you really want to work here?"

"Is there something wrong with my answer?"

"It's so . . ." Mr. Grissly starts to say.

". . . common," Mrs. Grissly finishes. "Our Residents need healthy stimulation in their day. We don't want common at Dignity Place."

"Haven't I seen you here before?" Mr. Grissly asks.

"Possibly. My father-in-law is Sebastian Connery Sr."

For the first time, color shows in Mrs. Grissly's cheeks. She raises a distinct smile and says, "He's the gangster-guy, Mr. Grissly."

"The gentleman who keeps punching holes in our walls looking for, ah . . ."

"Gangster bones," I say. "Left behind by Al Capone."

"Yes," Mrs. Grissly says. "Three more holes this month. It will be added to your bill."

Mr. Grissly smiles. "A fascinating, lovely man."

I say, "Old Sebastian?"

"Who?" Mr. Grissly says.

"We call him Old Sebastian."

Their smiles vanish. "We don't call our Residents . . ." Mr. Grissly says, and hesitates.

"Old," Mrs. Grissly says in a whisper, like she feels guilty for swearing in church.

I say, "It's the way we distinguish between my husband and his father. They're both named Sebastian."

"Please don't say the 'O' word here," Mr. Grissly says. "They are Residents."

Lifting my pitiful resume, as if we were starting the interview from the beginning, Mrs. Grissly says, "So why do you want to work at Dignity Place?"

American Gothic glares at me, expecting wholesome life-on-the-farm values from me, which I suppose includes telling the truth. So I say something I want to be the truth, even though the words sound foreign as I speak them. "I want to show my father-in-law I love him."

Mrs. Grissly's thin eyebrows vanish into a fold in her forehead. "Show your love to him after all this time?" she asks. "The gangster-guy must be over ninety years . . ." She searches the air like it's a thesaurus for the 'O' word.

"He's ninety-one," I say.

"Well, yes," Mrs. Grissly says.

"It's a lovely reason," Mr. Grissly says. "Mrs. Grissly, we should hire Mrs. Connery on the spot for her answer. Not common at all."

"Three dollars over minimum wage," Mrs. Grissly says. "Will that be all right?"

"But I forgot," Mr. Grissly says. "What are we hiring her for?"

"The fitness programs," Mrs. Grissly says. "One in the morning, one in the afternoon, Tuesdays and Thursdays."

Mr. Grissly's stare seems to inspect me with microscopic jerks and his horizontal lips droop just a bit. "Oh, yes, well, I suppose," he says. "But don't say that word around here."

"The 'O' word," Mrs. Grissly says, again with the sinner's whisper.

"It's been a while since the last fitness instructor," Mr. Grissly says. "She was built like a fortress. I suppose you'll do."

"Bring your program in writing next Monday, nine in the morning, Mrs. Connery," Mrs. Grissly says. "First you present us with your program, gentle on our Residents' bones, but active, and Tuesday you can start whipping them into shape."

Mr. Grissly says, "I'll get Hairy Harry to get the fuzz off the bottom of our pool."

Mrs. Grissly laces her fingers together on the desk. "Do you have any questions for us?"

Watching their dour faces, I wonder. I have to ask. Perhaps they're the couple happily married for fifty years I can show to Lola Two. "Have you two been together long?"

"Wedded four years," Mr. Grissly says. "Engaged for three. A fellah can't be too careful."

Mrs. Grissly says, "Almost newlyweds. Why do you ask?"

Their faces look like driftwood cracking apart on the beach together. I suppose they might be smiling at the moment. "No reason, really. It's just nice to know."

Mrs. Grissly hands me tax forms to fill out and all movement seems to cease and it's just American Gothic watching me once more. I thank them as I leave, but hear behind me, "Don't you think we should have asked her about her qualifications?" And then, "But she's so uncommon."

How strange for Mr. and Mrs. Grissly to think I'm uncommon. Of course they should have asked me about my qualifications. Considering the cost of keeping Old Sebastian at Dignity Place, part of me is offended I could work here as a fitness instructor. Maybe it's possible American Gothic could be Residents themselves and they've mutinied and assumed the role of the real Mrs. Grissly and Mr. Grissly, who've been kept tied up in a closet somewhere in the basement and watched over by Hairy Harry. Then again, how hard could it be to exercise the Residents at Dignity Place?

Hairy Harry paces in the lobby, twirling a curl in his sideburn. He sees me and runs up in a hurry. His Shredded Wheat mustache seems to have grown over his lips. "That was quick, Mrs. Connery. Did you tell on me?"

"Not a word."

"Did you get the job?"

"I start Monday."

"Did you get two dollars over minimum wage? Did you get more than me?" He grinds the toe of his shoe into the floor.

"No, Hairy Harry. A dollar over minimum wage."

His chest suddenly expands and he looks to the sun shining through the skylight, smiling as if he feels grateful to be alive.

"So you got the job," Old Sebastian says, and he spends the next five minutes in his wheelchair at his window, pulling at his ears. I sit on the bed behind him.

"Old Sebastian?" I say, leaning to see his face, but his eyes focus on something far away, and not anything I can find out the same window. His *Goodfellas* video plays on the television set, the sound down low and Ray Liotta goes on about who's gangster-whacking who, and who's likely to get gangster-whacked next.

With Old Sebastian's back to me, in all his silence, I feel like a bug in his room, and Old Sebastian would swat me if he had the weapon to do it. My thought to spend more time with Old Sebastian begins to feel foolish now. All those years of disapproving looks from the first time we met, how I'm not Scottish enough or don't behave Scottish enough, worsened by my refusal to name his only grandson Sebastian. I'm the murderer of a link which went back at least six generations of Sebastian Connerys.

Old Sebastian raised the man who loves me dearly and I wish to put my hands on his shoulders just for that and for saving Sebastian from Little Nicky Number Two and for the toothless smile he gave me when I thanked him. But even with his thick Connery hair and his body straight against the back of his wheelchair, so near, his shoulders as places to rest my hands feel so distant.

On the television screen, Joe Pesci gets gangster-whacked and now Ray Liotta is frantic wondering if he's next.

"Julia," I hear from Old Sebastian, as soft as a thought. "I want to walk again."

"Old Sebastian?"

His hand reaches to the toggle and he turns the chair a bit, just enough so his stare can corner over to me. "I can lift my legs now, straighten my knees, and my bones don't hurt so bad, just stiff from sitting in this chair for nearly five years."

"I'm not your doctor. I wouldn't know what to do."

"You're the new fitness instructor."

"Well, it's probably all a misunderstanding. I'll be fired when Mr. and Mrs. Grissly come to their senses."

"They never come to their senses."

"Can't we hire a specialist? People who know what they're doing?"

"I already know what I'm doing. I need your help."

"Why me?"

Old Sebastian toggles a bit more to face me and I find his eyes looking rather blank, as if he were seeing me for the first time. He tells me, "Because it will do us both some good."

He catches the dumb look on my face, a look of doubt about whether I could ever help him walk again, and my disbelief that trying will somehow help us both. "You would know I'm right if you thought about it," he says and toggles back to look out the window.

I stand and see Hairy Harry on the grounds, chased by Residents with pink ribbons in their hair, taking turns poking him with their fingers and canes. But Old Sebastian's stare is again lost in some other place.

It's time I do it, I think, and I settle my hands upon Old Sebastian's shoulders.

"A few steps is all," he says. "Just to stand and walk a bit away from this chair on my own. That's all I ask." With his voice scratchy and low and his back stiffening, he begins to sing a folksy lilt about Scotland, about the misty Mull of Kintyre, with his mind, I suppose, visiting the other side of the world.

"Don't tell Sebastian," he says. "I have my reasons."

He continues on with his song.

13

Usually it takes the threat of military school to get Roby to go next door for dinner with Iris. This time, though, it's Roby hurrying us along a half hour early, and his pacing at our bedroom doorway has got Sebastian taking turns tying his tie too long then too short.

"There's only a small window of opportunity," Sebastian says to Roby, "to avoid Iris Newberry's scorn for being too early or too late. The lady says four-thirty, she means four-thirty."

"Can I bring the camera?"

"Whatever for?"

"For the moment we tell her. Can you imagine the look on her face when . . . we are going to tell her, aren't we?"

I slip on a pair of black dress shoes. "Tell her what?"

"How we saw Mr. Newberry, alive and looking a lot like Santa Claus."

"Roby," I say. "What in the world makes you think Iris Newberry doesn't already know he isn't dead?"

"Oh," Roby says. "Right."

"It's something psychological, I'm sure," Sebastian says. His tie reaches down to the bottom of his pants zipper. "Iris Newberry is nuts. Best we stay out of it."

Faster than a finger-snap, Roby transforms himself into a slouching, angst-ridden teenager, looking like we've taken his drivers license away for life. "Can't believe you guys."

Sebastian turns to me, frustration over his face. "Is this a trick tie?"

"That tie was a Christmas gift from Mrs. Newberry."

"Then it's a cursed tie. A vampire's tie."

Roby says, "I can't go, then. I can't go and say nothing about it."

"You'll go," I say.

"I won't."

"And you'll say nothing about John Newberry."

"I will."

Roby takes his angst-ridden teenaged self away, shuffling the floor like he's dragging a bedspread and all the world's thunderclouds behind him.

Sebastian struggles with his tie some more, flips it about in a fury and sags when he sees the skinny half reach to mid-zipper, the fat half resting on his belly.

"It will be hard not to tell Iris," I say.

"That it will," Sebastian says. "Almost impossible." He takes a scissors and snips a foot off the tie's skinny half.

At ten minutes to Iris Newberry, Roby is out the door and I watch him through the front window, pacing on the walk by her sign. House For Sale. I suppose Sebastian and I are lucky to have a teenage son who is wide-eyed and who takes an interest in something other than himself.

Sebastian stands beside me. "Ready?"

"I feel like Lois Lane," I say.

"Who?"

"Superman's girlfriend. How in the world doesn't she yell at Clark Kent, 'Of course I know you're Superman! It's just a stupid pair of glasses!'?"

"And how does Clark Kent feel, thinking he can hide Superman behind a pair of glasses?"

Roby turns toward our house, waving his arms, and mouths to us at the window, *C'mon. It's time.*

When I was a teenager, there was a show on one of the less popular television stations called *Creature Features.* The screen would show a monster, often a mix between a transvestite and Count Dracula, and an announcer made sophomoric jokes and said to stay tuned for the next segment of a B-grade monster movie. For the life of me, I cannot remember a single minute of any one of those movies on *Creature Features,* but for the rest of my life I will remember its theme music. A reverberating, bass-string variation of military taps, perfect for a walk through a cemetery on a foggy Halloween night. *Boom—boom—boom, boom-bah, boom—boom—boom, boom-bah—*

There sits Iris Newberry beneath her sombrero hat, wearing something like a muumuu and her pasty-face industrial-grade sunblock even though she's inside, at the head of her gargoyle-tipped dining room table with the shades drawn and the light bulbs begging for mercy. But she now glows with mystery and I can't keep the music out of my head. *Boom—boom—boom, boom-bah—*

Iris lifts the serving cover off the tray and shows us her creation. "In honor of Sebastian's victory in court."

Roby slouches. "Lobster tails again?"

"It was two weeks ago," Sebastian says to Roby, and then to Iris, "Looks even better than the last time."

"I found something I'm good at," Iris says. "Finally."

"Why do you talk like that?" I ask. "There's plenty you're good at."

"Plenty? Everything I do goes into this house and I haven't had a single nibble yet to buy it."

"But I saw a young couple last week."

"Came in, sat down on the sofa for a few seconds and left.

Didn't say a word."

I can imagine. Total strangers entering Iris Newberry's *Creature Features* house, looking around and thinking something might come alive to eat them up, and then they meet Iris and are sure of it.

Iris bows her head toward her empty plate. "They didn't even bother to see the garden. All my work. All these years."

"Do you have any pictures of Mr. Newberry?" Roby asks.

"Quiet," I say.

"Why?" Iris turns to Roby. "What do you mean?"

"Nothing."

"Of course I have pictures of my late husband," Iris says, now looking softly into Sebastian's eyes. "He always washed his hands, you know. Always."

Sebastian sighs with Iris and places his hand on her shoulder. "Of course. He was a good man."

Roby coughs, covers his mouth with his napkin, and coughs again.

"Did you say something?" Iris asks.

"No, Mrs. Newberry." But in a second, Roby covers his mouth in his napkin and grumbles through a harsh cough, *Dave Jones.*

"Stop it," I say.

"What?"

"You know."

"I don't. It's how I cough."

"Let's eat," Sebastian says.

Iris stiffens. "What's going on?"

"Did you ever listen to the Monkees when you were a teenager, Mrs. Newberry?" Roby asks.

"I listened to cavemen bang rocks when I was a teenager. What's this monkey thing you're talking about?"

"You know. It's in the history books. Peter, Mickey, Michael.

And, of course, Davy Jones. Davy Jones was the little guy."

"Stop," I say, and I turn to Sebastian for some help.

Sebastian looks hard into Mrs. Newberry's eyes, like she's a science experiment, and says, "You know. Davy Jones. He shook his tambourine and his fanny and made teenage girls swoon in the '60s."

"Don't listen to them," I say. "There's no such thing as a singing monkey."

"Of course there is," Roby says. "We met one yesterday in court."

"That we did," Sebastian says.

"You met a monkey in court?" Iris asks.

Sebastian says, "We met Dave Jones in court."

My dinner plate clanks with the drop of my fork and I've taken a chip out of the porcelain. Iris doesn't flinch. She stares at Sebastian, then at Roby, then Sebastian, and I'd say she's gone a shade more pale than snow if she hadn't started off that way.

"Let's eat," Iris says. I half expect the gargoyles on the furniture to spring to life and tear our flesh from our bones. She turns to the lobster tails and takes one. "Never heard of a singing monkey. Let's talk about something else."

"No Davy Jones?" Roby asks.

"No." Iris's eyes narrow. "Definitely not."

"Idiots," I say, stomping toward our house. "Both of you."

"What?" I hear, and it could be from Sebastian or Roby. It's hard to tell the difference I'm so angry. I spin around and face them both, stopping them at the House For Sale sign.

"Of course Iris has no idea who Dave Jones is. It's a disguise, a secret. Which means John doesn't want her to know."

"Oh," Sebastian says. "You could be right." He tries to hug me there on the sidewalk but I won't let him.

"You never can tell," Roby says. "A woman who buries somebody without somebody to bury could know almost anything."

"What would you have us do, Julia?" Sebastian asks. "We've got a vampire neighbor with a dead husband, and the dead husband lives only five miles from his widow and he's gone and named himself after a Monkee. It's the oddest thing I've ever seen and it's right next door and not asking Iris about it is like having a chocolate cake put in front of you on your birthday and being told you can't eat it."

Sebastian tries to hug me again. This time I let him and he starts singing a Monkee's song into my ear, something about love and fairy tales. Between his fake-Scottish lilt killing the song and his late-evening whiskers brushing against my cheek, I succumb to him and hug him back, and I'd start singing with him if it weren't for Roby shouting away.

"Look!"

It's like watching a machine turn on that hasn't been turned on in a hundred years and you're waiting for it to explode and kill somebody. The plush, sun-faded purple drapes which have sealed the Newberry's front picture window since Creation begin to lift. An inch or two, pause, then another inch or two, pause, and we're dumbfounded on the sidewalk, watching Iris Newberry's shins appear off to the side at the window. The drapes rise a bit more, painfully slow, and her something-like-a-muumuu dress reveals itself, at her knees, her waist, then chest.

I'm wondering if there's enough faded sunlight remaining to turn her into dust. Apparently not. She's just standing there pasty-faced, a vampire in a muumuu and sombrero hat, a widow who's not a widow. Of course she can see us. Her stare is right on us, and now I wonder if my little family and I are about to be turned into dust.

"She knows about Dave Jones," Roby says.

"That she does," Sebastian says.

Sebastian and Roby turn to me. Me, with my new job as the fitness instructor of all of Dignity Place, where John Newberry hides from Iris.

"What's Iris doing?" Roby asks.

"She's waving," I say.

Sebastian says, "Well, we better wave back."

We wave at Iris Newberry, my old tune pounding in my head. *Boom—boom—boom, boom-bah, boom—boom—boom, boom-bah—*

I can't fall asleep. To the left of me lies Sebastian, rattling his tonsils. How he sleeps with the mystery of John and Iris Newberry is beyond me. The thought of it all feels like a ball bouncing inside my head from one side to the other. Look at him, eyes shut tight, lips hanging loose. I suppose if I had said something nice about England's history he'd be awake all night.

"Sebastian," I say.

No answer. So I turn my lamp's knob two more clicks to the right and the light makes his face glow bright. He smacks his lips, turns over, and rattles his tonsils some more. I give him a shove and another. Then I pinch his ass hard.

"Chrissake," he says.

"Who was that woman at our door?"

Sebastian turns back to face me so fast his bed sheet seems to snap. His eyes flick side to side. "It's the quarter of you that's not Scottish driving me batty again, isn't it? I don't know about any woman at our door. What woman at our door?"

"I mean the woman at the door before we left for your trial. The teary one wanting to be with you and write about you and do Lord knows what else with you."

"The day of my trial? I didn't see anyone like that."

"Because I sent her away."

"Then how could I have seen her?"

I sit up against my pillow and pout. "She was one of your students. You must have known her."

"I'm sure there's a woman or two in my classes this term."

"This one stunk of perfume and looked about forty in a miniskirt. It was horrible."

"One of my former students then. How do you expect me to recall a student that old just by her stink?"

"Old?" I say loud enough to wake Roby. "She's at least ten years younger than me. How can you say she's old?"

"Chrissake, Lassie. You know that's not what I meant."

"I've got more body parts hanging from my bones than I can count. I'm a frump, an aging, sagging frump, and there you are being so irresistible."

Sebastian leans away like I just socked him one in the nose. "Me?" he says. "I'm an aging Scottish toot and I stand nearly shorter than your eyes. I color my hair and deny it, and I can't keep up with the hair popping out where it's not supposed to pop out, on my ears and a bit on my nose, and I swear when I'm standing at the mirror shaving, there's some fat ones in my eyebrows I can see growing. I'm a puffy, short man, and I've got my irritating ways. I'm not irresistible, Julia. I know these things about myself."

"You're in style. Your kind is very much the thing right now."

"Puffy, short, irritating men with hair growing in places where they shouldn't be growing at all?"

"Um hmm."

"I'll be out of style soon enough." He shakes his head in the center of his pillow and looks at the ceiling. "You're thinking about John Newberry."

"I am."

"You're thinking about me running away from you, like John did from Iris."

"Maybe."

"I know you are," he says, glancing at me, then back to the ceiling. "I can see how red your face has turned."

"What I'm thinking about is what you think about me. When you dream, do you dream about me? And when you dream about me, do you make me skinny and put my breasts back up where they used to be when I was twenty?"

"I can't control what I dream. Tonight, before you interrupted me, I started dreaming about lobsters. Huge lobsters. They were terrifying."

"I don't believe you. You were sleeping as calm as a cat in a sunbeam."

"That's because all those huge lobsters were terrorizing Iris, demanding she admit the truth about John or else they'd crack open her old shell and eat out her insides. I was enjoying it."

I fold my arms and plop back down to my pillow to watch the ceiling with Sebastian. "Where do you go after work?"

"Me?"

"I don't see anyone else in this room."

"I come home to you and Roby. I always come home to you and Roby."

"Not always. Once, a couple times a month. I have no idea where you've gone to after work. I've noticed ever since Old Sebastian went off to Dignity Place."

"You're bringing this up now?"

The sound of my voice floats over our bed, like thickened air I'm hoping isn't poisonous. "Where do you go, Sebastian? Please don't lie to me. A wife tends to know when her husband lies to her."

"Ah, Lassie," Sebastian says. His head sinks deep into his pillow. "Every once in a while, there's something I need to do."

"Tell me."

"If you don't want me to lie to you, then I'm not ready to tell you."

"Hardly an answer."

"You wouldn't understand. I don't understand it myself."

My body turns away from him, on its own so it seems. "You disappeared on me once before."

"It was a long time ago. We were engaged, not married. But I know you don't want to hear that excuse again." Sebastian's hand presses on my shoulder, moves me back toward him. "You found out because I told you. You asked me her name so I told you. You asked for how long and I told you. You asked me why and I told you she was from my past, and I had done something stupid to say goodbye. Something perhaps unforgivable. But you never would have known, Lassie, unless I told you."

"I would have sniffed it out eventually."

"But I had to tell you. I couldn't marry you keeping a secret like that." He kisses me on my cheek. "I asked you if you would still marry me." Another kiss on my cheek. "You said yes. Nothing's changed since then except for the better. There's nothing to worry about."

"Saying there's nothing to worry about when you won't tell me where you're going off to only gives me more to worry about."

He kisses my cheek again.

"That's not an answer either, Sebastian. Tell me."

"There's no woman involved at all. I swear it's the truth."

"This isn't fair."

"Why did you decide to marry me? Why if this bothers you so much now?"

"Your tweed coat with the patches at the elbows. The man inside begging forgiveness looked like he needed me. But I suppose John Newberry once looked that way to Iris."

Sebastian rolls closer to me, embraces me with the air around him, his musk cologne, his breath made clean by religious flossing, brushing teeth and tongue and swishing about mint mouthwash. His scent defines him, I suppose, and makes him mine. Nobody's allowed to be this close to him but me.

"Don't compare us to John and Iris Newberry," he says.

"Who then?"

"Romeo and Juliet."

I start to laugh. Sebastian brings his fingers to my lips. "Perhaps I dream of lobsters terrifying Iris. Perhaps I need some time to myself once in a long while, but the truth about us is this. When I see you, I want you. When I'm away from you, I want to see you. I don't have to imagine the way your breasts used to look when you were twenty because I'm in love with the way you look now. It's devotion, Julia. You've given yourself forever to this short, puffy, irritating man even when I'm not in style."

"That's a nice thing to say, Sebastian. Those are nice words. What proof do you have?"

He moves his fingers gently over my lips and I turn to look at him.

"My pajamas."

"Now you're kidding me."

"Do you know why I wear pajamas? You know I slept in the buff at one time in my life. The thought of wearing pajamas under a blanket feels as confining as prison doors shutting me in a cell. Do you know why I forced myself to get used to pajamas?"

"I have no idea."

"It's because when I'm naked under the covers with you, my body always feels ready to do something besides sleep. It's because I anticipate making love to you and I want our bodies to collide. And I'm telling you, Julia, whether things are hanging from your bones or not, it's still the only reason why I wear pajamas."

"Your proof is your pajamas?"

"My proof is if I were to take off my pajamas."

He's smiling. Scottish smiling. Irresistible. And I ask him to take off his proof. Then, with his touch and kisses so soft over me, everything I worry about vanishes for the moment. My Sebastian tells me, without words, things I need to know. He makes me feel beautiful.

In the morning, while Sebastian's in the shower, Lola Two appears, gushing on about what fantastic thing Dr. Plastic has done to her lately. Still under the bed covers, refusing to open my eyes, I wish her to go away. Her voice is like water freezing in my ears. *You had him cornered, Julia honey. But you really let Sebastian get away with it this time. What were you thinking?*

I wait for more scolding, but it doesn't come. I open my eyes, and she's gone. It's for my own ears, then, when I say out loud, "I don't want to turn into Iris Newberry. That's what I was thinking."

14

I suppose I have confidence. I think I have confidence. But driving to Dignity Place for my first day of work as a fitness instructor, it's so hard for me to tell.

I've told Sebastian I wouldn't listen to the program anymore, but he's not here and he didn't specifically make me promise, so as I drive, my hand drifts to the radio dial and turns the volume up on *God Investment.* I'd like to call in, I suppose, one day when I'm certain nobody who knows me is listening. I'd tell these men to go back to their mothers and beg for forgiveness. The two male hosts of the show are interviewing an executive from a financial planning company, a woman, and she's saying families shouldn't plan their investment portfolios based on biblical scripture. The men share a condescending snort and knowing chuckle at her expense, and one of them says, *Of course they should. Of course they must! It does a family no good to leave mortal life and earthly riches behind only to face eternal damnation. And that's what will happen if it's the woman, rather than the man, who puts the money in a 401K.* She snaps back, *Where do you get such garbage?* And she's hit with the snorts and chuckles again— *Obviously, it's in the Bible!* Then she snorts and chuckles back at them, only hers are snortier and chucklier. *Show me,* she says.

Some pages start rustling and one of the men clears his throat. I turn the volume up a bit more.

It starts right here in the beginning. Genesis, Chapter Two, Verse 22: And the rib, which the Lord God hath taken from the man, made

He a woman, and brought her unto the man. But she says, *Soooo?* He says back, *The woman came from man's rib. Eve was made from Adam, the first man, whereas Adam was made from God's hands. Man is subservient to God. Woman is subservient to Man. Man tells woman how to invest.*

She says, *That's just complete and utter chauvinistic, self-justifying, warped-interpretive, straight-from-the-mouth-of-a-moron bullshit.* Not a syllable is bleeped out an iota on *God Investment.* Neither are the gasps nor the sounds of chairs and tables shoved about as if the men were diving under them to hide from bolts of lightning. And then she goes on and quotes from scripture herself.

Genesis, Chapter One, Verse 27, she says, *A full chapter and 26 verses before yours: And God created man in His own image, in the image of God created He him—male and female created He them.* Then she tells us all how her beloved father is a Pentecostal Baptist Minister, and says for fact, *This was on the fifth day of Creation, gentlemen, female as well as male created at the same time, both by God's hands. Then and only then, well after the sixth and seventh days of Creation, with women already out and about, did God add his Garden of Eden and put Adam inside of it. And among all the women on Earth, not one would have a thing to do with Adam, so God made him fall asleep and pulled out one of his ribs to make yet another woman.*

Gentlemen, she says, sounding like she has her own lightning bolts flying from her mouth. *You haven't proven men alone should lead a household in financial planning. You've only proven, in a world already filled with women, Adam couldn't get a date, except with his own rib.*

Suddenly there's a commercial interruption, and when *God Investment* returns, she's not there, or at least she's not talking, or she's been bound and gagged or killed. *We're taking your calls now,* a man says.

Driving through the gates of Dignity Place, I see the crowd gathered on the veranda. Old Toots lined up in wheelchairs and walkers and leaning on walking sticks and some tottering against each other and Hairy Harry standing behind Old Sebastian's motorized chair, the both of them looking Neanderthal each in his own way. And in front of them stand Mr. and Mrs. Grissly looking young only by comparison to the backdrop. They all face forward as if in agony, waiting for an unwanted group photo to be taken, except there's no photographer and no camera. And I don't see Dave-Jones-John-Newberry.

I park in an employee space and take my time to gather myself together. Best blue dress, pleated, hem just below my knees. Makes me look thin. Simple necklace. My hair down, tied in back. Makes me look young. Sebastian left for work smiling at me. Roby left for school shaking his head, but he always does that. I had stood at my full-length mirror in the bedroom before I left and decided, all right. Not so bad.

Stepping from the car, my purse snug at my side, I walk the long path to the veranda. The path curves around bushes and trees for no reason at all but for show, and as I move, all the eyes on the veranda move with me. Like bloodsucking insects in formation, those dark eyes appear to swarm, waiting to eat me alive; and as I near them I feel my confidence fall through my body, to my legs and feet, and ooze out of my toes.

"Mrs. Connery," Mrs. Grissly says. Her voice sounds high up a pedestal. "Where's your uniform?"

"Maybe she has a gym bag," Mr. Grissly says, mildly protective of me. But he looks at me, my purse squeezed at my side, and shakes his head. "No gym bag."

I stand at the base of the steps to the veranda, the swarm of eyes leaning forward. Hairy Harry looks away, but Old Sebastian's there looking ready to lean out of his chair. I say like a mouse squeak, "Uniform?"

"Well, I don't mean a uniform per se," Mrs. Grissly says. "Gym shorts, gym shoes, T-shirt, a whistle perhaps, that sort of thing."

A voice from down the line of Old . . . Residents calls out, "Leotards!" and the swarm begins to laugh, at me, stuck at the bottom of the steps. If there were a button to push to make the earth fall away and drop me into Hell, I'd push it right now and be grateful.

Mr. Grissly raises his hand. "Residents!" he announces. "As I said before she arrived, this is Mrs. Julia Connery, our new fitness instructor." He looks at me, sympathetic beside the severe Mrs. Grissly. "Mrs. Connery, it is our tradition here at Dignity Place to greet new employees this way, so you can see all the smiles and faces at once." Then he nods to the end of the line and it begins, the same way it was done the first day of kindergarten and at every club, gathering, meeting and institution on the face of the planet I've ever been to. A roll call of self-introductions.

Elaine is eighty and doesn't like noodle soup and Marie is eighty-five and was once married to an IBM executive and, not to be outdone is Nancy who worked as a banker for fifty years and says so four times before she lets the next Resident say hello. And their names and histories begin to blur into my dread of what Old Sebastian's going to say, and then what I'm going to say back. Like falling dominos, I count twenty, thirty, forty Residents. Mack who's the youngest, Janet who's the oldest, Frank who's the meanest, Donita who's the toughest. Then to Old Sebastian. He says:

"She's my daughter-in-law," and he smiles and waves.

His smile stays there, as friendly and warm as his car-grille dentures allow, and I would leap over the veranda's banister if I could and hug him. He gives me the confidence to say to the crowd, "Residents. Today will be orientation day for all of us.

I'll meet with each of you and hear what you would like in your fitness programs and what you don't like. Then the next time, we'll get started."

The swarm of eyes backs off. Seems to change into soft raindrops floating in the air. Mrs. Grissly extends her hand forward and I climb the stairs to the veranda. The Residents separate into their groups, some shuffling inside, and Old Sebastian rolls by with another wave, stopping to show me how he's able to raise his feet and tap them on the ground. He says, "I'll see you later."

Mr. Grissly says how good it is of me to take the time to meet all the Residents individually. A great idea. A good plan. But as we walk into Dignity Place, Mrs. Grissly sizes me up and down, her face puckered as if she's thinking of lemons. "Dear," she says at the front desk, her hushed voice causing even the Residents in the lobby to pay close attention. "Please wear a sports bra with your gym outfit."

"Sports bra?"

Mr. Grissly nods. "Yes. I see you need one. Very much."

Mrs. Grissly hands me a box chart of apartment rooms in Dignity Place with the names of the Residents belonging to each box. "If they're not out and about," Mrs. Grissly says, "you can find them in their rooms." They wave me on to begin my task, my program, my great idea, of meeting each and every Resident in Dignity Place and to listen to their favorite exercises and stories of ten thousand grandchildren and great-grandchildren. I walk slowly across the lobby, looking at the chart, and I flip a page to the second floor and find Old Sebastian's room. And then I see on the chart, three doors down from Old Sebastian, the mark in the box.

Dave J.

Old Sebastian pops in a DVD, *Godfather II,* and turns the mute on through the movie previews, commercials and credits. He spins his wheelchair about and sees me sitting lumped on his bed. "There are seventy-two Residents here," he tells me. "Even if you talked with each one for only ten minutes, it adds up to 720 minutes, which means you'll be here today talking for twelve hours to . . . what do you call us?"

I raise my stare apologetically. "Old Toots."

"Yes, Old Toots," he says, turning to make sure the DVD is still showing commercials and previews. "Throw in lunch and dinner breaks and you're up to fourteen hours. I don't think you could stand spending so much time talking to so many Old Toots."

"No."

Less like a question, more like a quiz, he asks me, "Why not?"

I see his eyes, so blue and like my Sebastian's, and his hair and nose so similar to Sebastian's, and his voice and cheekbones, and then I see how much frailty ninety-one years of living has brought to all his features. Ever since he saved my Sebastian from Little Nicky Number Two at Andaggio's, ever since our talk, I've understood how much he knows about my fear. So I just say it.

"I'm afraid of growing old."

He wheels to me and puts his hand on my knee. "I know. It's all over your face. But I wanted to hear it from you."

I should laugh at the brown hair and the bit of the color stained into the skin below his hairline. When I set my hand over his, I feel his bones first, their brittle sharpness, and it's a discomfort and struggle to keep my hand there. But then warmth rises through his skin into mine and a light sense of his pulse. As if by magic, my fingers begin to curve around his hand and his fingers curve around mine.

"I love you, my daughter-in-law," he says. "I love you for all the joy you've brought to my son."

"You've behaved quite the bastard."

"And you the bitch."

Then I throw my arms over his shoulders and hug him and all his frailty, and it's like clasping a reed too hollow to squeeze, but I do. "I can't stand the thought of interviewing seventy-one more Old Toots."

"Don't," he says.

"I promised them all. I promised the Grisslys."

"Half can't remember their own names and the rest imagine you've already talked to them. Don't worry about it. Just interview the one."

"Who?"

"Three doors down."

I straighten and look at the chart beside me on the bed. At the box marked Dave J. "Do you know anything about him?"

"He doesn't do a thing around here."

"If he's doing nothing then he's doing the opposite of being forced to do everything. He's doing the opposite of living under the command of Iris Newberry."

"The next time you're here," Old Sebastian says, "when you've got your gym clothes and sports bra, you'll help me learn to walk again."

Moving to his apartment door, shaking my head, I look back at him and he jiggles his feet and lifts them nearly straight, one at a time. There's pride in his old face and hope and something mischievous, like a plan of sorts, but I don't ask what it might be. He's smiling at me, waving at me, and all the while *Godfather II* has been playing with the mute on even though the young Robert DeNiro as Don Corleone wanders the streets of his old boyhood town in Italy. "All right," I say. "The next time, we'll give it a go."

I leave him and wait outside his door, listening to the sound of *Godfather II* being returned to the start. All the parts Old Sebastian missed so he could talk to me. When I turn down the hall, I'm nearly thrown to the floor by the sight of him, and I drop my chart of apartment boxes. There, standing before me, three doors down from Old Sebastian's apartment, is the full-bearded, long-haired, wildly unkempt vision of John Newberry.

"How are you, Julia?" he asks, his voice raspy but John's just the same.

"I'm fine, Mr. Newberry."

"I won't be attending your exercise classes. Nothing personal. I've never gone since I've been here."

I try to walk toward him, but now my confidence has frozen to the soles of my shoes. He looks to the floor and scratches at his beard. It's as though he's got a question for me in need of asking, but it's taking some time to rise out of him.

"Were you at my wake?" he finally asks.

"I was."

"And my funeral?"

"Of course."

"Sebastian, Roby?"

"Yes."

"A lot of people there?"

"You were a teacher, Mr. Newberry. We all loved you. It was packed with people and flowers."

"And the eulogy?"

"Absolutely a tribute. Wonderful, and it was all so true."

"How many cars do you think followed my casket to the grave?"

"A-mile-and-a-half's worth, if not longer."

He shakes his head up and down, smiling, and his eyes go watery with some sort of joy. "That's good to know."

"You should have been there. I mean, not that you should've been dead in the casket, that's not what I'm saying."

John Newberry shakes his head. "Sebastian did a nice job at his trial."

"John," I say, and I manage to take a step toward him. "What happened?"

"You were there in court. We found him not guilty."

"I mean . . ."

"Are you asking me about Iris?"

"I am."

"Don't."

"You know how my family is. They're going to be on me like bees to honey, probing me for answers until midnight."

John Newberry pulls at his beard as if forcing himself to turn around and away from me and all my questions about Iris and every other obvious question hanging out there as big as skywriting. "It's nice seeing you again, Julia. You look lovely as always. But when you see me here in the future, please call me Mr. Jones."

And he's suddenly spun completely about and through his door. He slams it shut. Then I hear the deadbolt scrape and ka-thunk into the jamb.

I turn around, but I'm stopped by a thought to leave a message. In my purse, I find a pen and one of Sebastian's business cards with the junior college's address and his office phone number on it, which drives me crazy because what does a teacher need with business cards? But John Newberry, since his funeral four years ago, perhaps he's forgotten where he used to live, and that the Connery family lives next door, and all the phone numbers he once knew in his former life with Iris. I write a message on the card's back and slip it halfway under his door. Then I step away and wait, listening to *Godfather II* and laughter drifting through Old Sebastian's door and down the hall.

The card slips inside and I leave, knowing Mr. Jones will appreciate the thought I wrote:

We were all thrilled to learn you weren't in the casket.

15

When Sebastian returns from the junior college, I show him the sports bra I bought on the way home from Dignity Place. "Looks like a prison for two," he says. "Have you tried it on?"

I nod.

"Is it comfortable?"

I shake my head.

"What's it supposed to do?"

"Keep things in place when I jump."

"Were you planning on jumping at this new job?" Sebastian looks at the sports bra with doubt in his eyes, then takes it from me and feels its material and weight. "I don't think I like this."

"I found my old leotards, too," I say, and Sebastian's eyebrows float up his forehead.

"Oh?"

Then I fall into him and cry. "How can I wear leotards in public? How can I pretend to be a fitness instructor? What was I thinking?"

Sebastian drops the sports bra; the size of it billows full of air and parachutes to the living room floor. He holds me tight. "Why are leotards making you cry?"

"They make me look lumpy."

"Lumpy?"

"I put them on and looked at my thighs and I saw the surface of your sainted mother's homemade mashed potatoes."

"You're a goddess to me."

Bee Robb

"Goddess of puckering fat."

"You have no such thing."

"Your eyes have gone bad."

"Connery men have strong eyes," he reminds me. "Not even a need for reading glasses."

I lean back from him and cup his pinchable Scottish face in my hands. "Then you're insane."

"Not any more than a woman who thinks I'm irresistible."

I wipe the tears from my eyes. "I suppose tonight you'll be wanting me to put on the leotard."

"Just so I can peel it off you." He nods. "And the sports bra."

"Really?"

Again he nods and whispers with his lips patting at my earlobe, "I want to rescue your lovely breasts from prison."

There's a cough in the hallway, and Sebastian and I find Roby glaring at us. "Don't you guys even care I can hear you? Don't you know all the psychologists I'll need 'cause of this?" He picks up the sports bra and hands it to his father. "Are you too distracted to ask Mom about Mr. Newberry?"

"I suppose I am."

"I talked to him," I tell Roby.

"What'd he say?"

"He said hello."

"What else?"

"He asked about his wake and funeral, and I told him how beautiful they were and how many cars followed his casket to the grave. He seemed taken by that."

"And?"

"He told me in the future to call him Mr. Jones."

"Then what?"

"Then he went into his apartment, slammed the door shut and dead-bolted himself inside so he couldn't hear me ask about Iris."

Roby cocks his head to the side. "You're going to find out more, aren't you?"

"Not unless he decides to tell me something more on his own."

"That's not acceptable."

"What do you suggest?"

"Take Mrs. Newberry to Dignity Place."

"Please," I say. "She's what made him run away."

"She's a fright," Sebastian interjects. "But maybe you can make her look beautiful."

"You want me to give Iris Newberry a beauty makeover?"

"Maybe a sports bra and leotard," Sebastian says.

"They'll likely crush her."

"It's an idea," Roby says.

"It's a horrible idea," I say to them both. "A shallow, horrible idea. Typical men. If you think it's something as simple as her looks that chased him away, then you're not thinking about the obvious. I mean, what if I got Iris to take off her hat and muumuu and put on a leotard, and let's pretend she's got some sort of womanly shape left to her, and let's say I'm able to scrape off forty years of sunblock from her face and discover she still has eyebrows and cheekbones and find there's hair left on her head to shape into something flowing and remarkable, and let's say I take jackhammers and hand chisels and plaster and spackle and sandpaper and paint and turn Iris Newberry into Miss America, then what do you have? I'll tell you what you have—you still have an overbearing, demanding, self-righteous, self-appointed, big-mouthed opinionated shrew who never let her husband inhale let alone make a statement about anything as simple as the shoes he should wear to work."

Sebastian's leaning away from me and my rant. "I thought," he says, "that you liked Iris Newberry."

"Of course I do. Two minutes at a time. I was never married to her."

"At least she'd be a shrew who looked like Miss America."

I grab my sports bra from Sebastian and think about whacking him with it across his irresistible face, but the size of the bra might suffocate him. Roby stomps his feet about and moans, "I don't know how you can stand it. Working at Dignity Place, knowing he's there, and you let him avoid the question."

"It's his right," I say.

"Yes," Sebastian says. "But was it right of him to lead us on this way? To make all of us think he was dead?"

"How do you know it wasn't Iris's idea in the first place?"

"I know," Sebastian says. "That woman made him run away, of course. It's easy enough to figure out. And her pride made her concoct a story about him dying from the black spot and then put a perfectly good copper casket in the ground to prove it. And for the rest of us, we shed tears over losing a friend and neighbor and we've suffered these four years, not only at the pretend loss of John Newberry, but also because we've had to take up the slack keeping Iris happy. Every Friday, Julia. Every Friday for the last four years since John Newberry's pretend funeral, we've had to sit in her living room for dinner wondering if we were going to eat or if her gargoyles and vampires would finally spring to life and take our blood and flesh away."

"You're being dramatic."

"Am I?" Sebastian asks. "Nobody's stopping to look at her house. Nobody's going to buy it. She's going to live there forever, next door to us, and you'll have forever to spend the rest of your Friday evenings with Iris Newberry at her dining room table looking out for gargoyles and vampires."

"He's right, Mom," Roby says. "It's not fair."

I watch them both. Teamed up. Now it's not so hard for me to believe that Old Sebastian might be the sanest one of them all. "A beauty makeover for Iris Newberry," I say aloud, just to hear the words.

"She may yet be beautiful," Sebastian says. "John used to say so."

"John told you Iris was beautiful?"

"He said he never saw her lose her beauty. Only that she began to cover it up a while back and draw the shades and curtains tight and keep them that way and never go anywhere without encasing herself in her own version of a suit of armor." Sebastian folds his arms and shakes his head with tsks and more tsks, then says, "A week before he supposedly died of the black spot, he told me, somewhere along the line, he lost his beautiful wife and got a drill sergeant."

"You never told me this."

"Didn't seem so important a thing to talk about after he died."

Roby says, "Now we know he's not dead and we're going to do something about it."

"We?" I ask.

Sebastian and Roby nod together and tell me what I already suspect: "You!"

My own curiosity appears spread over their faces and perhaps some anger at being fooled by both John and Iris, and the fear of every Friday spent into eternity eating among the gargoyles in the darkness of Iris's dining room. I also know the lament, both in Iris and John. It's more obvious in Iris, but I saw it in John, even beneath his baggy clothes and full beard and hair gone wild; I know I saw the lament in him. It must be difficult for either to say I'm sorry, one to the other. More difficult to admit the need to change and the need to talk things over. And it's likely impossible when the world saw your wife put you six feet under in a beautiful copper casket.

"I'll make Iris into Miss America for our own sakes," I say, and the Connery men smile at each other like it's an easy thing to do and as good as done. For me, I think I could more likely climb Mount Everest blindfolded than turn Iris Newberry into a vision of beauty.

I feel October's bite in the air and there's no kidding myself any longer that I can hold on to summer. It's a relief, I suppose, when the frost comes hard, as it has this morning, because the weeds fade along with everything else in my backyard garden and I don't have to hear about them from Iris anymore. Of course she wants the leaves raked up and mulch mounded over the rose bed. But I say leave them be. There's no sense treating leaves the same way as discarded candy wrappers.

I sit with Sebastian outside on the wrought iron chair, a glider really, a double-seater which fits us well; the toes of our shoes gently work the ground and swing us. Soon we forget about everything but ourselves. We huddle beneath our oversized Highland Park, Illinois, blanket, nearly a quilt, the red and white one with the fringe. The print in the cloth shows all the important buildings in town and has Ravinia and the beaches stitched into a semi-cartoon and exaggerated fashion. Beneath-blanket-cuddling is a ritual we perform before all the wrought iron goes into the basement for winter. In his warmth, Sebastian in mine, we realize how we thrive on rituals and Scottish culture and holidays and the successes and failings of our son, and even the Friday dinners with Iris. It's funny, I suppose, how it's the structure that helps to keep our love for each other alive, so new and energized, or, as Roby would say, too embarrassing to have his friends come over.

We're busy making our breath steam mix together through a hole we've shaped in the blanket for our mouths. It's a time for silence, to hear the last call of Canada geese in a far away vee in the sky, to feel the touch of cold on our cheeks, to witness the sight of the slate gray sunrise dim behind a thin cover of clouds. And to watch the weeds in the lawn and flower beds die! die! die! Although I know they'll celebrate Easter with a resurrection mass larger than ever before.

To the right, Iris's flower beds are put away neatly, covered in mulch so perfectly round I'm convinced they were made by a computer-driven machine. Her lawn holds on to its unnatural green color right up to the fence, and where the fence ends, it's as though a line separates Iris's green and my browning sod as straight as a ruler.

Sebastian blows his steam across mine, as if making a misty cross, and I pull the blanket away from my eyes a bit to see farther to the right. It's Iris who Sebastian's blowing steam at. She's standing there in the center of her backyard wearing her sombrero hat, dressed in some sort of canvas tent that shapes her into a teepee. In the shadow of a cloudy dawn, I'm envisioning a scarecrow, a zombie, a bride of Frankenstein and, of course, a vampire. I can't see her eyes and I wonder if she's staring at the mound of steam-blowing blanket on the Connery swing or my pitiful yard or her magnificent *Home & Garden* fall landscape.

Then I hear the sobbing, and at once Sebastian's steam and my steam halt as if our lungs have seized up, and we're both frozen at the sound of something we've never heard before. Waiting, we hear it again and we know tears flow down Iris's face, her hands now raised to her eyes. Her cry, so soft and lovely. Gentle. Huddled with Sebastian under our blanket with our rituals and customs and everything else keeping our love strong, I can't help but feel our display is a felony before the crying eyes of Iris Newberry.

A wind blows through our yard and shakes the hedges rimming Iris's pond. It lifts Iris's sombrero from her head and the hat hovers and spins above her like a UFO, then flies over her

125

roof and beyond.

"She has a full head of hair," Sebastian says into my neck.

"That she does."

"A little too blue, though."

Her arms and hands stretch above her, her fingers buried in her thick tresses swirling aloft. Nearly lost in the wind with the last wail of Canada geese, Iris Newberry's lovely cry calls for John.

16

Jane Fonda looks good in leotards. At least she did on VHS videotape in 1985. So thin and tall and fat-free, with big hair, and the little bikini bottom she has over her leotard that makes her fanny look like something too hard to sit down on. I wonder what she'd think now if she were in my living room watching herself on my television set, bending and stretching and jumping her fanny about, discussing it like it's an exhibit in a science lecture. It's my hope, for her sake, that today she's somewhere enjoying scoops of ice cream on a sugar cone and sitting down on a comfortable fanny spread out some since then.

I can't imagine why I bought this videotape. Back then it seemed like a requirement for women all over the world. But now I lie on my living room floor, watching Jane Fonda on my television screen lie on her floor. She's lifting her right leg pointy-toed into the air and she's propped her head upon her left hand and elbow, and her boobs stay put in defiance of gravity. All the while she's smiling, draping her right hand down her hip and saying the words *gluteus maximus*.

On my floor, I stay inert, flat on my back, wearing a beige leotard I found in my basement, at the bottom of a box of clothes I never wear anymore. I remember feeling self-conscious and exposed when I first put this thing on and let Jane Fonda torture me. Now in my leotard, I feel like that cold, lumpy bowl of Mother Connery's mashed potatoes. But how I love the touch of Berber carpeting scratching against my back. While Ms.

Fonda works her steely buns, I fall asleep. And I stay this way until the old tape reaches the end and starts moaning and groaning and threatening to tear itself free from its spindle.

I shower, put on a dress and makeup. I hold the leotard out before me. Without me in it, the thing looks like a dehydrated octopus. In my hands, it stretches long and I shoot it into the garage where it lands inside the abyss of a garbage can, and the Jane Fonda videotape follows, and I slam the lid shut so the beasts don't escape before Friday's trash pickup.

It's after ten. Sebastian will be home from the junior college for lunch at noon, full of questions concerning what Iris had to say about my turning her into a beauty for John. My winter coat is full of wrinkles after a spring and summer stuffed in the closet and I know Iris will have something to say about it and that my shoes need polishing. My hair will be tossed about after I walk through the wind to her house. Then I'll stand in her living room in my wrinkled coat and unpolished shoes and wild hair and tell her I'm here to make her into Miss America. She'll ask me, "Who the hell are you to make any woman into Miss America?" And I won't know the answer.

At Iris's door, with my hair whipping across my eyes, I still don't know the answer. When she appears, she looks as though she's been expecting me. Weak smile, head bowed below the same hat which had orbited away earlier this morning, she steps back from the door and waves me in.

On my way over, I had walked with my face toward the ground, fighting to breathe the frigid air swirling about my head. But in her living room, with Iris shuffling to sit at her dining room table, I see the sunlight. It pours through the long-settled dust on the picture window glass. It penetrates the air inside in broad shafts, lighting up linty motes that dart about as if alive and in shock. It lands on the dark wooden floor, creating a soft, rounded oval which threatens to reach to the furniture, and the gargoyles etched into the feet of chairs and tables and couches seem to lean away in fear.

It's an overcast morning's light, but in Iris's home with the one curtain open, it's a floodlight. Iris sits at the far end of her dining room table, an area still in shadow, and she leans back so I can see her eyes and the pink below them where she has rubbed away her tears.

"What do you want?"

I sit at the table, pulling a chair beside her. Even in shadow, I marvel at the warm color below her eyes and how the cake of sunblock has given way. She repeats, "What do you want?"

"Iris."

"What?"

"Take off that hat."

"You came here to tell me to take off my hat?"

I think for a moment. I think about fifteen years of being Iris Newberry's next door neighbor, her war against my weedy garden and her discontent with nearly everything I do and her muumuus and gargoyles and sunblock and her husband living as someone else only five miles away and his funeral she made up for show. "Yes," I say after considering these things. "Your hat. Take it off."

Her head bows toward the table, the brim of her sombrero lowering and covering her face. "It's been a while," she says softly. "A long, long while."

"I know," I say. "But what do you do when you're getting ready for bed?"

"I turn off the lights first."

"When you shower?"

"I avoid the mirror."

"Please, Iris. Give it a go."

Hidden beneath her hat, she cries the same cry from this morning. "Do you mean to be cruel to me?"

"Not at all."

"Then why?"

There's a rush inside me, blood circulating audibly through my ears, and a thudding in my chest. A cold wave shudders in my legs, flies up my spine and outward to my arms and fingertips. It's the same feeling of expectation I had the moment before saying yes to Sebastian when he proposed to me, the instant before announcing I was pregnant, the heartbeat before beginning a speech before a crowd of men and women in business suits. I think the words first, what I thought I would never say, now appearing in my throat and about to pass through my lips.

"I'm asking for John's sake. I think he would like to see your hair done up nice."

Through her sobbing, she asks, "From heaven?"

"No, Iris," I say more firmly than I thought I could. "From Dignity Place."

Her sobs seem to catch on a hook, and she's silent. I see the brim of her sombrero hat jitter about, hear the flap of her hands rushing across her wet eyes and nose. I offer her tissues from my purse and she takes them and withdraws them beneath her hat.

It's like a curtain going up, or perhaps a veil coming down. Either way, it's a slow production I witness, of her sombrero lifting at a snail's pace, then falling forward and off her head. As it moves, her hair begins to spring from beneath it, like cake batter rising in one even chunk. And her hat slides down her face to the table, settling there upside down. Her hair continues to rise slowly as if uncertain of what to make of this voluntary release, then at once tumbles freely to her shoulders. Her stare appears lost in the hat. And I see the wavy strands, thick from her scalp to their ends, caked in the color blue.

"Iris," I say. "It's lovely."

She shakes her head. "Hardly."

"The color. It's so . . ."

"I have my own formula. It's not a dye."

"Oh?"

"It protects against the sun."

I search my purse for a brush and I stand behind her. From the shadows we face the sunlight invading her home and I begin to brush through her hair. There's a crust to it, generations of hair spray, I suppose, and the remains of applications of her formula. I feel the resistance in her neck when I pull the brush through. Lightly at first. Then the bristles work their way in, and as I gather Iris's hair in my hands and continue with the brush, I feel the hairs begin to give and turn soft.

"I've seen John at Dignity Place," I tell her. "We had a chat. I told him you did a lovely job on his funeral."

Flakes of blue begin to powder from Iris' hair into my hands. She says nothing. I continue with what I know about John. "He sat on Sebastian's jury trial. You might consider he was the fore-man."

Nothing. Iris sits and says nothing. I don't know what else to tell her, so I simply brush and brush through her hair. It's a wonder watching the blue fade away with each stroke. It reminds me of the time my mother ordered remodelers to come over to tear out all the 1970s faddish decorating from my childhood home. The avocado and yellow fixtures and dark kitchen cabinets and orange countertops and shag carpeting and wall tile mirrors and cork board and George Jetson furniture, to find the classic beauty in the wood floors and textured plaster walls which was there in the first place. Brushing through Iris's hair is like that, an archeological dig through a veneer of mistakes. In our silence, facing sunlight, the blue leaves her hair, settling onto the floor and staining my hands. In its place appears lustrous silver.

"Iris," I say, placing the brush on the table. "Your hair is gorgeous."

"It's horrible," she says.

I spin her chair about, as easy as if she weren't there, toward the mirror over her dining room bureau. Of course rimmed in figures, faces of gargoyles with mouths agape, bearing fangs, the mirror catches a bit of the sunlight and shines back at us. Iris turns away from it, back to her hat. I bang the brush against the table, knocking blue powder free, and return to stroke it through her hair. I'm like a little girl on a play date with a friend, experimenting with beauty and discovering for the first time the loveliness of hair. How it feels in my hands, how it rests softly on the head and neck. It's something that feels as though it should go on for hours.

Iris glances back at the mirror, then away. "See, Iris? It's lovely." I watch her in the mirror and her stare drifts slowly back toward her image. "Truly lovely," I say, and I feel the give in her neck.

"Gray is a color, I suppose," she says.

"Silver," I say. "This, Iris, is precious silver."

Our reflections, my face above hers, smile at each other. I take more tissues from my purse and begin to wipe her face tenderly across her forehead to her cheeks and chin. The pasty white sunblock tears at the tissue, pulling out tufts that stick to her skin. Light pink spreads from below her eyes to the rest of her face where I wipe. Another archeological dig. And I notice, although there's a bit of a sag at her jaw and she's somewhere in her early seventies, she has few wrinkles.

"Why did you cover up all these years?"

Iris looks at me in the mirror. Studies my face as if I should already know the answer. "Why, dear," she says. "I didn't want anyone to watch my beauty fade away."

We stay frozen, watching each other in the mirror. I'm as

large as a battleship behind the wispy size of Iris, and the gargoyle faces appear stunned by the bit of sunlight in the room and the sight of Iris and me on our play date. I stare at myself, my expression not much different from the ones on the gargoyles.

She says, "John's not dead from the black spot. He's not dead at all. He ran away."

I hear her confession. I hardly notice it. Five minutes ago, I would have fallen to the floor in a fainting fit. Now, though, it's impossible for me to tear myself away from looking at our images, together, and feel overpowering comfort in the absolute beauty of Iris Newberry's silver hair.

You're going the wrong way you know.

I stop and blink into the cold, feeling frumped up by my size twelve flats and the wind chill inflating my overcoat. Ahead of me sits the rest of my block, away from my house. And there stands Lola Two in her miniskirt and halter, unaffected by the weather, striking an offensive pose with her rump thrown to one side, her hair now streaked long in gold highlights. "Now what have you done to yourself?"

Lola Two pouts and complains, *Why, honey, can't you tell? It's my cheekbones. See?* She smiles and blinks at me and I see now how her cheeks ride up to her eyes, nearly squeezing them to her forehead. I wish to turn about and head for home, but she stomps her stiletto shoes on the walk and shakes her golden-streaked hair at me. *I can't believe you thought the Grisslys were happily married for fifty years and would make me go away. What the hell were you thinking? They're nearly eunuchs. If they've ever had sex, I'll give up my new boobs.* She looks fondly to her Dr. Plastic breasts. *Not even Dr. Plastic could save the Grisslys. I mean, look how hard it is to tell which one's the man and which one's the woman. I think she's got the heavier moustache.*

"What are you?"

I'm this and I'm that. I'm the truth living inside your brain. I'm proof that you know just how much men wish to see a woman looking like me coming around the next corner.

"Can I go now?"

She cocks her head to the side. *Listen. Do you hear that?*

"Of course I do."

It's the Screamers. Claire and Theo Unkers. Bean Dip's parents. Their voices waver with the cold breeze and I catch pieces of their latest argument: "Bitch" "Dumb bastard" "Why don't you . . ." "The same to you and your mother's horse." It's the usual song trumpeting from that two-story house with the ivy covering the brick. People living within a hundred yards of the place consider this background music and have come to accept it. I tell Lola Two, "I'm not pointing to Claire and Theo Unkers for proof of a happy marriage."

Still, Lola Two says. *They're worth a closer look.*

I follow her another three houses down toward the Unkers' house and I'm horrified by her shaking fanny, looking a lot like steroid-enriched biceps flexing from inside her skirt, and the thought that men might like such a thing. *Beautiful home,* she says, stopping at the Unkers'. *The ivy and huge porch and the Lexus in the drive and the Jaguar in the garage.* She shakes her head some, almost out of pity. *Nice kids, too, if you like kids.*

Brian sits on the bottom step with his elbows daggered into his knees and his face resting heavily on his fists. His skin around his mouth looks aflame, and he's frozen even as his twin brothers skip behind him on the porch and throw acorns at his head. None of them wears a coat in the cold, just their jeans and baggy sweatshirts. I cut around Lola Two since I can't bring myself to pass through her.

"Brian," I say.

He barely moves his eyes. "Call me Bean Dip."

"I like 'Brian.' "

"Whatever."

"Why aren't you in school?" His brothers couldn't be more than five, blond hair and light complexion, so different from their dark, brooding brother. They throw more acorns at him.

"Woke up late. Missed the bus. I'm always doing that."

Behind him, his parents' fight flies through the air: "It's your fault. It's always your fault." "My fault? You're the dumb bastard who lets him sleep through the alarm." "Me? What about you, with your damn ear plugs?" "It's 'cause you snore like a diesel truck."

Something fragile crashes, and the fight rages on: "Missed." "Like hell. If I really wanted to hit you with it, you'd be bloody by now."

On it goes while Brian's face sinks deeper into his fists. "I had a trig quiz first period. I was getting an A in trig till now."

"Want me to drive you?"

"Nah. The teacher'll let me make it up. All the teachers do 'cause they know." He blinks and wipes at his eyes. "My teachers have met them." He sighs, hearing their noise. More crashes of breaking things. More insults. Always a bitch-bitch here, and a bastard-bastard there. Lola Two laughs from the sidewalk. *Can you believe they won't divorce for the sake of the kids' well-being?*

"Are you sure I can't drive you?"

"No," he says, and finally his face comes off his fists. One of the twins runs up and pops an acorn in Brian's ear, laughs, and scampers away. "I've got my own car. A lot of rust, but it runs. There's a hole in the floor. I call it my sun floor, and when I run it down the center of a street, I can see the yellow stripes zip beneath it. It's a great car."

He's got a nice shape to his smile, delicate and sincere, and I wish there were some way to mute his parents and make the mouth pimples go away. He looks back at his brothers and they both launch acorns at his head, one missing, the other striking him in the nose. He's like a father lion letting his cubs nip at him, and all he does is look at them and keep a sweet smile on his face. But then it's gone when he tells me, "I can't drive them in my car. It's too old for air bags and I don't have safety seats or belts for little kids." He shakes his head and plants his face back on his fists. "I can't leave my brothers alone with them. It wouldn't be right."

Lola Two counts the Unkers' children. *One, two, three. Claire and Theo must've done it at least three times. Twins? Well, at least twice. Now listen to them. Their marriage makes them turn bad. They'd be happier if they both had an affair.*

I want to take this boy home with me and feed him and tell him it's all right, how we'll figure something out, and he nearly knocks me off my feet when he tells me, "I wish my mom and dad were like you and Mr. Connery. That's what I want."

"Brian," I say. "It'll be all right."

He closes his eyes like he's heard this sort of advice before or wished for it many times before and all right has never come true.

Lola Two yawns and turns to the Petersen house next door. *Retired,* she says. *Both of them. They're free to have all the talk and hand-holding and sex they want with each other, but all they do is sit on opposite ends of their living room couch and watch TV. And that's also why you won't visit the Bakers 'cause they've got their fat asses on their couch, their backs to the front window, while they watch Vanna White spin consonants and vowels forever, even as they rot.*

"Brian," I say. "Come to my house whenever you feel you need to." He says nothing. Eyes closed, he winces at his temples to the crisp sound of something shattering inside his house.

Lola Two waits for me and follows me toward my house. She points to the Garpuchis' front porch. *Remember when you caught him at his computer? He wasn't expecting your visit. If only Mrs. Garpuchi would check out his E-mail, she'd know what you know about Mr. Garpuchi.* And the next house. *The last time the Winklers talked to each other Bill Clinton was still denying he had sex with that woman. You see, there's no couple on your block married happily fifty years. There never will be 'cause it's impossible. I'll be hanging around forever.*

When we reach the Newberrys' house, I stop and turn around.

"Maybe them."

I know I've caught Lola Two off guard. She falters on her high heels. *Damn, if I weren't a figment of your imagination, I might have sprained something.* Even though Dr. Plastic has stretched them toward her temples, lifted them toward her forehead and squeezed them with her cheekbones, her eyes give away a hint of worry. She looks to the Newberrys' house, its picture window curtain left open ever since my family learned and hinted about the alive and well John Newberry.

She coughs and the worried look vanishes from her eyes. Still, I hear the worry in her voice even when she laughs and tells me, *Julia, dear. Don't even think about Iris and John Newberry.*

Sebastian knocks on my bathroom door. I've locked it. I've never locked it before, and Sebastian asks me if I'm all right.

"I'm fine," I say.

"Can I come in?"

"No."

"Why not?"

I tell him the thing I know scares a man away, even a man like Sebastian. "Woman's problems."

"Oh, then, all right. Do you need to go to the hospital?"

"No."

He says, "I'll just make my own lunch," and his feet scamper away from the bathroom door.

I stand before the mirror, makeup-remover pads soaked in makeup-removing gel littering the sink and counter. The colors in them look like the pastel swirl of Easter egg paint. Like Iris, I suppose, I find it hard to stare into the mirror straight away. A glance, a glimpse, a peek. I can only bring myself to dip my toe in the frigid water.

I take a deep breath and look at the picture again. A photograph of me and Sebastian at our wedding reception. Bride and groom. White gown and black tuxedo. We stand side by side in front of a window in the Drake Hotel, all of Lake Michigan's blue and the sky behind us to serve as a backdrop. From our first apartment to our second, to our townhouse, to our home in Highland Park, this photograph always finds its place edged into the frame of our bedroom mirror.

All these years, day after day, this photograph is there, and it looks as fresh and new as the day we received it with the rest of our wedding photo proofs. I've always thought we looked the same ever since. Haven't aged a bit. We weren't going to. Friends say such lies to each other, genuinely so. It's as though we all make a wish for ourselves, and since we don't see the difference one day to the next, we begin to believe our wish has come true. But the truth is, it's like watching grass grow. There's nothing to see, but by the end of the week, the grass has grown tall and needs to be cut. Or like watching Roby grow. I didn't see things coming, but suddenly all my wishes for Roby to walk and talk turned into prayers that he would finally sit down and keep his mouth shut.

I remember the moment of this photograph, Sebastian refusing the photographer's riser and insisting it's all right if he's an inch or two shorter than his bride. He smiles broadly and reaches to my shoulder and I can still feel the energy of his gentle squeeze to hold me at his side. He told me a thousand times that day I looked beautiful. He still tells me. And from then until now, I suppose, I never expected the grass to grow.

All right then, I decide to look in the mirror. Straight away. Open my eyes. No makeup. I see what's there at age fifty-three.

I press my palms on my jaw and pull my skin toward my ears. I reach my fingertips to my temples and tug there, too. Tightening, pulling, lifting, stretching. Trying to find the Julia Connery in the wedding day photograph. My lips draw long and taut, my eyes narrow, and instead of finding the young Julia Connery, I see a fish-face staring back at me.

I see the awful similarity to Lola Two after what Dr. Plastic has done so far.

Letting go, everything flops back, from Lola Two, to the real me.

I study myself. Raise my chin. Smile. I brush my hair and make it full and wild, and I watch it fall over my face, reddish brown with gray here and there at the roots.

Sebastian's at the door again, speaking as he chews something he's made for lunch. "Still got woman's problems?"

"No."

"Can I come in?"

I think of John and Iris and my wedding day photo with Sebastian, and I unlock the door. The knob turns and slowly the door opens. I stand there ready to receive him. No makeup at all, my skin settled as nature would have it after thirty-three years of marriage. He steps in and sees the makeup-remover pads and their gooey pastel colors. Then he looks at me and I'm lit up by noon through a skylight, and light fixtures blazing over the bathroom cabinet. He faces the truth of the aging woman sharing his bed.

"My," he says, holding a tuna fish sandwich.

"What?"

He looks at his watch then winks his Scottish best at me. "Do you think we've got time?"

"No."

He steps to me, drops his tuna fish sandwich in the sink and brings his hands to my face. I feel the softness of my skin in his touch, and he somehow knows. "Did you have a bit of an experience with Iris this morning?"

"Yes."

"Are you all right?"

"I think so. Are you all right, Sebastian?"

"That I am."

"I don't look the way I used to."

"Neither do I." He holds me tight, presses into me with his smell of the tuna fish sandwich. "We at least have time for this."

Over his shoulder, I see the wedding day photograph atop makeup-remover pads. It suddenly feels as though the photographer has just held up his camera. I close my eyes.

17

For dinner tonight Sebastian says it's his turn to feed the family and opens up the yellow pages. "Chinese, Mexican, or pizza?"

"Dad," Roby says, slouching in the bench seat at the kitchen table. "I'll make something from the freezer."

Sebastian studies a menu listed in the phone book. "This is for your mother."

"I'll make something," I say. "I don't mind."

"But it's my turn. Why can't I do this?"

Roby groans and tsks his tongue at his father. "Then let me place the order."

"Are you telling me I don't know how to place an order for pizza delivery over the telephone? A grown man, your own father, history professor and head of the department at the junior college, can't say 'extra cheese' and 'no anchovies'?"

"It's what you say after that, Dad."

"Oh?"

Roby stands and places his hand by his face as if talking into a phone. "Hiya, Laddie. Listen. Do you wear gloves when you mix the dough? Do you wear gloves when you mix the sauce? Do you wash the preparation table after each pizza pie you make? Does your bathroom have the sign that says, 'All employees must wash their hands before returning to work?' And do you obey it and wash after using the bathroom, with sudsy soap and say the alphabet before you rinse? Do you promise not to spit on my pizza when I get off the phone?"

"Spit on the pizza?" Sebastian says.

I begin to scold Roby, but he slouches back down on the bench with a thud of teenage protest. "It's what Brian Unkers tells me."

"Ah," Sebastian says, his voice lilting high. "Your friend with the mouth pimples and static-electricity hair knows about spit on our pizza pie?"

Roby's eyes squint at his father, full of confidence in his facts and details. "Brian used to work at China Delight, and he used to work at Mia Senorita. He says they've got your name by their phones next to their lists of bounced checks."

I say, "A standing order to spit on our food?"

Roby taps his fingertips on the table. "It's what Brian told me. People don't like to be asked about their bathroom habits."

Slapping the phone book shut, Sebastian begins to pace in our kitchen. "So I have the choice of food made by dirty bathroom hands or spit?"

"Why do you assume," I say, "that people don't wash their hands before making a pizza?"

"Chrissake, Julia," and Sebastian paces some more and launches his hands into the air. "These places hire Brian Unkers to make our egg foo yung. Now what are the chances that boy washes his hands with soap and water and sings the alphabet before he rinses?"

"He delivers," Roby says.

"Ah! Great one, son. He delivers spit in boxes touched by his bathroom hands."

"I'm sure," I begin to say, but I'm stopped by the fire in Sebastian's eyes and his quick paces over our kitchen floor. He's ready to mount an offensive of a thousand phone calls to restaurants and Brian Unkers' parents and health inspectors, and I know if restaurant workers weren't spitting in our food before Sebastian launches his attack, they will do so after.

"I'll make dinner tonight," I say. "Please. It's easier this way."

Then Roby makes his announcement. "Brian helped me get a job."

Sebastian's jaw goes slack. "A job? Where? Why?"

"A warehouse by the high school."

"What about your studies? You've got your ACT this year. College, son. We're talking about where you go to college!"

"It's only a part time job."

"School is your full time job. Studying is your full time job. You don't have time to work in a warehouse. What does that get for you?"

"Money," Roby says. "My own money."

Sebastian stops his pacing. "Don't we give you what you need? Don't we provide everything? This house is paid for by the history of Connerys working and slaving and dying and passing their wealth down through the generations to us, to you, and my own work day after work day at the college just so you can have the time to study and learn and make something of yourself."

"Ah," Roby says with his own horrible Scottish lilt. "But it's not really my money now, is it?"

"We give it to you. It's yours."

"With strings attached."

"We're your parents. We don't hand over tons of money and say do with it what you will. Good parents attach strings."

Roby stands and I see for the first time he's got a half inch over Sebastian. Not a great height in any case, but something to notice. And he talks in his teenage way which lets us know he's not asking for our opinions. "Brian Unkers got me a part time job at a warehouse by the high school. Two hours, every other day, including Saturdays." And he says to me, "I already ate a peanut butter and jelly sandwich when I got home," and leaves the kitchen with his shoes scraping over the floor like sandpaper.

Sebastian's fiery eyes look doused. He leans on our kitchen table and stares at it as if it held secret battle plans for dealing with a teenaged boy. "I've got to do something about this," he says. "This Brian Unkers and his part time job at a warehouse."

Of course with all their rants and their pitched fights of iron will, the Connery men have abandoned the hunt for food. I open the refrigerator and remove the roast I began to thaw this morning. "Dinner in two hours," I say.

And two hours later it's another torment to me to sit at my kitchen table across from Roby's empty spot on the bench seat he usually takes and to watch my Sebastian eat his roast with eyes looking meanly into my prepared dinner. I know he imagines Brian Unkers and his pimply mouth ordering Roby to lift potato sacks onto greasy delivery trucks while bosses with fat cigars shout out language not allowed in our home. Sebastian rants on about Old Sebastian's grandfather and Old Sebastian's father and Old Sebastian, and himself; and it's all a tale of woe through the centuries of slave labor and the downtrodden and whips and chains and disease and famine.

"You're a college professor," I say.

"That I am."

"Old Sebastian was a high school teacher."

"That he was."

"His father taught math, and his father's father taught math."

"That they did."

"You make it sound like a history of black lung disease."

"Teaching a room full of children," he says with his eyes now wide, "can be worse than black lung disease."

I reach for his hands and hold them in mine. "You love your job. Your students love you. The young women graduate and show up at our door asking for your interview."

"You don't understand."

Tightening my hands over Sebastian's, I tell him I do

understand. "It's a warehouse, Sebastian, not a prison labor camp, and it's two hours after school every other day. It'll be good for him. It'll teach him about having his own money and responsibility, about what it's like to work." Sebastian tries to interrupt me with his pleas of fatherhood and respect, but I won't let him. "It's not about the job itself, now, is it?"

He looks at me like he's an abandoned lamb.

I say, "It's about our son making his own decision about something important without asking his father's permission first."

Sebastian kisses my fingertips, stands and scratches his head. "That it is, and it's spoiled my appetite." He leaves me at our kitchen table, alone with my prepared dinner. Not a single question about Iris or John or my job at Dignity Place.

What is it about men no matter their age, when they've got a thought, a project or a problem, the whole world around them vanishes and the only thing that exists or matters is their thought, their project or their problem? I look at my dinner table and conclude it's simply a way for them to get out of helping with the dishes.

Tonight, though, I'm going to leave the dishes. I'm going to let them stand and the gravy and butter can cake up and the meat can breed disease and the potatoes and green beans can turn hard as cement. My little protest.

Upstairs in the hallway, I see my bedroom door closed and Roby's bedroom door closed, and thin strips of light at their bottoms glowing horizontal like thin lips over gritted teeth. I knock on Roby's door and get no response. I say, "It's not your father."

"Then come in."

I have a habit of closing my eyes whenever I enter Roby's room. I suppose it's my wish to see the simple blue walls and neat desk and bed from years before. Maybe even my memories of the crib and stuffed animals and molded plastic toys and blocks and Sesame Street Muppets. Then I open my eyes and see the walls lost beneath posters of angry men and women rock stars with their mouths twisted into shapes of vulgar words, and they're standing tilted and postured as if ready to fight something floating in the air, and a desk and bureau littered with Roby's own mutilated sense of organization. It could cause a mother to faint.

Roby sits on his bed and occupies himself studying his headphones and iPod. He says, "What?" without looking at me.

"Do you love me?"

My question forces him to look at me. "Why do you always ask me that when there's a problem?"

"So we both know what's important before we start."

"Start what?"

"Talking about your father."

He looks back to his iPod. "Yeah."

"Yeah what?"

"Yeah, I love you."

"Good. I love you too. And your father?"

"Sure."

"Say it."

"I love my father."

"Good. It's important we begin with that understanding."

"Fine."

"Can I sit with you?"

Roby moves to the side of his bed and I walk over tossed-about CD cases and clothes and papers and something crunching beneath my shoes. Beside him, I feel his warmth. "Tell me about this job. What's it like?"

"I don't know. I don't start till tomorrow."

"Didn't you ask anyone about it first?"

"Guess not."

"Not even Brian?"

"Call him Bean Dip."

"I prefer Brian."

"Whatever."

"Did you ask him?"

"No."

"What will you be doing?"

"I don't know."

"How much does it pay?"

He shrugs then asks, "What's new with Iris Newberry?"

"Don't change the subject."

"Minimum wage."

"I see."

"Um hmm."

"So you're getting paid minimum wage for a job you didn't ask about, doing something you don't know about."

"Mom," he begins nearly in earnest. But his voice drops back into its mask. "That's right."

I run my fingers through his hair, so thick and brown like his father's. He doesn't seem to mind. "Will you manage school?"

"Yeah."

"Your father wants you to go to college. Some place important and special."

"Dad teaches at a junior college." Roby turns to me. "Don't you think he's hypocritical?"

"No."

"Does he look down at his students because they go to a junior college? Does he think he's better than everyone he teaches?"

"Your father thinks a student can be a fool at Harvard, an ass at Yale and a dropout at Stanford. But other students can be Einsteins at a junior college. The books are the same. The opportunities are there. It's all in how people apply themselves."

"Are you telling me Dad would be happy if I went to his junior college?"

"I am."

"I don't think so. He acts like a part time job is going to ruin my life."

I take Roby's head and hold it against my cheek. "Imagine it this way. You're the father. Over seventeen years you've bathed your son, diapered your son, cried his tears, washed his wounds, worried his illnesses, cheered his successes, and watched him grow into a person who shares your features and voice. Then your son makes a decision about something important without asking your permission first. What do you do? What do you think?"

Roby's shoulders rise in a shrug, and I tell him, "Of course you know."

"It's not fair," he says. "You're smart at this."

"This weekend, I'm taking Iris Newberry to shop for new clothes."

"Don't change the subject."

Releasing his head and his lovely thick hair, I tell him to think things through. "Don't be angry at your father for being a father."

I stand to leave, over the CD cases and clothes and papers and things that go crunch beneath my shoes. At his door I look back and see he's at his iPod again with the headphone pads poked into his ears. I hear the wisp of music begin to play. I know the melody going into Roby's mind. A lovely, lilting folk song, so ancient, singing the praises of Scotland's Mull of Kintyre.

> *Green hills I once roamed*
> *Oh, my lovely Kintyre*
> *As your son, my dreams,*

Fill with your sweet memories,
One day to come home

Roby's head weaves to the melody and his lips move to the words. And it seems as though the faces of the angry rock and rollers on the posters have turned to me with expressions of dismay, perhaps fear that, like the Sesame Street Muppets which came before them, their stay in my son's room will come to an end.

In my own room, I find Sebastian in bed early, claiming exhaustion. On his side, he curls around the box holding the Urns of Connery. He asks me, "Is everything all right?"

"Roby says he loves you."

"He's grown a bit taller than me." Sebastian hugs the box with the Urns of Connery inside tighter to his chest. "It's not about strength. When have I ever hit the boy or threatened to? Never, that's when. I'd cut my own hands off before I'd strike him."

"He loves you."

The Urns of Connery rattle inside the box. "Listening to your father shows you love your father, that's what I'm saying here."

"I'm telling you, Sebastian. Your son loves you."

He peeks over his shoulder at me. "Is he quitting that job?"

"I don't think so."

"Good night," he says and falls asleep, or pretends to, facing his map of Scotland on the closet door. Tonight he'll dream about the moment he releases small piles of the ashes of Connerys into the mist rolling over the shore of the Mull of Kintyre. I should tell him about his son, about the song he plays on his little iPod. But my motherly instincts insist I let it go for another day.

I awaken late in the morning. About eight. Sebastian and Roby have gone to school and, thankfully, the house isn't torn apart. I wobble down the stairs in my slippers, feeling my face and shoulders droop toward the floor two hours before I turn into the fitness instructor at Dignity Place. The dishes left out from dinner have been washed and put away and the food saved and packed in sealed containers in the refrigerator. There's a note on the kitchen counter, saying simply, "Sorry," and it isn't signed. Father and son have the same handwriting. Both have something to apologize for.

At the sink, I splash water on my face and pat it dry with a dish towel, hoping dryness and morning sunlight through the window over the sink will make my skin tighten up. Opening my eyes, I see Iris at her kitchen window, looking down, doing her own dishes I suppose. And I notice.

Beautiful silver hair. No hat.

18

Mrs. Grissly sizes me up.

Imagine. A woman looking carved from battered driftwood, dressed in a black suit, gives me the once over. "That will do nicely," she says with a sniff.

What does nicely, I suppose, are my navy blue sweat pants and gray sweatshirt, the little bit of makeup around my eyes and blush upon my cheeks, and my hair tied back. Dressed this way, I imagine I must look like my Catholic School gym teacher, whom we made shameful fun of and called Sister Mary Mustache behind her back.

I wear a whistle hanging from a suede string around my neck. Sebastian's old whistle from his protest days. It has a sound to it like a thousand hecklers spitting raspberries, and he blew it in the early 1970s at Young Republicans and other Nixon supporters. Something about the cracked pea inside of it, he once told me. Now it rests against my chest, ready to blow against the Residents of Dignity Place.

"Sports bra?" Mrs. Grissly asks.

"Yes."

"How does it feel?"

"Like my boobs are on vacation," I say, and I don't know why I say it. It's something I'd say to Sebastian, but not to the formal Mrs. Grissly, whose eyes awaken with spirit and lightning. She inhales and holds in the air as if considering how to fire me on the spot. Then she smiles. "I've never had a need for one," she says with a wink, "to the disappointment of Mr. Grissly."

She takes me by the hand. Her fingers feel so foreign touching mine, as if our hands are opposing magnets forced together despite their mutual repulsion. Walking across the lobby, her shoes click sharp authority over the stone tiles while my gym shoes pad meekly behind. I look around me so as not to look at her, so my thoughts aren't coaxed into thinking about what she might look like under the covers with Mr. Grissly, who wishes she had a need for a sports bra.

Marble pillars reach to tall ceilings, lush drapes of ivy hang green and yellow from lofty places and herds of potted ferns, two stories high, arch their fronds into pretend paradise beneath the skylights. Water runs over molded rocks into bucolic ponds filled with goldfish and soft-bubbling fountains and filters and pennies thrown in for good luck. Over the years, I had never bothered to notice this beauty before. Just hurried to Old Sebastian's room for our little visits and left. Noticing the loveliness of it all makes me wonder whether John Newberry's pennies lie beneath the goldfish, spent on thoughts of Iris.

Residents gather together behind ferns and sit on benches alongside ponds of pennies and goldfish, discussing something as they flick their stares toward me trailing behind Mrs. Grissly. They start to move, to gather, and to follow, like guerrilla warriors in the jungle.

As we leave the lobby into a broad hallway, the smell of chlorine strengthens, and soon we pass a door with a sign, *Natatorium,* then a sunlit, tiled expanse lined by a long row of glass. Inside, a flock of Residents floats in the pool, all wearing white swimming caps decorated in bright plastic flowers, their heads bobbing about like potted plants adrift at sea.

"Of course you have a watercize program this morning," Mrs. Grissly says.

"Of course."

"Two sessions of low-impact aerobics in the afternoon."

"I thought it was one."

"It's two."

"Of course."

We pause at a smoky glass door designated for employees only, then enter. In the narrow hallway beyond, the chlorinated humidity engulfs me and soaks into my sweat clothes and makes my armpits come alive with perspiration. "I have a swimsuit for you to try on, of course," she says.

I think to say, *Why didn't you tell me about this? Why did you talk about leotards and sports bras and gym uniforms but not this?* And again, with my words of capitulation, I say, "Of course, Mrs. Grissly."

We enter an office, a closet-and-a-half really. It has a cement floor, small metal desk, four-tiered metal filing cabinet, brown metal folding chair, and a reinforced window with horizontal blinds overlooking the pool and the potted plants dog-paddling about in the water.

"You can swim, of course."

A fine thing to ask me now. "Of course, Mrs. Grissly."

"You've been certified in some fashion."

Another fine thing to ask me now. "Of course, Mrs. Grissly." I don't tell her, in 1969.

"And I'm glad you brought your own whistle," she says, turning to the filing cabinets. "You've come prepared." She opens up the top drawer and pulls out a navy blue cloth shining like fish scales beneath the tiny room's fluorescent light. "This should fit you. It's pretty much one size fits all."

She lays the limp blue rag on the desk and draws the blinds shut for privacy. "I'll go to the pool and let our Residents know you'll be down in ten minutes." At the door, she asks, "Are you all right, Mrs. Connery? You seem a bit pale."

"Of course, Mrs. Grissly."

She smiles again, at me sweating in my sweat clothes, the beads of water on my upper lip and forehead and my whistle. "Of course," she says, and leaves.

I undress, all the while grimacing at the blue, one-size-fits-all rag. I pick it up and think of overcooked noodles. The unknown history of people who have worn this thing drapes over me like a plague. At least Sebastian's not here to see this. He'd have me fumigated before allowing me back in the house.

Opening the horizontal blinds, I catch Mrs. Grissly standing at the pool's edge, talking. The flock of floating potted plants turns toward my puny office and they wave their arms at the water's surface. Some bob their chins below and back up, spitting a bit of water in my direction. I wave at them and spy the white of my sports bra poking above the neck of the swimsuit and out around my shoulders. Looking down, I see the chipped toenails I painted bright red on a lark about two weeks ago. On the cinder block wall to my right, words in small brown-red letters, undated and unclaimed, say to my eyes, *They murdered me!*

I think of Old Sebastian and his stories of gangsters who once owned this place, and the horrible swimsuit on my skin and my sports bra poking out beneath it here and there, and my cracked, red toenails, and the Residents huddled in the pool, spitting water at me in their potted plant swim caps. Suddenly it feels so cold.

"Gather in the shallow water," I say, just as I used to say at Camp Sanunah when I was a junior lifeguard and swimming instructor. Camp Sanunah was a summer camp along a clear water lake near South Haven, Michigan. It had trees and a sandy beach and the children there were half my age and size. I figured then if they didn't listen to me, I and twelve other counselors and junior counselors could toss them about. The children knew it and for the most part obeyed my commands.

Along the tiled and concrete shores of the Dignity Place natatorium, my voice echoes back on itself and the Residents turn their heads about in confusion. I count twenty of them, all in the deep end, enjoying a float and conversations among themselves. Behind me, more Residents gather at the hallway window to watch, and I feel as though my own fanny, covered by a sagging rag of a swimsuit, is aglow and on display. I glance back and see—all men—standing pressed against the glass, their stares rising from my fanny to my eyes once they know I'm onto them. Mr. Grissly scoots the men along. A short one gives me a smile and a raised thumb.

The Residents in the pool begin to drift to the shallow end and I step to the edge to search for bodies on the bottom. Life preservers, torpedo floats and a rescue pole hang from hooks on the walls, but the bottom is clear and marked with four parallel black stripes for swimming lanes. I clutch my whistle, wondering what awful noise it would make released in this natatorium. A weapon, I suppose, should I ever have the need to use one.

At a corner of the shallow end of the pool, steps rise from the bottom to the edge with twin chrome rails for support. I sit on a foam kickboard above the top step, my legs stretched into the water, and I feel lukewarm heat more appropriate to a Jacuzzi. Exercising in this bath water will put these Residents to sleep for the rest of the day. Perhaps that's the plan of Mr. and Mrs. Grissly.

Of the twenty Residents floating toward me, I think I see three men among them. In their swimming caps, all adorned in plastic flowers, it's hard to tell. When their shoulders begin to break the surface of the water, I find seven are men, smiling their dentures beneath floral caps with black lettering at the sides claiming them as the Property of Dignity Place.

Natatorium rules loom large on a board bolted to the wall at the deep end:

1. No running. No skipping. No loud noise or music. No arguing.
2. All users of this pool must wear the traditional swimsuits and caps issued by Dignity Place, including bald men. No exceptions!
3. Nude soap showers are required before entering the pool area. No exceptions for anyone.
4. Please—No urinating in the pool.
5. No double bouncing off the diving board.
6. Enjoy!

"Aren't you coming in?" a Resident standing at the bottom step asks. She's slim in her swimsuit and has a face appearing more used to smiles than frowns, but it's the frown she gives me with her question.

"I thought we'd get acquainted first. My name's Julia Connery."

"We know who you are," she says. "Sebastian's daughter-in-law." She corners her stare to the Residents around her. "We've heard about you."

"Oh?"

"Sebastian says you call him *Old* Sebastian."

"It's the way we distinguish between father and son."

"Your husband's a junior. But you call his father old."

"I, well, yes. It's something the family does."

A heavier woman slaps at the water's surface, and the yellow petals on her cap flap about as she talks. "Isn't she the one who calls us all a bunch of Old Toots?"

"She's the one."

The Residents suddenly hush, a few fold their arms over their chests and their expressions turn sour beneath their swimming caps. My mind tries to come up with something to say through the broken smile on my face. Nothing arrives. I'm stuck in the humidity and glare of eyes.

"That's not a nice thing to call us," I hear from somewhere, but I can't tell because my neck and eyes have gone stiff.

"No, it's not," I say.

"Then why do you say it?"

"I don't know. I haven't said it in a while."

"Why'd you stop?"

"Because it's not a nice thing to say."

"We already told you so."

"I know."

"What's the real reason?"

"It's hard to explain right now."

"I don't think you should be teaching us Old Toots anything!"

"Please," I say, but the discussion intensifies around me.

"Leave her alone, Beth. By God, you are an Old Toot."

"And I'm an Old Toot, too, and I don't mind it a bit."

"It's not a nice thing for Mrs. Connery to say."

"Oh, please. Get over yourself. You've got a gallon of water caught in your wrinkles."

"I've got a name, and it's not Old Toot!"

I bow my head and wait for this civil war to finish. I'm thinking, if I survive, Old Sebastian may not. Peeking up, I find seven residents remain gathered around me at the pool's edge. All the men. The women drift off to the deep end to float and talk and glance back at me with mean looks in their eyes.

"Are there more kickboards around here?" I ask, hearing my voice shake. Two of the men stand straight in the water with their chests stuck out and their stomachs sucked in. They avoid the easy steps out of the pool and spring out over the side, running and skipping and arguing over kickboards set against a wall, breaking pool rules on my behalf. The remaining men watch me with differing levels of interest. And the Grisslys stand at the hallway window, looking in, frowning at the women floating in the deep end, frowning back at me and the men and how I've lost control of my watercize program before it's begun.

"I'm Paul," a man says, raising his hand. He's thick through the chest and hair sprouts on his shoulders, and his looks and voice say teddy bear to me. "You should apologize to them," he tells me. He looks down at the water and the reflected light flickers softly over his skin, as if angels busy themselves blessing his words. "Please don't quit."

"No?"

"They always quit on us. Always."

"Who?"

"Fitness instructors. One week, sometimes a month. One as long as a half year. But they all quit, sooner or later."

Looking at Paul, an elderly man in a floral swimming cap with tufts of hair on his shoulders and a pout like a child's, I'm drawn back to the memory and energy of Camp Sanunah. About a boy I offended. Short, skin pale as white chalk, made of bird-bones, so it seemed, and a face kinder than a saint's. But the other children ignored his sweet face and chose him as the camp outcast. I was thirteen, watching him ignored and teased and taunted and bullied. When I had my chance to do something about it, I chose instead to join the others. Funny how a thing like that, when you're thirteen and a junior counselor at a summer camp, can stay with you forever.

On a diving platform out in the lake, this boy found me and tapped on my shoulder. "You're mean," he said.

"I'm no different from anyone else around here," I said back in a snit, having discovered my newly acquired teenager voice.

"I thought you were . . ." He looked at his feet. "I thought you were better than everyone else here."

I remember those knobby knees and splayed awkward feet and his stomach like a small drum heaving with his breaths. I saw then his saintly face, and remembered myself. "I'm sorry," I said.

"Yeah? Prove it."

I looked at him with mountains of guilt on my shoulders and my hands gripped around the metal bars to the high-dive.

Standing on the concrete shore of the Dignity Place natatorium, I can still see that pitiful boy and his look of sadness wondering if I were different from the rest. I leave the men at the shallow end and walk away swinging my arms high, slapping my feet on the tiles. The women floating in the deep end turn to stare at me. They watch me at the diving board. They watch me climb atop and head to the edge. I raise Sebastian's whistle to my lips and blow a cursed sound of a thousand raspberries. Then I throw it to the floor behind me and shout:

"I WAS WRONG AND I'M SORRY!"

My apology and the whistle's raspberries echo about in the natatorium until they sound like an eternity. Then I take three steps back and run to the tip of the board. Bounding high, my arms aloft, I fall back to the edge of the board, violating Rule 5 on the wall behind me, and my double bounce takes me to the skylight, so it feels. I tuck, hands to toes, and the eyes below me stare with amazement, just the way that boy's eyes did at Camp Sanunah so long ago.

I begin my descent, tucked until the last moment, and open up to land hard, my stomach fully flat across the water's surface.

At the bottom of the pool, I curl up and let the water's current and bubbling around me soothe the sting. The remaining waves from my belly flop spread to the pool's edge, and the legs and arms of the women overhead work their way toward the shallow end.

As I walk back to my class, Mr. and Mrs. Grissly stand as American Gothic at the natatorium window. It's likely they've been counting the rules they've seen broken. They must wonder whether I've peed in the pool.

Slipping into the shallow end with the Residents, I find the men more subdued, the women more at ease. Smiles appear on their faces. The front of me flashes red, as if sunburned, and my ragged swimsuit seems ready to fall apart in shreds. A voice from somewhere in the middle of the group says, "Apology accepted."

"Thank you," I say, remembering the apology a small boy accepted from me at Camp Sanunah. "Now let's begin."

19

He sits so complacently in his room in his wheelchair turned toward me and with the press of a button on the remote, mutes Joe Pesci hyperventilating in *Goodfellas*. Old Sebastian asks me, "Are you ready?"

I stand there in my own stink of chlorinated water crusted over my skin, my hair frizzled so it sticks out like a satellite dish, the whites of my eyes turned red and my stomach still stinging from my apology. "Old Sebastian," I begin with a hiss. Joe Pesci screams a silent rant on the screen over Old Sebastian's head.

"What?"

His eyes blink wide with expectation of walking one day soon, his voice so much like a lamb's and his smile so endearing. I clench my hands and feel my fingernails stabbing into my palm. "Old Sebastian," I go on. "You shouldn't have told the world about my habits."

He looks down at his lap and fingers the toggle on the arm of his wheelchair. "I didn't tell the world," he says.

"Dignity Place is world enough."

It's like watching a draw bridge rise, taking its time, Old Sebastian's face lifting toward mine. "I know," he says, and water builds in his eyes.

"None of that," I say. "Tears aren't going to work."

"What will?"

I bring my clenched hands to my stomach. "An apology from you would do for a start."

"You want me to apologize because you called me and everyone else here Old Toots for the last four years?"

"No. For talking behind my back and for telling strangers our personal things. You made me feel like my soul was caught exposed in nothing but underpants."

"It was a moment of anger months ago. I asked you to stop and you didn't listen."

I look to the ceiling and feel water pooling in my eyes. I suppose it's the sting of chlorine enhancing Old Sebastian's impact on me. "Do you mind it when I call you *Old* Sebastian?"

"No. It's got its purpose, and its bit of charm."

"Can you say so to all the other Residents in short order?"

"I will."

"Do you want these walking lessons kept secret until you're ready?"

"Yes."

"Do you love me?"

"Yes, I do. But do you love me?"

He's thrown my own debating method back at me, and my stare falls from the ceiling to Old Sebastian. "Yes. Certainly I do."

"It's a good thing to say. Takes the wind out of a person's spit and vinegar."

Unclenching my hands, I see the streak of pink in my palms from my nails. Irritation, but no blood. Above Old Sebastian, Joe Pesci's face is like a maniac's and he lets someone have it with a gun. I take the remote from Old Sebastian's lap and turn off the television. "How do we do this?"

He moves his footrests apart to opposite sides and places his shoes, a pair of heavy wing tips polished into mirrors, to the floor. "Help me stand."

"Right off?"

"I know I can do it."

"How do you know?"

Old Sebastian winks at me. "Dave Jones."

"John Newberry's been giving you standing-up lessons?"

"He's got strong shoulders for support. And he keeps his beard washed. He's very clean even if he looks like a weed."

"How long have you known about him?"

"Since he got here."

"Why didn't you say anything at Sebastian's trial?"

"I promised to keep his secret, and I've obliged him. He's been a big help with my exercises."

"Then why are you asking for my help now?"

"It was Dave Jones's idea. He said it would be good for both of us. And he said he wouldn't help me anymore unless I asked you and you turned me down."

"I see. Considering he's run away from Iris, doesn't this seem a bit hypocritical of him?"

"Another man's marriage is none of my business. Even so, don't you think it's a good idea?"

Old Sebastian motions for me to step closer to him. "You need to get a feel for my balance."

He leans forward in his wheelchair, makes those grunts and groans men start to do in their late thirties. Bending toward me, he drapes his arms over my shoulders. He tells me to bend at the knees, which I do. There's his scented soap and my eye-stinging chlorine smell, and his grunting and groaning, and the pressure of his weight and strength upon my shoulders and my fear of dropping him and breaking him and my having to tell Sebastian I shattered his father's body all over the floor. I'm in a swoon about this, ready to faint. But then the world seems to rise, so slowly and easily, like the rise of a flower bud from the cradle of its leaves.

"We're standing, Old Sebastian!"

And we are. Steady, close together. He lowers his left hand to my side, keeps his right on my shoulder. "About saying things behind your back," he says, "I'm sorry."

He needs me for this, I can tell. His fingers on my ribs wiggle and jiggle, pressing to help keep his balance, and his hand on my shoulder flinches at the smallest lean to either side. It's his fear of failure, I know, mixed in with his hope.

"What do you think?" he asks.

"You're still short."

"Ah," he laughs. "But from here, I'll be able to see all of Scotland."

I lean back and witness the small pleasure in his smile and a faraway look in his eyes. "Scotland? What do you mean?"

"A secret," Old Sebastian says. "Now I'm keeping secrets. It's our new rule."

"All right," I say, and I feel how steady he's become standing at the foot of his wheelchair. "Does this hurt?"

"A bit in my knees and hips. Not too bad."

"I have fifteen minutes before my next fitness class."

"Let's stand a bit more."

"Fine."

"Julia. Take them for a walk outside."

"What?"

"Take the Residents for a walk outside. They don't want to march and step and swing their arms in a room. Have them march and step and swing their arms outside and off the trail."

"Old Sebastian?"

"It's what they want from a fitness class, to get out of here."

"It's turned cold outside."

"Have them put on their hats."

"Will the Grisslys mind?"

"Yes."

"Then I'll consider it."

"Julia?"

"What now?"

"I put another three holes in the wall behind my dresser."

"Find any gangster bones?"

"Still looking."

"John Newberry involved?"

Old Sebastian gives in on this one. "I hold the chisel; he swings the hammer."

Standing together as we are, we're like a father and daughter at a school dance and neither one of us knows the steps. We sway a bit, and it's Old Sebastian leading. Soon he begins to hum. Perhaps he means it as a hint about his secret, but I cannot imagine how he'd know. A coincidence, I presume. It has to be. He hums the same lilting tune Roby stuck in his ears last night. That ballad praising the Mull of Kintyre.

"Old Sebastian?"

"What?"

"You really need to stop making holes in the walls."

"I can't help myself."

"Old Sebastian?"

"What now?"

He hums off-key, rasping, and sweet in his own way. I give him a soft squeeze. It's all right, I suppose, his old bones creaking in my arms. Uncomfortable, but no longer revolting. I say, "Never mind."

I come home at four-thirty in the afternoon, make some toast with strawberry jam and stare at it on a plate on my kitchen table. Afterwards, I don't know. I have a vague memory of Sebastian lifting me off the chair and carrying me to our bedroom. It has to be a dream because he'd pop a dozen hernias if it were real. I wake up when it's still dark and Sebastian's telling me to go back to sleep. "It's two in the morning, Lassie."

"How long have I been out?"

"Nine, ten hours."

"There's toast stuck to my cheek."

"That's the way I found you. I didn't want to wake you."

Too exhausted to take the toast off my face, I feel myself drawn back into sleep even as Sebastian asks me how my day went at Dignity Place. "Hell, good, interesting," I say. My tongue and jaw turn limp. "Old Sebastian. He stood up today. We danced." I then remember it was supposed to stay a secret, but it hardly matters.

"Ah, Julia," I hear Sebastian say in my fog apart from reality. "You're still dreaming."

In my dream, Iris Newberry sits on a velvet chair, hidden in mist. Around her, music begins to play, but it's not the monster-gargoyle music I expect. Rather, I hear a soft tap, like someone snapping his fingers, and a haunting, deep, sexy, slip-off-your-clothes rumble from an upright bass. With the beat, the mist lifts, and there's Iris in full—absolutely gorgeous.

On her velvet chair, more like a throne, a light shines behind her, surrounding her in a golden glow, and birds flutter about chirping morning songs. Her silver hair shines like a neon light, thick on her head, wavy, lovely to her neck, and it frames her face. Now there's something. A lovely smile on Iris, and hazel eyes so dazzling they say come hither, and makeup done just right so her cheeks shine pink to her lips, and her lips so glossy and full. Shaped for a kiss.

She sits with her legs crossed, back straight, and her hands gently upon her knees. Soon trumpets and saxophones and clarinets begin to play along with the bass and finger-snapping. With the rise of the music, so rises Iris, slowly, and she makes a teasing flick of her head so that her hair swings about her neck. Black capri pants, a silver silk top, silver stiletto shoes. Iris has a shape to her, a shape to distract a man's eye and hold his stare for as long as she wants to. And when she walks, it's as though she moves to a soundtrack.

From her front door, she steps into sunshine. Beams of warmth from the sky surround her while the rest of town remains gray. As she goes, the sunshine and warmth go with her and the music gains speed with the sway of her hips. The sidewalk is her fashion show runway and crowds of cars slow and fender-bender into each other and the men inside turn to look and say in a rush of admiration—*Vah-voom!*

Vah-voom, Vah-voom! It's Iris Newberry strolling toward Dignity Place and the world stops to watch and listen. The music in the air builds in anticipation of drama. Trombones growl and slide their vibrato as she slips along, and the rest of the band crescendos, making the music spiral into the sky. Then suddenly it stops, and the drums take over and pound away as Iris reaches the gates of Dignity Place. She promenades to the veranda, meanders up its steps while a percussionist's brush circles the surface of a snare drum, hissing like a snake, and the soft thunder of a bass drum beats and rumbles beneath the walk of a woman who knows what she's after.

Into the lobby, the music follows her and her heels click along, gliding her over the marble floor. Residents stop their talk and card games and penny-throwing into the fountains, and they gawk upon the splendor of Iris Newberry and her music. Lowering her chin, eyes narrowing, she spots her prey. And with a flick of her hair once more, her smile and eyes flash a sultry attack upon him.

John Newberry stands in his denim overalls, wild, weedy, covered in hair. Through it all, his eyes grow huge and refuse to blink. The image of his lovely Iris in the paradise of the Dignity Place lobby, saunters toward him. He sees her smile, her eyes, her hair, her walk. All aimed at him. She's a missile moving to strike, and as she nears, the music builds and steam heat licks at his skin. The drums pound in his ears now, deep, and the reeds and the brass accelerate their pace and scream to the walls and ceiling. It's Iris Newberry! The world wants her but she wants only you, John Newberry. And you want her!

Before him, she stands curved and flowing like a dollop of soft-serve vanilla ice cream. With a clap of her hands, the music hangs on a precipitous note and waits as if teetering on the edge of a cliff. Her long fingers tipped in red-painted nails reach to John's face and part his beard, searching for his mouth. It's there, his jaw slack at the sight of her. Her lips reach to his, touching as the music and the Residents caught in the spell of Iris Newberry hold their breath.

She kisses him with the romantic tenderness of a first kiss, moaning soft her pleasure, eyes closed. In silence, he leans back, sees her expectation, her wonder at his response. Within him, the music warms again, pounding drums, an approaching scream of trumpets, and it builds and builds until all of Dignity Place can hear his shell crumble and excitement burst from his soul. With music suddenly flying about, a free-for-all of sound orchestrating wild romance, John Newberry grabs his bride around the hips, discharges a caveman's grunt of conquest and presses her against him, kissing her long and long and longer still, their lips and hands lost to each other.

Breathless sound, breathless sight.

I awaken in my room at dawn, Sebastian to my side in sweet sleep. I pull him to the middle of our bed and he's soon below me, his eyes opening, filling with light.

"Dreaming about my father standing again?" he asks, touching at my blouse.

"No," I say.

Sebastian removes the toast stuck to my face and licks the strawberry jam from my skin. Never in a million years would I believe that the thought of the Newberrys would one day drive me to such passion. Yet I again hear the music of John and Iris in the sanctity of my bedroom, and the breathless voice of my Sebastian calling out my name.

20

Brian Unkers rings our doorbell.

He's really not such a bad boy. He looks bad, though, with those pimples around his mouth and his hair dyed black and looking like he's still asleep and scrunched into his pillow. Today he wears an earring, a piercing in his left nostril, jeans and a T-shirt baggy over his body as if waiting for puberty to finish up and make him into a larger boy. He stands on my porch, smiling, his teeth made perfect by braces. "Is Roby ready, Mrs. Connery?"

"Ready for what?"

"For work."

"On Saturday morning?"

"Yeah."

Sebastian's voice booms from our bedroom. "Who is it, Julia?"

"It's for Roby," I call back.

"Oh."

"It's Brian Unkers."

"Oh," Sebastian says again from aloft. "I'll be right down."

Roby appears beside me, assumes the teenager slouch and begins his strange talk with his friend. Grunts and groans and shrugs and man this, man that. It's a collection of one-syllable sounds made with hanging lips that barely move, although they seem to understand each other.

"Who's driving?" I ask.

Brian steps to the side and points to this thing at my curb, more rust than car, a front bumper tied up by wire and stickers paying homage to evil.

Roby says, "Cool," and Brian smiles at his death trap with pride.

Sebastian arrives and rather than say hello, he asks Brian how he's doing in school.

"All right, I guess."

"All right? You guess? You mean you don't know?"

"My dad's mad about the B in trig. I told him it's an AP class so it counts as an A on my average, and I've still got the four-point going, but he's mad anyway." Brian grunts something Roby nods his head to, and says, "It's just the way dads are."

Roby steps to the porch. Together, the boys wear their ragged, oversized clothes and droop their way down the steps and walk to Brian's car.

"What is that thing?" Sebastian asks.

"It's the way they're getting to work," I say.

Sebastian calls out, "Wait! I'll drive!" but the boys react by not reacting. They keep going to the thing with wheels and Roby's off to a warehouse to work at a job without his father's permission. The sadness in Sebastian's eyes pains my heart. "I'm losing him," he says.

If only I could talk to Sebastian about the song Roby's been listening to and the song Old Sebastian hums; that his father's rise to his feet with my help after four years in the wheelchair was not a dream at all. And for all of Roby's work at a warehouse, three days already this week, his clothes show up in the laundry room clean enough to wear again. But it's not time, I know, even as Sebastian rubs his hand at the back of his neck, complaining of pain.

"Sebastian. Don't you have school papers to grade?"

"Ah. But it's a hard thing to do when you're losing your son,

171

your only child, and he won't say where he's off to."

"Now you know how I feel about your disappearances."

Sebastian glances back at me and sighs. By his eyes, I can tell he wishes to pretend he hasn't heard me. "Lassie, I can't," he says and hesitates as if wishing to tell me more. Instead he turns and leaves me at the door.

The torment I feel comes from the plotting of men, their secrets kept from each other and from me. If there's a finish line, where all things are revealed, I hope we get there alive and together. My complicity in this is clear, though. I open my purse and find my car keys. She waits for me on the walk, hidden in her tent of a trench coat and her woolen hat scrunched over her hair.

Despite what I see, the vision of her in my dream remains fresh, like an aspiration. It's time to take Iris Newberry shopping.

Iris sits in my car looking like a crash-test dummy. Stiff, bug-eyed, arms lifted slightly from her sides, waiting for disaster. Her hat, a woolen mushroom, smells like a wet dog's fur. With her slightest movement, the trench coat makes crumpling sounds like crushing a candy wrapper and I swear I hear a soft moan from her mouth that continues on without a break or her needing to breathe.

"Iris," I say. "This will be fun."

"Moooaannnn."

I feel as though I'm taking the wet dog to the vet for neutering.

When I turn onto Central Avenue, Iris's head begins swiveling from side to side. Downtown Highland Park is gorgeous even as the rest of the world slips toward winter with bare branches and late-October gray. This seemingly artificial universe of boutique shopping roots itself in downtown

Highland Park and makes quaintness into something to behold. Shop after awning-fronted shop, deserving of the spelling *Shoppe,* with names found in the scores of classical music. A parade of clothing stores and beauty salons and shoe stores and specialty food stores and gift stores and pooh-pooh-pampered pet stores, and not a Wal-Mart in sight.

This is make-believe, a section of town you'd expect to see as an exhibit at Disney World called Perfect Place. Perfect cleanliness and gingerbread-capped red brick two-story buildings and brick walks and thick-branched trees and shrubs and David Copperfield lamp posts and manicured lawn street medians, and the whole thing makes a Norman Rockwell Americana scene look slummy by comparison. This is real, and it's all in downtown Highland Park. In the gray of a dismal October day, downtown Highland Park still stands as heaven.

"I see Christmas lights everywhere," Iris says.

"It's beautiful."

"But it's not even Halloween." We roll toward a parking spot at the far end. "I should have brought a camera."

"Iris, haven't you been here before?"

"There was a place I'd always go to when I needed to get my hair done. All the people inside knew my name. But that was twenty years ago."

"Where do you get your clothes?"

"Catalog shopping. Sears and K-Mart. You know, the usual stores."

"Um hmm."

"Pants, shirts, and parts for the furnace. You can get anything you want mail order from Sears and K-Mart."

"Great."

She adds, "*Super* K-Mart, of course."

I park the car and turn to Iris. Her right hand grips the door handle, pulling it toward her as if trying to keep the world out. I ask, "Do you want to do this?"

The mushroom atop her head flutters. Neither a shake no, nor a nod yes. She pushes the door open and steps out, and a cold breeze swirls in, fluttering her trench coat back like a cape. On the street, split in two by a centered median filled with trees dangling a galaxy of small, white lights, I take Iris by the arm. "Do you go shopping here often?" she asks.

"On special occasions."

"Do you come here with your husband?"

"When I can drag him here. Sebastian claims the perfumes from the shops make him sleepy and cause lung disease and the smell drugs people into spending money on things they would never buy if they were standing in fresh air."

"He says such things?"

"He calls what he suffers Mall Face."

"Is that really an illness?"

"It's a reason to leave him at home."

"Julia," she says, looking down. "Do you know what agoraphobia is?"

I watch her, her eyes nearly closed, and wonder if I've made a damaging mistake. "It's an unreasonable fear of going outside."

"That's what they claim on TV shows," she says, wiping at her face. "But it's not really true. It's an irrational fear of being helpless or constantly feeling embarrassed or intimidated by the smallest things. It can happen even inside your own home."

"I'm sorry, Iris. Maybe this isn't a good idea."

"I don't have agoraphobia."

"Oh."

"But I looked it up just to see. I'm afraid," she says, and now she's staring at me with her hazel eyes all full of tears beneath her mushroom hat, in her trench coat, like an urchin from *Oliver Twist*. "I'm afraid of what I did to my husband for so many years, and it's not an irrational fear."

"Let's take a walk," I say. "Let me know when you're ready."

She smiles, and I notice that she wears no makeup and no paleface sunblock. She's a blank slate wrapped in a canvas from head to toe. Beneath awnings and trees decorated for Christmas two months before Christmas, Iris Newberry walks with me along the boutique shoppes on Central Avenue, her elbow hooked around mine. People we pass nod at us, some wishing us Merry Christmas and Happy Hanukkah and Happy New Year a month before Thanksgiving. They smile at Iris, at her hat and trench coat, and her head and body lost inside.

Behind us, a little girl's voice asks, "Mom, who is she? Think she's important?" And a woman's voice answers, "I bet she is. Traveling incognito like that."

Among the crowd and their voices, Iris seems to shrink at my side. I place my hand on her arm and whisper to her, "Perhaps we should go home."

"No," she says. She stops walking. "Here. Let's go in here." A hair salon combination clothier, *For Petites Only,* so the plate glass makes clear.

"Why here?"

"This was the place I'd go to, to get my hair done. This was the place where all the people inside said hello to me back when I used to do this sort of thing."

"Twenty years ago."

She says with a low tone of conjecture, "Maybe their children work here now."

"This place is for petites."

"I'm a size two."

In my battleship, 12-D flats, I say, "Oh, congratulations."

I open the glass door for her and we enter to the sound of the bell jingling at the transom. A wave of scented shampoo, conditioner, and permanent goo rushes up my nose and makes my head swoon. We're immediately at a podium staffed by a teenaged girl in a bare midriff knit shirt, bell-bottom jeans with fake fade marks dyed onto her thighs and the thick of her fanny. She greets us with pink gum popping out the side of her teeth while she chews. The white rings around her eyes prove her tan comes from a sun bed, and her bi-colored hairdo reminds me of a chocolate-vanilla ice cream twist on a sugar cone. "Do you have an appointment?" she asks, eyeing us like we're something contagious.

I say, "No."

"And you?"

Iris clings to my side and shakes her head.

"No walk-ins."

I see a row of four salon stations, their chairs occupied by women topped in clear plastic hats filled with brown gel. The women flip pages in their magazines to the music of timers ticking away atop the vanities. Beside them, three unoccupied salon stations and their three empty chairs. "Don't you know who she is?" I tell the gum-popper, smiling at Iris.

"Should I?"

With urgency in my voice, I say, "You better get your boss. Certainly your boss will know."

She considers us for a moment, pops her gum and sucks it back in with a squish. Roby, I suspect, would give up his iPod for her telephone number. "All right," she says, and she's gone through the door to this boutique's clothing section and soon returns with a skinny man dressed in black, form-fitting clothes. He's young and tall, his narrow face shaped as if designed in a vice grip, and he raises his straight nose with the confidence of a man successful before his thirties. I hate him on sight.

"This is Mrs. Newberry," I say.

"So?"

I tell him, "This is Mrs. *Iris* Newberry."

He's suddenly confused. He obviously should know her, so

my tone implies, and he raises that straight nose of his higher up, then down, and begins to softly say, "Oooh . . ."

"Yes," I say. "Iris Newberry."

"Of the . . ."

"That's right. Exactly."

"I'm Phillip," he says and smiles and reaches back with his right arm, showing Iris to a chair facing a salon station built for a goddess. "I'll do this one myself."

At the chair, red leather facing a porcelain basin and crystalline mirror, Iris unbuttons her trench coat. It falls from her, crunching and crumbling to the floor, and she stands in her pastel-blue muumuu. The customers beneath their goo-caps turn and gasp at Iris, and she lifts her hat from her head with her silver hair free of her blue formula.

Phillip says, "Oh my!"

"Do not dye this hair," I say.

"No?"

"Her husband wouldn't be happy."

"Mr. Newberry, of the same . . ."

"That's right."

"Of course. And the clothes?"

"Something tasteful. Elegant."

Iris opens her purse and removes a photograph. She sits in the chair and turns from me, facing the mirror with her eyes closed. "Like this," she says, raising the picture in the air. Phillip takes the photograph, studies it with care, then looks toward Iris as if transposing a miracle.

"This is what you want?"

"Yes," Iris says. "If you can do it."

Phillip shows the photograph to the gum-popper and she joins him in a look of constipation. Stepping to a phone on her podium, the gum-popper raises the receiver to her ear and presses a single number. "We have an emergency," she says.

"Yes. Get Bruce."

"Who's Bruce?"

The gum-popper tells me, "Our best wardrobe specialist. He's from Tahiti."

Phillip takes me by the arm and leads me to the front door. "Come back in three hours."

"What?"

"Three hours."

"For what?"

Phillip winks at me and leans his head near mine. "This lady. This Iris Newberry. She has the possibility of being my greatest work." I look at him and he smiles. "For free," he says. "The hair, the makeup, the clothing, all of it free. It will be my best before-and-after ever. We'll advertise the result!"

"Three hours?"

"At least."

Phillip assumes my approval and leaves me, and he spins Iris's chair slowly about, hovering over her as if studying her for exploratory surgery. "Do not dye the hair," I say.

The gum-popper pops a wad. Phillip shoos me away.

What have I done to Iris? She seems so frozen beneath the lights and the attention of Phillip. "Go," Iris says. "I'll see you in three hours. And, thank you."

The picture from Iris's purse remains on top of the podium, upside down. I slip it into my hands and turn toward the door. I wait until I'm outside and down several stores before I flip the picture over. John Newberry, clean-shaven and square-jawed in his black tuxedo. Beside him stands his bride. Iris in a wedding dress, a lovely off-the-shoulder gown. She's full-bosomed with a narrow waist and has her slender arms slipped into silk gloves. Her smile is as beautiful as an angel's, and her face, both sweet and haughty, fits the delicate shape of a heart to her chin. I close my eyes and think of Iris and I hope this woman in the photograph, now at age seventy-something, is still there, somewhere, in some lovely form beneath years of hiding.

Holding the photograph to the Christmas lights trimming S*hoppe* awnings two months before Christmas, I see it. I don't believe it, although perhaps I should. John's left hand, gentle on Iris's left shoulder, pulls her softly into him with a tender embrace for the ages, just as Sebastian did on our wedding day.

I pray in this Highland Park heaven of perfumed boutique *Shoppes*, all of it sparkling in premature Christmas lights and Hanukkah menorahs, filled with gum-poppers and skinny men named Phillip dressed in black, form-fitting clothes, and wardrobe specialists from Tahiti named Bruce. I pray for Iris, of course, and for John. But more to the point, I pray for myself and my Sebastian.

21

Three hours to the unveiling of Iris.

I have to leave town. I know I'd window shop for a time, but I'd only be faking it and soon arrive back at Phillip's *Combo Salon For Petites Only Clothier* peeking through the window for glimpses of Iris being hacked apart and put back together. The question why I'm drawn to Dignity Place probably has a dozen answers for social workers and psychotherapists to explain. I decide it's to sit in my miserable pool office and draw up a plan for Tuesday's watercize program.

On weekends, the Grisslys are gone, their office door behind the front desk closed, lights out. Hairy Harry sweeps the lobby floor when I walk in and approaches me with a question. His voice is soft enough to ignore and I keep my head down, too afraid of seeing John Newberry and screaming at him, *Do you know what you're putting your wife through?* And I'm fearful of what he would say in return. Hairy Harry sighs and brooms himself away from me.

Today the chlorine from the pool smells refreshing. Considering the smells inside a combination salon-petite-clothier, at least the smell of pool chlorination is unpretentious and easy to identify. It's honest. It's there to kill germs and do nothing else. It doesn't pretend to be a mysterious aroma from the fountain of youth or pheromonal aphrodisiac. Pool chlorine strips the skin clean, clears the sinuses and brings the blood to the eyes. Perhaps I should have dragged Iris here for a swim. Lord knows what Phillip, Tahiti Bruce and the gum-popper have dipped her in by now.

I sit at my desk, pulling out drawers and closing them. Empty. No pen. No paper. I lean back and close my eyes, listening to the sound of a rhythmic splash of water. I walk to the window blinds and open them. There in the center of the pool, a Resident front-crawls through the water, capped in her rubber flowers with tinted goggles over her eyes. At least I think the swimmer's a she. Could be a he, I suppose. Regardless, this Resident moves through the water without effort, arm strokes relaxed, kicks even as if tickling the surface. Nearing the deep end, the swimmer's head goes down and legs rise toward the ceiling. Flip turn. Push off the side. Underwater for five, ten seconds, the body submarining the other direction a good distance before re-emerging. Beautiful strength and technique. It makes me wonder why this Resident is in a retirement home, swimming better than most people in their twenties. Perhaps John Newberry isn't the only one running away, or perhaps it's laziness or convenience for the families.

When Old Sebastian lived with us, he made his demands and shouted his uninvited opinions on everything. His opinions on keeping house and raising a child were too much for me, sins against my domain only an obstinate old man could make. All I could do was pretend to look him in the eyes, all the while concentrating on the fake brown in his hair staining down his forehead. The absurdity kept me from screaming his eardrums into oblivion. His fall nearly five years ago was the reason we put him in Dignity Place, for his own safety and well-being. For my sanity. Sebastian had said it first. "Lassie, now I think we have to." But here I am, full of guilt, taking comfort in the recent memory of his body rising in my arms, standing with me at the foot of his wheelchair. If he walks again, he might ask, *May I move back in?*

The whine whistling in my ears seems natural enough. Born from the guilt in my heart, traveling out my lungs to my throat, mouth and nose. The sound turns sour, off-key, and I hold my breath, yet the whine goes on. Two notes not matched for each other, honking like geese in a tiff, and then it stops. Through the office window, I see the swimmer climb the steps at the shallow end. Thick-chested, tufts of hair on his shoulders, Paul removes his swim goggles and waves to me. I wave back, and I know he has no need for my watercize class.

With two hours to the unveiling of Iris, I turn back to my desk, prepared to sit out the time in hiding. The sound returns. Not a whine this time, more of a growl breaking into a pitiful cry. The ceiling, the walls, the filing cabinet, the desk show me nothing. They give me no hint. There's no radio or stereo or anything of the kind. When I open the door to the hallway, the sound fades. Stepping back in my office, I hear it as though it were a distant wail floating at my feet. And there are those horrible words etched reddish brown into the cinder block—*They murdered me!*—and the horrible noise from the vent beside it seems to prove the case.

On my knees, huddled by the vent, I hear the pain and the agony of what I imagine could be the sound of murder. The noise stops and I'm frozen there in wonder. A voice seeps through the slats of the grate, angry and upset—"This isn't easy!"—followed by a second, deeper voice, calm and soothing—"Try it again. More relaxed this time."

I don't recognize this second voice, but the first one I know. Through a vent in the floor, although faint and far away, it doesn't matter. Beneath my feet, somewhere in Dignity Place, Roby complains again—"But I'm already relaxed!"

"Try again!"

Then, a moment later, the sound of goose honks in a tiff.

★ ★ ★ ★ ★

Hairy Harry follows me through the lobby. He doesn't know I know this. He trails his broom behind, stopping to sweep when I stop to glance back at him. Whistling, he swishes at the tile and I turn back around and head to the stairs to Old Sebastian's room. On the second floor, I glance back and Hairy Harry returns to sweeping his broom at nothing, this time over the carpeted hallway. It's a silly sight, but I have too much on my mind to bother with him just now. Behind Old Sebastian's door, the sounds of DVD-television bullets fly through the air.

I knock and he calls out for whoever it is to enter and be quick about it. As I come in, Old Sebastian says from his wheelchair, "It's you."

"It's me." I look at my watch. "I have ninety-seven minutes."

"One minute to spend with me for each year of my life?"

"You're ninety-one."

"Feels like ninety-seven."

"What's the difference?"

"You'll know when you get there."

DVD-television bullets keep rat-a-tat-tatting, jumbling up my spine. I turn the gangster movie off. He growls, "You better be here with some magical walking exercises for me."

"I'm not."

"Then what?"

"Come with me."

He taps at the remote and turns his show back on. "Where?"

"To my pool office."

"Why should I?"

"You'll know when you get there."

"Fine."

Old Sebastian freeze-frames on a body falling out a high-rise window, cocks his wheelchair's toggle forward and rides out the door, nearly into Hairy Harry. Hairy Harry says, "Can I ask you a question?"

"What?" I say, chasing after Old Sebastian. I swear his machine could pop a wheelie the way it's cruising toward the elevator.

"I heard your husband teaches at a college."

"That he does."

"Oh."

I join Old Sebastian in the elevator and turn around. Hairy Harry stands frozen at the threshold as if we might snap the door shut on him if he tries to enter. When the door begins to close, Hairy Harry disappears behind it, but he blurts out his question so it slips inside the elevator.

"Can your husband teach me how to read?"

The elevator moves as though waiting for speed to be invented. Old Sebastian plays with his toggle and inches back and forth. "The boy's a pity. He could use Sebastian's help."

"I'll talk to him."

"I'm not kidding."

"All right," I say.

"Are you mad at me about something?"

"No."

"Could you be mad at me about something pretty soon?"

"Yes."

Old Sebastian grunts and laughs and grunts some more. I look at my watch, seeing seventy-two minutes left to the unveiling of Iris. "You should leave it alone," he says.

"You know something?"

"Don't ask. It's for your own good."

The elevator lands with a thump and a bounce, and we wait another moment for the door to slip open. Hairy Harry's there to greet us, sweeping at something else he imagines. "Taking the stairs is faster," he says, pretending a bit of shock, as though the elevator could go anyplace else.

"Where are we going?" Old Sebastian asks.

"To my pool office."

"Yeah, yeah. That's right."

I walk ahead and Old Sebastian follows. He says back to Hairy Harry, "She agreed to talk to him about teaching you how to read."

"She did? Wow! Did you tell her to tell Mr. Connery I wasn't stupid or nothing? I'm absent-minded is all."

Old Sebastian doesn't answer. He wheels in close behind, following me into the hall toward my pitiful office. "He looks like an ape," Old Sebastian says, "but he's not stupid."

"I said I'll talk to Sebastian."

"Even if you get mad at me?"

"I'll talk to him."

Once inside my office, I close the door and sit at my desk. Silence. Old Sebastian asks, "What are we waiting for?"

"Goose honks."

Old Sebastian looks at my metal desk and my metal chair and my metal filing cabinet and the cramped space and cinder block walls. "This office really sucks."

"Why do you talk that way?"

"I'm old enough to be dead twenty years ago. It's my privilege."

"There!" I say

"What?"

"Goose honks."

"I didn't hear anything."

Again the pitiful wail floats beneath my feet. "Wheel over there," I say, and I stand from my chair and shove the desk aside to make room for him to roll to the vent. I hear it again, I swear. Old Sebastian inches to the vent then halts.

He shouts, "Holy shit!" and rolls up his sleeves. He digs into his shirt and removes a hammer, and, reaching in once more, a chisel. "Help me!" he says.

"Help you how?"

"Don't you see? Those words, *'They murdered me!'* They've been here all along. Right here in your shithole office." His eyes are ablaze and he rocks in his seat, trying to get out of his chair. I hold on to his shoulders.

"You're not ready! What if you fall?"

He leans back, the chisel raised in his left hand, the hammer in his right, and the muscles in his forearms shudder beneath his skin. "Don't you see, Julia? Don't you see?" And he growls low as if someone might be listening in. "Gangster bones! Help me with the hammer. I'll hold the chisel."

"I'll do nothing of the sort."

"Then get Dave Jones."

"I will not."

"Blast it! I know there're bones stashed in Dignity Place. Little Nicky said so. He said this is where they murdered his grandfather. And look!" He chants the scream on the wall— " 'They murdered me!' "

"The Little Nicky you ran into at the restaurant?"

"No, no. Not number two." Old Sebastian raises his chin. "Little Nicky Number One. The worst of them all."

"Stop lying to me."

"The hell I am. Little Nicky Number One told me the first week you put me into Dignity Place. He's the reason why I stopped complaining how you shipped me off to die. And he's the reason why I've been punching holes in the walls."

"Of all people, why would he ask you for help?"

"Because he swore the bones were behind the walls in my room."

"I see."

"But he was wrong. They're here. Says so right on that cinder block."

"In my little pool office?"

"Makes sense to me now. By God, look at this dump, it was a torture chamber for sure, and they walled people up and let them starve to death."

"Who?"

With a hiss and respect for the dead, Old Sebastian says, "Al Capone and his men."

I take the hammer from his hand and he clutches the chisel against his chest. "Give it back. Help me or get Dave Jones!"

"They're just some words on a wall, a sick prank."

"They're written in blood, I tell you. Look at the color."

"It could as easily be a marker."

"Touch it."

"What?"

"Touch it. What are you afraid of?"

"Nothing. I don't want to appease your obsession with gangster bones."

"Go on. Do it and I'll shut up if I'm wrong."

"No!"

We stare at each other, the sounds of our breathing filling the pool office, or the torture chamber, or whatever it might be. But I know when you're with someone you've known for a long time and you're cramped in a small space with nobody else to listen in, your mind can let you believe all sorts of silly things. A campfire at night when a screech owl shrieks, a sleepover with a best friend when the furnace groans in the night. It doesn't matter that I'm fifty-three and Old Sebastian is ninety-one. He wants to break down some walls and find gangster bones, and his singular obsession has its pull on me.

"All right," I say. "I'll give it a touch."

Slowly, I turn and lower myself to my knees. I hover there

beside the vent, nearing the words colored reddish brown over unpainted cinder block—*They murdered me!*

Old Sebastian inches his chair behind me and leans far forward in his seat with his breath at my ear. "Go on."

I raise my right hand and hold it before the words, afraid somehow that Old Sebastian could be right and Little Nicky Number One would enter our lives and claim his indebtedness to us and ask whether there's a deal we cannot refuse. Then, a sound. Not goose honks; neither a whine nor wail, nor the cry of the tortured, but a sweet, deep hum. It pours through the vent, softly at first but unfurling into something fantastic, and encouraging words flow along with it: *"That's it, Roby! That's right!"*

Roby? *My* Roby? I manage that single thought before I hear . . .

One sound holding the power of a nation, like one seed blossoming into an entire forest. It rises and grows and gains strength until it vibrates my bones and sets my three-quarters-Scottish soul afire.

"Lassie," I hear gasping above me and the clank of the chisel dropped from on high to the floor. "There's the sainted voice of the Tartan bagpipe."

When I turn around, I cannot believe what I've just heard . . . what I now see. "Old Sebastian," I say. "You're standing!"

Old Sebastian stays transfixed on the sound, his stance steady and his stare to the heavens, or what he can see of the heavens in my pitiful office.

I stand to hold him and I tell him I love him, how I'm sorry for anything bad I've ever said to him. His arms wrap around me and he begs within the music of Scotland, "Please don't tell Sebastian. None of this. Not a word."

"All right," I say. "I promise."

"It's for your own good."

"Old Sebastian. The words on the wall were written by a felt-tip pen. I'm sorry."

He holds me. Says nothing more. Over his shoulders, I see my watch and the time telling me it's fifty-five minutes to the unveiling of Iris. And my fingertips bear small flakes of something brown. Could be dried blood from long ago, I suppose, but I already have enough torment in my life. So I won't tell Old Sebastian.

22

I'm late for the unveiling of Iris. A good twenty minutes late.

It takes time to settle a man down when he stands on his own after nearly five years in a motorized wheelchair. Old Sebastian tells me back in his room, smiling and full of energy, "I feel like I'm eighty again."

When I was a little girl, I played the double-your-age game with my friends again and again. We'd sit around and double our ages so when I was seven, I would still be only fourteen. At ten, I would be twenty. At fourteen, I would be twenty-eight. And by the year two thousand, I'd still be fifteen years younger than my grandmother was then. My girlfriends and I would find comfort in our math and we'd laugh because we knew we were going to live forever and never lose our girlhood. Boys could wait, makeup could wait, the year two thousand could wait. We'd have each other day after day just the way we were and always would be. Those years off into the future, double what we were, seemed so far away as to be impossible.

I can't remember how old I was when I abandoned playing the double-your-age game.

If I double my age now I'd be a hundred and six, fifteen years older than Old Sebastian and at least thirty-six years older than Iris. Somewhere along the line, I graduated from high school and all the babies born that year have since graduated from high school and many have had babies themselves who are about to graduate from high school. Unbelievable.

On my last birthday, Sebastian told me middle age is always ten years beyond whatever age he happens to be. It will always be this way for him, even when he's as old as his father. And if he doesn't make it to a hundred and ninety, he figures he'll be the last to know. "A birthday simply celebrates another trip around the sun," he likes to say. "And considering some people live a life worth a hundred years even if they die young, and others live to a hundred still waiting for something to happen to them, the number of trips a person takes around the sun may not matter so much in the end."

I have often asked Sebastian, if he believes what he believes about birthdays, why he bothers celebrating my birthday every year, taking me to fancy dinners, giving me thoughtful presents. His answer is always the same—"Because I know there would be dreadful consequences if I didn't."

That, of course, would be true.

"Besides," Sebastian says, "a birthday doesn't celebrate your age, it celebrates you, and that I still have you."

When it comes to raising our son, Sebastian can be an honest-to-God booby, king of the booby hatch. As a husband, he can be pure gold. These wonderful things about Sebastian make me think of Iris and John, and I walk into *Phillip's Combo Salon For Petites Only Clothier* for proof that when I'm a hundred, I could then double my age and still find Sebastian at my side, the both of us shrunk and shriveled into rotting prunes, telling me I'm forever beautiful to him.

The gum-popper looks up from her podium, at me, then back down with a sigh of frustration. "Phillip," she says, almost a shout. "She's back."

Phillip approaches from the clothes department, his face flush and his lips clenched thin. "Come with me," he says, and I follow him into the clothier section. I'm surrounded by size one mannequins, and they pose with their plastic hip bones stabbing at hip-hugger jeans and minis and midis. Their heads are set as if to avoid my size twelve stare, and their noses, all the size and shape of a Hershey's Kiss, angle toward the ceiling. "She's in here," Phillip says, brushing aside a curtain to a suite of dressing rooms. "It's sad, really. This Iris has potential if only she'd let go."

I thank Phillip and he sniffs out an "Of course" and leaves me.

Through the curtain, down a small hall with saloon-styled doors on either side, I step slowly, listening for Iris. Her cry comes from inside the last dressing room on the left. She sits on a bench in her trench coat looking half melted into it, and her woolen mushroom cap droops low over her eyes.

"Julia?"

"It's me."

Makeup smears across her face and covers her fingertips. "Take me home."

"All right."

"Now."

"All right."

She stands and I walk with her beneath my arm, our eyes cast down so as to see the way out but not the stares of other people. We push through Phillip's door, jingling the bell at the transom, into the cold air. We walk under lovely awnings decorated in holiday cheer into the heaven of downtown Highland Park and move through the chocolate smells of the confectionaries, the perfumes from the other *Shoppes,* the aroma of freshly baked breads and cookies, and the sounds of the steps of the people around us.

In my car Iris settles back, tucks her chin to her chest. "I never told you," she says. "I should have told you before we came here." Her breath shudders from her mouth. "I had a mastectomy twenty years ago."

I turn quickly to her and look back to the road, unable to think of anything to say. I know I cough and hem and haw and make all sorts of nervous sounds.

"My left breast. Complete removal. The doctors told me it was a success." Again her breath shudders. "Imagine something like that being called a success."

At a stop light, I look down at the steering wheel, my hands feeling as clumsy as oven mitts. Iris must know what I'm thinking. She tells me there's nothing to say.

It's true. After fifteen years living next door to this woman, I never had a conversation with her which led to anything important. Not until this year. Not really until now. What can I do but feel ashamed?

She clutches her hands together at her lips, wipes at the remains of makeup on her fingertips and wrings her knuckles white. "I thought I could do this today," she begins, then coughs and tells me she had a fit and fell apart when it came time to try on a dress for strangers to see.

In our silence she turns on the radio set to my oldies station. She presses a button to another oldies station. The next button she presses finds *God Investment.*

The woman of the house must remain subservient in all things to the man of the house-uh, regardless of circumstances. It is so written in the Scripture-uh. It is the word of our Lord-uh.

Iris is quick to the radio and turns it off. "Damn fools," she says.

Driving us away from man-made heaven, I imagine standing before my own bedroom mirror, slipping off my clothes and wondering if I could look at myself if I were Iris. Would I avoid my image or would I look? Would I catch an unintended glimpse of the absence of something so important and find my face angry or flooded with tears, or both? Without the strength of a thousand angels, I'd be lost in the absence of something I anticipated in my girlhood, something I came to take for granted as there forever, helping to define me as a woman, and something Sebastian would touch as a man who tenderly loves his wife.

"Can we cancel the Friday dinners?" she asks. "For now?"

"Of course, Iris."

"I know it's Sebastian and Roby, but I'd rather not have men at my house for a little while."

As I should have done long ago if my own worries hadn't have gotten in the way, I think of Iris now tucked away beside me inside her ridiculous coat and hat. I slide my hand between us, and after a moment her coat crumples and crunches as she moves to take my hand in hers, and squeezes with the warmth of a friend.

When I come home, Sebastian's at the kitchen table eating pizza with a knife and fork, a napkin on his lap, another tucked under his chin, and another napkin beside his plate. A pile of school papers he's graded sits stacked like a new ream of paper at the center of the table. He asks me how my day went, which he immediately regrets because I flop beside him on the bench seat and turn into a thunderstorm of tears. "Chrissake," he says. "Did you put a scratch on your car?"—which he regrets saying even more because I convulse into a laughing fit the devil would be proud of.

Men can't handle a woman's tears. They react by doing silly things. Sebastian offers me a perfectly square cut slice of his pizza as if it were a cure of some sort. "Tastes pretty good," he says. "Made it myself. No spit."

I'm overloaded with the secrets of other people. Old Sebastian rising from his chair on his own. Roby somewhere in Dignity Place learning how to blow the Tartan bagpipe, getting lessons from somebody even as he lies to his father and aggravates him about a part-time job that doesn't exist. And the drama of the words—*They murdered me!*—on my office wall that in fact crumbled like dried blood when I touched the letters. And Iris and John, and Iris herself. Especially Iris. So I eat Sebastian's bit of pizza, and cry some more and laugh some more until I settle into an exhausted pile of flesh.

"Sebastian," I say. "Hairy Harry wants you to teach him how to read."

"Who's Hairy Harry?"

"A young man working at Dignity Place. I promised him I'd ask you."

"Chrissake. You know I'm not a remedial reading teacher."

I lift a slice of pizza from Sebastian's plate by my hands and let tomato sauce drip over my lips and chin. Sebastian's quick with a napkin to my face. "You're a good teacher," I say. "Plain and simple."

"But I don't know how to teach an adult to read. It takes a specialist, I'm sure."

I slurp the cheese and smack my lips. "He was mistreated growing up. His teachers called him an idiot."

"They were wrong to say so out loud, but were they wrong?"

"Your father insists the boy's only absent-minded."

"I've got enough troubles with our own son."

"Sebastian."

"What?"

"Do you love me?"

He smiles. "Did you put a dent in the fender?"

"No."

"Then I love you."

"Why?"

No more smiling. "Chrissake."

"I mean, which part of me do you love?"

"I love all your parts."

"Do you love my legs?"

"I love your legs."

"My hips, my waist, my arms, my hair, my elbows, my nose?"

"I love the nails upon your tiny toes."

"But what if I lost my toes in an accident or to a disease; would you love me then?"

"Why are you asking me these things?"

I take the napkin tucked below Sebastian's chin and pat it at the tears on my face. "I don't think they're unreasonable questions for a wife to ask her husband after thirty-three years of marriage."

"What if I lost my legs?" he asks.

"It wouldn't matter to me."

"That's exactly how I feel."

"Are you sure, Sebastian? I mean, which parts of me can you do without?"

"None of them. I mean all of them. Julia, for God's sake. Is there a right answer to this question?"

"What if I lost parts you love, like my legs and my arms."

"I'd love what's left of you."

"What if my body fell off and my neck and head, too, and all there was left were my lips yapping on this seat. Would you love me still?"

"It depends upon what your lips were yapping about."

I take Sebastian's hands in mine and kiss his fingers smelling clean and washed even after he has eaten most of his pizza. "Iris Newberry told me she had her left breast removed twenty years ago. And don't you dare tell another soul about this."

"Ah," Sebastian says. He looks smacked in the face. "That would explain things."

"Like what?"

"About her and John and the darkness and the gargoyles and the muumuus."

"It's not that easy," I say, dropping his hands.

"No, I suppose not. But don't doctors have plastic surgery for this sort of thing? Can't Iris get an implant?"

"You're being shallow."

"But that's the thing to do if she feels she needs it; am I wrong?"

"Maybe she had one and it didn't work out. Maybe she's too old now for implants."

"I suppose age could be a problem. I mean one side grows old while the other side doesn't." He scratches at his chin. "It's an interesting thought, really, when you consider it. All these women getting big breast implants in their younger days turn into grandmothers and great-grandmothers sooner or later. And then what do you get? A ton of gray-headed wrinkly old ladies hunched over their fantastic pairs of boobs."

"We're talking about Iris."

"An alien race will come to Earth one day and do an archeological dig, and they'll find all these caskets full of bones and twin jelly-filled orbs fallen to the skeletons' armpits. I wonder what the aliens might think they are."

"What if—"

Sebastian surprises me. Proves he's been listening even as he talks about breast implants and space aliens and orbs in caskets. He stops me and says, "I'd love you the same."

"How would you know until it happened?"

He stares at me with his blue eyes topped by furry eyebrows. "I'll be an old man one day," he says. "I might totter and teeter and topple, and I might need to be walked to the bathroom, or worse, cleaned up afterward and bathed like a baby, and I know you'll be there to take care of me as long as you're able because you'll want to. Because you love me. And I know if everything about you were lopped off and discarded and all there was left were your sweet lips yapping beside me on this seat, well I'd lean over and tell them to stop yapping so I could kiss them, and then I'd kiss them even if they went on yapping."

I lean back, his hands over mine in my lap and his stare upon my eyes. "You'll teach Hairy Harry how to read?"

"If you want me to, I'll give it a try."

"All right then."

"You had quite a day."

"I did."

"Are you sure you didn't dent your car?"

"I'm sure."

"Iris must really like you."

"I suppose she does."

We share the last piece of pizza together, cutting neat squares, chewing in silence. "You know," I say finally, "I can't promise you I won't bring this conversation up again."

Sebastian leans into me. He says, "I know, Lassie," and swoops in to kiss my yapping lips.

23

All evening long, Roby won't talk to Sebastian. Sebastian won't talk to Roby. The quiet is peaceful enough on the surface. Maybe I should enjoy it. In truth, the silence is so loud the air between father and son stretches and strains. When Roby slams his bedroom door shut, the echo pounds at my heart and Sebastian's toughness melts away with a sigh and a slow shuffle to the basement where he'll put too much soap in the laundry and I'll itch for days.

I bet you think you're making progress, sweetie.

Lola Two stands in the hallway, blocking my way to Roby's room. I know I could pass through her and her mini-skirt and halter, but the thought of it makes my skin revolt. "I don't have time for you."

Ah, honey. But here I am just the same. I'm not going away. She bows her head and flings her golden-hair-from-a-bottle back as if a seashore breeze blew by just for her. She tries to pose her fanny to the side but bangs it hard against the wall. *You need a bigger house.*

"Your fanny's overtaking you, dear."

Oh my, no way. T and A are all men want to see. As long as Dr. Plastic sucks the crud from my waist and thighs, you know this sort of thing drives men wild. I lean forward and inspect something new about her face. *Chin job. A Dr. Plastic specialty.*

"You've completely disappeared."

I'm new and I'm improved. Exaggerate the positives, so says Dr. Plastic.

"Smile."

What?

"Let me see you smile."

What are you trying to pull? Lola Two straightens as much as her fanny allows and she stares at me with her new chin and hoisted cheekbones and cat-like eye tuck and brow lift and elfin nose job and with her boobs lifted like missiles ready to fire. Even when her lips move, there's no expression to see, just the mask she's created. So much the feminine robot. *Sugar,* she says, *I've been smiling at you the whole time.*

"Frown."

All right, how's this?

I wait to see a change. There isn't any. She tells me, *Well, whatever. It's not important. Men don't want to see an expression on a woman anyway.*

"You're a pity."

My, aren't you something talking to me like that. Getting confidence from Iris Newberry, are you? You think you're gonna prove something to me with Iris?

"I might."

Lola Two stares at me for a moment. *If you think Iris and John are the ones to make me go pop, then you're a bigger fool than I thought. I know you can't tell but I'm laughing at you right now.*

I approach her. My once waif-like creation so utterly sucked away or chipped away or covered by something phony. With my eyes straining to stay open, I pass through her, a mist and a buzz and a whispering gasp. Such an odd sensation, to actually be inside a figment of my imagination. A moment when my mind has been turned inside out. On the other side, facing Roby's door, I say, "I saw nothing inside you."

Bitch, she says. *I'm coming back forever and you know it.* Look-

ing over my shoulder, I see the length of my hallway empty of
Lola Two, but I fear she's never too far away.

This time when I sit beside Roby on his bed, the angry posters
seem to shrink away from the power of a mother. He holds his
arms folded tough-guy style over his chest and pouts in an
angry way so easily softened by the boyish fuzz on his face. "I'm
sure Dad thinks I'm doing drugs."

"Are you?"

"No."

"I knew that."

"Then why'd you ask?"

"A mother's supposed to. You get arrested these days for not
asking your child about drugs and sex."

"I'm not having sex either, so don't even start with the babies
and diseases talk."

I brush my hand through his tangling brown hair and he lets
me do it. "You didn't eat dinner."

"I'm not hungry."

"Of course you are, working in a warehouse all day long."

There's a rush of heat and moisture to Roby's scalp. He lies
to me. "The warehouse has a cafeteria. I ate plenty today."

"I suppose it's going to be a good-sized paycheck. What will
you do with your money?"

He grunts something for Brian Unkers's understanding. I
think it stands for I don't know.

"So. What do you do at this warehouse?"

"Stuff."

"Stuff?"

"Things."

"You stuff things?"

"Right," he says, folding his arms tighter over his chest.

"What things do you stuff?"

"Things into boxes. Boxes into crates. Crates into trucks."

"Big things?"

"Some big things. Some not so big."

"Sounds like a dirty job."

"Definitely."

"What's the name of this company?"

Roby shrugs. "I don't know, I just work there."

"Well, I see. I suppose it will be on your paycheck in any case. In about two weeks."

"No." Roby's eyes search his ceiling for something more to say. He finds it. "We don't get paid until Christmas. Christmas day."

"Everything's closed on Christmas day. Even warehouses."

"I mean the day after Christmas."

"That's two months away. Seems unfair. Maybe we should have a lawyer look into this situation."

"Maybe."

"I was at Dignity Place today."

Roby undoes his arm-folding and stretches his hands to his knees. "Why?"

"Because I work there."

"Not on Saturdays."

"You seem to know my schedule."

"I guess I do."

"I had a talk with your grandfather. And I sat in my office and heard things through an air vent."

"Things?"

"Yes."

"What things?"

"Some big things. Some not so big."

"Oh."

I kiss him on the head. "Between now and Christmas," I say, "be tolerant of your father." Roby nods, and I tell him, "If you're going to insist to me and your father that you're doing your dirty job at a warehouse, you at least ought to come home with some of the dirt under your fingernails and a smear more of it on your shirt and pants."

Without looking for his reaction, I leave him in his bedroom and close his door. But I stand there in the hall, stepping in place loudly at first, then slowly softer until I'm standing still and waiting. Soon enough, I hear the beeps on Roby's phone and then the grunting which serves teenage boys as communication—"Bean Dip there? Um, Bean Dip. Yeah, uh-huh, yeah. Look, she knows. Yeah, uh-huh. Figured it out somehow. Christmas, yeah, Christmas. Uh. No. I don't think so, no. Uh-huh. No, she's not telling my father—I'm not sure, uh-huh, yeah. It seems like she wants to help us out. Uh-huh. Yeah. Uh-huh. Christmas."

I inch away from his door and pray the floor beneath the carpet doesn't moan and groan, which it doesn't. In my retreat, I hear Roby tell Brian Unkers to my satisfaction, "Yeah, my mom, yeah, uh-huh. I guess she's not so dumb."

24

My family hasn't been to church but for Christmas and Easter and weddings and a funeral or two for as far back as I can remember. This Sunday morning, I insist, and it's not Roby giving me the battle. Roby says "Fine" and smiles at me and washes up and puts on pants and a shirt nearly good enough to be seen in public. But Sebastian still wears his pajamas, stands in our living room, arms folded tight over his chest, and says like a child, "Why?"

"Because I need this right now."

"Why?"

"Please. Your son and I are going."

"But why do you need me to go with?"

"Because we're a family and you're my husband."

Roby walks in, smiles at me again, sees his father and grunts, "I'll start the car," and leaves.

I say to Sebastian, "This will be good."

"But you know how I feel about church. It's a huge stone building on ten acres of tax-free Lake Michigan shore land and its walls are lined in marble and the woodwork is the finest cherry and the organ and the choir and the flowers—what in God's name does God need with such a palace? Jesus never had a palace of any kind. He had tattered robes and sandals and slept in stables and the outdoors. Can you imagine all the good charity the church could do if they sold all their palaces and gave the money to the poor?"

"Then there would be no church."

"God is everywhere. That's what they say. I can be dressed in my pajamas here with God in our living room. He doesn't need me in a suit and tie sitting in a palace to hear my prayers."

The engine to Sebastian's sedan starts up and revs down our drive. "The boy's going to honk the horn at eight-thirty in the morning," Sebastian says, and sure enough the horn blares for our neighborhood to hear.

"You've got fifteen minutes," I say. I turn around in a bluster and my skirt sweeps at Sebastian's legs so high and mighty up on his soapbox.

"Or what?"

On my way through the door, I tell him, "You'll miss your chance to say a prayer for Iris in church."

Outside, it's one of those North Shore Chicago mornings in late October after a cold spell when it's suddenly warm again and the sun feels powerful shining on my face. Although leaves lie scattered on lawns that no longer wish to grow until April, it feels as though buds will be popping open on tree branches and robins will soon return. I look down the block of beautiful old homes and their front porches. The crowd of age-old trees and bushes seems to curve thick around brick and mortar, as if embracing old money and good taste. Except for my own and the Newberrys', the homes are dressed up for Halloween with monsters in windows and scarecrows sitting on porch swings and goblins hanging from branches and witches on brooms looking as though they flew smack into trees. The decorations remind me of the season, and despite this morning's return to spring, like it or not, winter's coming.

I open the driver's side back door and get in to sit behind Roby. He asks me why.

"Because your father sits in front."

"Are you sure he's going with?"

"Yes."

Roby groans. "Then maybe I should get in back."

"No."

I lean forward to look through the car window at Iris's house. Her porch appears barren and the House For Sale sign on the lawn tilts far forward. "When you were a boy, did you ever go to the Newberry house for Halloween?"

"Never."

"No?"

"None of us did."

"Why not?"

"We were all too scared."

"Of what?"

"Well," Roby says, tapping on the steering wheel. "We thought a real monster lived there."

"I see. So you always stayed away?"

"Once or twice we'd play tricks on a dare. Ring the doorbell and run away. Scream like bloody murder on the porch and run away. Leave a sign on the door and run away."

"What signs?"

"I don't know, Mom. I guess signs about the monster living there, that sort of thing."

"Iris?"

"Yeah."

"That's terrible."

"It was long ago."

"You're not old enough to have a long ago."

"I was a kid."

"Still, it's a good thing you're going to church today. You'll ask for forgiveness." Roby nods some more and I rub at my forehead, whispering, "That poor woman."

The front passenger door opens up with a whoosh and Sebastian climbs in and slams the door shut. "Guilt!" he announces. "This church business is all based on guilt."

He sits wearing a shirt collar half over his sport coat collar, and a tie showing in back over both. Leaning against his door, he complains he's had no time for a shower or proper shave, he had to use the electric razor and it barely had a charge left in it and he feels unwashed and unkempt and he hopes God appreciates the fact that he's going to His glorious palace under these circumstances. In the silence following Sebastian's tirade, Roby shifts into drive and rolls us to the curb. He stops us there and turns to his father.

"Put on your seat belt, Dad."

"I'm going to pray for Iris," Sebastian says, "and then I'm going to pray your warehouse goes out of business."

I thank God they've finally said something to each other. Sebastian buckles his seat belt.

St. Rita of the Holy Annunciation is everything Sebastian described. I sit between Sebastian and Roby on a cherry wood pew and the smell of plush, vacuumed carpet and flowers brought in fresh engulfs me thick in the scent of holy luxury. We're surrounded by men and women, well-fed, well-bred and satisfied to be in a crowded, palace-sized church on a day that's not Christmas, Easter, or a wedding or funeral. Sebastian says to my right ear, "You could have a major league baseball game played in here, it's that big."

The choir begins: *Praise to the Lord in the highest!*

Sebastian complains about the choir. "They all smile when they sing, even when they're waiting to sing, like they're politicians on Prozac." Then Sebastian complains about the service. "Stand up, sit down, stand up, sit down. It's like a gym class."

Jesus on the cross bears witness to my torment, hanging centered before the congregation, and I hear again in my right ear, "So many dipsy-doodles and secret handshakes in this place."

"Shh, Sebastian. These are traditions."

He beats his hands on his knees and looks around. "Right. Traditions."

"Like Scotland."

"You don't have to drop a twenty in the collection plate to appreciate Scotland's traditions."

"There are three of us. A twenty dollar donation is reasonable."

"We could've fed a homeless family with our twenty dollars."

Roby whispers in my left ear. "Are you taking Communion, Mom?"

"I don't know."

"Why not?"

"Because I haven't been here in a while. I'd feel guilty."

Sebastian's at my right ear again. "If you're going to drop a twenty in the collection plate, the least we should do is get our wafers."

"It's the Holy Body of Christ."

"This church buys its wafers from the A&P. They all do."

Roby leans forward and looks at his father. "Do they?"

"They do," Sebastian says.

I'm going to Hell, I know. I'm in Hell right now, right here in my church pew on Sunday. Jesus on the cross seems to know, looking down at me, forlorn and aggrieved.

The priest takes the lectern and raises his gilded Bible aloft and pronounces: *The word of the Lord!*

Sebastian: "Right."

Roby: "Where do the wafers really come from?"

I close my eyes and sit and listen to the sermon about the true meaning of wealth and how doing for others is the only everlasting venture we can perform on this Earth. Act as the

Lord acted, believe in the Lord by what you do. That a man says he believes in the Lord as our Savior pales to the man who not only says it but also proves it in the way he lives each day of his life.

My right ear hears, "For this speech they want a twenty?"

I ask, "Are you suddenly an atheist, Sebastian?"

"No."

My left ear hears, "I think we all should take Communion. Let's see what the Body of Christ tastes like today."

My right ear: "I'm not an atheist. I'm agnostic."

"What's the difference?"

"We have our doubts but are willing to listen to answers."

My left ear: "Do the wafers come in flavors? Can you pick a line to stand in for the flavor you want?"

My right ear: "I don't know what to believe. But I know a man does not have the ability to determine the details and thoughts of an omnipotent being."

My left ear: "I should have brought my own jelly jar."

My right ear: "It's nothing but arrogance, like a frog telling other frogs what humans are all about."

My left: "Maybe they'll have jelly jars put out."

My brain screams.

The priest: "So sayeth the Lord, Amen."

The congregation responds to the priest: "Amen."

The priest: "Now rise and turn to your neighbors and greet them as you would our Lord."

We're suddenly surrounded by smiling faces and extended hands, and we stand and we're told by all of them, "Peace be with you." I say, "And also with you." Roby says, "All right, thanks." Sebastian looks at his hands, grimaces and tells me, "You can't prove everyone washed their hands today, and now it's been spread around this room like a plague with these handshakes."

The congregation: "Peace be with you. And also with you."

Communion lines form in the aisles. Roby asks me if one line has chocolate wafers. "No," I say. "The wafers all taste bland."

"Are you going to take Communion?"

I nod and head for the line leading to the priest. I stand there, my head feeling blown up by embarrassment to the size of a blimp, and everyone in church stares at it, I know, with pity or scorn or something else I can only imagine. I stay focused on Jesus on the wall. In the distance, I hear, "Body of Christ." "Amen." "Body of Christ." The Communion line moves forward and the words become nearer. I dare to move my eyes to the side and see people retreating back to their pews, hands in prayer, their lips closed together lightly and their mouths gentle around dissolving wafers. Serenity glows upon their faces.

"Body of Christ."

I accept the wafer in my hands and bring it to my lips with the taste of guilt sharp on my tongue. But when I take in the wafer, it rests there in my mouth in all its tasteless wonderment, calming me, softening the bite of guilt, giving me the most personal of feelings to share with my faith. I spin away, only to find Roby and Sebastian have lined up behind me.

I hear in advance, in my mind, Roby's request to the priest for grape jelly or marmalade or strawberry jam or a condiment menu or to have his wafer lightly toasted with butter. But Roby gives me a covert wink and makes the sign of the cross.

"Body of Christ."

"Amen, Father."

Roby retreats behind me with his hands pressed together in a stance of prayer. He smiles at me, shows me he knows not to chew.

"Body of Christ."

Sebastian remains standing, his knees and back straight, and stares firmly into the priest's eyes, the offered wafer hovering unaccepted. "Father," he says loud enough for the surrounding pews and people halfway down our line to hear. "I have a question."

"Oh? Must it be now?"

"Please."

The priest frowns at the line of people standing behind Sebastian. Sebastian asks, "Is it a sin for a boy to disobey his father?"

I fight the urge to scream, there in the center aisle in a crowd of people and the Body of Christ still on my tongue. I stomp up to Sebastian and pull at his suit coat. Roby scampers down the aisle, shaking his head, and out the congregation door. "It depends," the priest says.

"Really?"

"Yes."

"On what? What sort of a son's disobedience against his father isn't a sin?"

"Perhaps you should make an appointment with me for another time."

"Will it cost another twenty bucks in the collection plate?"

"Sebastian!" I say, and I flame with heat under my skin and the knowledge I have shattered my wafer to pieces. "Please, Father. Forgive him."

The priest looks at me. He's an old man, perhaps ready to retire after this service and has a face as craggy as a rock. But he smiles and his eyes seem to know my torment. He turns to Sebastian and says, "The Lord, our Father, the Son of God, came to the same question as his earthly body hung dying on the cross. As much as it may be a sin for a son to disobey a father, it is equally sinful for the father not to listen to his son. And, as a son yourself, perhaps it's a sin for you to forget what it was like to be a young man in your father's home. But I advise you now that to carry a stern heart over your own child is not only a sin against God, but also a risk to your own flesh and blood, and the love I am certain you have for your family."

Sebastian parts his lips. No sound comes out.

The priest pops the wafer into Sebastian's mouth and says, "Body of Christ." People behind us start to applaud, and the applause spreads down the Communion line and into the pews, and everyone looks and starts clapping probably because they think it's part of the program. Upon the cross, Jesus still looks down at me, but now I see the agony is gone from his face, and the heat in my body becomes a chill along my spine. Sebastian brings his hands together at his chest, flat, in prayer. I suppose he's now an agnostic with an answer.

I lead him down the aisle and hear the priest's fading voice. "Body of Christ."

"Don't chew," I say to Sebastian. "And whatever you do, until the wafer completely dissolves, don't talk."

25

We've reached an understanding in our house this afternoon. If Roby keeps his grades up, he can keep his warehouse job. Sebastian will keep a check on things exam by exam.

This particular understanding's not the same thing as a peace agreement. It's more like a temporary suspension of hostilities in the Father versus Son War. Sebastian still seethes on occasion and is poised to strike at the first A-minus Roby brings home. Roby agrees to it because it's all a big lie, and the lie, as far as I know, will be over by Christmas. My incomplete understanding of Roby's lie, though, feels like I've seen my Christmas gift box, and I've untied the ribbon, but I still can't see what's inside.

While Sebastian's outside slamming garbage can lids at the curb for Monday's trash pickup, I tell Roby, "Christmas may be too far away."

"I don't know what you're talking about," he says, twitching and fidgeting at the kitchen table in his bag of clothes as he lies to me some more. It's okay. I don't mind. I go on.

"Your father may explode before Christmas."

"From what?"

"Do you think you can get done whatever it is you need to get done before then?"

"Get what done?"

"I know it may not be easy, but Thanksgiving would be a good time for this plan of yours."

"You've lost me."

"Thanksgiving then?"

"Whatever."

I kiss Roby on the cheek and say, "I'm glad we had this talk."

When Sebastian comes in, he sees Roby and me breaking away from our little huddle. Roby says, "Hiya, Dad. Need any help around here?"

Sebastian takes a deep breath and forces a smile. He says to Roby, "Shouldn't you be studying?"

Some have tension in their homes thick enough to cut with a knife. Here in my home, the knife could be a machete and the blade would shatter against the strain. "All right," Roby says on the edge of shouting. And he looks at me and talks with the same angry tone. "Maybe Thanksgiving. Maybe not at all!" He stomps to his bedroom and slams the door shut.

"You know," I say. "It's only a part time job. It's not as though your son goes out and beats people on their heads."

Sebastian looks at me with hurt in his eyes and asks, "Do you think he's doing drugs?"

Monday.

Still sunny and warm. And it's Halloween.

By three in the afternoon, children come home from grammar school and soon take to the streets in their costumes. I'm dropping candies into bags held by the usual monsters grouped on my porch, some with rubber knives in their heads and bug-out eye masks. One girl arrives dressed as Paris Hilton and a few boys dress up as somebody they claim is a fellow named Simon Cowell. It's all very frightening, really.

When I turn to close the door, I see children gathering on the walk by Iris's sagging House For Sale sign. They kick at it and point at her porch and whisper in each others' ears. They don't approach her house. Rather they laugh about something and run away.

I look down at my bowl of candies and sigh. Nearly gone already for the second time. There are more bags of it to dump in. So I do. And I grab my bowl and more extra bags of candy and step outside, closing the door behind me.

A boy half my height, dressed in black plants and shirt and a black cape, jumps to my porch and shouts, "Trick or treat!" He holds out his bag.

"I'm going next door," I say. "You can get candy there."

He looks to the north and says okay, and I tell him no, the other direction.

He slowly turns to the south, toward Iris's house. "See you later," he says, and runs away.

I think of Iris and her most personal secret kept for twenty years and how she squeezed my hand warmly in hers inside my car, so gently and lovingly after she had told me. So in need of a friend while the world around her bolts from her in fright as if she were Frankenstein's monster.

On Halloween and every other day, I cannot imagine the horror Iris sees.

When I knock on her door, it's unlatched and ajar and swings open slowly. There Iris sits on her living room couch, soaked in sunshine, and the darkness and gargoyles appear scattered back to the corners of her dining room. A large bowl of colorful hard candies balances on her lap, full to the rim, and her right hand rests on top.

No makeup. No paleface sunblock either. And no muumuu. Plain black pants and peach shirt. Sweet, really, with a belt tightened to prove she has a waist belonging to a petite.

She droops her head toward her bowl. "No trick or treaters yet. Not one. I don't know what I'm going to do with all this candy. Happens every year."

I hold out my bowl. "I thought I'd come over so we could sit on your porch and give away our candy together. It's warm outside, Iris. A beautiful day."

"I never understood why the children wouldn't come to my house on Halloween. I've had my curtains closed for nearly twenty years. Now I know."

"They're just kids."

"I see them. I see how they look at my house. Every neighborhood has an evil house and a bad person living inside it. I never knew it was my house. I never knew it was me." She brings her hands to the left side of her chest and her hair falls over her eyes.

"Did John treat you badly after your surgery?"

She shakes her head, sniffs, and looks off to a place in this room I cannot see. "When I came home from the hospital he asked me to take off my shirt. I didn't want to but he pleaded so earnestly, I eventually gave in. He dropped to his knees and brought his face to my scar and what was no longer there. He kissed my wretched scar and told me he loved me and I was forever his beauty. By the graces of angels, he said, my life was spared from that horrible cancer, and he broke down and wrapped his arms around my hips and fell to crying like a baby." Her chin quivers and her eyes soak full to the lashes. She asks me, "What do you suppose makes a woman a woman?"

"Iris?"

"We go through menopause and get old and take pills to replace the hormones that are no longer doing the job on their own, and we get our ovaries and uterus yanked out, and cancer seems to keep its devil's eye on the rest of our bodies. After all that, Julia, what in the world makes me a woman?"

There's a moment to speak, but it passes and anything I say now would come too late. I wonder about her question, whether she had expected an answer from me at all.

"I slapped him," Iris says. "I slapped John in the face twice. There he was kissing my scar and holding me and crying over me and I struck him hard and told him never to lie to me. And I told him if he said it wasn't a lie I'd strike him again."

I stand there with my stupid bowl of Halloween candy in my hands and I want to run to her and hold her but wonder if it's the right thing to do. I don't know. I just don't know. She tells me she's hideous, a hideous woman, the evil monster on the block children run away from on Halloween, so I risk it. I set my bowl on the floor and I set myself beside Iris on her couch in the sunshine. "Don't slap me for this," I say, and wrap my arms around her.

She laughs. I don't know, maybe it's a grunt and I'm hoping it's a laugh. What I know, though, is that I feel her hands on my sides, hugging me back. "I'm sorry for what I did in the salon."

"You weren't ready," I say.

"But it's been twenty years."

Children again gather by the House For Sale sign. Five, then more arrive. Masks rise up from their faces, and the children point and talk to each other. "Let's go outside with our candy bowls."

"What's the use?"

"Because I think you want to."

Iris leans back and dries her eyes with the backs of her hands. She stands and I hold her at my side, her bowl in her arms raised over her chest. "Try to relax," I say. "Think of something good."

"All right." She breathes in deeply and lowers her bowl of candy to her waist. "Something good."

I open the door and lead Iris through to the porch. The children have huddled low, their heads together in a circle, making their plans, I suppose, to ring the bell and run or leave a nasty sign on the door. Halfway down the sidewalk, Iris says to me, "You forgot your bowl."

"I know," I say, and the children hear us and rise at the sight of Iris.

The smallest girl, a pretty blondie in a ballerina tutu, holding a wand and her bag of treats, stands from the others. "Do you live here?" she asks Iris. Iris nods and extends her bowl of candy. The ballerina blondie turns to the other trick or treaters. "She don't look like a monster to me. She looks like my grandma, but not so wrinkly."

I tell Iris, "Go to them."

She toes a few steps forward, breathes in deeply again, Iris, in her plain black pants and peach shirt tied at the waist by a narrow black belt. There's loveliness to her shape when the muumuu's gone. She bends down toward the ballerina and asks, "Would you like some candy?"

The ballerina reaches into the bowl and asks, "How many?"

"Take as much as you want."

The other children say together, "Aw-right!" and they're at the bowl taking and grabbing and laughing and telling Iris thanks. The air fills with repeated plops of Halloween candy into bags. The bowl now empty, the children stand back on the sidewalk and stare at Iris. A skinny boy dressed as Batman lifts the mask off his face. "Are you really moving?" he asks, glancing at the teetering House For Sale sign. Iris nods. "Well, I hope you're still here next Halloween."

The children don't run or scream. They walk and skip away, their bags dragging with the weight of candy received from the house of Iris Newberry.

I ask her, "What good thing did you think of?"

She watches the children, their voices saying happy things about Iris and all her candy. Her empty bowl at her side, her hand through her hair, she tells me, "My legs. I've still got a damn good pair of legs."

"Does John remember?"

A rise at the corners of her lips, perhaps a smile, her voice as distant as the children when she says, "That will be up to John."

I lie awake in bed tonight, roll my head left toward the clock on my nightstand, and see the red letters glow 11:06 beneath the dim lamp. I roll my head to the right and see Sebastian's pillow, his side of the covers still tucked in place. I wonder why Lola Two hasn't sauntered out of my brain. Certainly this would be a perfect time to add to my torment.

A crush of wheels over pavement, the drone of our garage door opening then closing, and I lose track of the moment. Suddenly Sebastian's in our bed, washed, brushed and in a fresh pair of pajamas, but I cannot recall the time and sounds that brought him beside me.

"Where were you?" I say to the ceiling. "And before you answer, I called the school six hours ago."

There's a hesitation before Sebastian speaks, the sort of hitch preceding an answer guaranteed to make a wife want to scream. "I saw Dad after work."

"You've never stayed at Dignity Place this late before."

"That man, a boy really, cornered me. Hairy Harry. He wanted to know about reading lessons. He wanted to know if it's true I'll teach him to read. I swear to God I thought he was a Halloween costume from head to toe."

"What did you tell him?"

"I said I wasn't sure I could fit lessons in my schedule just yet. Maybe sometime down the road." Sebastian laughs a bit. "That boy really knows how to drag himself away in sadness."

There's relief in my chest, embarrassment over what I was thinking. But when I roll toward him, to embrace him, a scent hugging Sebastian's skin rekindles my doubt. It's the outdoors. The unmistakable odor of hours spent in the woods or in a field, by a lake or stream; the aroma of fallen leaves and moisture penetrates deeply into flesh and hair. Even Sebastian can't scrub it away. "Where were you after that?" I ask flatly.

Sebastian raises his head slightly off his pillow and stares at me over his cheeks. I wish I could see anger in his face or sudden humor or something discernable as an immediate and innocent reaction. But I get nothing. "Please, Julia," he says, his head back to his pillow. "I love you more than I can say."

"But you won't tell me where you've been. Not till you're ready."

Silence. A slight mumble expressing a thought of words perhaps, but nothing spoken.

I reach to my nightstand light and turn it off. In the darkness, Sebastian feels for my hand. There's firmness to his grip, a gesture begging for trust. Although I gently squeeze his hand back, I sense Lola Two somewhere in the darkness, her voice in this room. *Poor Julia. And you thought everything was going so well.*

26

I have to say, I'm feeling pretty good about myself this Tuesday morning. About a lot of things.

There's an odd satisfaction in letting Sebastian know I'm on to him, surprising him with my intuition. Surprising myself with an ability to forgive yet without being naive. And of course making my family attend church last Sunday with the priest's sermon about living as Jesus would live, but more the priest's ability to silence one of Sebastian's rants.

Most of all, though, there's the transformation of Iris Newberry.

My good feeling soars higher when I don't talk about Iris to Sebastian and Roby, even as they speak in one-word sentences to each other before heading off to their schools. Something about not wearing success on my sleeves makes my good feeling more satisfying.

Iris joins me for coffee in my kitchen before I head off to Dignity Place. We don't talk much. I compliment her white slacks and black blouse. She tells me the slacks outfit is from Sears, the blouse from Target, an eclectic ensemble. I tell her thank you for yesterday.

"I think I'm ready now."

"Iris, are you sure?"

"Pretty sure." She slurps from her coffee cup, and she looks lovely with a gentle touch of mascara around her eyes and gloss over her lips. "As sure as I'm ever going to be."

I say, "I'll see what I can arrange."

There are quicker ways to drive to Dignity Place from my house, but I take Sheridan Road with my windows rolled down and the freshness of Lake Michigan filling my lungs. The start of November fails to chase summer weather away and sunlight shafts through the sky as if made just for me.

This street is a magical place full of brick and stone mansions, with garages and guest homes large enough to put my house inside them several times over, and ivy-laden masonry fences with wrought iron gates and spires and glimpses of the water and shoreline. It goes on for miles and miles, starting from Chicago's Lake Shore Drive nearly to the Wisconsin border, meandering as the lake shore and age-old property lines demand, through twisting ravines and under bridges of interlocking tree limbs, past beaches private and public and Jewish synagogues and churches of every faith and the Baha'i Temple. Always one twisting lane in each direction, compelling drivers to go slowly, to see and admire, to appreciate and dream.

It's a moment in time and place for me to bottle up and take with me so I can drink from it when my next torment arrives. But now it's time to turn onto the road west toward Dignity Place. Not a bad road, but typically straight and facing away from Lake Michigan. The smell of the water's freshness comes through my car's windows in less frequent puffs, and I wave my nose about to hunt them down and breathe them in.

An ambulance passes around me with its siren off.

A second.

A police car. Another police car.

This could be almost anything. It doesn't have to be about Dignity Place.

A Channel 7 News van with a retractable pole antenna on

top. Channel 5. Channel 9. Fox News. They turn the direction I'm going to turn. They turn onto the next street. Another turn right puts them on the final road to Dignity Place. They take it. All of them. Of course they could go on past the drive.

They don't.

They join a fleet of cars already gathered at the veranda in violation of Dignity Place parking rules, and Hairy Harry's all about waving his arms at them to move to the appropriate lot. He's ignored in the swarm.

A police squad takes up my assigned spot, parked on an angle as if the officer couldn't wait to jump out. I park behind it. I block it in, feeling justified. Before I leave my car, I lean back and close my eyes, thinking of Sheridan Road and wishing I could have a swig from my imaginary bottle of bliss right now.

When I near the veranda, Hairy Harry shouts my name and the reporters turn to me like a wolf pack grown far beyond hungry. They run with their microphones held forward as if they were lances aiming to spear me through. Their questions are all the same: "Are you *the* Julia Connery?"

"I am. Why?"

"Did you know about this?"

"I rarely know anything."

A man I recognize from the Ten O'Clock News smiles his perfect teeth at me. "How do you feel?"

"Me? I'm feeling pretty good. Why do you ask?"

"No, no. I mean about your father-in-law?"

"What?"

There's a hand grabbing mine and I'm pulled through the crowd, stumbling up the stairs to the veranda. The hair thick on his wrist, Hairy Harry pounds on the entrance door for the Grisslys to let us in. Mr. Grissly works the lock and cracks the door open enough for me and Hairy Harry to pull through and we turn and push the door shut before reporters can barrel their way in.

Mrs. Grissly stands in the middle of the lobby, arms folded, her eyes and lips and nose looking folded up too. "Did you know about this?"

"Whatever it is," I say, "I'm sure I'll be surprised by it."

"Come with me."

I follow her across the lobby to the hall leading to the pool. A police officer stands by the pool window, looking at his note-pad. A second officer stands guarding the door to the passage leading to my office. He asks Mrs. Grissly, "Is she okay?"

Mrs. Grissly shoots me a doubtful look and sighs. "She's all right."

It's like entering a bank vault, our entrance guarded, a third officer inside the passage, turning and escorting us forward. He speaks into a shoulder radio. "Two citizens approaching, ten seconds."

In ten seconds, we're at the threshold to my office. Along with the humidity and chlorine comes the smell of police busi-ness, of wool suits and polished shoes and words inked upon notepads for an investigator's eyes only. There's a crowd inside my pitiful pool office, like a contest to see how many people can fit on the head of a pin, and I feel as though I'm passing through a sweaty armpit. Our police escort announces, "Coming through!"

The bodies begin to part, pressed to the walls, my desk upended on its side and the chair atop the filing cabinet. The oxygen in here feels as though it's been used up and my head grows dizzy with the sound of shuffling feet and someone call-ing my name. Men and women in jeans and white lab coats hold things that look like paint brushes. They nod and turn away. And the final two people I see . . .

Old Sebastian. John Newberry.

John blushes through his beard and looks absently at his

shoulder. It's Old Sebastian, in his chair, who toggles forward and speaks to me. "Julia!" he announces as if he's discovered gold. "Look!"

In my near faint, I follow the direction of his finger, pointing to the wall. The block proclaiming—*They murdered me!*—is gone, as are many others, banged out and chiseled away, cement crumbs littering the floor. And there, standing pressed between two boards inside the wall, is a brown suit. Pleated slacks and double-breasted coat with wide lapels and a dried, encrusted flower pinned on one side; polished brown shoes with spats, white shirt, wide blue tie, cuff-links, fedora hat with a feather in its side. And inside all these clothes stands a man, his skeleton, a ring on the pinkie of his left hand.

Old Sebastian gushes, "It's Little Nicky Number One's grandfather!"

The skeleton's head seems to hold a nod of agreement and aims its morbid grin Old Sebastian's way.

A woman in a white lab coat, holding a brush, says, "We don't know that for sure. Not yet."

"Like hell it ain't!" Old Sebastian raises a dried-leather wallet from inside his shirt. "Driver's license. Picture ID."

"Why are you hiding that?" the woman snorts. She snatches the wallet from Old Sebastian's hands.

There's a pull on my arm and I spin around, and a man tells me to smile. John Newberry is pushed to my side and Old Sebastian toggles to my legs.

A rise of a camera. A flash. A photo. Last I remember, John Newberry catches me before I hit the floor.

Mrs. Grissly says I'm fired. Mr. Grissly tells her not to be so hasty. Old Sebastian tells them both not to mess with me because I'm the daughter-in-law of the man who found Little Nicky Number One's grandfather.

I lie in the aroma of old-man odors. Old Spice, Aqua Velva, Epsom Salts, original Listerine. Ahead of me, mounted on the wall, is a television set with its built-in DVD player. A bookcase beside it holds gangster DVDs. A window to my left, pictures of Scotland beside the window, and to my right, on the bureau, the tuxedoed Don Corleone leers at me over his cotton ball cheeks. Old Sebastian wheels to my head and asks, "Comfortable enough for you?"

"Your bed's lumpy."

"The lumps fit my lumps."

Mrs. Grissly steps to the foot of the bed and stomps on a pedal. Slowly, the head of the bed rises, lifting me into the full power of her glare. I suppose I could touch her face anywhere and I'd feel her pulse, both racing and floundering, her heart threatening to either shut off or detonate. "We have a responsibility to our Residents, Mrs. Connery. Dignity Place is meant to bring calm and order to the lives of the functioning elderly. It's not a place for a media circus. The Residents need peace and quiet. That's why it's called Dignity Place."

"How do you know what we need?" Old Sebastian grumbles.

Mrs. Grissly raises her index finger and stabs at him through the air. "Your privileges here are hanging by a thread."

Mr. Grissly begins to pace, arms behind his back, as if a condemned man deciding over his last supper. He halts and turns to stare at the back of Mrs. Grissly's head. He tells her, coughing and stammering, "Shut, uh, up."

She spins about.

He says again, planting his feet and raising his chin, "I said shut up."

"What do you mean?"

Mr. Grissly looks away, his body deflating before Mrs. Grissly. He says, "It's the most excitement the Residents have had since we took over the place."

"Fun? You think a bunch of Residents having strokes and coronaries is fun?"

"Who had a stroke today?" Old Sebastian asks.

Mrs. Grissly answers, "Nobody."

"Who had a heart attack?"

"Nobody. Nobody yet. With all this excitement, it's a matter of time."

"Well," Old Sebastian says, "if you wait long enough, everybody's going to go ker-plop sooner or later."

Mrs. Grissly sniffs into the air at me. "Mrs. Connery, did you or did you not take the Residents on a walk outside last Thursday evening?"

"I did."

"What do you suppose the temperature was at the time?"

"I have no idea."

"It happened to be the one cold evening of the month. Thirty-five degrees."

"Was that with the wind chill?"

"No."

I say weakly, "They all wore hats."

Old Sebastian asks, "Who caught a cold?"

Mrs. Grissly blinks. "Nobody. Nobody yet."

Old Sebastian toggles toward her. "Nobody's caught a cold from Julia's walk."

"She took them off the path."

"You mean she took them out of the rut."

Old Sebastian stops his chair a yard away from Mrs. Grissly's shins. I can tell he's making ready to ram her. I know what ramming her would mean. He'll be kicked out of Dignity Place immediately and be back in my house, and although that doesn't sound as bad to me as it used to, I'm not ready for it.

"I quit," I say. "That's right. I quit."

"Fine," Mrs. Grissly says.

"No," Old Sebastian says.

Mr. Grissly says, "The phone's ringing." And it is, the sound no match for the tempers flying about this room. Old Sebastian heaves forward, saying he'll get it because it's still his room for the moment, and Mrs. Grissly dodges out of the way into Mr. Grissly. Picking up the receiver from the phone behind Don Corleone, Old Sebastian says, "Oh!"

He smiles into the mouthpiece with a slew of "Yes, sirs," and "You're welcomes." Then he turns to Mrs. Grissly, extending the receiver toward her. "It's for you."

"What?"

"Don't say no, Mrs. Grissly. For God's sake, don't say no."

Mrs. Grissly takes the receiver from Old Sebastian and barks into it, "Yes, this is Mrs. Grissly." She goes pale, repeating as did Old Sebastian, "Yes, sir" and "You're welcome, sir."

I hear the voice through the earpiece, not the words but the tone. It's deep enough to vibrate my bones and, by the looks of her, Mrs. Grissly's bones as well. She says goodbye and slowly lowers the receiver to the cradle behind the Godfather.

Old Sebastian tugs at Mrs. Grisslys' arm. "Little Nicky Number One."

"Yes," she says, clucking her tongue.

"Julia keeps her job if she wants it."

"Yes."

"Nobody's getting kicked out."

"No."

"He was extremely grateful?"

"He was," Mrs. Grissly sniffs.

"A substantial donation is in the mail?"

"It is."

Mr. Grissly seems to have recovered somewhat. He tells Mrs. Grissly, "Shut up means to let other people have their say." He leaves the room in long strides, reflecting either his confidence or his hurry not to wait for Mrs. Grissly to regain her senses.

"At least," Old Sebastian says, offering her some sort of consolation, "I'll stop knocking holes in your walls."

She blinks and smiles at him, at me, at the picture of Don Corleone. Then, as if her opinions were never in the room in the first place, she leaves.

Old Sebastian shows me, with a press of his hands on his wheelchair's armrests and a chorus of old man grunts and groans, how he stands on his own. "I'm getting pretty good at this. Soon you'll start teaching me how to dance."

"Old Sebastian?" I swing my feet about and sit up on the side of the bed. "How does Mrs. Grissly know who Little Nicky Number One is just from a phone call?"

He sits accompanied by the same volley of grunts and groans. Settling back in his wheelchair, his right hand at his chin, his head back and slightly turned, he looks at me with his eyes sneaking out between his lids. "Oh, Mrs. Grissly knows Little Nicky Number One's voice all right." He's posing as does Don Corleone in the photo beside him, touching his pinkie to his lips while he replies. "She definitely knows."

27

Old Sebastian's famous.

Interviews for television news, newspapers and magazines. The works. One reporter nicknames him the Gangster Bone Hunter. He holds court in the center of Dignity Place's grand lobby until noon, the ponds and ferns and pillars to the skylights all serving as his backdrop. He makes jokes. Reporters laugh. He waves to Mrs. Grissly standing behind the front desk and she smiles back one of those smiles that lets you know she'd rather have her hands around his neck if the circumstances were in her favor.

For my first afternoon fitness class, Old Sebastian wheels into the exercise room and takes over. More adulation. More smiles. Requests for autographs. I don't bother changing into my gym clothes and shoes. Instead, I hunt down John Newberry. Unlike Old Sebastian, he's hidden himself from the attention in the aftermath.

I knock on his door. Inside, he coughs and tells me it's unlocked and to come in. When I do, he's in a chair by his window, a second chair to the side, and he's brushing off the seat with a handkerchief. "I've been expecting you," he says. "Sit."

Through the window, I see reporters milling about their vans and cars, talking things over among themselves and with police officers. A pair of men in suits takes the body of Little Nicky Number One's grandfather away on a stretcher. I notice the skeleton's right arm is uncovered and a bony finger points slightly to the sky, at the window. At me.

"That picture they took of us in my office will be in the papers," I say, sitting down.

"It likely will."

"Iris will see it."

"She never reads the newspaper. Never."

"Think she'd recognize you if she did?" I look at John Newberry, at the gray beard thick over his face, indistinguishable from the thick hair on his head. Just his nose, eyes, balled-up cheeks and forehead show through.

"She'd recognize me."

"What would she do?"

"It wouldn't make a bit of difference. She's known I've been here from the beginning."

"The Grisslys know who you really are?"

"They do."

We sit for a time. So many questions in my head, but it's so hard to speak my thoughts to this man. After a weak cough, I ask, "Why were you expecting me?"

He pulls down at his beard. "You're going to ask me to go home to Iris."

"No."

"Yes."

"Probably."

"What has she told you?"

"The worst of it." I place my hand on his broad back. "How you were an angel. How terribly sorry she is."

"I see."

He stands, engulfed in his hair and his baggy overalls, and leans his forehead against the window. "I think most of all I remember our honeymoon. Not a grand place, but nice. A bed and breakfast on a bay in Michigan. It was all we could afford

231

back then. But I remember it was beautiful. Iris was beautiful, and the fact we were poor on a poor couple's honeymoon didn't matter at all. We were in love."

He looks at me over his shoulder and I can tell by the shape of his beard that he's smiling at the memory of his honeymoon. "You and Sebastian have a lot of personality in your marriage. You have your ways about you, how you swing on your glider together in the back yard, how you laugh and kiss so much just to do it, and talk to each other as if you were still children."

"It's not always easy between us."

"Still," he says, looking back out the window, "it's what keeps you young and in love."

He tells me about the history of Iris, how she declared war on dirt, dust and disorder by the age of seven. "It was endearing, really, the way she would take care of things, and me. Let me tell you, on our first night at our honeymoon bed and breakfast, I challenged her demand for order. We started to make love for the first time after our wedding and I whispered in her ear that I had left a glass out on the floor in the common hallway just to do it. Just to see which she would choose. Me now, or organization first then me later. She said she didn't care about the glass in the hallway and started to laugh, and laughed louder, all the while loving me. Then she asked me what kind of glass I left out in the hallway, and I told her it was just a glass. We went on making love, but soon she started asking me to be more specific about the glass. I told her it was the memento glass the bed and breakfast gives its guests. She's fine with things for a while until she has to ask me which one because the bed and breakfast has three kinds."

John's shoulders shake, his head moving side to side. "I told her the one with the bed and breakfast Victorian home etched into it that said 'Welcome to the Traverse City Bed and Breakfast, Enjoy Your Stay,' and I kissed her all over, and I mean all over, all the while telling her to enjoy her stay.

"I can't tell you how long it lasted, likely well into the morning hours. Finally we were exhausted and she rolled off our bed and ran out of our room like she couldn't help herself. She dashed back in with the glass and told me she thought someone might have seen her naked in the hallway on our honeymoon night. I remember her laughter, with a hitch in it like a hiccup, and how tightly she held that glass to her bosom.

"Falling asleep in my arms, Iris told me the next time we start to make love to be sure that I first leave the glass out in the hallway and tell her I put it there. She said not to ask her why, but I asked anyway. She kissed me one of those kisses a man never forgets. Then she said, 'Because it was fantastic.' We fell asleep with nothing but that glass between us."

Before me stands a Neanderthal telling me about honeymoon sex and his bride's obsessive-compulsive disorder. He turns around and says, "Those were the kinds of things that kept love young between me and Iris."

I consider his story, how it fills this room as if he lives it even now. "Iris gave away Halloween candy yesterday, John."

"Really?" He looks doubtful. "She came out of the house and talked with children?"

"She was lovely. The children adored her."

He makes a sound, somewhere between a grunt of disbelief and a squeak of surprise. Back in his chair he slumps and tells me he hasn't seen Iris for twenty years. He's seen her in her horrible clothes, hat, and sunblock, of course; but he hasn't *seen* her.

"The truth is," I say, "I didn't come to your room to ask you about Iris. I'm here to ask about Roby." Again with a pull at the beard. I wonder if he means to tear it off his face. "I want to know if he can learn his Tartan bagpipe by Thanksgiving instead of Christmas."

"I don't know what you're talking about."

"That's the same thing Roby told me. But I expect the truth out of you, John. Roby and Sebastian won't last until Christmas. I need whatever Roby's planning to happen as soon as possible."

He squeezes his fingers between his knees. "The bagpipe is a difficult instrument to learn, Julia. I've never taught it before."

"It was a sweet note rising through the vent in my office last Thursday."

"He needs to learn more than one note."

"Please."

He starts to nod his head and says, "Maybe. Roby's a smart boy. Can he come here more than three times a week?"

"If he needs to."

"Five times a week. Six would be better. Then Thanksgiving is possible."

"It's interesting that you thought I came here to talk about Iris." I stand and leave him in his chair by the window. But before I go, I tell him what he needs to know about himself. "You weren't simply expecting me. You were hoping I'd talk to you about coming home to Iris. You had your door unlocked and a chair waiting for me, John Newberry. That's a fact."

He remains staring at his hands clasped between his knees. He doesn't move or say a word. I suppose in the depths of his mind, he will always remember the bed and breakfast glass, and how much he enjoyed his stay with Iris.

Sebastian asks me at the dinner table, "Anything new happen today?"

To each possible answer, I consider Sebastian's possible reactions. "Nothing," I say. "Nothing new happened at all."

I keep the television set and radio off and, in the morning, throw our newspaper onto Iris's porch. My picture is on the front page with Old Sebastian's and John Newberry's. Old Sebastian's smiling, I look ready to vomit and John looks like a man with a shotgun pointed at his head. Sebastian wants me to call the Tribune people to complain about our missing newspaper. I tell him I will.

28

Before she leaves my car for Phillip's salon, Iris tells me, "Come back in two hours." Her eyes and voice express the same mixed emotion about this deadline. Wonderment and fear.

As I drive from downtown Highland Park heaven, a man's voice over the radio announces that *God Investment* is on hiatus for the time being. He sounds as though he's a second away from crying, yet gives no explanation.

I don't know how I feel about this. It's all right, I suppose. I'll be fine. Still, I play with the buttons on the radio in case I've made some sort of mistake. It's the right station. Then the announcer tells me the news about a suspected gangster's skeletal remains found hidden in a retirement center outside Chicago and says Residents named Donald and Old Sherwood, with the help of June, Sherwood's sister, found the body inside a discarded refrigerator. Makes me grateful for the accuracy of modern media. I press a button on the radio for an oldies station. Elvis Presley sings *Amazing Grace*.

I have an hour and forty minutes left.

It's just as sunny as yesterday, just as warm, but this time Sheridan Road gives no comfort to me. I give up trying to find bliss and take the direct road to Roby's high school. It's a large block of a building made of off-white brick with few windows, and if it didn't say Highland Park Central High School on the large sign along the school bus drive, it would be easy to mistake it for the warehouse Roby pretends he's been working at.

I get my visitor's pass at the administrative office and stand in the hallway, looking left for the staircase. There's not a soul around but for a hall monitor on a chair, eyeing my pass and asking me if I need help.

I ask, "Where's the music room?"

"Up the staircase to the second floor. Room 280A. Two rooms down to your left."

My heels strike the tiled floor with the sound of a librarian's foot, an adult, someone a student sees in the hall and looks at with a sneer that says, What are *you* doing here? Up the first part of the staircase, I make the turn and a girl in a pink sweater and denim bell bottoms gives me such a look. She rolls her eyes at me and goes on her way and I want to tell her she'll be fifty-three one day soon enough.

I look at my watch at the top of the stairs. Ninety-seven minutes left.

Two rooms down I find a green metal door with a small window at eye level and I peek in and see four risers of students singing. A man in a suit stands centered before them, holding his hands out level. I lean back and look again at the sign on the door, just to make sure it's room 280A. When I push the door open, the sound comes at me in a rush. A beautiful harmony hanging on the word "Oh." The conductor pulls his hands in and extends them again with a snap. The students hike up "Oh" another pitch, another harmony. Such talent from a gathering of baggy clothes.

I sit on a folding chair against a blackboard and listen to their voices and I gaze to the ceiling two stories high made of something I could throw a pen up to and expect its point to stick. The conductor turns to look at me, a young man, trim in his dark suit, smiling and rosy cheeked. With a quick grip of his hands at the air, the chorus ends their chord, and he says to me, "I'm Mr. Kaufman." He turns back to the students. "It appears we have an audience."

A blush rises to my face. I wish for a pen to throw to the ceiling. Mr. Kaufman's arms go up then gently fall into a slow, waving rhythm and the chorus begins. It's a soft piece, full of chord progressions and minor harmonies. I've never heard the tune, and certainly not the words.

You'd expect the boys to be in waistcoats and the girls in Victorian gowns to hear them sing this melody. But there they stand in all their torn denim and violently damaged hair. About fifty of them, heads with wide-opened ovals crooning harmonies. Mr. Kaufman slows the tempo and raises his arms toward the top tier, to a boy in a black shirt with black hair wildly uncombed after a night's restless sleep. With a hushed harmony below him, this boy begins his solo:

> *Come to me softly, my love of my life*
> *Don't worry the years long gone by*
> *The years gone by add charm to your ways*
> *They make you the love of my life.*

> *Your kisses enchant me, I'll never forget*
> *Tastes sweeter the years long gone by*
> *The years gone by add charm to your kiss*
> *Your kiss is the kiss of my life.*

Without any doubt, it's Brian Unkers. Bean Dip. While the rest of the chorus sings harmonies, he waits silently, slouched and angry. The chorus croons toward the end of the melody, and Brian's shoulders rise strong, his eyes softly closed, and his face shows the passion of a love song. He sings:

> *As I wait for you now, the love of my life*
> *Remember the years long gone by*
> *A day in heaven will join us once more*
> *Once more the life of my life.*

How a person people know as Bean Dip is chosen to sing like the angels is not in my power to understand. Brian Unkers has been chosen. He tries to ignore the fact that I have leapt to my feet to applaud him. The slouching and the anger he typically displays tries to come, but they won't stick. Other students begin to applaud him along with me. What Brian does is smile and wave at me and run his hands through his hair in a way that knocks over the spikes.

Mr. Kaufman loans us his office and closes the door on his way out. Like Roby and John, Brian denies knowledge of a plan. "There's not a warehouse anywhere near this high school," I say.

"It's by the expressway."

"Roby said it was by the high school."

He smiles. "Bet he didn't say which high school."

His father is an orthodontist yet this boy has crowded teeth. His mother is a dermatologist yet he has pimples around his mouth. The neighborhood knows his parents as the Screamers, and he lives his life so silently. Right now, though, Brian doesn't look so bad, and his smile doesn't look so foreign on his face. There's a handsomeness about this boy when you get a good look at him. It defies the crowded teeth and the mouth pimples, the slouch and the anger. "You have a beautiful voice."

"Thank you, Mrs. Connery."

"People shouldn't call you Bean Dip."

He turns crimson from his chin to his cheeks. What an odd compliment for him to blush at. I get to the point. "I need whatever Roby's planning to be done by Thanksgiving."

"Why are you telling me this at school?"

"Sebastian's good at finding things out. I couldn't call or drop by your house without risking things."

"What things?"

"You know."

"I do?"

"This plan is for Roby's father. We can't have him finding out."

"Finding out what?"

I think to say my son does all right choosing his friends, but I don't. What's the use? I tell Brian again, "You have a beautiful voice."

He looks at me like I need medication. "By Thanksgiving," I say. And I see it, subtle, but I see it. Brian nods his head.

I remember Iris, look at my watch, and realize I'm running out of time.

Phillip waves a hair duster brush at me. I think he intends to look menacing. "Iris told me you're late," he scoffs. "Twenty minutes late."

"I'm sorry."

"That's twice now."

"I said I'm sorry."

What is it that causes a flimsy young man to think he's such a tough guy? I could wrap my hands twice around one of Phillip's scrawny biceps and squeeze it until he begs for mercy.

There's a soft pop behind the curtain to the dressing rooms and a voice says, "Ready?"

With a snap of his fingers, Phillip commands the curtain to slide open. The gum-popper steps through, then moves to the side. First in shadow, then inching forward into the dazzling lights of *Phillip's Combo Salon For Petites Only Clothier*, Iris Newberry is at last unveiled.

Lovely pleated blue skirt, high heels and a silver blouse.

It's still hard for Iris. She shakes and keeps her stare down toward the floor. Phillip applies a soft, lifting touch to her chin, and it's like watching the sun rise over a meadow.

A light application of makeup, mascara and soft blue around her eyes. Blush upon her cheeks and gentle peach gloss over her lips. Silver necklace, pearl earrings.

Phillip says to her, "Iris Newberry, you are now the beauty Mother Nature intended a glorious woman to be." For those words and the glow it brings to Iris's skin, I forgive Phillip the fact he's a pompous ass.

I return the photograph to Iris, the one of her and John on their wedding day. She presses it to the left side of her chest.

The gum-popper pops her pink goo and says, "Awesome legs."

When Sebastian comes home from the college, he looks at me angrily and says, "I know." He doesn't say what he knows. He doesn't ask for dinner. He doesn't ask for anything. Instead he goes into the hallway bath. A minute later, the shower starts running.

I lean against the bathroom door, trying to listen to what he knows. All I hear is a song without lyrics, a jumble of hums and whistles and almost-words. If I were to ask him what he was singing, he'd ask me what I was talking about.

Roby appears over me, looking surprised to find me sitting on the floor outside the bathroom door. I don't recall sliding down. He asks me what's up.

"Your father knows."

Roby considers this for a moment and drops his book bag to the floor. His shoes are invisible beneath his saggy pants and the hems have turned brown from dredging the earth. There's worry on his face and dirt beneath the fingernails he uses to scratch at his chin. He asks, "Knows about what?"

"I don't know."

"What's he gonna do about it?"

"I have no idea."

He smiles and blinks so the hair dangling in his eyes twitches at me. It's endearing to a mother to witness a remaining habit from her son's childhood. "I can't tell you what I'm up to. Don't ask."

"I won't."

Roby coughs a bit to clear his throat which doesn't need to be cleared. "I know you talked to Bean Dip."

"Are you mad?"

"Not really. But please stop investigating."

I stand and bring my hands to his cheeks. He has no choice but to take his mother's kiss on the lips and another on his forehead. I ask him, "Is Thanksgiving going to work out for you?"

He nearly goes limp in my hands, I suppose out of frustration with me. He gives in and answers, "We're trying."

"You and Bean Dip and who else?"

"Quit asking."

The bathroom door opens behind me with a whoosh and a blow of humidity. It makes me leap and spin about. Sebastian stands in a towel around his waist, his chest flush from his hot shower, and a small patch of pale hair between his nipples. Steam swirls over his head and he looks past me to Roby. "I'm your father. You're grounded until I say you're not."

Roby stammers out, "But why?"

"You know why."

"I don't!"

Sebastian glares at me, more proud than angry. "I called every warehouse and business that could possibly have a warehouse near the high school. Then I tried nearly the entire North Shore business district. I missed my lunch and my break periods for a week to do it. Nobody has a Roby working for them. Nobody." He scowls back at his son. "Give me the name of the warehouse you're working at."

Roby looks at the floor.

"I knew there was no such place," Sebastian says. "Wash that phony dirt off your hands!" The bathroom door whooshes shut and the hair dryer goes on.

Raising his stare to mine, Roby hangs his jaw slack and the reddening flush moves up his neck looking ready to pop his head off. I ask him, "Son, do you love your father?" I smile as best I can, knowing he knows my tricks. This time, though, he says nothing, absolutely nothing. It's the first time in his life he hasn't answered this question. His dragging pant hems and trailing book bag slip into his bedroom and disappear behind the door.

Inside the bathroom, the dryer goes off. Sebastian bellows, "And I know about the gangster bones, too."

29

Whatever Roby had planned, it's over.

He bangs through the front door after school the next day and slams his bedroom door shut. There's a click of the handle lock, although I could pop it open with a point of a pen through the hole in the center of the knob. These are the noises of protest and an announcement to me that there's no more work to be done at any warehouse, and there will be no more music rising from the floors of Dignity Place.

The day after, a piece of notebook paper goes up on his door. In red, drippy letters, it reads:

The Torture of William Wallace Now In Progress.

Brian Unkers comes over after school with a backpack and the corners of his mouth weighted down by the need to study. For a moment in our living room, he smiles at me then catches himself as if his smile were a mistake. He shifts his eyes and his body toward the staircase and drags himself up to Roby's room, pounding the floor as he goes as if gravity pulled especially hard at his feet.

I hear him grunt, "Roby." I hear Roby grunt, "Bean Dip." Then the bedroom door closes and a second later, the click of the handle lock. Sebastian arrives home and immediately flies up the stairs. He's gone for a minute or two then sits next to me at the kitchen table for a cup of coffee. "They're studying," he says with the self-satisfied smile of an overlord snuffing out the spirit of his subjects. "I heard them through the door talking trigonometry."

I set my cup on the table and study the murkiness of the coffee and cream. I say, "You've ruined things."

He looks at me out the corners of his eyes like I could be a traitor in his little overlord army. I think to tell him what he may have ruined and decide not to. It's up to Roby to do it. To one day break his father's heart with the news of his father's own wreck of things. I say, "A tragic waste of time."

He sips from his cup, still looking suspicious of me. "A waste of time?"

"What you did."

His voice rises and his cup clinks hard on the saucer. "What did I do?"

Our cups look like chess pieces on our table, steaming, dark, and positioned by our hands. "You went through the phone book looking for businesses to call and you called them, one by one, all over the North Shore, looking for Roby. How many hours did it take you?"

"Not many."

"You said enough to take up your lunch hours and breaks for a week, calling and making a fool of yourself." He shoves his cup and saucer toward me and tries to speak, something about Roby and who's making a fool of whom, but I won't let him go on. "Just think," I say, pushing my cup and saucer against his, "of all the other things you could have done with that time."

"Like what?"

"Like come home to me."

Sebastian broods over our saucers touching rim to rim. "I hadn't thought of that."

"A shame. Now you've lost the time forever over your little obsession, your mistrust of your own son."

"He lied to me."

"So what if he did?"

"I never lied to my father."

I glare at Sebastian, waiting for him to raise his stare from his coffee. When he does, he closes his eyes and says, "Maybe once or twice."

"About what?"

"A girl. A long time ago."

"Which girl?"

"You."

"What lie did you tell your father about me?"

Sebastian sighs and opens his eyes. "When I first told him about you, I said both your parents were Scottish through and through."

"But you knew my mother was half. Would it have made a difference?"

"Back in those days, I don't know. I didn't want to bother with it."

"You should know I told your father about the one quarter of me being a mystery."

Sebastian moans. "I know. Why'd you do it?"

"He asked me, and my answer didn't seem to matter. Your mother and father still kissed me at our wedding and wished us well. Did they say anything behind my back?"

"One time."

"Oh?"

Sebastian pushes our cups and saucers aside and takes my hands in his. "This is different. This is about my son putting lie upon lie. It's not about protecting the love of his life."

"What did your parents say behind my back?"

Softly, Sebastian tells me, "They said, 'We'll have to see about this woman.' "

"That's it?"

"It's what they said at our reception."

"Doesn't sound so bad to me."

"No. Not now."

"So you lied to your father about me and kept it from me all these years." I let that sink in a little. "Maybe what Roby's up to isn't so bad."

His fingertips move over my knuckles and in the grooves of the delicate skin between my fingers. He knows how I love the sensation this gives me. There's an unresolved thought in his eyes, a touch of hardness mixed in with a look of giving in. Sebastian says of Roby, "We'll have to see about this boy."

For the time being, Roby keeps quiet around his father, his shoulders and face slouched. Sebastian takes it as normal teenager posture, but I hear the hiss in the air.

It goes on like this for a week after the discovery of gangster bones, and the weather slips away from spring and turns back into November. The sky is constantly cloudy, misting rain and fog, and hurls down an occasional pellet of snow. I get regular visits from Iris, so silent and cautious in my kitchen, and she's always telling me before she leaves, more anxious each time, that she's ready. And Hairy Harry calls asking for Sebastian, and Sebastian takes the phone and moans with the realization of who it is. "Perhaps in a couple more days," Sebastian always says. "Yes, I promise," then puts him off two more days with the next phone call from Hairy Harry.

On Wednesday, Sebastian arrives home after ten-thirty at night. We pass each other on the staircase. He's going up, I'm going down. We nearly pause as we go by each other, our eyes glancing at something over the other's shoulder. He doesn't give me an explanation for his late return, and I don't ask for one. At the bottom of the stairs, Sebastian's swirling aroma of the outdoors, fallen leaves and moisture, engulfs me, and I think I should cry if only it would do me some good.

The news of gangster bones has slipped away from the Tribune's front page to page three, to ten, to a blip in the neighborhood section. Finally, on the Sunday editorial page, the Tribune declares the whole thing a likely fraud, Old Sebastian a relic lost in his fantasies of Al Capone and the 1920s, and Dave Jones a name so utterly common it has to be phony. Thankfully, there's no comment about me, and the editorial proclaims that only the results of forensic testing will prove the truth of the identity of the bones. Monday morning, the story disappears from the Tribune entirely.

Old Sebastian calls. He complains to me, "But I gave them the wallet! I gave them the identification!"

I tell him, "Who knows what a relic lost in his fantasies of Al Capone and the 1920s is capable of forging." It's an angry thing to say, but I've become an angry person for the moment. Old Sebastian hangs up on me. The phone rings seconds later and I answer expecting an apology from Old Sebastian. It's Mrs. Grissly. She says, "The investigation of the bones at Dignity Place is done. Things have quieted down. You can have your little office back and continue teaching your classes." Her voice is that of someone with a gun to her head reading from a prepared script. She hangs up assuming I want to keep teaching my classes. For Iris's sake, I suppose, I do.

On Thursday, two weeks before Thanksgiving, I sit in my pool office for the first time since John Newberry took a hammer and chisel to my walls at the direction of Old Sebastian. The hole is covered by brown plastic taped over the edges of damaged cinder block. My desk and chair have been set right but they are covered in dust and bits of cement, as is the floor.

When I teach my watercize class, there's no spark in my voice and the Residents have to ask me to repeat my instructions. The water feels cold and chills me to the point where I'm aware of the shape of my own bones. Paul with the hair tufts on his shoulders comes up to me by the diving board, his face serious and square-jawed beneath his flower-laden swimming cap, declaring him the property of Dignity Place. "You seem distracted, Mrs. Connery."

Despite the water clinging to his body, the coils of hair on Paul's shoulders rise up like sprung springs. I want to touch them, grip them, pull them out. I imagine a satisfaction sensing the roots tearing from his pores. Paul backs away.

Between watercize and my first afternoon program, I sit in my pool office and feel the cinder block dust and rubble grinding between my bathing suit's wet fanny and the chair. I have no idea what I'm going to do for class. I can't take them for walks outside. I can't be too rough with them. I can't be too gentle. So when the time comes, I stand in my sweat pants and sweat shirt and Sebastian's whistle hanging from a rope around my neck, and I ask them what they want to do.

They line up as best as they can in the day room, twenty-one of them, fifteen women, six men, looking tipped and tottered like a line of telephone poles sinking in mud. They come dressed for their fitness program wearing I ♡ Dignity Place T-shirts tucked into polyester pants with elastic waistbands. I say a second time, "What do all of you want to do?"

For a second time nobody answers.

I stand there like a fool, waiting. They tip and totter some more, peek at each other, whisper things I can only imagine. I'm a fraud. I'm an ignorant, angry fraud.

A hand goes up on the left end. A woman with the face of elderly sweetness steps forward, smiling, her right hand vaulted into the air asking for permission from me to speak. She wears earrings the size of small chandeliers, and settled into a fold of skin circling her neck, a heavy necklace looks responsible for bending her spine down toward my waist. I nod at her and her hand waving at me in the air.

"My name is Vivian," she says. "Can we dance?"

"Dance? This is an exercise class."

"You took us for a walk last time. How's dancing any less exercise?"

I consider her words and, of course, I don't have anything to disagree with. Fact is, dancing is not something I'm in the mood for. I think of excuses not to dance. "We don't have enough men."

Vivian still presents the face of sweetness when she tells me, "For all my life there's been nothing a man could do for a woman that a woman couldn't do for herself."

"We have an uneven number of people."

"You make it even."

"We don't have music."

"Paul can sing. He has a lovely voice."

Paul, in his brown plaid pants and I ♡ Dignity Place T-shirt, looks shyly away from me. He asks, "What should I sing?"

Vivian says, "Something to a waltz."

"I don't know any waltzes to sing."

"Then count. One, two, three. One, two, three."

"Count? I suppose I can count out a waltz."

Vivian asks me, "You know how to waltz, don't you?"

I look upon their faces, fifteen women, six men. I ask them, "Does anybody not want to dance?" Their arms stay down. Nobody says a thing. "So. You all want to dance the waltz?" Twenty-one arms rise into the air.

In our years of marriage nearly to the day before Roby was born, Sebastian and I danced in the evenings. A spontaneous thing, really, Sebastian sidling up to me with his eyes dilated and his lips swelled around a grin. He'd wrap an arm behind my waist and take my hand in his, and slowly he'd move me across our living room floor just to do it. A waltz, always a waltz, a low hum from his chest our only music. He would remind me how the waltz was at first considered scandalous and was quickly banned by churches and governments alike, and for good reason. There's something about the repeated one-two-threes of a man and a woman locked in each other's arms and embrace, the motion of two bodies as one, sharing the air between their lips. "A waltz is so natural to human rhythm and touch, like a prelude to making love," he would whisper in my ear. And I would whisper back, "It is making love." Then he would slip his right hand down to cup at my fanny, still counting, and the two of us moving together. One two three.

After Roby's birth, evenings meant passing out when the baby finally fell asleep and the dances were something gone from our lives. Standing before my class of Residents wearing I ♡ Dignity Place T-shirts tucked into polyester pants with elastic waist bands, I've lost myself in these old thoughts and memories of Sebastian's touch over my body, leading me across the living room floor.

"Mrs. Connery?" I blink and see Vivian's hand still extended in the air. "Are you all right?"

I smile at her head and neck extending horizontally from her chest. "I can dance," I tell her. I begin to demonstrate, stepping my left foot to the left, my right to meet it, the left in place, the right back to the right, and repeat. "This is the basic waltz step."

The teetering, tottering line begins to move with me. At first disjointed, they soon form a coordinated motion as if proving the human nature of the waltz, as with making love, is never completely forgotten. I tell them to pair up. Let one person lead.

The six men are swept up immediately and the remaining women turn to each other to join in our little dance. Vivian, the excluded odd number out, walks toward me with her arms and head stretched out. I take her hand, put my arm on the hump of her back, and we begin etching over our small spot on the floor.

Paul sings, "One two three, one two three." He does have a marvelous basso voice. The others whisper beneath him, "One two three . . ." and Paul turns from his partner to wink at me. Instead of numbers, he sings these words:

> *My bonnie young teacher*
> *She waltzes with me*
> *The grandest fair maiden is she*
>
> *She teaches this young man*
> *Held close to her breast*
> *Things finer than one two and three.*

With Vivian, it's like I'm dancing with a Butterball Turkey held in my arms. Why this makes me long for Sebastian and our evening dances, I'll never understand.

30

To my way of thinking, if there's one thing worse than eating an egg salad sandwich, it's watching someone else eat an egg salad sandwich.

It's the rotting sewer smell even a fresh-cooked egg gives off, sharpened by mayonnaise, and the sight of the yellow and white goo and bread gathered on a tongue and gnashed between teeth. Horrible. What man in history invented that sandwich anyway? Considering the insane formula, it had to be a man. Hopefully there was no trial. He was taken directly from his kitchen and shot.

Mrs. Grissly has two egg salad sandwiches on the desk in her office, smelling like egg salad, looking gooey like egg salad. I decline her offer of one of her sandwiches and she talks even as she chews.

"I heard you taught dance lessons in your fitness program today."

My empty stomach feels the urge to gag out the egg salad sandwich bite she's swallowed. I press my hand over my mouth and feel my lips curl. She looks at me as though she knows I could vomit at any moment but won't let it happen in front of her. So I suffer with the illness of it all, and it seems to make her happy. She pauses to smile at me, the spaces between her teeth mortared in egg salad goo, and takes another bite.

There's a paper beneath glass, framed in dark wood hung on the wall behind her. From my seat at the beach of her mighty desk, it looks like a hat over her head. It's the state certification of Dignity Place. Renewal comes due in two more months. I don't recall seeing it there when the Grisslys first interviewed me. Beneath the expiring certificate, Mrs. Grissly asks me, "Why dance lessons in a fitness class?"

"They told me it's what they wanted to do."

"Who did?"

"The Residents."

"Oh?" Mrs. Grissly wipes her mouth with a napkin. A bit of yellow goo on her lower lip remains and it shakes at me while she talks. "But why did you agree?"

"Mrs. Grissly," I begin, dropping my hands to my lap, but I stop at the noise I make. It's the sound of a mouse squeaking at a lion. Gazing at the egg salad on her lip, I hold my breath and raise my stare directly against hers. I narrow my eyes. She blinks. I tell her, "You don't care for me much."

She sets her sandwich down on a napkin unfolded over her desk and she fans her hands over the napkin's ends as if ironing out wrinkles. "You misunderstand me, Mrs. Connery."

"I don't think so. You hired me because nobody else would take the job. Everyone else you hired quit soon enough." I wait for her reaction, but all I get is her woodenness, her usual ability to appear inanimate. "You know I'm not qualified."

Her eyes nearly closed, she says, "Of course I know."

"Why'd you hire me?"

"The truth?" she asks. I nod. "Sebastian Sr., Old Sebastian as you say, asked us to." She studies my reaction, my hanging jaw and spread eyelids and the small thud of my back against the chair. "There's the honest truth for you."

"Does this have anything to do with Little Nicky Number One?"

She goes back to her sandwich and finishes it off, then picks up the other one and takes a heaping bite. Leaning back in her chair, her head appears as if it were a vertical rectangle blown out at the bottoms by egg salad sandwiches stuffed inside her cheeks. She chews with her mouth closed. I tell her, "We danced today because it's low impact. It's done indoors." I look to the ceiling, and then back at her. "The truth is I did it because I wanted to."

I watch her chew and swallow and chew some more remnants, working her mouth and tongue, finishing with a suction of air through the spaces between her teeth. "Mrs. Connery," she says. Her elbows now on her desk, hands folded, and her chin upon her fingers. She claims she likes me. What's more, she admires my family. The bit of egg salad still shakes on her lower lip.

"I don't believe you."

"That's all right. Nobody believes me when I tell them I like them."

"Not even Mr. Grissly?"

She grins over her knuckles. "I'm grateful for the one exception."

"You want to fire me."

"No."

"You did the other day."

"I was a bit upset about the dead man in your pool office wall. I've gotten over it."

"You won't fire me now because of Little Nicky Number One because Old Sebastian found his grandfather's bones."

"I don't know who or what you're talking about."

"Of course you do."

"Even so, I'm denying it."

"But you know."

"Mrs. Connery," she says. "Julia." She settles back in her chair, her arms folded over her chest. She's flush, her eyes reflecting light, looking nearly alive. "I just wanted to talk with you about the dancing."

"You don't seem to like me."

"Because of the way my face is. It's stuck in a frown. But I like you."

"That's a laugh."

"Go to your pool office and see."

"See what?"

She looks at her watch. "Just go to your pool office. Give it twenty more minutes once you get there."

"I'll go only because I left my purse there."

I stand in my sweat clothes, and they are full of sweat from doing battle with the incredible Mrs. Grissly, who claims she likes me even though her head looks at me like the bottom face of a totem pole. At her office door I tell her there will be more waltzing in my fitness classes as long as I'm in the mood for it. As long as I decide to stay on, and if I decide to stay on.

She tells me, "That's why I called you into my office. Keep up the good work."

My office remains littered with piles of cement crumbs. I suppose I leave it this way because I don't expect to be the Dignity Place fitness instructor much longer. I expect I'll quit like all the others. I brush the cement bits and dust off my chair with my hands and sit. My purse glows black over the little boulders of rock on the desk. I'm ready to go, but I sit some more, waiting out Mrs. Grissly's twenty minutes for her proof that she likes me. Nothing yet. Whatever it is, if it comes, I'm sure I'll still quit.

There's splashing going on and I open the window blinds and see Residents jumping into the pool. I look at my watch. It's nearly four-fifteen and less than five minutes away from Mrs. Grissly's deadline. Roby must be home, locked in his room, happy to study so he can escape to an out-of-state college, happier still to have abandoned his plans to surprise his father.

Vivian waves at me; I can tell it's her from the curve of her spine and her smile. She still wears her heavy necklace, but now I notice the Cross and the Lord Jesus Christ in gold hanging well below her fallen bosom. Paul waves at me too as he floats in the water, the coils on his shoulders submerged. There's another by the diving board I know as Marie, and also the men who ran for a kickboard when I had asked for it during my first watercize class, George and Aaron. Some I still don't know. But I realize, despite the disguising swim caps atop their heads, each with pastel plastic flowers declaring its wearer the property of Dignity Place, I'm recognizing shapes and habits and the names that go with them.

There's a rustling behind me and I turn to see the plastic over the gaping hole expand at once into the room, then flag. It's as though the building took a breath. The plastic does this once more, rustling and crinkling, expanding, fading back to limp.

A vibration starts beneath me; it's hidden when the plastic again expands with its own noises. But soon the vibration turns into sound. It becomes something I recognize and pricks at my skin. One note, then two. Full and emotional, an intentional change of one rich timbre to the next. With this music, the plastic stays inflated, arched into the room like the tattered mainsail of an ancient and battle-weary warship still able to catch the breeze.

Beneath the bagpipe calls of Scotland, from the Highlands to the Lowlands to the Mull of Kintyre, John Newberry's voice rises to my office—*You've got it! Roby, you've got it! By God, we'll get this thing done for Thanksgiving yet!*

I look at my watch. Mrs. Grissly has proven she likes me with one minute to spare.

31

On the drive home I roll through four stop signs and make a left turn on red. I squeal the tires on my street and bounce over the curb to my driveway. There's no time for pulling into the garage and, as I rush into the house, I realize I may have left the car keys in the ignition.

Sebastian's at the dining room table sorting out books and I slow down. I blurt out, "Bathroom," and rush up the stairs.

At the top step, I find that Roby has taped a new piece of paper to his door, another sign written in drippy red ink:

Whipped Peasant At Work. His Shackles Cut The Flesh.

I inch to his room, hear only my breathing. There's silence on the other side of Roby's door and I wonder why there's no bloodshed, why Sebastian's so calm downstairs. Suddenly there's laughter inside the room and Brian Unkers' voice: "I hate trigonometry." And Roby's: "We have to get ready for the quiz on chapter seven." They talk about sines and cosines and tangents, then pages turn in a book, and one of them sharpens a pencil.

Perhaps Roby practiced the bagpipe at Dignity Place, put it away, jumped in Brian Unkers's wreck of a car and blew through more stop signs and red lights than I did just to come home before for his father's return from the junior college, and leapt into his room for his studies. I press my palm on the door handle and consider other possibilities. Then I consider turning the knob. I should rush in with an offer of lemonade or chips, or to ask if they're all right or in need of anything. It would be innocent enough. But I suppose Roby locked the door so I really couldn't rush in at all unless I first poked a pen in the center of the knob, and that wouldn't look innocent at all.

From where I'm standing, I could call in and ask how they're doing.

But I don't.

I find instead my hands held up and my fingers splayed out and I tell my brain to stop. Stop investigating things, is what Roby asked of me. Through the door I hear him, "We're supposed to figure the arc-type co-angle of the Talmudic hypotenuse."

I think to myself there's no such thing, and then I hear Brian Unkers's and my son's noses snort out laughter.

The climb down the stairs takes me some time, each step slowed by my thoughts jumping from one fact to the next. I heard the tartan bagpipe at Dignity Place. I heard it plain as day, and John Newberry's voice congratulating Roby on his progress. And the mention of getting things done by Thanksgiving. Now so soon at home I hear Roby's and Brian's voices on the other side of Roby's bedroom door. The boys laugh, likely at the sound of my feet creaking down the stairs. They let a spy know they know about the spy. I find myself at the front window without remembering how I got here. All I know is that I don't recall seeing Brian's car on the street when I pulled in and I don't see it now.

There's a cough behind me. Sebastian at my shoulder, his eyes blinking quickly. "Are you all right, Lassie?"

"I am."

"You seem preoccupied."

"I had to hurry to the bathroom."

Sebastian coughs again. "That's what you said when you ran

by. But I didn't . . ." He stops and his throat struggles as if it's suddenly impossible for him to talk.

"What? Tell me."

"Nothing."

"The boys are upstairs studying?"

"They are," Sebastian says.

"Did you see them?"

"No. They were in Roby's room when I got home. Trigonometry. You know I don't understand it. Something about a Talmudic hypotenuse."

"I see."

Another cough. Sebastian looks at me embarrassed to say what he's about to say. "I didn't hear a flush."

"What?"

"You know the pipes in this old house make terrible noises. You said you were in a hurry to use the bathroom. You came down but I didn't hear a flush."

"Oh."

"I didn't hear the sink either. I mean, I know you're good about washing your hands . . ."

"I am."

"I didn't hear it."

"It isn't what you think."

He looks at my hands. "Was it woman's problems again?"

"Sebastian," I begin with a rise in my voice, as though I'm about to say a whole lot more to him, that there's no such thing as a Talmudic hypotenuse and our son has split himself in two. His furry eyebrows lift in expectation. I grab his cheeks in my palms and pull his lips to mine. He relaxes against me. "Remember when we used to waltz in the evenings?"

"I do."

"We should dance again."

"You're keeping me from asking my questions."

"My hands are very clean."

He whispers in my ear, "Let's go upstairs. The boys are locked away in study."

I'm frumped up in my sweatpants and sweatshirt, and I carry the Dignity Place pool's smell of chlorine in my pores. My hair's so ragged I can see it shoot out from both sides of my head though I stare straight into Sebastian's face. I'm tired and haven't yet forgiven him for losing his mind over his son, or for making me lose mine over his occasional late returns home.

He doesn't offer to waltz me around the living room. "All right," I say.

As we turn at the top of the stairs, Sebastian hesitates with a glance at Roby's bedroom door. Brian says, "Take the remainder of the cosine and substitute it in for beta times alpha over the arc of the Talmudic hypotenuse." Roby answers, "Of course."

Sebastian squeezes my hand and smiles, and I don't have the heart to tell him what he doesn't know about trigonometry.

We're together and he loves me, and we fall asleep in the early evening in each other's arms. There's a soft knock on the door and I struggle to open my eyes, to look at the clock's red numbers on the nightstand. 7:53PM.

"I'll make my own dinner," Roby offers. "Don't get up." His feet patter lightly down the stairs.

Hairy Harry calls in the morning. Sebastian and Roby have already left for school.

"How'd you get my home number?"

"Is he or isn't he going to teach me?" Hairy Harry asks. "I need to learn how to read."

"He is. How'd you get my number?"

"I need to learn how to read real soon."

"By when?"

Mrs. Grissly's voice sounds distant through the phone. "Hairy

Harry, don't use the phone for personal calls!" He shouts back to her, "One more minute!" Then he says to me, "Thanksgiving."

"Really? Why by then?"

"I can't tell you. It's a secret."

"Seems rather soon to learn how to read."

"I've already told you, I'm absent-minded is all." He goes through the ABCs, even the song after Z, inviting me to sing along with him next time. "See?" he says. "I never bothered to learn to read because, like I said before, I'm absent-minded."

"Whoever said you were absent-minded?"

Hairy Harry breathes heavily into the phone. "I never went to school. I mean, I went to school for a while, and then I went to school at home. And my parents, they're absent-minded too."

"Your parents can't read?"

"It's just my father now, but he owns four new big black Cadillacs. He's owned four new big black Cadillacs as long as I can remember."

Mrs. Grissly grouses, "Hairy Harry! It's been over two minutes. Hang up!"

"I'll take you to meet Sebastian at his college," I say.

"When?"

"Today. Three o'clock. I'll pick you up at Dignity Place."

"But you don't work on Fridays."

Hairy Harry!

"I've got to go, Mrs. Connery. See you at three. Oh!—please don't say nothing to nobody about the four new big black Cadillacs. Dad hates it when I brag."

"How'd you get my home number?"

There's a bang through the earpiece and I hear voices, Hairy Harry's becoming softer with the sound of footsteps moving away and he calls out to Mrs. Grissly that he needs to get off of work by three because Mrs. Connery's taking him to college. I expect Mrs. Grissly to say something impolite and threaten to fire him if he leaves. But her faraway voice sounds composed: "That's great, Hairy Harry. Could you please get the telephone receiver out of the trash can?"

32

I arrive at Dignity Place before two-thirty. Mr. Grissly works at the front desk, writing on a ledger. Mrs. Grissly stands behind him, pointing things out, telling him he should have used a pencil first. While Mr. Grissly scratches something out, Mrs. Grissly raises her head and looks right at me walking across the lobby. Her lips stay level then creak into a bit of a smile that looks more like a rectangle sagging in the middle.

There's a familiarity here for me now, much more than when I came only to visit Old Sebastian. The bubbling from the ponds soothes me, and the towering lobby skylights with the ivy cascading down and the ferns stretching to the glass feel exotic and comfortable at the same time. The matt slate tiles in the lobby and the carpeting fluffing over the staircase far exceed what I have at home, and the brass banisters rising with the stairs to the second and third floors must have cost a bundle. It's open and inviting, rich and beautiful. Standing before the elevator door, waiting for it to slide open, I wonder whether Old Sebastian would want to leave this place even if he were able to cartwheel to my house.

Inside the elevator I look at the numbers and letters for the floors and wonder what the difference is between LL and B. I push both. Only LL lights up. The door doesn't close and I push LL again and again as if it might make a difference. The elevator starts to emit nagging bursts of buzzing, sounding like *uh-uh, uh-uh.* I say, "Uh-huh," and press LL three more times.

The door pokes out a bit, then a half foot. "I'm sure," I say. "Take me down." The buzzing stops and the elevator door lumbers across.

I've never taken this thing below the first floor before. It makes a groan beneath my feet as if complaining to somebody, and takes its sweet time. When it settles, the door stays shut and LL glows at me yet. There's no emergency phone in this thing and no emergency button. Above the button panel is a Certificate of Good Condition signed by Earl. Just "Earl." The paper is faded and worn and tells me Earl hasn't been here in two years.

Outside the door, I hear the noise of laundry being washed and someone whistling *If I Only Had a Brain*. I pound on the elevator door and call out for help, and when the door slips open, Hairy Harry stands on the other side, sweating at the pits of his white uniform. A row of front-loaders in wash cycle face me with bed sheets and pillowcases and soap suds tossed about behind glass. "You're early," he says, wiping his brow.

"Does this thing go down another floor?"

He stutters something close to a "yes," and catches his breath. "No."

"Why is there a B button below the LL button?" Hairy Harry leans into the elevator and looks at the inside like he's never seen it before. "Take me down to B."

"I can't," he says. "Please go back up."

"If you don't, I won't take you to the college for your reading lesson."

"Yeah you would. You're a nice lady."

I fold my arms. "Hairy Harry, take me to the very bottom basement of Dignity Place."

Even in the shadows of the laundry room, his face mottled by black hair, Hairy Harry manages to go pale. He steps into the elevator, removes a key from his shirt pocket, and inserts it in a hole beside the B button. Turning the key, Hairy Harry makes the B button light up. "If Mrs. Grissly finds out, I'm in deep trouble."

"I won't tell."

"They might."

"Who?"

"Please. Don't make me say."

The elevator door grinds closed and we thump a bit up, then begin our descent. The light inside flickers and there's a chattering sound like the ratchet of a crank. Hairy Harry shakes his head. "This could mess things up."

"I already know. Some of it anyway."

In flickering light, he says, "Oh," and shakes his head some more. "You really surprised me. It takes a key to get the LL button to work, too."

When the door slides across, blackness swims at me beyond the elevator. Hairy Harry turns the key and leaves it dangling in place. "It'll stay open for us. Don't worry about that."

He takes my hand and leads me forward, walking smoothly. It unnerves me the way we speed over a floor I cannot see through a vision of the abyss. The clicks of my heels echo back on themselves like gunfire. I think of gangster bones and more gangster bones and how they could pop out from anywhere right now and howl at me with their empty heads. Blackness eases a bit to dark gray and far off there's a vertical sliver of light. Its distance is something unfathomable, but Hairy Harry knows. He leads me on and the light turns into the shape of a door ajar. A voice off in the distance: "Now try it again."

John Newberry.

An amplified strum of a guitar fills the darkness and the chord lingers in my ears, then the whine of the tartan bagpipe starts and climbs to match its pitch. The bagpipe's belly holds the sound of all the deep-voiced angels in Heaven humming in harmony, and above it sing the pipes, soaring a single note aloft. I want to cry at the splendor of it all, at how this beauty is made by my own son.

The music falls and eases, and there's silence but for the music's echo, which I don't think will ever leave my ears. John Newberry, his voice behind the door, says, "Well done, Roby."

I pull at Hairy Harry's arm. "Let's go back."

"But why? I mean, you seemed so sure."

His face is nearly the ghost in this darkness. "I wanted to tell Roby something. I wanted to tell him that you, Hairy Harry, will be keeping his father busy after school from now until Thanksgiving. He can practice all he wants." We turn around and the elevator glows small in the distance, its flickering light suspended in the black. "You'll tell Roby for me, won't you, about his father and the practicing?"

Hairy Harry says, "There's no worrying to do, Mrs. Connery. Your son's already got it taken care of."

"How do you know?"

"It's what he told me."

"Do you know what he's up to?"

"Yeah. Well, no. I used to. I didn't understand most of it when he told me. I forgot the rest." Back inside the elevator, Hairy Harry works the key and the door begins to slide closed. He pushes the first floor button. As we rise, he says, "Like I was telling you, I'm absent-minded."

I take Hairy Harry's hand and pet the fur on his wrist. I tell him he's all right.

33

We pull into the parking lot at the junior college. Hairy Harry's got his head sticking out the window and he attracts the attention of strolling students along the walk. With dark hair popping out nearly everywhere on his head and his tongue hanging over his lower lip, he looks like a sheepdog enjoying the breeze.

"Hairy Harry," I say. "It's freezing."

"This is so cool."

What's cool to Hairy Harry became ordinary to me long ago. A bunch of one-story, brown-brick buildings sprawled out over acres of lawn with a forest preserve and pond beyond. The campus is attractive enough, I suppose, but nothing compared to the grounds and main building of Dignity Place. Hairy Harry draws his head inside the window. He tells me as I park, nearly giddy, "I smell books."

"Of course, Hairy Harry. It's a college."

"College," he says, pushing his head and tongue back out the window. "Wow."

I suppose the overcast skies and mist in the air give the place a serious look, and there's ivy still green clinging to the brick outside the entrance. When we leave the car, Hairy Harry seems to shrivel beside me the moment we walk through the main entrance. Moving along the hall toward Sebastian's office, he pats his white uniform, self-conscious of the students in jeans and sweaters glancing at him momentarily and smiling into their little groups of friends.

"They're staring at me, Mrs. Connery. I should've brung my coat."

"You're a working man, Hairy Harry. That's what your clothes mean. I'm the lady walking with the man in the white clothes. Perhaps they think you're escorting me to the school psychologist. Maybe they're all staring at me."

Hairy Harry smiles. "Yeah," he says. "That could be it. I'm the psycho-worker, and you're the crazy lady I brung." He darts from my side toward the hall window lining the library and presses himself to it like a moth against glass trying to get to a living room lamp. "Look at all of them, Mrs. Connery. All them books."

His lips and nose leave steam on the window, an uneven circle growing and fading with his breaths. He says, "E-X-I-T," and laughs. "I can spell things, Mrs. Connery. I can spell." He spells out the large red letters hanging over the emergency exit door across the library's main room and turns around to smile at me. He doesn't see the students at the library tables staring at him with looks that wish him to go away.

In the days when Roby first began to understand the meaning of letters, I recall the wonderment of it all. I don't know how or why it happens, only that it happens. Roby's first reading of a word, understanding what he's done, saying the word over and over to me as if he's teaching me what he knows. It was magic. My joy of the memory still lives in my motherly heart, and it makes me wonder what happened to Hairy Harry, who tells me again why he's unable to do more than read letters. He's absent-minded.

I ask him about his parents. After looking at his shoes for a time, shaking his head, he tells me.

Hairy Harry and I sit and pass the time in the waiting room in front of Sebastian's office. Cinder block walls like my pool office. Bigger space, freshly painted light yellow, and no claim of murder written anywhere. A door leads to the office Sebastian shares with three other professors, and the front area is for the secretary. The secretary's desk is empty. The clock against the wall behind the secretary's desk nears three-forty-five. Roby's at home by now, studying with Brian, and he's also at Dignity Place learning the bagpipe with John Newberry. I must have birthed twins and didn't realize.

Sebastian leans his head through the door. "Hiya, Lassie."

"I brought Hairy Harry with me."

"I see."

Hairy Harry waves his hand and spells out the secretary's name plate. "I can already spell, Mr. Connery." Hairy Harry smiles.

"Great." Sebastian walks slowly toward us, explaining things while his posture bends into an apology. "It's not a good time of year. Exams before the Thanksgiving break, and all that." He stands at Hairy Harry's feet. "You can understand, son, can't you?"

Hairy Harry looks down at his hands clasped on his lap.

I say, "Hairy Harry, tell my husband who your parents are."

Hairy Harry shakes his head.

"Do it, Hairy Harry. It'll be our secret with Sebastian, I promise."

Sebastian looks at me like I'm wasting his time.

"All right," Hairy Harry says, still looking down. He draws his lower lip in as if gathering up his childhood memories, and gasps at them. "My real mother's dead. My real father's dead. Nobody came to get me. Not nobody." Hairy Harry wipes at his eyes and sniffs. Sebastian slumps his shoulders, looks softly at the space between me and Hairy Harry. "I was two then, and it's what I was told. I don't know for sure myself, but everyone's said so. I stayed at foster homes for six years, four of them, then he came and got me. He said I was the runt, the underdog, and he likes underdogs because he was an underdog once too. So he took me."

"Who?" I say. "Tell my husband who you're talking about."

"My new dad never went to school, so he said I didn't have to go, and he owns four new big black Cadillacs. He's always owned four new big black Cadillacs since I've known him. And he didn't need school for them neither."

"Hairy Harry. Tell my husband who he is. His name."

Hairy Harry begs, "Promise you won't tell no one?" He raises his stare to Sebastian and sees him nod. "Mr. Nicholas Garva. He's got four new big black Cadillacs. He always has as far back as I can remember."

"Go on," I say. "Tell him."

"People don't call him Mr. Nicholas Garva, but that's his name. I call him Dad 'cause that's who he is to me, as much as any other dad could ever be. He's always been good to me, and to Dignity Place." Hairy Harry says this with pride and finishes his story. "People call him Little Nicky. Little Nicky Number One."

Sebastian's face and body have been taken over by ice. He doesn't move, not even his lips when he asks Hairy Harry, "You mean there's really a Little Nicky?"

"Uh-huh. Number One. My Dad. He owns four new big black Cadillacs. He always has. I'm hoping he'll give one to me some day, but he says I have to learn to read things first."

"Check on Roby," Sebastian tells me. "Make sure he's home with his studies."

"I need to read by Thanksgiving, Mr. Connery," Hairy Harry says. "I already know the alphabet. I'm just absent-minded is all."

Sebastian finally blinks and says, "We'll start right now."

271

★ ★ ★ ★ ★

At home, the note on Roby's closed bedroom door now reads in drippy red letters:

Lincoln Freed The Slaves. Would Someone Please Tell My Father?

On the other side, the boys discuss trigonometry. The Talmudic hypotenuse and all that. And they snort their laughter. This time, I already have a pen in my hand and I don't hesitate to use it. It's in the doorknob hole and the door unlocks. Inside, they're still snorting laughter out their noses, and I look around and see what they've been up to. With what I find, I can't help but snort out my nose too.

34

Saturday morning, Old Sebastian calls and tells me to turn to the news on the radio. He's having a happy fit from what I can tell by the laughing and hooting through the phone.

"Which station?"

"Doesn't matter. They're all talking about it."

So I flick on the radio in the kitchen, to an AM news station, where I learn right away that the Bears are ten point underdogs and still can't decide which quarterback to use for tomorrow's game. The highways are clear and the weatherman expects rain and a high of forty. Then a reporter says her name is Lise Dominique and tells all of Chicago and everyone in seven Midwestern states that the news of the moment is this:

Preliminary testing of the full skeletal and dental remains of a man in a double breasted suit, fedora hat and spats found inside the walls of a Highland Park, Illinois, retirement home indicates they are of a man named Nicholas Garva, a member of Al Capone's rum-running crew. He had disappeared without a trace in 1927.

Then the radio switches to an interview and the man speaks as though he's gargling rocks.

"I'm grateful to hear my granddad's been found at last. Grateful to Dignity Place, but most of all I'm grateful to Sebastian Connery Sr. and his entire family. Now I can give Granddad the proper Christian burial he deserves."

The reporter asks, "Proper Christian burial? Mr. Garva, are

you aware of your grandfather's dealings with Al Capone and why he may have met the fate he did?"

There's a shuffling and some puffing and I can almost see through the radio speaker how Little Nicky Number One grabs the reporter by the throat when he answers, "Granddad was a business man, a beloved father. That's all there is to it, understand?" Then an Empire Carpets commercial cuts in.

I've been holding the telephone by my side and Old Sebastian's happy fit comes through louder and bounces around my kitchen. I place the receiver to my ear. "Did you know Hairy Harry was Little Nicky Number One's son?"

"Yup," Old Sebastian says. "Adopted."

"Do you know Hairy Harry's expecting Sebastian to teach him to read by Thanksgiving?"

"So I've been told."

"Do you know what's going on with Roby and John Newberry in the basement of Dignity Place?"

"I do."

"Old Sebastian?"

"What?"

"Tell me what's going on for Thanksgiving."

"You'll get your invitation," he says abruptly, and hangs up.

Behind me, Sebastian's gasping for air. After nine-fifteen in the morning, he's standing at the threshold to our kitchen, still dressed in the pajamas he fell asleep in, although I'm not sure he ever really fell asleep last night. He rubs at his face and scratches at his hair. I ask him what I already know. "Did you hear the radio?"

"What am I going to do?" he sighs. "Hairy Harry, he's a nice enough young man and it's a sad story, but I'm telling you, that boy, well, I don't know how else to put it but the truth. That boy's duller than dull, and he wants to read something to his father who happens to be a gangster, and he wants to do it for

Thanksgiving and he won't be able to learn, not by then, and did I tell you his father's really a gangster? A gangster, Julia! I'm going to fail teaching Hairy Harry how to read by Thanksgiving and his gangster dad is going to know I failed and then you're going to be a widow."

Sebastian turns around, stumbles into the hall and mumbles things about cement shoes and sleeping with the fishes and a rat-a-tat this and a rat-a-tat that, and he sounds as though he's Old Sebastian watching one of his gangster movies rather than my husband whining up the staircase. Maybe I should console Sebastian or worry by his side. But there's an odd comfort for me in all of his imagined troubles. That Roby could sit with me in the kitchen earlier this morning, eat the eggs and toast I made for him and kiss me on the cheek and tell me as loud as he pleases that he's going to Dignity Place with Bean Dip, knowing his father could be nearby to overhear, and how none of it seems to matter right now. Sebastian's too distracted. Because of gangster bones, I think this family can make it now all the way to Thanksgiving.

Lise Dominique is back on the radio to give me another bit of news. "This morning, federal agents seized the bank accounts and other assets of two radio talk show hosts suspected of embezzling client funds. Harvey Jarcoveny and Brenner Nicholman are best known for their controversial and long-running radio show, *God Investment*. Their station manager said he stands behind his men and their program. Their lawyer had no comment."

Sebastian and Roby say they're too busy for church this Sunday morning. Roby's off to Dignity Place by eight for, "Well, you know," he whispers. As Brian Unkers's wreck pulls to our curb, I tell Roby I don't really know anything for sure. "Oh, then," he says, and he's gone.

Sebastian's ready to go to his college by eight-thirty to meet with Hairy Harry for an emergency reading lesson. He's rumpled about the face, shaven in spots while overlooked stubble pokes up in other spots and there's shaving foam behind his ears. Although his pants and shirt look all right, the blue sock on his left foot stands out next to the black one on his right. Before Sebastian closes his briefcase, I see the collection of Dr. Seuss books inside it, the covers and pages torn and tattered and drooled upon during Roby's long-ago days. I kiss Sebastian's lips before he's on his way, telling him, "You remembered where I stored Roby's books."

"Of course," he says, holding the briefcase by the handle in one hand, the satchel with the Urns of Connery inside in the other. "He's my son."

"But the Urns of Connery?"

Sebastian looks puzzled at me as if I should know why he takes them to meet Hairy Harry. "Inspiration," he says. "I may be ashes in an urn myself soon enough."

He sets the satchel and the briefcase down and kisses me as though he were a soldier off to meet an uncertain fate in battle, and I have to say it's a damn fantastic, lip-sucking kiss that makes me glad, for the moment anyway, of gangster bones, Hairy Harry, and how Sebastian overreacts to just about everything.

I suppose the priest at St. Rita of the Holy Annunciation will be glad I'm in attendance for Sunday mass without Sebastian and Roby. He wouldn't admit it, of course. Not out loud. But I know I'll see the relief in his eyes when he hands the Communion wafer to me and I tell him *Amen* and he sees there's no family with me and he says *Amen* to that.

Still, I feel lonely sitting in my car at the edge of the drive, dressed in my best blouse, skirt and heels. I turn to look at Iris Newberry's house, the drapes open but the lights off and the front window looking dark within the porch, like a clean slate blackboard waiting for words to be written upon it. The House For Sale sign lies nearly bent to the lawn, flopping around in the wind with dead leaves collecting and piling up where it sticks into the ground. Through the raindrops landing on the car windows and in the morning's dull and damp, Iris's house appears so lonely, as if lost in thought; like Iris herself, I suppose.

I find myself dashing to Iris's porch, my clothes windblown and my hair threatening to collapse under the raindrops sticking to it. Knocking at the front door, I'm thinking perhaps she'd like to go to church with me. I'll pretend church is my reason, but I know it's my curiosity again, and it grows and grows waiting for her to answer my knocks. When she arrives, it's only to inch the door open a bit and poke her face through. I should be used to the new look about her, but with her head leaning forward at me, like a figure jutting forth on the prow of an ancient sailing ship, I cannot get over her transformation from vampire bat to loveliness.

"Julia," she says in a whisper. I smell the coffee on her breath. But there's also perfume, like lilacs, and mascara around her eyes and gloss on her lips and rouge on her cheeks.

"Good morning, Iris. I'm thinking perhaps you'd like to join me for church."

She blinks at me and her eyeballs flutter in their sockets to one side. It's the telltale effort of someone trying to come up with an answer to get out of something without hurting anybody's feelings. She sighs and looks straight at me, and I'm guessing she's about to give me the truth. "I can't," she says. A man within the house calls out, "Iris, who's there?"

"I have company," she says to me, and she's blushing. Iris Newberry is blushing.

I blurt out, "A man?" which is stupid enough of me to ask

considering this voice sounds foghorn deep.

"Yes. A man." And now she smiles so girlish along with her blushing.

"A relative?"

"No. He's handsome and two years younger than me."

"Oh, but Iris, what about John? You said you were ready."

"Of course I'm ready." She jerks her chin up and stares at me in nearly an angry way that shuts me up. She says, "This gentleman's only company, Julia. For now. But I can't wait forever."

I debate if I should say it, and I know I shouldn't but consider the consequences if I don't, so I go ahead and blurt it out. "John told me about the glass. The bed and breakfast glass."

She says nothing at first. Her stare drifts off over my head, and a smile comes to her so pained and loving at the same time. "John told you about the glass?"

"He did."

"That was sweet of him to think of it."

"Do I know the gentleman inside?"

Iris says, "Yes," and closes the door.

In the aftershock of hearing another man's voice inside Iris's home, I sense Lola Two has leapt from my brain and stands behind me, dressed in something vivacious and disgustingly sexy while the rain passes through her without a touch. She's probably got her arms folded tight under her bosom so her fake cleavage rises to meet her chin, and her red, collagen-injected lips set to flip-flap at me as huge as throw pillows. When I turn around, Lola Two is just as I imagine her. She wears a gold mini-skirt squeezed over her hips and a pink halter, and those lips of hers do go flip-flap at me over the valley of her bosom.

He's probably the mailman or the neighbor's husband from across the street. You know the guy. Yes, you think it's the neighbor's husband. You recognize his voice. He's another one who promised his bride 'til death do us part.

I storm past her and her taunting trails behind me.

You know who I mean. Across the street and four houses to the north. Wally Lisherman, father of two, grandfather of one, who married the widow Liz, who tricked him into marrying her three years ago with her collection of Wonderbras. And all he ever thinks about day after day is how he was fooled and wonders what happens to his wife when the Wonderbra comes off.

"Iris had a mastectomy!"

Poor Iris. It will be a cruel moment all right if things go that far, and they probably will.

"You don't know."

Iris said he was handsome.

I stand by my car, let raindrops gather on my hair and skin and clothes, and the wet begins to seep in. "Go away," I say, and I fumble my car key at the door lock.

You left it open.

I know she's snarling behind me in all her plastic allure, sneering her bleach-whitened teeth through her red throw pillow lips. Her words crawl up my spine and make my shoulders hunch. *Every marriage fails in some important way. The Newberrys will fail. Then you will know for sure that for you and Sebastian, it's only a matter of time.*

I plunge myself into my car and drive away. The rain soaked over me oozes through my dress and puddles in the car seat, and I can only imagine what I look like now because I won't look in the rearview mirror. Lola Two's in the back seat, tapping her feet against my backrest.

While you're driving to church, why don't you ask yourself how many self-proclaimed religious leaders have cheated on their wives?

"It's a Catholic church."

Okay. Priests don't count for now. But as soon as the Vatican gets rid of its vow-of-chastity thing, then you'll see. The percentages will be just like the rest of them.

St. Rita of the Holy Annunciation looms before me, its spire aloft, crossed at the peak. A line of cars draws toward it and a policeman in an orange raincoat and hat guides the traffic through, motioning with his flashlight. He points cars to the left, to the nearest parking spots. With me, it's the same, but I turn right and find a spot in the back of the lot, alone. The cars fill up row after row and it feels as though I'm watching a movie through my windshield about an attacking horde and the rows of cars are columns of the enemy and they draw nearer and nearer to me.

Lola Two leans forward and dangles her arms over the front seat. She sees a group of five men in trench coats, standing beneath black umbrellas, talking before they head in, and she kisses at them. *Did you know the average man thinks about sex every twenty-five seconds? You read it in Cosmo a while ago, so it's got to be true. There's no exception to the rule, not even while they're in church.*

Long after mass begins and Lola Two is thankfully gone, I'm still in my car in the back of the church parking lot, sitting in the puddle of the driver's seat. I press my palms together and pray.

35

This time, under these circumstances, I should not have any doubt where Sebastian is and who he is with. I call Sebastian's school office anyway and exhale when he answers the phone.

"You've been at it for hours now. How's it going?"

"Pretty good," Sebastian says loudly at first. Then he excuses himself to Hairy Harry and whispers back to me, "Horrible. Just awful."

"Has he learned to read a thing?"

"Titles."

"It's a start."

"Short titles. *Hop On Pop. Horton Hatches the Egg.* Some Grimm's fairy tale books. I can't tell if he's truly reading the titles or memorizing their pictures and saying what I expect to hear."

"Sebastian," I say. "Wait."

"What?"

I don't answer him, but listen to the silence through the phone. Hairy Harry says, *"The Cat In The Hat."* Then another, *"The Cat In The Hat Comes Back."* And he says, "See, Mr. Connery? I can read the longer titles now, too."

It's good to hear Hairy Harry's voice for myself. It's a relief that calms my silly nerves and keeps Lola Two at bay. "When will you be home?"

"About seven or eight, maybe a little later. I don't know. We're ordering in Chinese food. Hold on, he's turning the page."

Hairy Harry's voice again, distant, monotone, and stilted. "Puh-bished in 1966, by Ran, Ran, Ran-dom Hoses."

"Hairy Harry!" Sebastian says like he's discovered gold, and he hangs up the phone.

There's a cough behind me and I spin about ready to shout at Lola Two, but it's Roby and Brian at my bedroom door. Roby raises his hands in defense, as if I were about to give him a kiss in front of his friend. "I'm home," he says. "Just wanted to let you know." He looks around the room and asks, "Dad here?"

"He's with Hairy Harry at the college."

Brian's shoulders look hitched to a nail and the rest of him hangs down. I ask him, "How are your parents doing?"

"Fine."

"Fine?"

Brian shrugs. "Okay, I guess."

They're arguing all the time, and loud loud loud, Lola Two whispers in my ear. *Divorce is only a matter of time.*

I approach these boys, dressed ragged in their bags of clothes, and I kiss my son on the cheek. Brian looks sadly at his feet and I turn to kiss his cheek, mouth-pimples and all.

"Mom," Roby says, groaning.

Brian tells Roby it's all right.

"Make your parents breakfast early tomorrow morning. A good, big breakfast." Brian looks at me, confused, like I know something I couldn't possibly know. Lola Two is still at my ear, laughing. *It won't make a bit of difference.* "Make them huge omelettes tomorrow morning," I say, "and report back to me how it goes."

"Sure," Brian says. Although his mouth refuses to smile, I can see something like a smile form in his eyes.

We have a funeral to go to this Tuesday; it says so on our

telephone answering machine in our bedroom. I play the message for Sebastian. Home after eight from his work with Hairy Harry, Sebastian collapses into his clothes as he listens. He says nearly in shock, "How'd he get our home number?"

"We're listed."

Sebastian licks at his lips. "Oh. Right."

He rewinds the machine a bit and plays the message somewhere from the middle:

". . . and Mr. and Mrs. Connery, it would mean a great deal to me if you could attend. Tuesday morning at ten sharp, St. Peters Cemetery on Coron Road. You must know the place. Bring your son. Sons are important to me."

The caller didn't leave his number or his name, but the rocks rumbling in his voice made matters clear. Little Nicky Number One expects the attendance of Julia, Sebastian and Roby Connery at the proper Christian burial of the gangster bones, now known as Nicholas Garva the First.

"We're going," Sebastian says. "We all have to go." He gets into bed fully dressed, unwashed, and turns out the light.

"Sebastian," I say, and I undress for him the way he likes, nice and slow at his bedside, and I kiss him full on the lips.

He says, "I can't, Lassie. Not tonight." He touches my hair and tells me I'm beautiful from head to toe, but still, not tonight. Instead, we lie in bed together with a foot of space between us. Sometime in the dark, I manage to fall asleep.

36

Tuesday morning brings clear skies and warmth. Ten days before Thanksgiving, it's like summer again, and the sun shimmers above the east horizon so bright and strong I expect songbirds to fill the trees.

I drive my sedan with Sebastian to my right, Roby in back, both excused from school and dressed in dark suits. Roby leans his head out his window and makes his observation about the summer weather in mid-November. "Nature has no choice but to obey. Today is Little Nicky Number One's grandfather's funeral."

Sebastian groans about forgetting to bring the Urns of Connery with him.

"It was a beautiful service at the church," I say. "And you both behaved yourselves."

"It was strange," Roby says. "I've never seen so many sunglasses worn at a church service before."

In truth, the church wake could have been anybody's church wake. I don't mean the casket up front, which looked made of gold, nor do I mean the forest of red roses engulfing it, nor the priest appearing shell-shocked as if afraid to say the wrong thing in front of all those men looking so square-jawed and serious beneath their dark suits and sunglasses. And Nicholas Garva the First, deceased sometime in 1927, his church wake in the twenty-first century, done with an open casket.

Mourners wept over the skeleton in its fedora hat as if death happened yesterday, and somehow its brown double-breasted suit looked dry cleaned. No, none of it seemed particularly normal.

The priest, though, stayed strictly to the traditional, adding nothing else to the service beyond his repeated calls to render the chants of Our Father and Hail Mary and Amen, and a sermon sticking to, without details, how the deceased was a good man. He was a good husband. He was a good father and provider. He was a good friend. All those basic things we hear at the funeral of a nasty person with a nasty history, who gets improved only in death by the strength of generalities. The priest finished in less than half-an-hour, sweat pouring from his brow. He said nothing about the fact that Nicholas Garva the First died breathing his last with the smell of chlorine in his lungs from a pool Al Capone owned at the time, or how he was cinder-blocked into darkness because of something even the likes of Al Capone didn't approve of.

Roby says in the car, "Who do you think was Little Nicky Number One?"

"I couldn't tell," I say. "All the men dressed the same."

"He probably wasn't going to show himself so the cops couldn't shoot him. I'm sure there were undercover cops there ready to shoot him on sight."

Leaning over the front seat, Roby stares through the windshield. Ahead of us drives the white van with the words *Property of Dignity Place* printed on its back, carrying Old Sebastian, John Newberry, Hairy Harry, and the Grisslys in the procession. As Sheridan Road curves, so too does the ride to the cemetery, and the cars ahead stretch far into the distance, the hearse and lead cars long out of our sight. The line must stretch just as far behind us.

"This gangster bones guy would be at least a hundred and twenty years old today," Roby says. "And there must be hundreds of cars going to his funeral. I bet none of us would get a fraction of that even if we died tomorrow."

I think to say, *Your father might, he's a teacher,* but I keep my mouth shut. Sebastian's groaning again, this time about how Hairy Harry's reading regressed on Monday compared to his sudden progress on Sunday, and he can't believe how his fate is in the hands of an especially dull boy, even if Hairy Harry's a nice dull boy. So I concentrate on following the cars to the cemetery, the Dignity Place van and all those hundreds of new big black Cadillacs. Inside one of them sits Little Nicky Number One.

I've never been to a golf tournament, but I've seen them on TV. Sebastian likes to watch them sometimes on Sunday afternoons because he says it's one of the few sports where spectators dress up reasonably well and stay respectful throughout. And, of course, he reminds me how golf came from Scotland. If you can imagine dark suits and sunglasses on all the spectators, including, so it seems, most of the women and children, the funeral of Nicholas Garva the First looks just like a golf tournament, the hush and the silence and the packed distance of the crowd waiting for the final putt on the eighteenth hole that will decide who wins a million dollars.

By the time we arrive, park and head toward the grave site, the crowd has already thickened with mourners. We make our way around to a distant edge where it's only six rows deep, and Sebastian, Roby and I peek around heads and shoulders to catch glimpses of the burial.

The golden casket lies upon the straps of the device that will soon lower Nicholas Garva the First into the Earth, and the priest stands at the head, chanting, "Ashes to ashes, dust to dust." Rows of chairs extend from the foot of the casket with the most frail and the closest relatives filling them up. In front of them all, though, sits a man in a dark suit and sunglasses. Old Sebastian in his motorized wheelchair. His love and obsession for all things gangster have been more than satisfied by his role in the discovery of the gangster bones, having made all of this possible, earning him his placement before an entire gangster clan. Even from this distance, I can see the curl of his lip, the posture of his head, the working of his chin. Much more than my wedding day with his son, this is one of the happiest moments of Old Sebastian's life.

The Grisslys stand behind Old Sebastian's wheelchair, their dour faces and dark suits making them into the stubby remains of twin trees shorn of leaves and branches. And John Newberry tries to hide behind them, as if it were possible in his overalls and string tie in a crowd of gray and black Armani double-breasted suits.

I can tell by his eyes flying around in their sockets that Sebastian has a thousand questions. He doesn't dare speak them now, not among a thousand guests standing among thousands of headstones, where a whisper would carry as far as a siren. When the casket lowers, heads bow, and I look to my shoes and listen to the creaks and cranks of Nicholas Garva the First's final descent. Somewhere and far away, a cry comes out: "No reporters! No photographers!" and the sounds of a scuffle and what could easily be the smashing of an expensive camera and someone being dragged away. I wait for the gunshot. Perhaps a silencer keeps me from hearing it.

A hand grips at my shoulder and I turn to Sebastian; his pupils appear lost swimming in the whites of his eyes. He jerks his head for me to look forward and mouths, "Chrissake!"

Between the rows of heads and shoulders, I make out Hairy Harry in his dark suit and sunglasses. Already he needs another shave and the thick of his black hair presses down on his face with the weight of cement. He reaches the hole in the ground, looks down for a moment at his—at his what?—at his great-grandfather by adoption, dead in 1927, and crosses himself. Then he turns to the crowd and smiles. He calls out, "I've been asked to read something."

Only by the strength of Roby's hands does Sebastian not fall backwards to the ground. Roby holds on tighter to his flagging father when Hairy Harry announces, "I could hardly read nothin'. Not until Mr. Sebastian Connery started teaching me last week."

From within his suit coat, Hairy Harry raises a book aloft and pivots it about for all to see. The colors, the yellow and white and blue and the letters in bright red, but most of all I see the edges gnawed and drooled to oblivion. I would know this book even if I stood a hundred yards away in a snowstorm. So would Sebastian, who leans into me for more support.

Hairy Harry opens the cover and holds the book before him as if it were the Bible itself, and he brings a hand to his mouth to cough importantly before he begins. Then Hairy Harry reads in halts and fits:

"Once upon a time."

That's it.

Hairy Harry beams and the crowd stands as still and as serious as can be, as if Hairy Harry were in the midst of singing *Ave Maria*. He turns back to the hole of Nicholas Garva the First and bends low, dropping Roby's long-ago copy of a *Grimm's Fairy Tales* into the grave.

From the middle of the rows of chairs, a man slowly rises. His black hair shines slicked back and his lower jaw looks hinged to his sunglasses like a menacing shovel to an earth-moving crane. Barrel-chested, he appears taller than all of the people around him even though he's not. He tugs at the front of his black suit coat and slips its two buttons through matching slits, then he moves among the crowd parting for him in advance. He stops at Old Sebastian's wheelchair and rests his left hand upon his head. I would expect Old Sebastian to float to the clouds once this hand is lifted. He turns momentarily to the Grisslys, who nod back with their eyes closed, then walks toward Hairy Harry at the grave.

Hairy Harry rises and turns, and the lips on the shovel jaw say something to him. Hairy Harry points, and the rows of people ahead of us part. The slicked-back hair, the black suit, the sunglasses, the jaw, the barrel chest; the whole package heads for us Connerys. There's no smile or warmth to be seen and the grass appears to crush to the soil yards before the approach of the wing tips on this man's feet.

It seems like a blur and slow-motion at the same time, this man imposing himself before my Sebastian. I won't let go of Sebastian's hand. The huge jaw moves.

"Are you Sebastian Connery?"

Even as Sebastian's hand sweats in mine, there's a stiffening of his spine and a squaring of his own overmatched, pitifully boyish jaw. Sebastian says in his poor Scottish lilt, "By the strength and courage of the Highlands to the Lowlands, I tell you I am he."

The sunglasses look confused.

"I am Sebastian Connery."

"You're the one?"

His sweat makes a puddle in my palm. "I suppose I am."

The square jaw breaks into the smallest of smiles, and says, "I'm the boy's father."

In his next breath, Sebastian finds himself engulfed in the embrace of Little Nicky Number One. And just as the million-dollar putt on the eighteenth hole receives applause from the spectator gallery, so too does Sebastian reap the applause from a thousand friends and relatives of the gangster bones.

Dirt rains down by the shovelful over the casket, with Roby's boyhood copy of a *Grimm's Fairy Tales* upon it.

We walk the headstones and he tells me as we pass them one by one: gunshot, gunshot, bludgeoned, stabbed, drowned with rocks in his pockets, poisoned, pushed off a cliff, gunshot, stabbed, gunshot. A house-lot-sized area of cemetery land full of Garva men born soon after 1900, all dead by the 1930s. He removes his sunglasses and bends low at the one man who made it into his seventies. Nicholas Garva the Second. "Hello, Dad," he says, and picks a last purple mum off a plant turned brown. When he stands, he forgets to put his sunglasses back on; I'm witness to his large brown eyes with lashes sweeping low to his cheeks.

I tell him, "You're not a gangster."

Nicholas Garva smiles and his jaw turns into something less frightful. His voice runs over my ears like velvet. "You've seen my commercials?"

"When I've had trouble sleeping."

"It's the best time to advertise on television."

"Why do you want to talk to me?"

"I'm grateful to your father-in-law." Placing the last mum of the year into his coat's breast pocket, he pats his hand over it at his heart. "There hasn't been a Garva in a gang since 1936," he says. "It wasn't good for our health." He expands his barrel chest and slips his sunglasses over his eyes. Nick Garva, the Cadillac Sales King of the Midwest, transforms back into Little Nicky Number One and his voice rattles its rocks at me. "But the persona," he says, "is useful. It gets a thousand distant relatives and my employees to come to a skeleton's funeral. It makes the owners of a retirement home give a job to my boy." We walk from his father's grave past the last Garva grave, a man who died in 1924. "Gunshot," Little Nicky Number One says, pointing at the headstone as we slip by. "And it makes a college professor sweat and teach my boy how to read."

He takes my hand and weaves with me around headstones and trees and benches, and his pull tells me he knows where he's going. Over my shoulder I spy my family gathered by Hairy Harry and the Grisslys at the fresh earth over the gangster bones. They watch me walk with Little Nicky Number One with their mouths hung open so much like bottle tops I expect the breeze to blow over them and play a tune.

As we walk, I begin to sense familiarity. The shapes and patterns of the headstones and trees and shrubs. It fits a powerful memory from more than four years ago. Soon I'm the one leading us forward. Around three burr oaks towering into each other, I recognize the low headstone, its nearly white granite reflecting the sun into sprays of light. A lump of a man crouches at the stone, touching its surface, and he startles at our approach. Standing, John Newberry stares at us for a moment, then tries to find something else to look at. His lips part, close and part again, as though each time the words he thought might explain things evaporate in his mouth. He walks from the grave, away from us, faster, until he's in a run. We say nothing to him.

Little Nicky Number One stands at the foot of this grave, again taking me by the hand. His voice rumbles, "You can't come to Dignity Place for the time being."

"No?"

"Then you must come on Thanksgiving with your family. Five in the evening. Sharp."

"Why?"

"A dinner and a show."

"The Grisslys will fire me."

"No," he says, squeezing my hand. "That won't happen."

"Is this Little Nicky Number One ordering me or Nick Garva the Cadillac Man making a request?"

He releases my hand, takes off his glasses, saying softly, "I'm asking."

"Then I'll consider it."

Something snaps in the distance and I turn my head about. There's John Newberry peeking at us from behind a tree. Nick Garva the Cadillac Man asks me not to tell Old Sebastian he isn't a gangster. It wouldn't be fair to ruin his fantasy. "One more thing about Thanksgiving at Dignity Place," he says, and the sunglasses go back on and the gravel in his throat returns. "You have to invite Iris. Drag her there if you must, but make sure she goes."

I suppose I should be surprised by his demand, but I'm not. I look back at the headstone of John Newberry, its etched words proclaiming he died four years five months ago. Until this morning I've overlooked a few things. In this case, the headstones around this spot, all with names of other Newberry men, filling a house-lot-size of cemetery land. Little Nicky Number One begins to point at them one by one, saying, "Gunshot, stabbed, poisoned, drowned with rocks in his pockets, gunshot . . ."

Like the history of Garvas, each Newberry, to the last, lay dead and buried since the 1930s.

37

Brian Unkers comes calling at the house after school. I tell him Roby's out with his father and grandfather at a party celebrating a burial. "That's okay, Mrs. Connery," he says. "I want to talk with you." He turns to his twin brothers sitting on my porch swing and orders them to stay. They watch him suspiciously, as if aware of a new power he possesses. They nod and fold their hands over their laps like angels.

I stand aside at the front door and let Brian in. Still a dragging pile of clothes, with spiked hair atop of his head. He sits on the living room couch and Lola Two appears beside him in a shambles, looking as though her face has been dragged down a street. *Dermal abrasion,* she says. *I had a couple scars to get rid of, one on each side of my face. I'll be perfectly healed in a week.* Her face oozes clear fluid, a syrupy sweat, and she holds a bowl of water and soaks a cloth in it then dabs at her raw skin. She looks at Brian and says, *Handsome boy. Even the mouth-pimples are fading. I should get him a sun lamp to finish the job.*

Brian sits hunched over his knees, fingers interlaced. When I sit on the chair beside the couch, one side of his mouth breaks into a smile. "It worked," he says.

"What worked?"

"Omelettes. My omelettes worked. I made my parents breakfast yesterday morning and they went into shock." He shakes his head and a laugh leaks from his lips. "My mother kissed me." Looking at me with admiration, running his hands through his hair, he says, "Then they kissed each other right in front of me, the way you and Mr. Sebastian do in front of people."

Lola Two pats her cloth on her chin. *It's a temporary thing. They'll be arguing about nothing again in no time.*

"When I came home from school today, Dad's car was in the garage and their bedroom door was locked."

"What did you make them for breakfast this morning?"

"Apple pancakes with powdered sugar." He whispers his secret. "They're busy right now. I could tell from the noises."

Probably another woman in his father's bed is all this is.

"Then my mother opens the door a crack and asks me if I could leave the house for a little while with my brothers." He looks at the clock over the television set. "I've got twenty more minutes."

They'll fatten up and have heart attacks.

Brian leans back and cocks his head. His eyes look ablaze with relief. "How did you know, Mrs. Connery?"

"I didn't."

"You knew something."

"It was a guess."

"I don't think so."

Lola Two, beside him in all her dermal abrasion torture, shakes her head and laughs. *You're a cruel one, misleading the boy. Like everything else in a marriage, breakfast will get dull dull dull, boring boring boring.*

"Brian," I say. "Look at you. Grown up into a teenager. Almost a man. Dressed in clothes nobody else but another teenager understands and your hair styled to look unstyled and an attitude of defiance. But your parents know you as their baby, their newborn, their toddler. The fat cheeks and pudgy arms and legs, the first crawl and the first step. The first word and first sentence. They remember when they picked you up and you wrapped your legs over their chests and your arms around their necks and you said Mommy and you said Daddy. And they remember the fat of your face, your cheeks they called kisspads, pressing cool and as soft as a kiss against their necks. Don't you know, Brian, how parents forever remember their children? Their love created you. Do things to remind them and make them grateful."

Oh, freakin' hell, Julia Connery. What kind of Dr. Phil-Oprah-Mr. Roger's Neighborhood-show did you pull that load from?

Brian nods his head and stares into the black of the television screen. I say, "It doesn't work for everybody, I suppose."

With a full smile, Brian stands and gives me a quick kiss on the cheek. "Call me Bean Dip," he says.

I'd pinch the young man's ass if I wasn't invisible.

I see Brian to the front door. On the porch, his brothers leap off the swing and stand on either side of him. They touch lightly at his waist, raise their stares toward his face as if waiting for instructions. Fear does not appear to be their motivation. What I see is gratitude.

Before Brian goes, he hesitates on the porch as if considering himself, straightens his back and levels his shoulders. He asks me if I'm going to Dignity Place for Thanksgiving.

"I am."

He leaves me with another smile, springing over the porch steps with his brothers, and runs down the walk. To me, he has the look and energy of a child who knows his parents still love each other in spite of the shouting and arguing. Beside me, Lola Two whines, *Well, I know it's temporary. It always is.*

Her skin has recovered, smoothed over, polished and taut as if stretched upon the rack, done over in gaudy makeup. "You said it would take a week to heal."

A minute felt as long as a month, listening to the hot air you gave the boy.

"Lola Two," I say, peering closely at her face. "Those weren't scars you removed. Those were your dimples."

Dimples, scars. Whatever. They were obnoxious.

She laughs. She laughs so hard the collagen and man-made parts all over her face and body threaten to orbit away. "What?" I say, and she points over my shoulder and laughs some more. Following the length of her arm and finger, I step out on my porch and see. A new, big black Cadillac leaving Iris Newberry's driveway. Dealer's license. NICK E 1.

So Little Nicky was over at Iris's house. Just think about what that could mean, honey. Then think about this. Bean Dip's screaming parents had sex today, and you and Sebastian didn't. Your man's given you no sugar all week.

"He's too tired and too drained from all the worrying he's done lately. Perhaps tonight."

You thought the same thing yesterday.

"Tonight."

At night, Sebastian quickly falls into a heavy snore.

Lola Two's voice floats in the dark. *A fake snore if ever I heard one.*

I turn away from Sebastian and wrap the pillow around my head to cover my ears. We buried gangster bones today, and Sebastian faced down a gangster. At least he thinks the man's a gangster. Under these circumstances, there's nothing to worry about. Nothing at all.

Muffled through the pillow, my imagination scolds me. *Yes, plenty of distractions lately. But we know, there's still damn plenty to worry about, honey pie.*

38

I miss Dignity Place.

I can't believe I'm feeling this way but it's true. If only I could go there promising to visit Old Sebastian and sit in my pool office and teach a swim class but not snoop around, maybe they'd let me in. I call Mrs. Grissly's office. "Not on your life," she says. "And not on my life." I should reveal the truth to Mrs. Grissly. Little Nicky Number One is a car dealer, that's it. But something tells me I'd be exploding a myth that shouldn't be exploded, not for the sake of Hairy Harry and the financial health of Dignity Place. So I keep my mouth shut about it and tell her I'll see her next Thursday evening. She is firm. "Not a minute before five."

Since Sebastian meets with Hairy Harry every other day now, Roby's gone and put his signs back up on his bedroom door on the days when his father comes home early.

Wednesday's was: *Call My Lawyer!*

Friday's: *Yesterday's Wounds Haven't Healed Yet.*

And Sunday's: *On the 7th Day, Dad Told God He Couldn't Rest. So What Chance Do I Have?*

These signs make Sebastian smile. The discussions through the door about Talmudic hypotenuses make me laugh.

Tuesday afternoon, though, Sebastian comes through the door at three.

"I thought you were teaching Hairy Harry today."

Sebastian slips out of his trench coat and carries it over his arm. "We rescheduled for tomorrow."

"Oh?"

I'm unable to move, imagining a scene that will happen moments from now, and Sebastian looks at me kind of odd. "Anything wrong?"

I shake my head.

"You look like something's wrong." He kisses me and steps toward the stairs.

"Sebastian," I say, following him. "It's been a while."

"I'm sorry, Lassie." But he keeps going up the stairs.

I reach to my chest and tear at my blouse. "Look, Sebastian!"

He peers over his shoulder, then turns to face me with a smile. "Why, Lassie, it has been a time. Why don't you come up here?"

"Down here, Sebastian." I unsnap the front of my bra.

"But where down there?"

I wink, I smile and I tell him anywhere he would have me.

He gazes at my cleavage with his dilated eyes and his smile of expectation. He says, "Upstairs."

"Downstairs."

"Upstairs."

With a sighing breath, I say, "Sebastian." I roll my blouse off my shoulders.

He takes a step down. I drop my shirt to the floor, unsnap my bra. Another step down. But then he says, "No surprises, first let me check on Roby." He turns around and looks to see the door open, the lights out, and his son in violation of a promise.

I shout, "It's been over a week!" but he's not hearing it. He flies up the stairs to Roby's room and I follow him with my breasts unleashed and there for the taking. Sebastian takes nothing. He glares at my eyes and yells, "Where is he?"

"I said it's been over a week."

"Do you know where he is, Julia? Tell me if you know!"

"I know."

"Where?"

I work the bra straps back over my shoulders and press the front snap together. Covered and leashed. "I can't tell you."

"It's me asking. He's my son. My son has lied to me. Don't you understand?"

"If I tell you now, you'll never forgive yourself."

He stares at me, enraged. "You tried to distract me with your weapons."

"I did. The offer's still on the table."

I turn around to our bedroom, fall on our bed and wait for him to make his move. Pattering noises are all I hear, his pacing the hall and his throat-growling "Chrissake almighty!" Then I hear his feet run down the stairs and the sound of our front door open and shut. I close my eyes, hear the sound of the car engine fading down the street.

"If you appear and say a thing," I say to Lola Two, "I'll find a way to kill you."

The phone rings and I flop my arm to the nightstand to answer. It's Little Nicky Number One. "Have you asked Iris yet?"

"No."

"When were you going to?"

"Soon."

"Thanksgiving's in two days."

"Soon."

"Now."

"Are you wearing those damn sunglasses?"

"Which would you prefer?"

"Thanks for asking my opinion. I'll do it now."

"Good."

"Couldn't you have done it yourself when you were at her house?"

He hangs up.

I drop the receiver beside me and flop my head down on my pillow. There's my chest, looking reasonably well-pointed skyward even if I'm fifty-three and flat on my back. I circle my fingers around my nipples beneath my bra, but my girls know the difference, when it's Sebastian's touch at play. They very well could have been in his hands right now. Are you thinking about them, Sebastian? Tasted by your lips? Are you regretting the choice you've made tonight?

Nothing but ceiling above me. Nothing but disappointment within. I suppose I'm in the right state of mind to speak to Iris.

39

"I've missed your company," I say.

Iris stands at her door in blue capri pants and a white knit sweater. "I thought you were mad at me."

Of course I was mad at her, but I'm not going to say so to her face. I'm not going to tell her she's turned into something lovely, and I'm responsible for it, but I never meant for her to use such loveliness to lure other men into her home. "Are you alone?"

"Yes."

"It's cold on your porch."

"Are you here to talk to me about John?"

"Perhaps I am."

Her eyes go adrift. With her next breath, her chin drops and her shoulders slump. She steps away from the door, motioning me to enter.

The wind rushes in with me and I think to leave my long coat on. In her living room, with the sun down early, the lamps throw their pitiful light against the darkness. She has her furniture pushed back against the far wall, the china cabinet, sofa, dining room table and chairs, and all their gargoyles look placed in a lineup to stare me down. "What's going on?"

Although she has closed the front door, Iris remains facing it with her hands pressed against the panels. "Tell me what you came here to say."

She's nearly gone in the darkness, her gargoyles at my back.

"I've come to ask you to Dignity Place for Thanksgiving dinner."

"No."

"Iris?"

"Absolutely not."

"You said you were ready."

"Being ready isn't the question anymore."

"Little Nicky Number One insists you come."

With a hiss, she shakes her head.

"I'm asking you for myself."

She leaves the door, shuffles toward me with such heaviness I wonder if she longs for her pasty sunblock and blue hair formula and sombrero hat. "I was dancing."

"What?"

"You asked me what was going on. I assume you mean about the furniture. So I'm telling you. I was dancing."

"By yourself?"

"Don't be ridiculous."

We stare at each other, both knowing the answer. She speaks up first. "With Nicholas."

Iris Newberry, so lovely on her wedding day, so lovely now, takes my hands in hers and smiles. "Would you comb my hair again, dear?"

She leaves the dining room and returns with a brush, hands it to me and sits in a chair by the line of gargoyle furniture. "Comb my hair the way you did before."

I'm still cold in my long coat and, as I stand behind Iris, I'm certain some of the fangs and claws on the gargoyles brush against the cloth. Her hair feels like silk in my fingers, as if she's been running the brush through in a rush to make up for twenty years of neglect. In her dining room, with the dim light and gargoyles and furniture pushed aside for a dance, I feel warmth return to my skin and a new urge to know her secrets. But I wait, feeling at first her neck without give slowly ease and sway to the rhythm of the brush. She says, "Nicholas wanted to apologize."

"I see."

"Then he wanted to dance. No fooling around. Just a dance."

"What did you do?"

"I accepted his apology. Then we danced."

The silver of her hair flows in the shape of running water over her head. My thoughts get lost in its thickness, though of course I ask her. "Apologize for what?"

"You know exactly," she says, which I don't, but I consider the possibilities under the circumstances and accept them all as equally in need of an apology.

"Sebastian had an affair a long time ago," I say. "When we were engaged."

"Forgive him."

"But he disappears on me now and again."

"Follow him one day. If it's innocent, then apologize."

"If it's not?"

"Julia," she says, reaching to pat my hand. "It's Sebastian."

I sweep the brush lightly over her ears and gather her hair in my hands. Drawn back is the way she had it styled in her wedding photo. She says, "Do you ever wonder what I buried inside John's casket?"

Her eyebrows, their shape, and the shape of her chin and cheekbones, turn into a smile with her question. "I assume nothing but air, perhaps a photograph."

"You shouldn't assume."

"Then I'm asking."

"Does John want me to come to Dignity Place?"

My brush strokes halt on the crown of her head and I consider her question. "I've never asked him directly, and he hasn't exactly said so, but he's hinted."

"Hinted how?"

"He left his door open for me, said he expected me to ask about you. And he went on to tell me the things he loved best about you, and what he remembered before the cancer."

Iris leans back in the chair. Her head feels relaxed enough to wobble off her neck. "I've decided," she says.

"Decided what?" Although I expect she's about to say yes or no to Thanksgiving at Dignity Place, Iris surprises me.

"Now I know what makes a woman a woman."

"Oh?"

"I have."

"Mind if you tell me?"

She sounds so sure, and I pray the phone and doorbell won't ring. I listen with my head bowed toward hers, the brush at my side. Iris taps lightly at my wrist and gets my brush strokes going again. Tilting her head, the brush at her neck, she tells me.

"Being a woman means having someone who thanks God for me."

Our silence lasts a few minutes, or perhaps it only feels that way. I don't know if I have the brush going through her hair or through the space over her hair. All I imagine is John on his knees, his arms around Iris's hips, thanking God he has her and grateful that her horrible cancer is gone. And Iris slaps him hard on his face.

"Do you think that's a good answer, Julia?"

I set the brush down and fluff Iris's hair at her shoulders. "Since you've said it, I think I believe the very same thing."

"There's something special I buried in the casket."

"Are you going to tell me what it is?"

Iris turns to look at herself in the mirror on the wall. "Forgive Sebastian," she says evenly. "Otherwise you'll turn into a vampire."

★   ★   ★   ★   ★

On my way home, the start of a storm catches me between houses. There's Lola Two sitting with her legs crossed on my front walk, her face pouting on her hands. She's blurred by the streaks of rainfall. "What's today's surgery?"

I had eyeliner tattooed into my lids.

"I didn't notice." She raises her head and I see the black lines and the sock-in-the-eyes swelling. "It's true what Iris said," I tell her. "About what makes a woman a woman."

Dr. Plastic makes a woman a woman.

"I don't think so."

Lola Two goes back to pouting. *You'll see.*

I smile at the sound of her uncertainty.

Roby comes home before Sebastian. He leaps up the stairs, grinning wide, and tells me things went well at Dignity Place.

"Your father didn't teach Hairy Harry today."

"No?" Roby's grin loses support from the rest of his face and he goes blank.

"They switched days. Your father was home at three."

Roby turns to his bedroom, sees it wide open with the lights out, and groans from his chest, "One more day. Just one more day." He plods to his room and closes the door. By the time Sebastian arrives, Roby's posted a new drippy-red sign for him to read:

Grounded Until AARP Eligible

I stand in Sebastian's way at Roby's door. Soaked from the rain, he says, "Do you know where I've gone to looking for that boy?"

"Everywhere."

"That's right."

"You should have stayed home."

"What?"

"He was back minutes after you left. Said he forgot a book at school and got a ride from Brian Unkers."

Sebastian looks at me with water dripping from his hair and his eyebrows, like soaked sponges, sag over his eyes from the weight of a flood. "Gone to school to get a book, is that what you're telling me?"

"That's all."

"Why didn't you tell me earlier?"

"I didn't know until he came home with the book."

"Julia," he says. "When I first left, I forgot my wallet. I came back to get it and the house was empty. No wife and no son."

My lips must look like they're hanging from a noose. Maybe it's all the rain he's absorbed, but he can hardly lift his chin to look at me. "First time I know of that you've lied to me, Lassie," he says. "I'm going to sleep."

It's like watching the Lord Jesus carry the cross to our bedroom and I'm alone in the hall and sit on the top stair wishing I could be the type of person who smokes and drinks to oblivion. There's nothing to say to him, nothing at all. I'll soon have to dress for bed and slip in beside a man who doesn't want a thing to do with me right now.

There's a creak behind me and I turn about. Through the sliver of light at the edge of the door, one of Roby's eyes blinks at me. He thanks me for trying.

"You're welcome."

"One more day, Mom. That's all." He closes his eye, then the door.

I sit there and wonder what I'd do if Sebastian ran away and I decided to fake his funeral. What would I bury in the casket? For revenge, perhaps the Urns of Connery if he left them behind. For spite, I'd first mix the ashes with used kitty litter.

For symbolism, I'd bury my engagement ring and wedding band, but first I'd squeeze them flat with pliers, remove the diamonds and use them to pay for a month-long massage.

For sorrow, if I were to lose Sebastian, I would bury myself. It makes sense to me now that I'd turn into a vampire, just the way Iris once did. Just the way she has warned me.

40

Thanksgiving Eve and the men in my house have vanished.

It's a half day at the junior college today, but Sebastian calls to say he and Hairy Harry are working late into the evening. He wants to say something more to me, I can tell by his small breaths, like sobs, through the receiver. But there's pride in men which sooner or later gets in the way of what their hearts wish them to do.

"I'll wait up for you," I say.

He says, "You don't have to." A weak goodbye, and he hangs up.

All day long, the same paper sign hangs on Roby's door.

Will Someone Please Post My Bail?

The voices of Roby and Bean Dip vibrate into my kitchen, discussing trigonometry behind Roby's closed bedroom door while darkness falls. I sit at the table with the same cup of coffee gone cold hours ago, listening to sines and cosines and theta this and theta that and the squares of the angles of the Talmudic hypotenuse and the laughter and the "C'mon, seriously, Bean Dip," and I swear I could figure out the trajectory of Mars by now. Twice I've seen Iris at her window over her kitchen sink. The first time she waved at me and smiled. This second time she looks puzzled at the way I sit in the same spot hour after hour. I call her and ask her if we're still on for tomorrow.

"Are you all right?" she asks.

"Yes. No. I mean, not really."

"Neither am I."

We look at each other through our windows, both of us with a phone at our ears. Like children playing with walkie-talkies, we could just as easily open our windows and have the same conversation. I ask her, "Are you nervous?"

"A bit."

"So am I."

"Why would you be nervous?"

"I feel responsible."

She looks away from her window, her lovely hair falling over her face and phone. "Whatever happens," she tells me, "thank you. You're my best friend."

Her best friend? Hearing these words, I think right away, poor Iris. We hang up and smile at each other through the space between our homes.

She's gone from her window, hours now, I imagine, lights out, and I'm in the same spot thinking of her and my family and Thanksgiving Day.

Footsteps behind me stop, a kiss at my ear, and Roby says, "Another good day. I think we're ready."

"What's ready? Who's ready?"

"I can't say."

"Go to bed before your father comes home." Another kiss at my ear and his steps patter away and up the stairs to his room.

I turn on the radio and listen. *God Investment* is gone. There's no station manager making excuses or claims of innocence. A woman welcomes me to the North Shore's newest classic rock station. Greatest songs, fewest commercials. Then she breaks to a commercial.

A part of me will miss listening to those evil men and the silly women who followed their advice and the other women who gave them hell. All along I had made excuses for listening.

Was it an accident or background noise, or was *God Investment* just the show that came on after the show I really wanted to listen to, even though it was on all the time? In truth, it was like being witness to a train wreck. Even with all the carnage, how could I look away?

That's how I feel about you.

Lola Two sits across from me at my kitchen table. She talks but her face doesn't move.

"Botox injections?"

All over the place.

She doesn't have the strength to move her pillow lips, and her voice sounds as though she's holding on to her tongue. I lie and tell her she looks good.

Leaning back, she folds her arms beneath her torpedo breasts, and her cleavage looks so much like a fanny protruding its twin lumps through the cut of her blouse. A wax museum face now shaped nearly into a heart. Not a wrinkle to see, no dimples, no cleft in her pointed chin, her cheekbones pressed up to her eyes, and her eyes hoisted and shoved to her brow and pulled toward the sides of her head.

I ask her, "Has Dr. Plastic finished with you?"

Pmmmf.

"I'll take that as a no."

She watches me with her mask-face and waits. When Sebastian comes home, he washes his hands, makes himself a cheese sandwich on the counter, puts it on a plate and washes his hands again. He sits across from me on the bench seat not knowing he's blended half into Lola Two. "Good session with Hairy Harry?" I ask.

"That's where I was," he snaps.

"I'm not accusing you of anything."

"Good."

He chews a bite of his sandwich with his mouth closed until

the bite is gone and swallowed. He looks at me momentarily, part Sebastian, part Lola Two, and takes another bite. The blend of them hurts my eyes. Worse yet, his hands hold his sandwich at her left breast when he bites, and Lola Two moans as if it's so much fun.

With his sandwich gone, Sebastian wipes his lips and hands with a napkin and sweeps up crumbs only he can find. Finally, he looks at me, half of him anyway. "I'm waiting for an apology," he says.

"I'm sorry."

"Do you know what for?"

"I do. And what about my apology?"

"Is the boy home?"

"Upstairs. No apology from you?"

"Are you sure he's upstairs?"

"I'm sure."

"How can I trust you?"

"See for yourself."

Sebastian stands, separating himself from Lola Two. "I will," he says. "These days I have to see things for myself."

Without touching me, he rushes by, and I ask him, "Do you love me, Sebastian?"

He hesitates in the hallway. "Yes," he says like a pre-recorded message, and he thumps up the stairs to check on Roby.

Lola Two manages a grin. *That sounded convincing.*

"Botox easing a bit?"

Um hmm. If only Sebastian knew what he was chewing on. But you saw. What did you think of the sight of it? It's the sight of the inevitable dream of any married man coming true.

After witnessing Sebastian's coolness toward me, Lola Two appears impenetrably plastic. She's the woman Sebastian confessed to me about, the fling he had during our engagement. A woman I never met. Scorn and resolve require a target.

311

Someone I can see. In his rush to confess to clear his conscience and preserve our wedding day, Sebastian had failed to provide an image I could hate. Now I realize he's as guilty as I am for creating Lola Two.

Well, it's clear your ass has spread a bit more sitting there all day. Do you want to talk to Dr. Plastic?

My fanny is spread and numb, it's true. The thought of Dr. Plastic examining it with a marker and scalpel makes it uncomfortable to sit on.

"Lola Two," I say, standing. "I believe I saw your upper arms wiggle."

Among the sculptures of her man-made face, an emotion leaks through. Part uncertainty, part shock. She touches at her upper arms and squeezes, and she groans as if she's touched the flesh of a thousand elderly schoolmarms in sleeveless blouses, jiggling and wiggling their upper arms while they write on blackboards.

To my ceiling, Lola Two calls out, *More liposuction!* and she vanishes.

It's past ten. I'll never get this day back. I slip beneath the covers beside my occasional torment, who softly snores and whispers dreams between his lips.

41

Brian Unkers stops by at noon. He tells me he made a morning buffet of scrambled eggs, sausages, hash browns, raisin muffins, fruit salad, and mimosa cocktails. He doesn't expect to see his parents out of their bedroom until tomorrow.

"What about Thanksgiving?"

There's a rush of blushing to his face that makes what's left of his mouth-pimples nearly disappear. "It's all right." He smiles at me. "I like them this way, even without a turkey."

"Where are your brothers?"

"With our grandparents." Before I can ask, he says, "I thought I'd stick around here. Get some school work done with Roby."

"You look good, Bean Dip," I say, and his stare skims my face in a grateful way as if my fifty-three-year-old-lady opinion of him actually matters.

"Roby home?"

"Locked in his room."

Brian hurries to the stairs. Halfway up, he says, "Thank you, Mrs. Connery." His head leans far over the banister and everything is so serious on his face. I'm stuck between answering him either with thank you or you're welcome, but he's gone and in Roby's room before I'm able to decide.

Rather than close the front door, I step outside on my porch to see what the weather's doing. A mix of gray and blue in the sky, and I wonder what the difference is between partly cloudy and partly sunny. The wind blows strong and its chill makes it to my skin through my slacks and sweater, but it's hardly the chill late November typically brings to Highland Park. This indecisive weather is so much like Iris and John Newberry.

Brian's rust bucket on wheels faces south on the other side of the street, insulting the neighborhood's Norman Rockwell brick and trim. Over my shoulders, Sebastian huffs, "That boy couldn't walk four houses to ours?"

I tell Sebastian I'm surprised to see it parked there, even though I'm not, and in my mind I thank him for talking to me but don't say so out loud. For a moment I wish I had on the sort of clothes Lola Two wears, the mini and the plunging and the clinging and the revealing, but I wear frumpy brown slacks and a lumpy white sweater, and Sebastian looks at me without the energy I've grown used to. He's told me in the past how he likes ordinary clothes on me because undressing me was like tearing apart a plain Cracker Jack box to find the terrific prize inside. Not today.

"C'mon in, Lassie," he says. "It's cold."

At the threshold of our door, I kiss him on the lips then lean back to see his eyes, but stay near enough for our breath to mingle. He seems so sad and defeated. "They're locked in Roby's room, studying," I say, and he gives in a little with his own soft kiss to my lips.

Although he smiles, he says nothing. His disappointment in Roby will take some time to get over and the thought I would lie to him to protect our son's disobedience of him may linger forever.

I should scream about husbands and wives cheating on each other, slugging each other, and taking each other to divorce court to drain their finances into their lawyers' pockets. And what, Sebastian, is this tiny thing you're obsessing over? How does this particle compare to your refusal to tell me where you go off to now and then? How can you justify your anger under these circumstances? But I don't want to hear my voice speak these thoughts or the rage that would accompany my words. To me, it would be the sound of defeat. Mine and Sebastian's.

I'll take his kiss, far too short, far too silent.

Upstairs, Sebastian knocks on Roby's bedroom door. I hear through the living room ceiling, "Yes, Dad?"

"We're leaving at a quarter to five."

"Yes, Dad."

"You're to stay put in your room till then."

"Yes, Dad."

"Then we're going to Dignity Place for Thanksgiving dinner as a family, all of us dressed up nice, and none of your baggy, draggy, saggy rags. You've got a handsome suit. Put on your suit."

"Yes, Dad."

"And your friend can come with if he wants to, if he's got a suit or something else nice to wear."

"Yes, Mr. Connery. Thank you, Mr. Connery."

There's a pause in the conversation, but no footsteps go anywhere. Sebastian says in a higher tone of voice, "Don't you boys study anything besides trigonometry? It's getting a bit on my nerves."

"Yes, Dad."

"Yes, Mr. Connery."

"What?"

"History, Dad. A report on ancient Scotland's defeat of the Roman invasion."

"Really?"

"Yes, Dad."

Again a pause, and no footsteps to anywhere.

"Well, then," Sebastian says. "Feel free to get something to eat if you want to. There's a new cherry pie in the fridge."

"Thanks, Dad."

"And ask me any questions if you need to."

"Thank you, Mr. Connery."

One last pause, then Sebastian says in a warning tone, "I'll be expecting to read a copy of your report on Scotland."

Roby's fast to say, "Yes, Dad."

Four-thirty and Iris isn't answering. I call. I knock. I ring. I take the door handle, turn it and push. Locked. I try the back door and it's also locked. I peer into her garage window and see her car parked inside. In my heels, dress and overcoat, it's hard for me to kneel down to take a look through her basement windows, but I do and I can't see a thing through the darkness. Back on her porch, I look through the front window and see the furniture the way I last saw it, pushed back to make room for a last dance with Little Nicky Number One. The gargoyles shoved to the far wall appear nearly vanished, and their eyes, like a wolf pack staring out from the edge of a forest, seem to hang in mid-air, finding a way in the dark to glare orange light at me.

I find her.

With my toes stretched high in my pumps outside her bedroom window and my big head so obvious if only she'd look up, Iris sits on her bed holding her sombrero hat. Dressed in a lovely peach gown, she stares at the hat's peak and slowly, so painfully slow, she sets it on her head, and it's as if the weight of it sags everything into her lap. I sag with her, off my toes and below the window sill.

Of course. I understand now. She's been thinking things over, weighing the pros against the cons of going to Dignity Pace. I recall seeing the pillows side by side on her queen-sized bed, looking as though two people would arrive home late this evening. But at twenty-five minutes to five, the cons have apparently won her over.

Everything had been so promising up till now. The obedience

of the boys, Roby and Brian, their kisses on my cheek at the front door. Even the way Sebastian looked at me when I got dressed for dinner. His favorite dress, inches above my knees, curving neckline, low shoulders, blue with nearly invisible red cross-stitching. Sexy Scottish. It's as though I successfully got his plug back into its socket, and his batteries have begun to recharge.

Well, I think, breathing deeply. It's Iris's decision.

As I slip toward my house, I look across the street, at the porches and the trees and the way the sun has set in a sky now cloudless, leaving a line of silver and deep blue over rooftops and intertwining branches. Somewhere a flock of geese talks in the sky and the honks turn into something musical. It reminds me of the first bagpipe blasts I heard in my pool office and my swings with Sebastian on our glider chair before we took it to the basement for the winter season. When I inhale, the air tastes moist with the scent of fallen leaves beginning their change back into earth. Sweet sights, sounds, and smells, and none of it feels right without Iris. Then I notice. How could I miss it?

Brian Unkers's car is gone.

I rush to my porch and through the front door, and I hesitate at the foot of the stairs to listen. Roby talking to Brian. "Take the square of the root of the Talmudic hypotenuse," and Brian's snit of laughter, "Yeah, yeah, the Talmudic hypotenuse."

Climbing the stairs, listening to them, I feel as though I'm running up a down escalator. My heart's a hammer pounding against my rib cage and air catches in a lump in my throat. It's a scene I thought could happen but wouldn't. Now it does. Escaping the stairs, I see the door open enough for a person to walk through, and the new drippy-red-letter sign.

The Party Has Just Begun

I ease through the opening, hands first, then arms, then my

legs, and my head and body, my eyes shut tight. I listen to them.

"Bean Dip, this is hard."

"Figuring out the angle of the Talmudic hypotenuse is always hard."

When I open my eyes, there's Sebastian, alone among the ruins of Roby's room, the tossed-about clothes, the angry rock star posters, and the things that go crunch beneath footsteps.

"They're making electronic gadgets too small these days," Sebastian says. "And the sound these recordings make are too good for their puny size."

He lifts the piled clothes off the stereo, no larger than a car stereo, and hits a button. The trigonometry talk ends and, slowly, the black plastic lid atop rises. Sebastian lifts the CD disc in his fingers then drops it in his other hand. He stares at the letters written across it and sighs. Then he stares at nothing, or at everything written on dust motes, it's hard to tell. Turning to me, he shows me the drippy red letters scrawled atop the CD: *Talmudic Hypotenuse Defeats Tyrant King.*

I thought it clever and funny when I had first seen it, but now it represents another lie told to my husband of thirty-three years in support of our son's disobedience. So I expect anger and accusations of betrayal. But Sebastian has nothing to say. His shoulders slump into his charcoal suit, the best suit he had put on for me and our Thanksgiving dinner at Dignity Place.

Five minutes after five, we begin our drive in silence. Without Iris. Without Roby.

42

Perhaps it's the uneven shadows in what's left of daylight thrown over the horizon. Or the leaves on the ground, allowed to blow here and there, or the invasive plants in the lawn which have overcome the last spread of weed killer and now grow well enough in November weather while the grass shrivels into dull greens and browns. Whatever the reason, Dignity Place appears to have let loose a little bit. The grounds feel less controlled, less symmetrical. Beside me, turning off our car in a sea of parked cars filling the drive, sits the opposite. A man tightly curled into his own circle of despair and suffering.

I wish to slap him off his woe-is-me pedestal so high in the sky I'd expect his nose to bleed. And I wish to shout, Get over yourself! But I don't slap people and I don't shout. I'm surprised I'm considering such things, and more so at the satisfaction I feel imagining doing them to Sebastian.

We walk together toward Dignity Place, elbow to elbow but not touching. The posts on the veranda are twined in stalks of corn and a scarecrow man and woman sit close beside each other in Adirondack chairs set alongside the stairs, their heads made of pillow cases topped in straw hats. In jeans and flannel shirt, he smokes a pipe. In a frock and apron, she darns a sock. They look happy.

Carved pumpkins lie in small groups at the scarecrows' straw-filled work boots, showing more than a bit of shrivel. Strung up along the length of the eaves, icicle Christmas lights glitter in nightfall and wreaths with gold bows hang between window frames. Colored paper made into turkeys and Happy Thanksgiving signs and Pilgrims carrying muskets shaking hands with Native Americans cover most of the glass. It's lovely, really, this odd combination of holidays. One gone nearly a month, one here today, one yet a month away.

As we go forward on the walk, I sense energy between Sebastian and me, the suction of a vacuum working to hook our arms together and clasp hands. But there's nothing strong enough right now to make it happen. He's so determined in his sadness. While the veranda glows in celebration of multiple holidays, Sebastian stomps heavily up the steps, resigned to despair.

He does open the door for me and politely stands to the side. I ask him to smile and he ekes out a constipated sort with his lips. "Keep your face that way," I tell him, "and people will think you're forever wishing for the toilet."

Sebastian pity-whispers to himself, "Was it too much to expect a son to be with his dad on Thanksgiving Day?"

It's a party inside Dignity Place. The atrium drips with shimmering streamers strung from the balconies and staircase. And a Christmas tree at the center towers over two stories toward the skylight, its branches filled with silver tinsel and gold garland boas and colorful ornament bulbs the size of softballs, all of it soaked in a mesh of small lights. The skylight, its glass shaded black by evening, domes over the lobby's display and makes me feel as though I'm walking into a galaxy of stars.

Perhaps two dozen round tables cram the lobby, arranged to circle the Christmas tree. Each table has its own white tablecloth draped to the floor, and a centerpiece of silver Mylar balloons announcing Happy Thanksgiving strung to a base of blue and white carnations. The residents and their families crowd around their tables, smiling, laughing and clinking their fine silverware against fancy china plates and serving bowls and their own teeth and dentures, too busy to notice the arrival of the Connerys. These small sounds gather together into a symphony of one note, continuous and happy.

"It's lovely," I say to Sebastian.

In this burst of galaxy light, Sebastian's a barren asteroid drawn to nothing. He says through the weak smile I've ordered to his face, "Was it too much for a son to obey his dad on Thanksgiving Day? That's what I'm saying."

From the opposite side of the lobby, a shock of dyed brown hair moves along level through the crowd, appearing, disappearing, and reappearing. Old Sebastian swings his wheelchair around the last set of tables and makes his way to us. "They brought out the turkeys a while ago," he says.

I say, "Turkeys?"

"Twenty-three turkeys. One for each table."

"Hello, Dad."

Old Sebastian wheels to Sebastian's shoes and scowls at him. "You look like someone's peed in the Urns of Connery."

"I feel that way."

"Something you ate?"

"No."

Old Sebastian cocks his head and his eyes seem to wizen at the sight of his son. He says what I couldn't. "For chrissake, son, this is Thanksgiving. Get over yourself."

I take Sebastian by the hand and he lets me. We follow Old Sebastian around the tables to the other side of the atrium, to a row of chairs arranged in a line. The chairs face away from the Christmas tree toward three black canvas curtains hung taut in a row, suspended by wire cables and pulleys from a balcony. I imagine they're ten feet high and thirty feet long taken together, and they block off the atrium's ponds. Old Sebastian snarls at the size of them. "They think with so many Old Toots drinking

Thanksgiving booze, we might start jumping in the water to steal the pennies."

I say, "Who thinks that?"

"The Grisslys."

"Where are they?"

"I have no idea."

"Who's serving all this food?"

"Little Nicky Number One's taking care of everything," Old Sebastian says. "Even Hairy Harry gets a rest."

I count ten chairs in a row facing the canvas curtains, no table, no food. Signs taped to the backrest of every chair announce the same thing: *Reserved For The Connery Family.* Paul with the hair tufts sits at the farthest one. Even though he wears his gray slacks and blue cardigan sweater, it's the thought of his hair tufts beneath his clothes prickling at my nerves reminding me it's him. He raises a full champagne glass, winks at me, and sips. Then he says, "You're late."

I look at my watch. "Only by twenty minutes."

"An hour and twenty minutes."

"Mrs. Grissly told me five."

"Now, Julia," Paul says, meaning to lecture me. "Everybody knows Old Toots all over the world start dinner by four." He looks at me, surprised I've forgotten about the Residents' compulsive migration to their television sets by five-thirty. "Even if it's a Thanksgiving rerun," he reminds me, "The Wheel starts in ten minutes."

"Wheel?"

"You know. The Wheel. The first half hour of *Wheel of Fortune* starts at five-thirty."

"The Wheel, um-hmm, I see. Then Mrs. Grissly lied to me."

Into his champagne glass, Paul says, "I suppose she did."

"No dinner on Thanksgiving," Sebastian moans beside me. "Was it too much for a father to have dinner with his son on

Thanksgiving? That's all I'm talking about here."

I look at Old Sebastian. He's parked to the right of me and smacks his lips and pats the small bulge of his tummy packed with food. "The Grisslys told me five," I say.

"Nope. Four," Old Sebastian says. "We always eat by four. Although I think Pat Sajak reminds me of an elf."

Paul finishes his glass of champagne and looks at the pitiful gathering of Connerys, then frowns at the nine empty chairs running down the row with the reserved-for-Connerys signs. "I was expecting more of you."

Sebastian wobbles to the chair beside Paul and sits. "An absent son and no Thanksgiving dinner," he says. "That's what I'm talking about here." Sebastian looks less like a man and more like a balloon once in the shape of a man before it lost half its air. His eyebrows sag over his eyes and his head tilts one way then the other as if bouncing off his shoulders in slow motion. All the while his lips and chin pout toward his chest. He peers into the three rows of black canvas lined up for him to see and finds companionship there rather than with me or Old Sebastian.

"It's just us," Old Sebastian says, wheeling to the other side of Paul. "The Connery family."

There's Old Sebastian full of food, all the while knowing Thanksgiving dinner started at four and he never bothered to tell me. And there's Sebastian deflating into his shoes as if he intends to sag all evening long until he's melted flat across the floor. Between them, Paul tries to smile at me and the empty chairs far outnumbering the Connerys. I sit beside Sebastian and swear I can hear the high-pitched whine of air leaking from his body.

I say, "Mrs. Grissly insisted not before five, I know it."

Sebastian tells me with a sigh, "It's not as though I'm hungry anyway."

Leaning past Paul, Old Sebastian says, "I'm sure there are leftovers somewhere."

Sebastian says, "Leftovers on Thanksgiving day?" and groans his face toward his knees.

"Well," Old Sebastian says with a sniff. "It's not as though we've been licking the turkey meat and putting it back on the serving trays."

"At least the Grisslys could have kept our table here," I say.

"There was never a table here," Paul says. "Just the chairs in a row." He stands up and, without a look to any of us, leaves our gathering overwhelmed by empty chairs and walks to the right side of the canvas curtains.

"What's he doing?" I ask. Sebastian grunts to himself and Old Sebastian acts as though he doesn't hear me. I say louder, "What was Paul doing sitting in chairs reserved for the Connerys?" Again a grunt. Again I'm ignored.

Paul disappears behind the three canvas curtains and suddenly the entire length of them comes alive as if bumped by a parade of arms and legs. Old Sebastian says to Sebastian, "I ate your slice of cheesecake and saved mine for later. And you can't have mine 'cause it's mine."

"My own father steals my Thanksgiving cheesecake," Sebastian says, drooped toward the floor. There's a momentary self-righteous rise in Sebastian's shoulders. It's like watching the final surge of a fatally wounded beast, and he wails out the cross he bears. "I'm a father without my teenaged son, my only child, on Thanksgiving Day, and no turkey and my cheesecake stolen by my father, and all I'm offered are leftovers from someone else's dinner plate; that's exactly what I'm saying here." Then his body sinks below the surface of life and becomes a lump of limp misery.

"Pisser," Old Sebastian says.

I say to Sebastian, "Why are you making this so hard?"

He glances at me with a look of blame in his eyes, but he knows better than to say anything close to blame in front of his father. So he gasps out a sigh a mile long and I expect him to flop to the floor on his back and kick his arms and legs up in the air and roll his tongue out his mouth in a final convulsion of death. And I bet he assumes all the policemen and firemen and ditch-diggers and emergency room nurses and doctors who have to work Thanksgiving Day will drop everything to crowd around and take pity on Sebastian Connery before he finally passes on in all his woebegone glory.

"Roby loves you," I say. "More than you know."

"Right," he says. His face and soul disappear into his cupped hands.

The Connery men have fallen silent, and without their noises, it's as though my sinuses have popped open after being plugged for days from the flu. Suddenly I'm aware of the people filling the atrium behind me and their talk feels as though they have packed together in my ears. Hushed with excitement, they murmur, "When's this thing getting started?" "It better be soon." "The Wheel comes on in nine minutes."

There's a noise behind the three broad bands of black canvas, a gathering of some kind. Old Sebastian straightens over the top of Sebastian's wilted head and gives me a wink. On the other side of the canvas, voices whisper. "Ready?" "No." "Yes?" "No." "Now?" "Hold on" "Okay, okay, okay." "Ready."

Around the left canvas curtain, Hairy Harry appears carrying a microphone. He stumbles over the cable, nearly falls, but makes it to stand before the center canvas. Wearing his dark suit from the gangster bones funeral, he coughs and clears his throat and smiles nervously at me. He's likely shaven twice today but the dark forest is back on his face and he's in need of another. When he lifts the microphone to his mustache, the feedback nearly knocks me out of my chair. Hairy Harry looks back toward the canvas. "I thought this was ready!"

From behind the canvas—"Hold on. Okay. Try it now."

Hairy Harry turns and smiles at all the people at the tables. "Hi." He waits for Residents to say "Hi" back. A few of them do. "You all know me, uh-huh, and I got somethin' I got to read to you." He shoves the microphone under his upper arm and the sound booms as though he's got thunder stored in his pits. Pulling a paper from his coat pocket, unfolding it, he brings the microphone back to his mustache. "I can read this now, thanks to Mr. Sebastian Connery."

Hairy Harry pauses to stare and smile and extend his arm toward the lump beside me, and there's a sweep of applause throughout the atrium. Sebastian, even as he sits crushed in his chair, remains aloft in his self-pity.

Poor Hairy Harry. I'm sure he expected more from Sebastian than rigor mortis. So he coughs again and raises the paper before his eyes and reads, in fits and stutters, aloud into his microphone. "Dear Mr. Connery. We sons can be tough sometimes, but we try to be good. Happy Thanksgiving."

Hairy Harry drops the microphone to his side, smiling so proudly, but then snaps it back to his mustache, far too close. He rumbles into the atrium:

"So please stop being an ass."

Hairy Harry takes a quick bow, then another, and the Residents and their families laugh and applaud him. Walking to the canvas strip on the left, he crosses himself and mouths an "Our Father." He crosses himself once more and disappears behind the canvas.

Sebastian says to me, "Did that boy just call me an ass in front of a hundred people?"

"Probably two hundred, yes."

"Chrissake. I teach him to read and he calls me an ass in front of two hundred people on Thanksgiving Day." He presses his fingertips against his forehead and covers his eyes.

The canvas on the left begins to shudder. Like a window blind, it begins to curl off the floor into a roller at the top. Ever so slowly, it lifts, and behind it two pairs of legs appear as thin and as straight as flagpoles. I already know who stands on those spindly things before the curtain rises past their knees. The Grisslys. When the shadow of the canvas passes on high, they look as scared and as stiff as wooden boards can look. She stands holding a triangle and a metal bar to bang it. He stands behind a snare drum with drum sticks in his hands.

Already the center canvas has begun to lift, and I sense the crowd of people moving from their tables to crowd behind the row of chairs reserved for the Connerys. Over the slump of Sebastian, Old Sebastian smiles his brilliant dentures. His hands press down on his wheelchair's armrests and his feet slip off the wheelchair's footrests to plant themselves squarely on the floor. "Old Sebastian?" I say.

"I'll do it soon enough, Lassie," he says.

And there before me, the two canvas curtains nearly rolled to the top, the third on the right still down, stand the Grisslys, Brian Unkers, Paul with the hair tufts, and John Newberry. Brian up front holds an electric folk guitar strapped over his shoulders. Behind him, Paul wears an accordion across his chest, and John Newberry stands partnered with an upright bass. The Grisslys smile stage fright smiles, their stares jerking toward Brian. Brian lifts his microphone stand off the floor and walks forward.

"How you all doing?" he says.

The Residents and their families, surrounding us, shout out "Fine!"

Brian strums one chord and the rich sound floats down from speakers set high above. "Look behind me," he says, and he sweeps his arms to John Newberry in his gray hair and overalls and Paul with the tufts and the Grisslys like firing squad targets with their blindfolds removed. "Here's the reason why the Rolling Stones better quit before they turn eighty."

I nudge at Sebastian. He doesn't move from his frump.

"Mr. Sebastian, sir," Brian says. "Someone special thinks you deserve this. But I think you've been a pain in the ass."

This makes Sebastian stir a bit. He moans to me, "Did that boy just call me a pain in the ass?"

"He did," I say.

"Before two hundred people, I'm called an ass and a pain in the ass on Thanksgiving Day, that's what I'm saying."

"Mrs. Connery," Brian says. "We apologize for the noise in your pool office." He looks back at his odd band and calls out, "Ready?" The lot of them shrug doubtfully at each other and shake their heads. "I know," Brian says. "We thought we had till Christmas to practice, but let's give it a go." Then he looks to the audience. "Ladies and Gentlemen, we call this band The El Cheapos, but I have no idea why."

Turning to glance behind the final curtain, Brian nods, counting in a slow waltz, "One two three." He strums alone in a lazy rhythm, and the deep hum of his guitar fills the atrium. He begins to sing:

> *Green hills I once roamed*
> *Oh, my lovely Kintyre*
> *As your son, my dreams,*
> *Fill with your sweet memories,*
> *One day to come home*

As Brian strums another measure, the effect of this song is immediate. Sebastian's head begins to climb, chin from his chest, like first sunrise peeking over the horizon to see if mankind is still in one piece. Paul starts in with harmonic chords

from his accordion and John Newberry thumps deep notes from
his bass. Brian sings:

Though I once left you, in youth gone astray
Your valleys and sea sides live with me today
With eyes closed I listen to my heartbeats inspired
By misty blue sunsets
Of my lovely Kintyre

Brian, now with his eyes closed, sings the chorus, this time
with Paul's voice reverberating deeply below. The spines on Sebastian and Old Sebastian stiffen and they've thrown back their
shoulders because they can't help themselves.

Green hills I once roamed
Oh, my lovely Kintyre
As your son, my dreams,
Fill with your sweet memories,
One day to come home

Stepping back, Brian strums his guitar hard and turns once
more to look behind the final canvas curtain. Mr. Grissly begins
to bang a simple waltz rhythm on his snare drum and Mrs.
Grissly strikes her triangle every third beat. They hold this sound
together measure after measure, each time louder than before,
building as if to launch a revolution.

Already inflated with pride for Scotland and his Mull of Kintyre, Sebastian looks as though a wick has been lit at his feet
and the flame rolls toward gunpowder within his heart. For
with the sound and beat of this unlikely band, the last canvas
begins to rise, and, finally, the mighty blow of a Tartan bagpipe.

Tartan slippers, socks, and calf tassels, the bare knees, then
the hem of a plaid kilt and the red and gold plaid of the
instrument's bag, the curtain continues to rise. The song and

sound from the sole bagpipe, one powerful note which holds and intensifies, descends upon the room from the skylight in an engulfing embrace. It's full of Scotland's soul as if it sweeps down to Dignity Place from the Highlands themselves.

"Such beauty!" Sebastian exhales.

Everything else in this world has been displaced by the music from this ancient machine. And I can only imagine the explosion in my Sebastian's plaid heart when the canvas curtain and its shadow finally rise above the young man in full Scottish regalia and he sees the arms at the bag and pipe, the head in the hat and the cheeks and lips at the reed sending forth the wind giving birth to it all. His son, Roby Connery.

> *Listen to voices I knew as a child*
> *Winds over oceans reach me*
> *Ever so mild*
> *A wish I have prayed for each night I retire*
> *To return to the shores of*
> *My lovely Kintyre*

Sebastian rises slowly from his chair, lovely devastation vibrating his bones to the sound of Roby at the beloved bagpipe carrying the melody throughout the atrium. He babbles out, "That's my son!" and staggers forward like Frankenstein's monster taking his first steps off the life-giving table. He looks up to Roby just as a father should when a son shows him how much he is loved.

This pitiful looking band gathered before us lurches its song forward and holds us in the rapture of what it has done to Sebastian. Sebastian stands firm before his son, his eyes full of salt water from the Atlantic. There's nothing I can do but cry with him. It's a mother's dream and a wife's hope to see her husband and son together like this. I have it now, for real, and if Lola

Two were here I'd squash her beneath my frumpy size-twelve flats.

Green hills I once roamed
Oh, my lovely Kintyre
As your son, my dreams,
Fill with your sweet memories,
One day to come home

The song ends, yet it remains. It's in the walls and glass and floor and every holiday decoration in the place. It always will be. There's no applause but a held breath of anticipation. Surely everyone in Dignity Place knew about this plan and put up with the repeated honks and bleeps coming through the vents in their rooms until Roby came to learn the instrument. And now the Residents are at the point they've waited for. Roby successful and out of breath, standing before his father.

"Roby," Sebastian says, breathless himself. "I tell you and everyone here right now that in the history of the world, there has never been a son who has given his father a finer gift." Sebastian rushes to him and the bladder on the bagpipe squawks in the middle of their embrace. "I've been an ass," Sebastian says. "And I've been a pain in the ass. Why'd you do this for me, son? Why'd you do this even after the way I behaved?"

Roby leans back, wearing his father's tears on his cheeks. In a voice grown deeper than I remember, Roby says, simple enough, " 'Cause you're my dad."

"That I am, Roby." Sebastian wipes at his eyes. "Can you play another song, son?"

"It's the only one I know."

"Can you play it for me one more time?"

Roby looks to Brian and Brian nods back. "If that's what you'd like, Mr. Connery."

Sebastian stands watching the band regroup itself and begin

anew. This time, with the first chorus, I'm up on my feet and I walk behind my Sebastian. I whisper in his ears, "We're dancing like we used to dance in our living room." He raises his hands and I take them. Together, we waltz slowly to the music played by our son, his friend, and the odd people our lives have brought us to.

I used to fear Dignity Place. I once believed it held the proof of time's ravages on the body and romantic love. Now around me and my Sebastian, the Residents and their families sing the chorus of a song from my family's heritage. And somehow it seems inevitable that Dignity Place is where I hear the words from Sebastian's lips I know will carry me through to death do us part. He bites at my earlobe in the rhythm of our little waltz, and he tells me:

"I thank God for you."

With our kiss, there's a hush on the other side of the atrium lobby, and it's as though people there have heard Sebastian's words to me and begin to faint one by one. The silence sweeps toward us and the music falters until there's no more singing and no more music. I turn from Sebastian, toward the crowd of heads looking away, moving in unison along with the patter of shoes walking forward on the marble tiles, and I see . . . Iris Newberry holding the elbow of Little Nicky Number One.

He's in gangster mode. The dark suit and sunglasses, and his face working as if something horrible moves beneath the skin over his huge jaw. Iris slips her arm away, kisses him once on the cheek, and then walks toward the band.

She's not slinking forth. She's not wiggling about. There's no sweat-making saunter or pounding beat to her steps. It's nothing at all like I had dreamed. Rather, in her peach gown and black high heels, she moves as lightly as a wispy cloud, her silver hair flowing thick and glorious over her shoulders. Iris floats with the innocence of a lamb, and her eyes stare upon

John Newberry with a plea for forgiveness.

Brian steps away, as do Paul and Roby and the Grisslys. Gripping his upright bass as if it were some sort of safe haven, John Newberry stands alone, and he sees her as the rest of us do. Loveliness, pure and simple.

As she nears, she slows, approaching him cautiously. His softening stare upon her recognizes his bride the way she was before cruel circumstances in life began to tear them apart. "Hello, John," she says.

He hugs his bass close to his side. "Iris," he says. "You look like a dream."

It feels as though I'm so close I can touch them, and with Sebastian's hands warm in mine, I wish to shove John and Iris together and tell them to get a room.

"Please forgive me," she says.

John lowers his chin. "I see you came with him."

"I'm afraid, John. Nick gave me courage to come here tonight. Please forgive both of us."

Iris Newberry rises on her toes and she moves her lips glossed in soft red lipstick toward his beard. Her hands work the hair, parting it to find his lips. John leans down toward Iris, his eyes nearly closed, and there's a gasp held in the air waiting for the moment they touch.

"John," she says.

"Iris . . . I . . ." and he suddenly straightens, and passion disappears from his eyes. It's a cold look he gives her. He lets loose from his bass and the instrument comes crashing down with the thump of a fallen animal. "I can't do this, Iris. I can't!" He leaves her there, like a bride abandoned at the altar. John Newberry runs away from Iris, and Little Nicky Number One heaves himself in his path with his barrel chest and threatening jaw.

But there's no waiting for John Newberry. He hauls off a

powerful blow to Nicky's nose and sends him to the floor. Dignity Place lets loose a collective shudder at the sight of John Newberry standing over the man known as Little Nicky Number One.

"What are you all staring at?" John Newberry yells at the rest of us. "What?" He shakes his fist over the dark suit and sunglasses beneath him. "This is for show! He sells Cadillacs, that's it! There hasn't been a gangster in his family for seventy years!"

Hairy Harry pushes through the crowd to help his father from the floor and John Newberry rushes off and out of Dignity Place.

"Don't be a fool!" Nicholas Garva the Cadillac Man calls after him. "Take Iris back. Take her!" But the hair and the overalls leave without hesitation, bursting through the doors and into the cold.

"What just happened?" Sebastian says.

Iris gazes into the bright lights on the Christmas tree, tears in her eyes, and she shakes from the pressure of two hundred pairs of eyes pitying her. Beside her, Lola Two stands with her hands on her hips and her breasts like blimps pushing hard against her blouse.

You thought you had your proof, Julia Connery. You thought you were rid of me. But look at what really happens to a woman who thinks a man can love her after fifty years!

Old Sebastian pulls at my sleeve. I bend down to him.

"In all the excitement," he whispers, "I forgot to show Sebastian I can walk."

"I'm sorry."

"Now's not a good time?"

"Not really," I say.

"Nope. I don't think so either."

43

Tonight, I cannot fall asleep. I don't know why Sebastian thinks I can. How easy it is for me to follow his sounds.

Past midnight, Sebastian lifts his head off his pillow and studies me. "Julia," he says softly. Louder a second time, and he waits. I let my jaw go slack and give a bit of a snore.

His noises create images in my fake-sleeping mind. The careful opening of our bedroom closet, the slow slipping on of shirt and slacks. Frequent hesitations, repeated inspections of my sleep. The faint creak of our bedroom door, a patter down the steps, and the brush of our living room closet door over the carpet.

He's putting on his overcoat, boots, and hat, I know.

A rush of wind from the opening and closing of our front door brings a touch of pressure to my skin. A few minutes later, he's pushing his car down the drive before he starts it. Rolls it a bit over the lawn.

He doesn't know I'm at the front window, putting on my overcoat, my car keys in hand.

My car is like so many other sedans. Something close to brown. A boxy style. My four-door bore. Whenever I leave the grocery store or shopping mall, I wander among cars looking the same as mine and I squeeze the door-lock button on my key chain. I try to recall where I've parked, and I wander and press that button until I hear the beep and hunt it down. A half-hour past midnight, a mist beginning to fall over the windshield, I drive an anonymous distance behind Sebastian's sedan, grateful for my four-door bore.

Through his rear window, the top of Sebastian's head peeks over his seat's backrest and gives the impression of a car driving itself. It seems to know where to go along narrow side streets, taking us away from Highland Park neighborhoods to Forest Way Road and toward the Arboretum in Glencoe.

I wonder about so many possibilities, and why, after the evening we just had, he needs to go to a place he refuses to tell me about. Or to a person.

There are things, I suppose, a wife has to do even though she knows the dangers. In making the confrontation, asking the question and demanding the truth, it is possible that the honest communication people talk about as being fundamental to a good marriage is the very thing that can destroy it.

Blackness appears molded together, overhead, on all sides, to the road. Mist covers my windows and I hear only the beat of intermittent wiper blades and the whoosh of wheels over wet pavement. I cannot help feeling as though I'm caught in a tunnel and my hips make it too difficult to back out, so I drive forward.

Sebastian's left directional begins to flash and he turns into the Lagoons, a forest preserve south of the Arboretum. I drive past the entrance slowly, then come to a stop to peer behind me. Easing his car around a pathetic wooden barrier, Sebastian heads along the narrow drive inside the Lagoons.

A speed limit sign a few feet ahead of my car says 30 mph. I'm motionless on Forest Way Road, alone with my thoughts. So many places to meet someone here in the dark. Covertly. My quiet surprises me. No gasps for breath. No sobs. Warmth crawls over my skin where there should be cold. I suppose if I were to look at myself in the rearview mirror, I'd see Lola Two glaring back at me.

Not reluctantly, but inevitably, I pull my car far off the road onto the dirt shoulder and gather myself tighter in my overcoat. On the passenger side floor, the mushroom hat Iris wore on our trip into Highland Park lies folded upon itself. It's only fitting, then, when I leave my car for the preserve, I press it tightly over my head to protect me from the mist.

Headlights on Sebastian's car shine in the distance among trunks and leafless branches, their glow guides my walk down the path and hovers along with me between trees, remaining distant even as I approach. My rubbery sneakers, my stealthy shoes, fill with moisture and the right begins to send out a little squish and whistle with each step, the left suddenly sounding like the bleat of a whoopee cushion. Iris Newberry's mushroom hat droops from the weight of a heavier mist, a drizzle really, and my hair strings down over my face. Despite the chill in the air, my warmth turns to heat, my skin like embers beneath my overcoat. Perhaps Sebastian will laugh at the sight of me. And perhaps whoever is with him will do the same.

I close my eyes at the trunk of Sebastian's car and say a little prayer to myself. It begins with "Our Father," ends with "Amen." In the middle are words that could send me to Hell.

When I open my eyes, the headlights seem to light up the forest like a ghost-storyteller's flashlight held under her chin. The folds of craggy bark over burr oaks, the reach of their angling branches, accentuate into their unnatural shadows and the earth at my feet feels as though it has fallen away. I blink and focus forward.

A length of gray floats horizontally among the darkness of near and distant trees. With my squeaks and my bleats, I step around the car toward this shape. Slowly, it takes the form of a lagoon and its shoreline. Forward, to the left, Sebastian says in the darkness, "Over here, Lassie."

On a log at the shore, Sebastian sits huddled up in his overcoat and hat, his boots sunk into mud at the bank of the lagoon. He cradles a fishing pole in his bare hands.

"How'd you know where to find me?" he asks.

"I didn't. I had to follow you. How'd you know it was me?"

Sebastian rotates stiffly on the log, his eyes flashing below his pitiful hat brim. "I'm familiar with the music your shoes make."

There's enough room on the log to sit beside him, and I do. His pained look, though, lets me know his thoughts are overcrowded. So I keep my own thoughts to myself.

"There's no one else here," he says after a time. "There never has been." We sit in silence with our thoughts, his hands around his fishing pole, mine stuffed in my pockets.

I've noticed in books I've read how writers often describe the beat of rainfall. Never a word about the sound drizzle makes. Drizzle does have a sound. Powerful in its subtleness, it touches delicately upon barren trees and the earth covered in decaying leaves and prickles the surface of a lagoon. Drizzle makes the sound of nature's whisper. Neither crass nor apparent like a hard rain with its boastful lightning and thunder, its softness portends more important matters. When Sebastian finally speaks what is on his mind, the sound of drizzle parts like a curtain, simmers like the hush of an audience caught in rapture.

"I used to fish with my father," he says. "When I was a small boy. His hands worked the line, hook and bait like magic. His casts to the water were poetry. Mind you, we hardly caught a thing." He lifts the pole and beams at the line I cannot see in the gray of the lagoon. "But to a boy, fishing with your dad is always like magic. Fathers are like magicians to their young sons. Good fathers are precious. When a precious father hands his boy his best fishing pole for the first time and says, 'Here, son, you give it a go,' it's enough to make the boy's heart burst with joy and hold on to the moment forever."

"You could have told me," I say.

Sebastian's hands grip tighter around the fishing pole, a battered thing I notice, pieces of cork chipped off the handle, the reel nicked and dented here and there. "Four years ago," he says evenly, "closer to five now, I made my father fall."

"Old Sebastian fell on his own accord. It's what he told the paramedics."

"You weren't there when it happened. You weren't in the precise spot at the precise time when it happened."

Sebastian tilts his face skyward, eyes and face awash, and he blinks into a memory. My hands feel foolish inside my pockets. They need to clasp around him, and they do. I plead through the drizzle, "Please tell me."

It's as though there's an earthquake inside Sebastian, a rumbling expanding from his core to his skin. "I yelled at my dad," he says with a rush of breath. "Truly yelled at him. Such awful things. I told him all the angry things a son thinks when he feels smothered in his father's grip." He lowers his head and nearly disappears into his overcoat. "At what moment does a son's amazement and worship of his father turn to anger and rebellion? How does such a thing happen? And here I am like the tyrant to my own son. A son who does something so beautiful for his father."

With my arms snug around Sebastian, I hold on to keep him from fading away. He shakes within my embrace and his words tumble forward. "I yelled at him. I yelled like I never have at anybody before or since. The way Dad looked at me, the way he stumbled, like I had slugged him in the chest. I might as well have pushed him down our stairs." Sebastian heaves out a breath. "It's why Dad can't walk. It's why he can't come to this spot, our spot, to sit on our log together and fish the way we did when I was a boy."

"He could fish from his wheelchair."

"Lassie." Sebastian slumps. "The boy inside me, sitting and fishing on this log, couldn't bear to watch what I've done."

Perhaps a minute passes by, perhaps two. It's so hard to tell. Sebastian straightens and extends his father's magical fishing pole over the shoreline. His words, I know, are for his own ears as well as mine. "Tell me how a son can ever forget something like that?"

I hold him and squeeze him and manage to find a spot on his cheek to kiss away a tear. "Don't forget a thing, Sebastian. It's more important you remember."

Sebastian lifts the pole and reels in some line, a sound of tumbling pebbles. "Our son's a good boy. A remarkable child. He never liked to fish, though. Feels sorry for the fish and worms. But I can let that go." He turns to me, a different kind of sadness clouding over his face. "For almost five years, every once in a while when too much thinking got to me, I needed to come here by myself. I'm sorry I didn't have the courage to tell you sooner, Lassie. I truly am."

I should sing the relief I feel, but my relief doesn't seem fair after listening to Sebastian's grief. I slip a hand over his, feel the attachment he has to his father's battered fishing pole. "What did you do in the winter?"

"I froze."

Sebastian reels in his line and his hook leaps from the water and slaps against the pole. "Fish took your bait," I say.

"Don't use bait. Just let the hook soak in the water. In winter, it lies on the ice." At last there's a bit of brightness in Sebastian's voice and, I suspect, a moment's laughter. "Dad was a good fisherman only to a small boy. Truth is, he had no talent for it. And he taught me everything he didn't know." His eyes, wet and filled with uncountable emotions, stare so fully upon my face. "Lassie," he says. "The whole point of a son's fishing with his dad has got little to do with catching fish."

I make a small sign of the cross over my breast. It's a necessary thing to do when a promise must be broken, even for the sake of a bigger promise. "About Old Sebastian and his wheel chair," I say. "There's something I have to tell you."

To someone passing in the distance, the sound Sebastian makes to my news, the sound I make to Sebastian's reaction and the sounds we make together, could be interpreted as many things. Wounded animals or drunken teenagers at play, perhaps a row of trees falling one into the next. I am grateful no one else appears in the woods to spoil our moment, how we don't care about ruined clothing, and that we aren't arrested. I am grateful for Sebastian's jokes about fishing poles, and how, in the morning, Roby doesn't grimace at the obvious way we look, or when we tell him we have to retrieve my abandoned car from Forest Way Road.

Most of all, though, I am grateful for the memory I know will always arise. Always. Whenever the sky turns gray and it begins to drizzle.

44

Over the two days since Thanksgiving, as a matter of routine in our conversations, Sebastian tells me what a lucky man he is to have me and Roby and how he's going to buy the borrowed bagpipe Roby used and have it enshrined inside its own curio cabinet set in the center of our living room.

I consider the horror of this. All the people who will come inside our home and smile a sort of smile that means well but will tell me they're glad not to have such a thing displayed in the middle of their own living rooms. And I know how Sebastian will retell to each and every visitor the story of what his marvelous son did for him on Thanksgiving Day, and he will go on forever like a never-ending slide show of vacation pictures. Soon we'll never have a visitor to our house again.

In my moments without Sebastian or Roby, I feel as though I'm forced to think about Lola Two in all her big-boobed, pillow-lipped, fat-suctioned, botoxed-collagened-dermabraided-rhinoplastied-nipped-and-tucked-here-there-and-everywhere glory, standing next to Iris who looked so small, defeated and utterly rejected. It's the guilty side of my own joy, knowing the way Iris Newberry became victim to a new kind of sadness and my fault in making it happen.

Guilt carries me awake through the night until light leaks around my bedroom curtains. By morning, I'm exhausted with the repeated rants from Lola Two playing inside my head. *You may have won a battle, Julia honey, but hardly the whole war. Sooner or later, all marriages turn into misery.*

After Sunday breakfast, I melt into my living room couch. Sebastian's and Roby's voices above me in Roby's room go on about the bagpipe, and then they play songs of Scotland on Roby's stereo over and over, their voices falling silent as if listening to a secret told to them from the heavens.

In my weariness and in the cheer of father and son, I miss his approach to my front door. His knock nearly flies lost over my head. I suppose he's been at it a few times before I hear the pounding and the doorbell well enough over the sixth and seventh consecutive playing of Scottish songs through my ceiling. I blink and rise from the couch. On the other side of my front door, Nicholas Garva wears his black suit and black sunglasses and his monster jaw.

"Good morning, Mrs. Connery," he says, using his gangster voice.

I offer to let him in from the cold. "No," he says. "I'm here to drop something off."

He reaches into his coat pocket, a motion which, until a few days ago, would have made me think of gangster guns. "Open this when I leave," he says, and he hands me a large envelope, sealed and packed thick with something that makes my fingertips tingle.

When he begins to turn away, I see there's a question remaining on his lips. I'm not surprised to find him turning back to me with his fingers pinching at his chin. This time, his voice is smooth. "You're really something, Mrs. Connery. Without you, none of this would've been possible." I must have enough energy left in my face to show him my confusion. He tells me, "The things men do because of you. Your son, your husband, your father-in-law." He pulls his sunglasses from his face and his brown eyes appear ready to cry. "And me," he says. "Especially me and my son. There's a magic about you, Mrs. Connery. It's the only thing I can figure out."

I look into his eyes and see how large they are and the length of their lashes. "Whatever happened between you and Iris," I say, "there's been enough suffering for all of you."

"John's still missing," he says with a sigh. He sets his sunglasses back over his eyes. "Nobody's seen him since Thanksgiving. Nobody."

Nicholas Garva leaves my porch and heads down the walk toward his Cadillac in the driveway. Like Sebastian, he seems to have crossed over his own torment, relieved somewhat but also saddened. I call for him and he turns around. "Mr. Garva," I say. "Why don't you stop wearing those sunglasses and dark suits? You don't need them."

He hesitates on the walk, his head cocked to the side. Slowly, his hands reach to his sunglasses and he holds them out as if he were considering his entire life. "I've thought about that," he says, and drops them to the cement. His shoe is soon over the sunglasses and falls deliberately, crunching, grinding, shattering. He steps back and looks at the pieces. Even in his dark suit, with his jaw thrashing at the sight of what he has just done, the once and former Little Nicky Number One looks no different from the confusion I saw in Roby the day he had given up his pacifier.

"Sorry about littering your sidewalk."

"It's my pleasure, Mr. Garva."

Still lost in the sight of his ruined sunglasses, he says, "John dug up his casket the night he ran from Dignity Place. I didn't see him do it or how he did it, but he's got friends out there and he did it. There's just the empty casket beside the hole now. Funny thing is, John left the lid open like he took something out and ran off in a hurry. He's gone. John's gone with whatever was inside the casket Iris buried." He blinks his large brown eyes at me and his lashes sweep to his cheeks so much the opposite of a tough guy. I suppose I understand why Iris took an interest in this man so long ago.

Before ducking into his Cadillac, he says in his soft voice, "Like I told you, Mrs. Connery. It's amazing the things you cause men to do."

I close my door and stand facing it with my lips brushing against the wood and I listen to the engine of the Cadillac fade away from my home. Considering things of late, I suppose I should wonder more about John Newberry. Why he seemed ready to give in to Iris then suddenly harden and run off. Why he dug up his own grave, if he was the one who dug up his grave.

Of course he was the one who dug up his casket, and I no longer wonder about what Iris buried inside it. I know what she buried. At least I'm almost sure. It's the one thing I can think of that John would want badly enough to dig out of his own grave on a cold Thanksgiving night.

In my thoughts of John and Iris and graves and caskets, the envelope Nicholas Garva handed to me slips from my fingers and falls to the floor. I nearly forgot I had it. But its heavy thud sparks my curiosity and I carry it back to the couch where I sink once more into my weariness. For the first time I see the words written on the flap:

To the Connerys,
Tokens of my gratitude.
From Nicholas Garva, the Cadillac Man.

Overhead, a Scottish tune plays on, and Roby and Sebastian are silent. It's likely their lower lips hang slack with their tongues poked out their mouths and their eyes have misted over, and even though they sit in the trash of a teenager's bedroom, I know they think they're in heaven. I tear at the tape sealing the flap and the little metal clip through the hole. I shove my hand inside the envelope without looking and pull something out. A boarding ticket. Round trip air fare. Then another and a third. There are more inside. I flip the envelope over and pour the rest out to the floor. Round trip boarding tickets. Six sets in all.

To Scotland.

I fall back against my couch and think of the ashes inside the Urns of Connery living forever inside my bedroom closet. "At last," I say, and sleep closes my eyes.

45

It's been a month since John Newberry ran out of Dignity Place and away from Iris. Nobody has seen him since. The undigging of his grave made page fifteen of the Tribune then disappeared for good.

Between my fitness classes and visits to Old Sebastian, I often stop by John Newberry's room and stare at his door and ask aloud, "When are you going to do it?"

Three days ago, I found his door left open and the room barren. All personal effects had been removed and a desk and chair and a stripped bed were all that remained. I suppose the Grisslys had no choice about it and Hairy Harry did what he was told. Standing in the middle of the room, I felt the smallness of the place, as if the walls crept toward each other a bit. And the faint smell of the man, the musk cologne that would float into my yard whenever he obeyed Iris and pulled imaginary weeds from a perfect lawn, faded more and more with each breath I took.

Old Sebastian coughed at the doorway. When I turned around, I smiled at his new habit of stretching his chin to the ceiling, as if trying to grow a jaw like Little Nicky's, or perhaps to stand as tall as he could now that he walked again with a bit more ease and a cane. "When can I tell Sebastian I can walk?"

"Soon," I said.

"You sure you haven't already told him?"

It was an easy lie to make. "I haven't."

I met Old Sebastian at the doorway and kissed him on his

cheek. With my arms wrapped around him, hugging him with a squeeze, I took comfort in the old bones creaking and groaning within my embrace.

Hardly anyone asks me about John Newberry. Sebastian wants to, I can tell by the way his eyebrows float to his hairline. But he stops himself and asks me about something else. There's a look in his eyes, a combination of dismay and pity. It reminds me of the look I had seen in my own eyes in my car's rearview mirror whenever I listened to women agree with the advice handed out on *God Investment*. It's my habit to tell Sebastian, "It'll happen soon enough," and he tells me back, "Lassie, I have no idea what you're talking about."

Between breakfast and school and studying, Roby sneaks out to our porch in his ratty jeans and shirt. I don't order him in from the cold. He stands there with his hands in his pockets, sometimes staring at the small lump of crusty snow around Iris's House For Sale sign, sometimes staring at the house. He waits for it to happen. We both know it will.

Christmas Eve morning, Lola Two knows it as well. She stands in my kitchen behind Iris, watching her finish her coffee and pour another cup. It's hard to describe Lola Two. At one moment she appears confident in her armor of cosmetic surgery and ready to knock Iris's head off with one swing of her plastic boobs. Suddenly she turns sour and she looks like a pornographic Mrs. Potato Head on the verge of dropping all her plastic parts.

Iris sips at her second cup of coffee. Her silver hair and the lines around her mouth and eyes fit her well now. Comfortable. Light dabs of makeup, a bit of hair spray, elegant clothes. With Lola Two at her back, Iris looks more real and lovelier than ever before.

"All of you are welcome to come over tomorrow for Christmas dinner. Lobster tails."

I smile and drink from my coffee cup. "We'll be over by four."

From outside in the cold, through crisp air, carried by the wind chill into my kitchen, a noise arrives both muffled and angry. It's a shout to pierce brick and mortar.

"Iris!"

Lola Two's arms fly up toward my kitchen ceiling. She moans like a wild animal and vanishes.

"Can you freshen my coffee?" Iris asks in her soft way.

I do, and we listen to the shouts and the screams coming from outside. "Iris! It's me! Iris!" Iris stays put in my kitchen. The shouts turn into bangs and thuds and pounding, and still Iris sits at my table and drinks from her cup.

After ten minutes, Iris rises with her coffee cup. She says, "All right."

I follow her from my kitchen to my living room to my porch. She doesn't seem to be in a hurry. Outside, Sebastian stands on our porch in his boxers and night shirt and Roby wears something that used to be a robe. They're too excited to notice the cold and Sebastian turns to Iris and me. "Chrissake, Lassie. You were right."

There's nothing to see but the Newberrys' house and the small crusty lump of snow around the House For Sale sign. It's a weak snow, hardly worthy of Christmas. There's not enough to show footprints on the walk. "He's up to something," Roby says, and the four of us gather at the railing to watch.

A growl, a rumble, an earthquake. It's all these things. We hear the crash and see the front window glass fly in pieces to the porch and a dark mass of wood twirl in the air over the hedgerows and break on the frozen ground. It's a chair. Followed by another. And another. Six of them gathered broken on the front lawn. Gargoyles at their feet turn gray toward the sunlit sky. Wind howls over their corpses. Smashed pieces of the dining room table arc over the porch and crush the gargoyles' remains, then bureau drawers and their frames, and more and more gargoyles lie wasted in the heap. End tables, framed mirrors and paintings, couch cushions and the couch itself. The china cabinet. All of it.

Iris stands with one hand tucked under an elbow, the other holding her coffee cup aloft. Her lips ease into a delicate smile.

Inside her house, screams accompany tearing and ripping. The living room's heavy curtains and rods soon sail over the porch and settle on the broken wood. There's stomping and thundering, and big hands appear at the upstairs windows, ripping away at shades and curtains and blinds, and more stomping and thundering until these shades and curtains fly over the porch to the growing pile out front. At last Iris's UFO sombrero hat frisbees into the air and the wind catches it and sends it across the street and high over the reach of towering tree branches. Gone.

"Iris!"

John Newberry appears on the porch and steam blows from his mouth and nose and ears and the pores on his hands and face. He's no longer wearing his overalls, but neither does he wear the slacks, shirt and tie Iris made him wear even on the most humid summer days to work in her perfect garden. He's in jeans and a sweatshirt, and he stomps his feet on broken glass spread over the porch and calls out.

"Iris!"

"He's shaven for you, Iris," Sebastian says. "Except for the mustache."

"I almost forgot what he used to look like," Roby says.

I say, "Handsome in his way."

"Um hmm," Iris says, and we turn in the cold to watch her take another easy sip from her cup of coffee.

Down the porch steps, John Newberry pounds the pile he's made. He glares at it and kicks at it and turns to his house with one foot on the ruins. He presses his foot on the heap of broken dark wood and thick cloth and shattered gargoyles and everything that had filled his house for twenty years and kept the sunshine away. He shakes his fists at the house and screams.

"Take me as I am, Iris, or leave me alone!"

He waits with the whites of his eyes so huge and steam rising now from his shirt collar.

"I know you're in there, Iris! I know you're in there! I'm keeping the mustache, do you hear me? I've always wanted a damn mustache, is that too much to ask for? And I'm never wearing a tie again, do you hear? For chrissake, I'm retired. No damn ties! Will you take me with my mustache and without my ties? And I'm gonna wear gym shoes without any socks and I'm not gonna wear ironed and starched boxers and I'm not gonna hide from the sun, do you hear? And you know what else, Iris? I'm gonna sleep in the raw, do you hear me? What do you think about that? Will you take me this way, Iris? Will you take me now? And I'm gonna say 'gonna' whenever I please, and 'ain't', and I'm gonna put my elbows on the table when I eat and I'm gonna keep the shades up and let the sun pour in and fade the carpet and furniture and burn my skin, do you hear me, Iris? Will you take me this way?"

John Newberry presses his foot on the pile harder and steps up with the other. He wobbles and shakes on the broken pieces, but he's soon upon the mound, stomping and crunching and crushing and cursing and shaking his fists to the sky. "Iris! I've done this to your damn vampire decorations! Will you take me now?"

Roby looks back over his shoulder, his eyes heavy with tears. I suppose it could be from the wind chill. He asks Iris, "What're you gonna do, Mrs. Newberry?"

"Iris!"

It's a scream and a wail and a lament all combined into one

eruption. Neighbors fill their porches and cars halt in the street and all these people stop to gawk at John Newberry, dead and buried four and a half years ago by his wife, now stumbling up the slope of a mountain in his front yard.

"Iris!"

"Mrs. Newberry, what are you going to do?"

On our porch, our stares upon her, Iris takes a last sip of coffee and hands me her cup. "Thank you, Julia." She kisses me on the cheek, pats Roby on the head, then kisses Sebastian on the lips. She turns from us and steps down our porch. She calls out, "Over here, John."

John Newberry turns to Iris from on high upon the slope, his mouth agape but silent. She seems to float toward him, her shining silver hair, her new clothes and her lovely shape. His eyes drink in the sight of her. "Julia," Sebastian says at my side. "Mrs. Newberry pinched my fanny."

"Iris," John says. "Will you take me this way? Will you take me the way I am?"

Iris says nothing, her arms reaching toward John. He hesitates, watching her. A smile blossoms on his face and he climbs down to meet her.

Up and down the block, husbands and wives watch this scene and I wonder if they think about themselves and all they've done in marriage. Will they go back into their homes and confess and mend and salvage and love each other the way they had once promised?

"Come with me," Iris says, and she walks with a bit of a wiggle toward her porch, and the force of her wiggle tows John in with her. On their porch, a moment before John Newberry disappears into the house with Iris, he reaches inside his sweatshirt. "Iris," he says. "I dug something up for you."

Cars begin to move off and the porches on the block empty

of people and I tell Sebastian and Roby, "Let's leave them alone."

I'm the last off our porch and I stay to watch. I know who's coming. She's there on the Newberrys' porch at the shattered picture window and I hurry over to meet her. "You're not looking so well," I say.

No, I'm not.

There's no expression to see on Lola Two's face. Everything about her bubbles and boils. Her botoxed brow and her collagened lips and her molded cheekbones and chin and nose job and tattooed eyeliner all melt together on this cold, Christmas Eve morning.

"I was right about what Iris buried in the casket."

Lola Two no longer has lips to move. She muffles in her throat, *Guess you've won.*

There's a small pop and a whine in the air and the right side of her sculpted fanny falls to the sound. A second pop and the other side falls. *No!* she says, and she looks at her plastic breasts and hears them go pop-pop. She starts to cry out gray tears from her melted, misshapen eyes. *Not Dr. Plastic's breasts!*

The right blimp falls to the sounds of pop-pop and goes crashing toward her belly. Then the other sends out a pop-pop and a burst. She gives me a tormented look from her gooey, twisted face and says, *You've got a hell of an imagination.*

The rush of air from her collapsing breasts lifts her off the porch and sends her spiraling away. She's caught in the wind chill and gives a faltering cry, shrinking into herself, a final blob twirling into the air until she vanishes. I stare into the final point of air she occupied, wondering about her and whether she could ever come back. Somehow, it doesn't seem possible.

I take one last look into the Newberry living room, through the picture window now gone but for the few remaining shards in its frame. The cold blows into the hollow space that used to hold all of Iris Newberry's vampire furniture and pictures with eyes watching my every move, all of it tinged in gargoyles ready to pounce. Rather than emptiness, I see daylight welcomed in all directions, wanted, streaming through the windows. The beams gather together to create a spotlight at the center of the living room floor.

Off and away in their bedroom, Iris and John Newberry are together again on Christmas Eve after fifty-four years of marriage. In the center of the hollow space, in the center of the spotlight, I see what I had expected all along. A glass, a bit yellowed with a cake of dirt at the rim. But I can make out the etching of the Victorian home and its words.

Traverse City Bay Bed & Breakfast. Enjoy Your Stay

46

Have you ever been to Kintyre? You really ought to go.

It's a peninsula, nearly an island, swooping off the southwest part of the mainland into the Atlantic. Start north at Tarbert into Skipness and Clachan, Tayinloan to Carradale, cross back to Glenbarr and down to Machrihanish, Drumlemble to Campbeltown. In Campbeltown, motor along the main road until you get to the sign that says, "End of the Public Road." From there, you walk to the Mull. About twenty minutes. Longer if you're pushing an ancient man in a motorized wheelchair with dead batteries.

The Mull is the headland of the Kintyre peninsula, where the landscape strikes you with green hills and cliffs and vast green meadows and deep blue sea. The whole of its near and distant splendor appears so close, you feel as though you could touch it all in one grasp, yet so vast you shrink away in the heavenly size of its beauty. If you go, you should take the walking path to the lighthouse on the Mull and stand on the edge of the cliffs there with your arms spread wide. You'll feel yourself in the breeze and in the mist that softens the sun into streams of pastel colors. You'll soar aloft in a rainbow and wish never to step away.

If you breathe in deeply enough you may inhale a piece of my family's ancestry released into the breeze one lovely day in April. And if you listen carefully enough, you may hear the captured echoes of Roby, Sebastian, Old Sebastian, and me whooping and hollering as we unleashed the ashes of the Urns of Connery and sang our poem in honor of the Mull of Kintyre.

Be sure to wet your lips and you may taste the ripe sweetness in the wind that blew around the held hands of Iris and John Newberry. At the Mull, they never let go of each other and, by the sight of them, you'd think they'd fall over if they ever did.

Should you take off your shoes and socks and curl your feet in the green grass, you may feel the moisture in the earth. That's where Sebastian cried when he first saw for himself his father's rise from his wheelchair and his steps into his arms.

For me, though, as a wife and mother, there was nothing as precious as watching my three men, sitting close together on a log, a pace or two from the edge of a cliff, with fishing poles in their hands. Their lips moved over smiles. Easy conversation able to last an eternity.

To them, it made no difference their hooks dangled, without bait, yards above the water.

Back in our home, there's dirt and stone in the Urns of Connery and Sebastian is careful to leave the black beneath the tips of his toenails alone. No thorough washing. Not like it used to be. I know this can't last forever, but Sebastian aims to try. I ask him, "What's with all the dirt?"

Sebastian holds me close and gives me his horrible lilt.

"Lassie, by God, it isn't dirt." Our lips a moment before a kiss.

" 'Tis Scotland!"

ABOUT THE AUTHOR

Bee Robb is the author's pseudonym, a *nom de plume,* a moniker. The following is why.

Bee wrote a novel in a genre that won a novel-writing competition. In a similar genre as the first novel, Bee's second novel earned particularly high praise and a starred review from book review publications that matter. Since then, literary agents have told Bee not to pursue publishing a novel such as *My Occasional Torment* because it would be outside Bee's expected genre. Mystery.

Expected genre?

Please.

Bee lives happily married, with a marvelous child, and therefore has written *My Occasional Torment,* a book inspired by romance thriving within marriage, and thanks Tekno Books and Five Star publishing for not believing that something as three-dimensional as a human being must live as an author inside a genre prison.

So there.